PRIMORDIAL

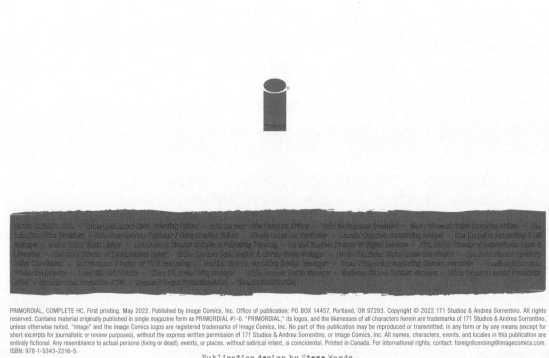

PRIMORDIAL, COMPLETE HC. First printing. May 2022. Published by Image Comics, Inc. Office of publication: PO BOX 14457, Portland, OR 97293. Copyright © 2022 171 Studios and Andrea Sorrentino. All rights reserved. Contains material originally published in single magazine form as PRIMORDIAL #1-6. "PRIMORDIAL," its logos, and the likenesses of all characters herein are trademarks of 171 Studios and Andrea Sorrentino, unless otherwise noted. "Image" and the Image Comics logos are registered trademarks of Image Comics, Inc. No part of this publication may be reproduced or transmitted, in any form or by any means (except for short excerpts for journalistic or review purposes), without the express written permission of 171 Studios and Andrea Sorrentino, or Image Comics, Inc. All names, characters, events, and locales in this publication are entirely fictional. Any resemblance to actual persons (living or dead), events, or places, without satirical intent, is coincidental. Printed in Canada. For international rights, contact: foreignlicensing@imagecomics.com. ISBN: 978-1-5343-2216-5.

Publication design by Steve Wands

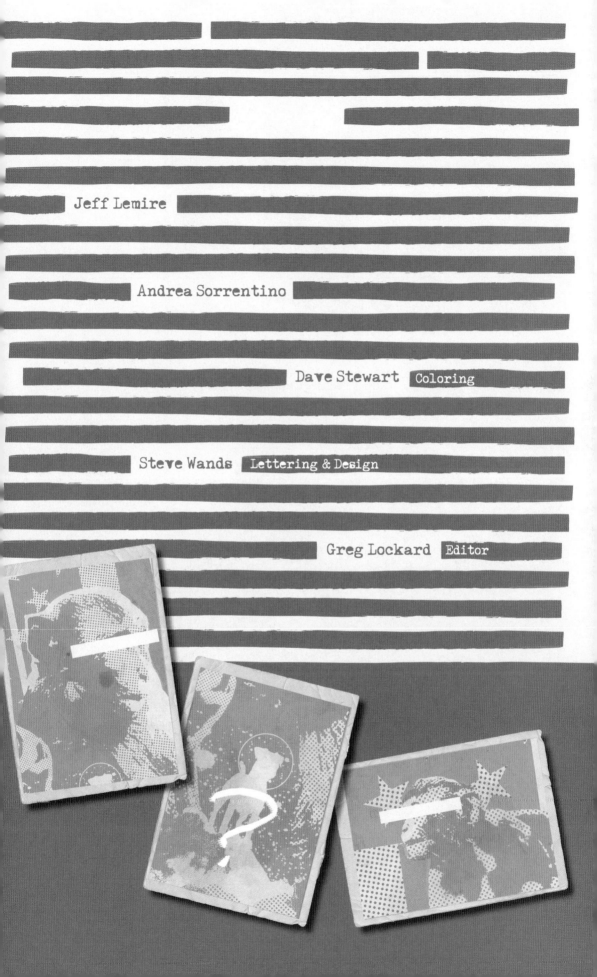

[redacted]

[redacted] Jeff Lemire [redacted]

Andrea Sorrentino [redacted]

[redacted] Dave Stewart Coloring

[redacted] Steve Wands Lettering & Design

[redacted] Greg Lockard Editor

[redacted]

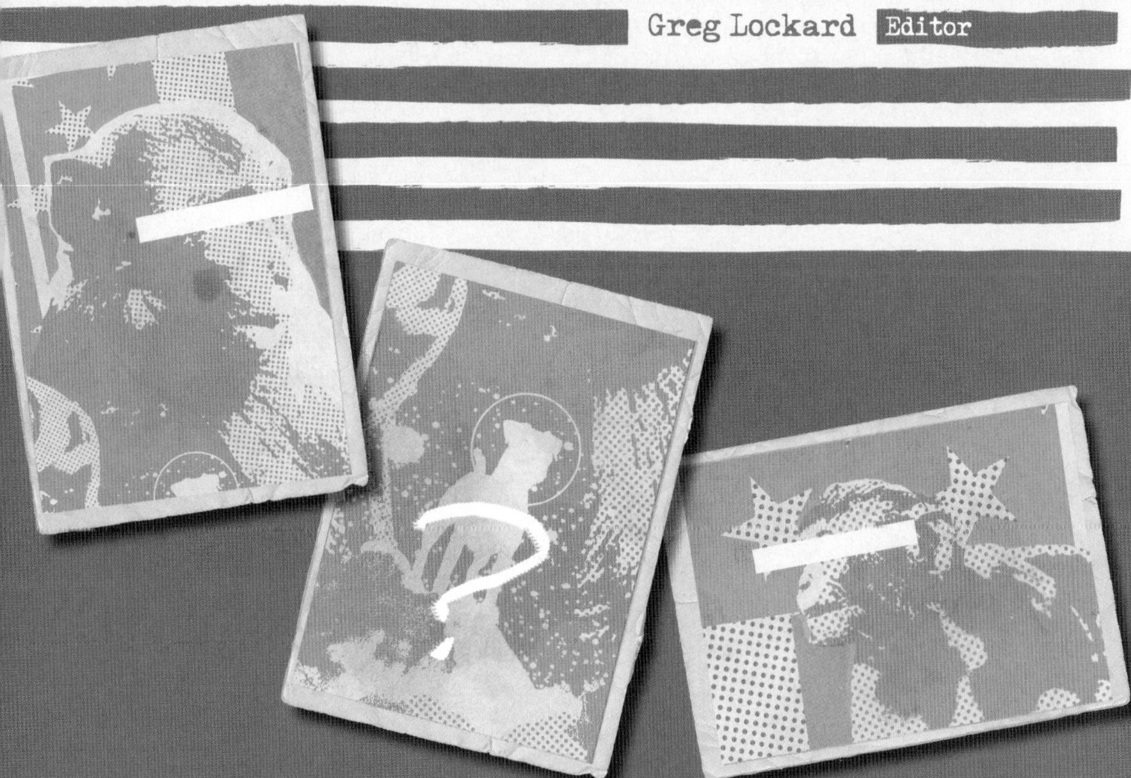

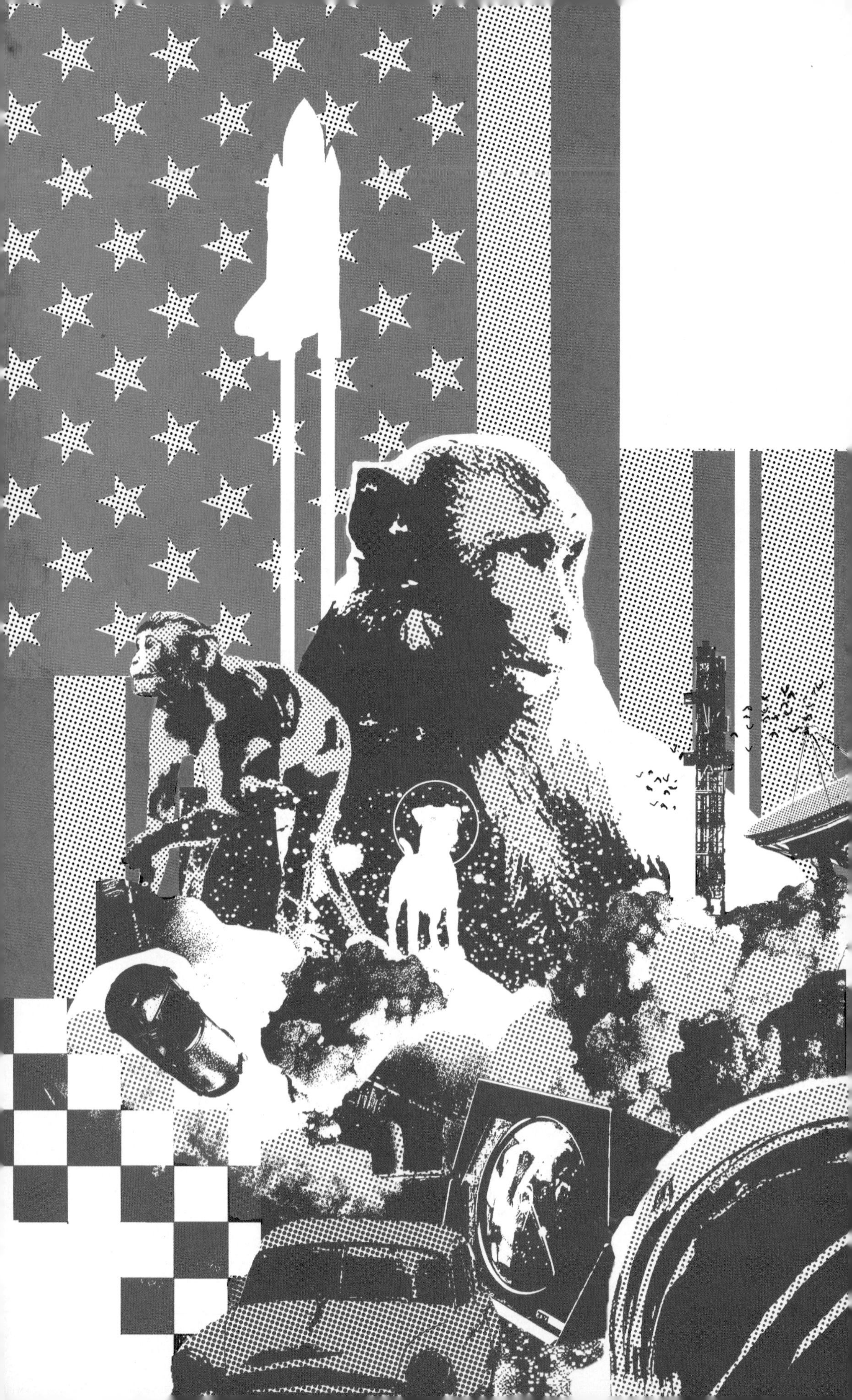

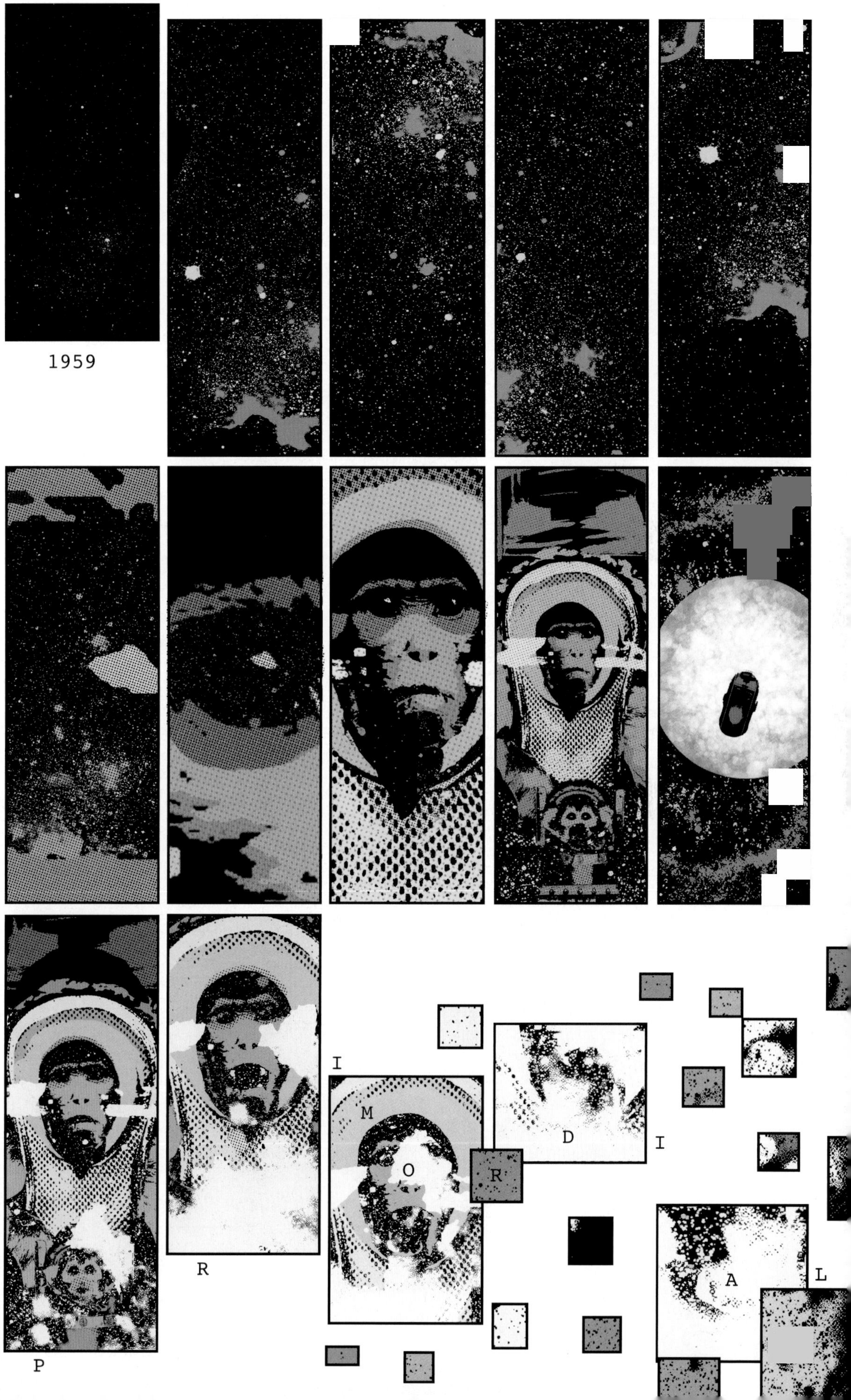
1959
P
R
I
M
O
R
D
I
A
L

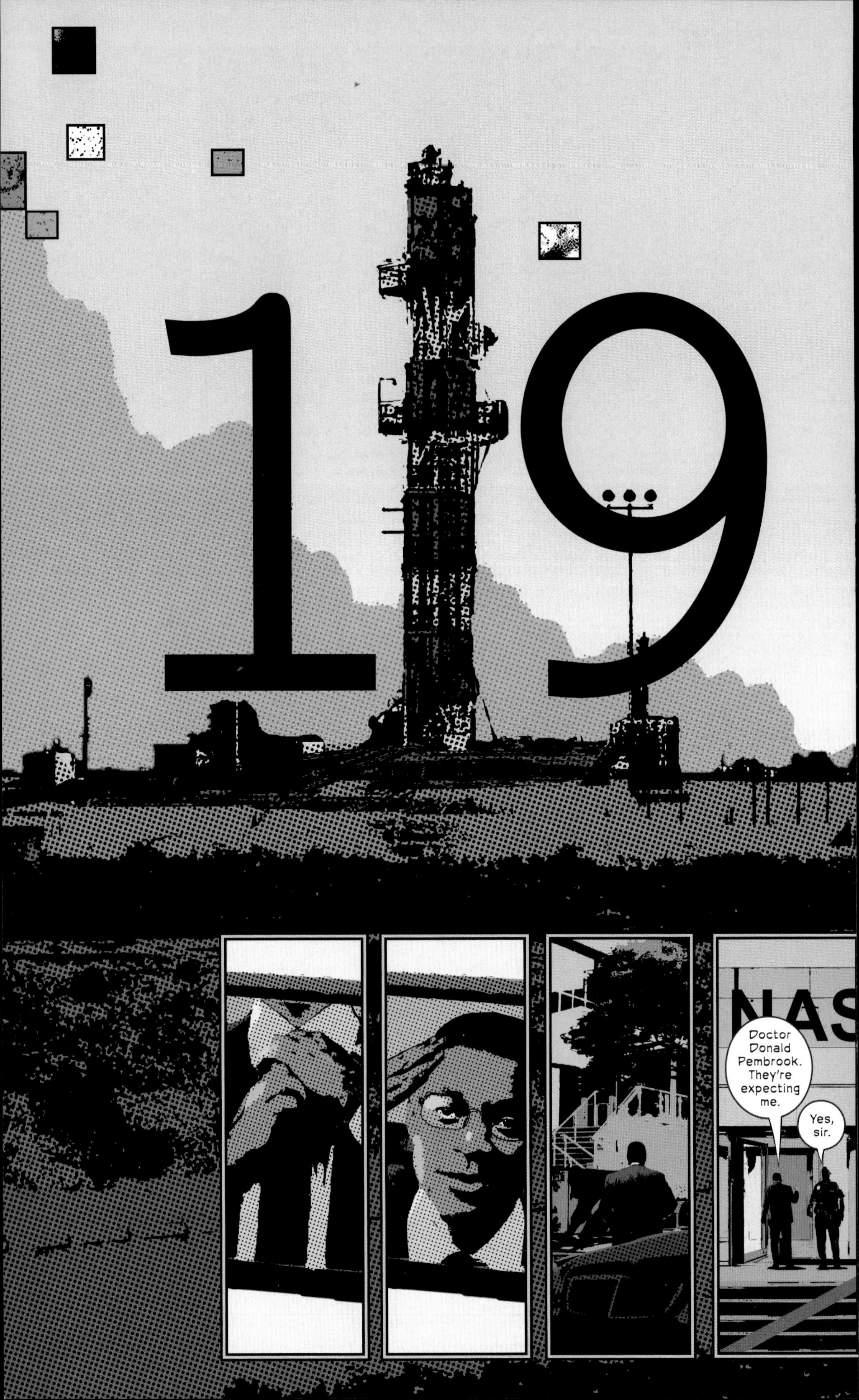
19
NAS
Doctor Donald Pembrook. They're expecting me.
Yes, sir.

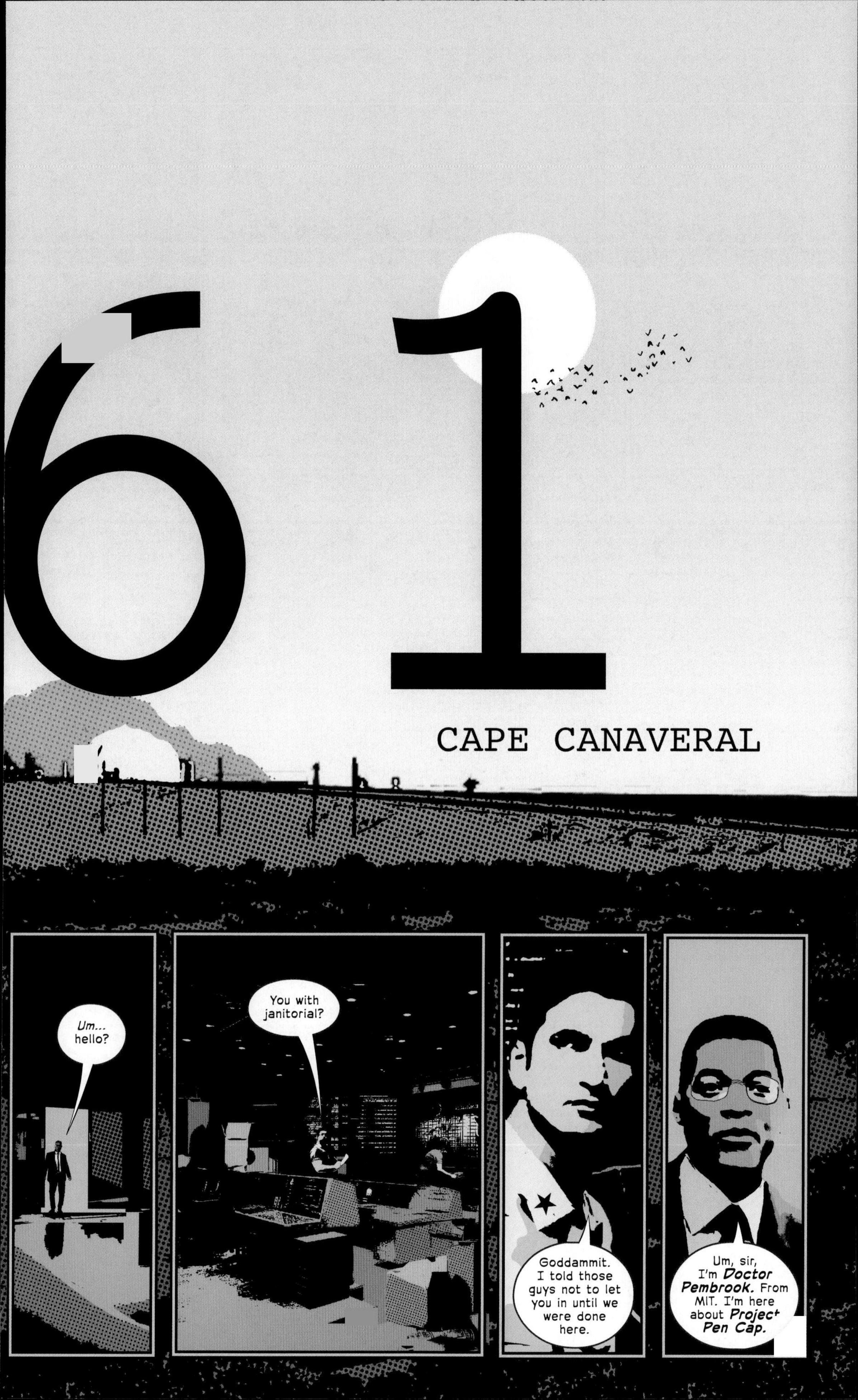
61
CAPE CANAVERAL
Um... hello?
You with janitorial?
Goddammit. I told those guys not to let you in until we were done here.
Um, sir, I'm Doctor Pembrook. From MIT. I'm here about Project Pen Cap.

Oh, shit. Sorry, Doc. I didn't--

Well, I didn't think that was you.

Right.

So, where should I check in? Will there be a debriefing or--?

Debrief?

Uh, what is it exactly is it you think we're *doing here*, Doctor Pembrook?

Well, when they told me it was a top secret operation at Cape Canaveral... I thought--

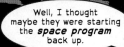

Well, I thought maybe they were starting the *space program* back up.

Ha! Shit, I'm sorry, Pembrook. We aren't starting *anything* here. We're *taking it apart.* For good.

Space race is as dead as *our careers*, pal.

Sorry, Doc. Project Pen Cap is just a *clean-up job.* We need to strip this place of any equipment that may still have military application.

Then Uncle Sam is selling the land off to the private sector.

But I--I have my *PhD in electrical engineering* from *MIT.* I led the *digital computation depart-ment* there for the last two years.

Which is what qualifies you to identify anything we can still use in the *nation's defense.*

Good luck. You have *three days* to get as much junk out of here as you can. After that it all goes to the *scrapheap.*

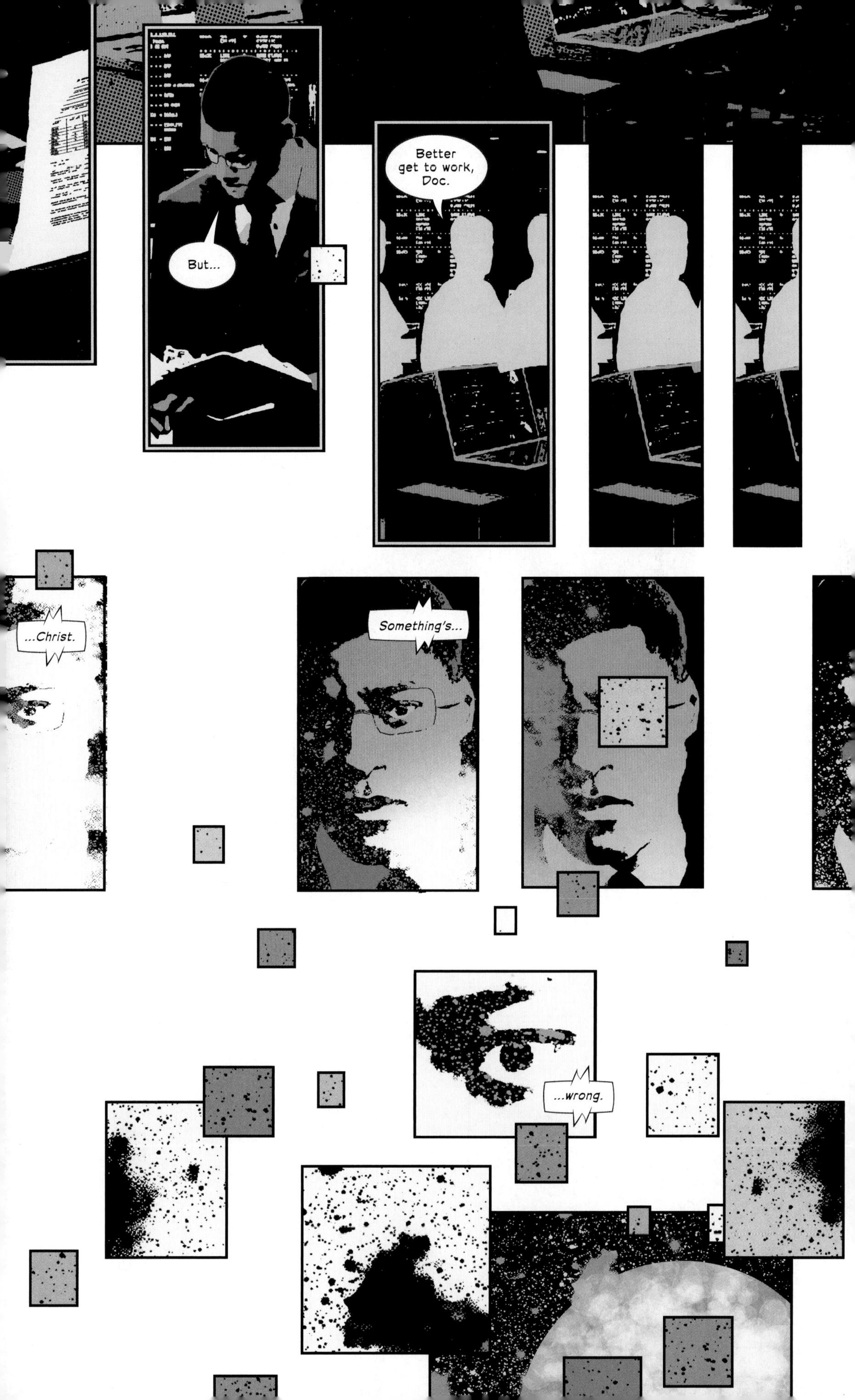
But...
Better get to work, Doc.
...Christ.
Something's...
...wrong.

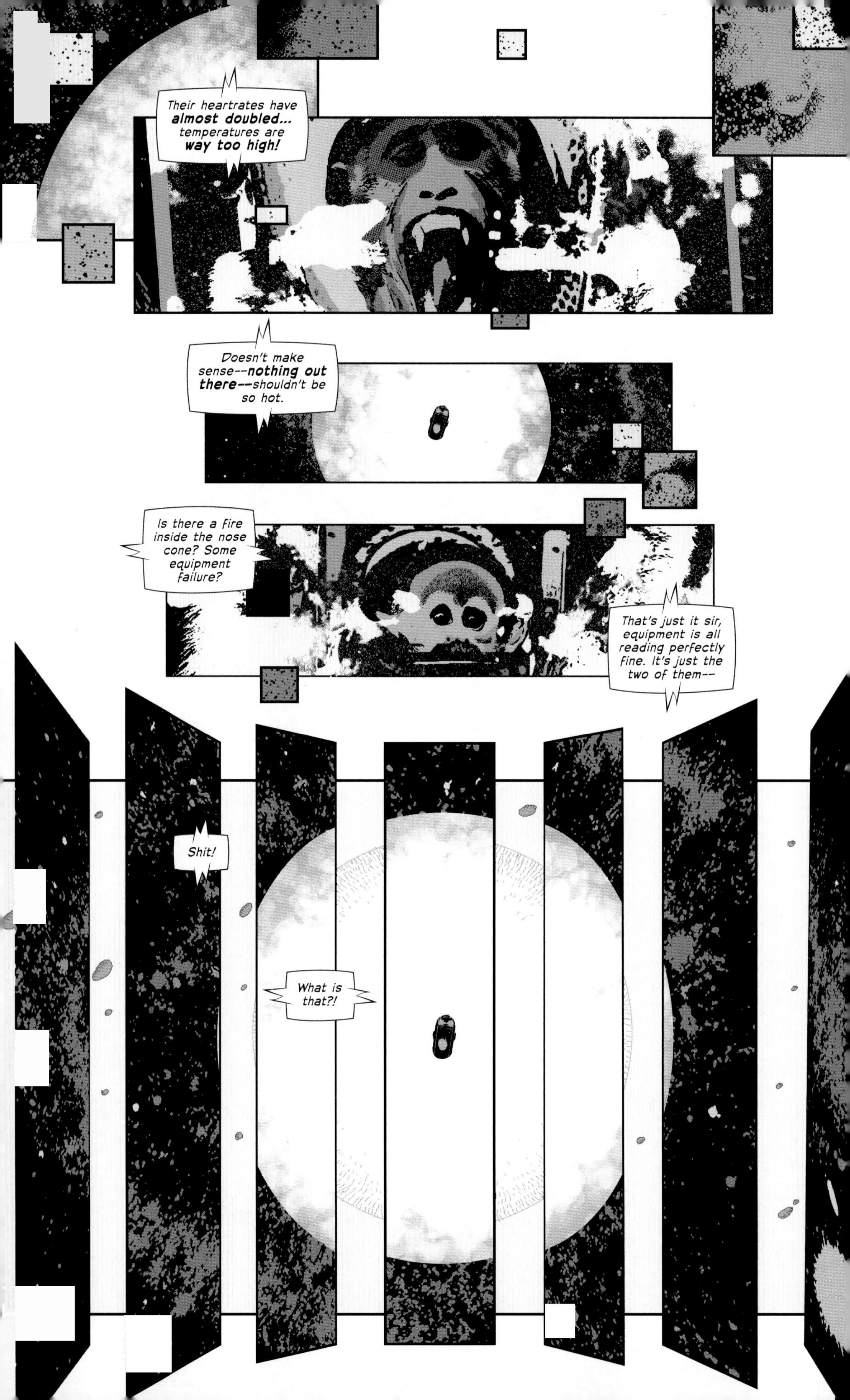
Their heartrates have almost doubled... temperatures are way too high!
Doesn't make sense--nothing out there--shouldn't be so hot.
Is there a fire inside the nose cone? Some equipment failure?
That's just it sir, equipment is all reading perfectly fine. It's just the two of them--
Shit!
What is that?!

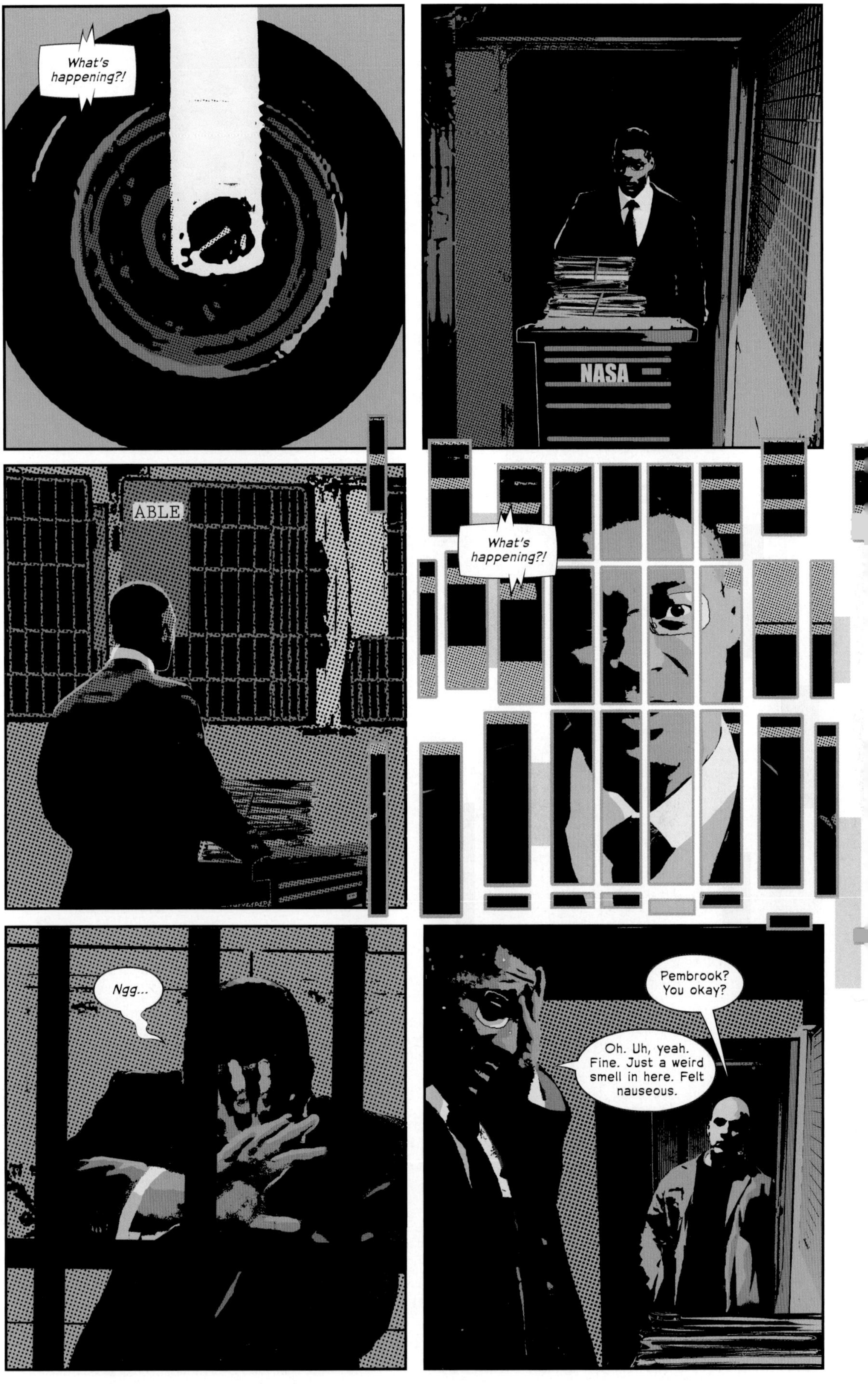
What's happening?!
NASA
ABLE
What's happening?!
Ngg...
Pembrook? You okay?
Oh. Uh, yeah. Fine. Just a weird smell in here. Felt nauseous.

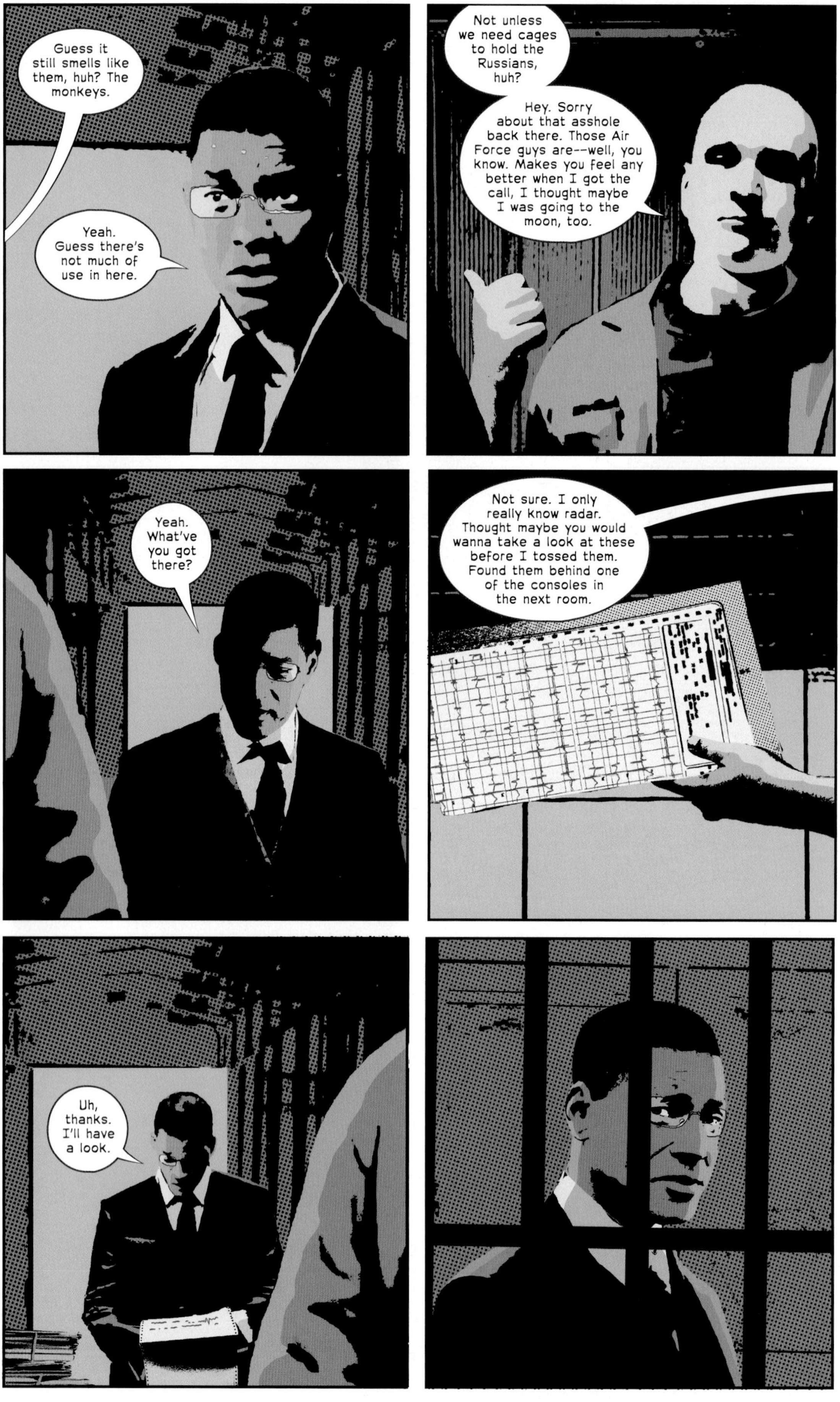
Guess it still smells like them, huh? The monkeys.
Yeah. Guess there's not much of use in here.
Not unless we need cages to hold the Russians, huh?
Hey. Sorry about that asshole back there. Those Air Force guys are--well, you know. Makes you feel any better when I got the call, I thought maybe I was going to the moon, too.
Yeah. What've you got there?
Not sure. I only really know radar. Thought maybe you would wanna take a look at these before I tossed them. Found them behind one of the consoles in the next room.
Uh, thanks. I'll have a look.

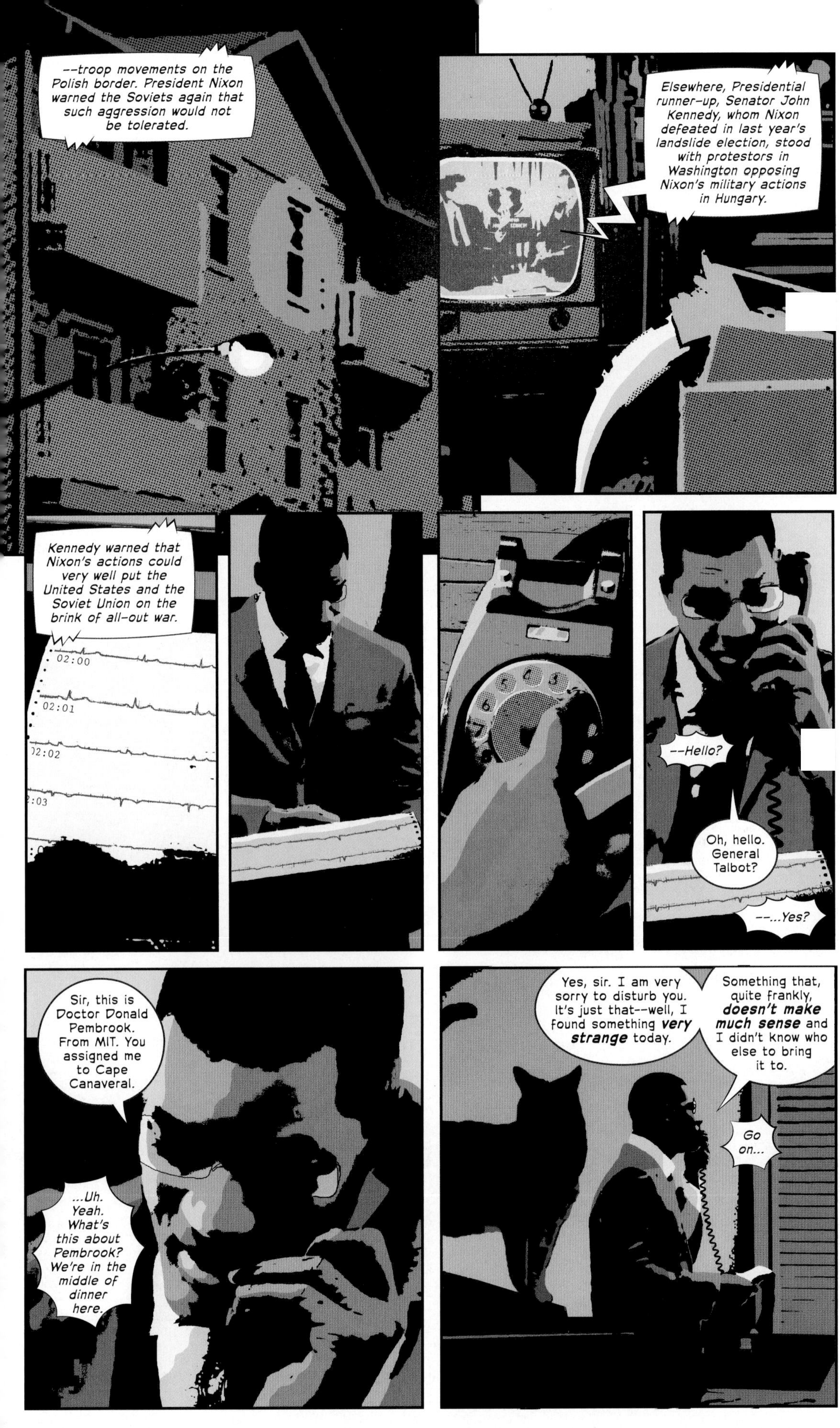
--troop movements on the Polish border. President Nixon warned the Soviets again that such aggression would not be tolerated.
Elsewhere, Presidential runner-up, Senator John Kennedy, whom Nixon defeated in last year's landslide election, stood with protestors in Washington opposing Nixon's military actions in Hungary.
Kennedy warned that Nixon's actions could very well put the United States and the Soviet Union on the brink of all-out war.
02:00
02:01
02:02
--Hello?
Oh, hello. General Talbot?
--...Yes?
Sir, this is Doctor Donald Pembrook. From MIT. You assigned me to Cape Canaveral.
...Uh. Yeah. What's this about Pembrook? We're in the middle of dinner here.
Yes, sir. I am very sorry to disturb you. It's just that--well, I found something *very strange* today.
Something that, quite frankly, ***doesn't make much sense*** and I didn't know who else to bring it to.
Go on...

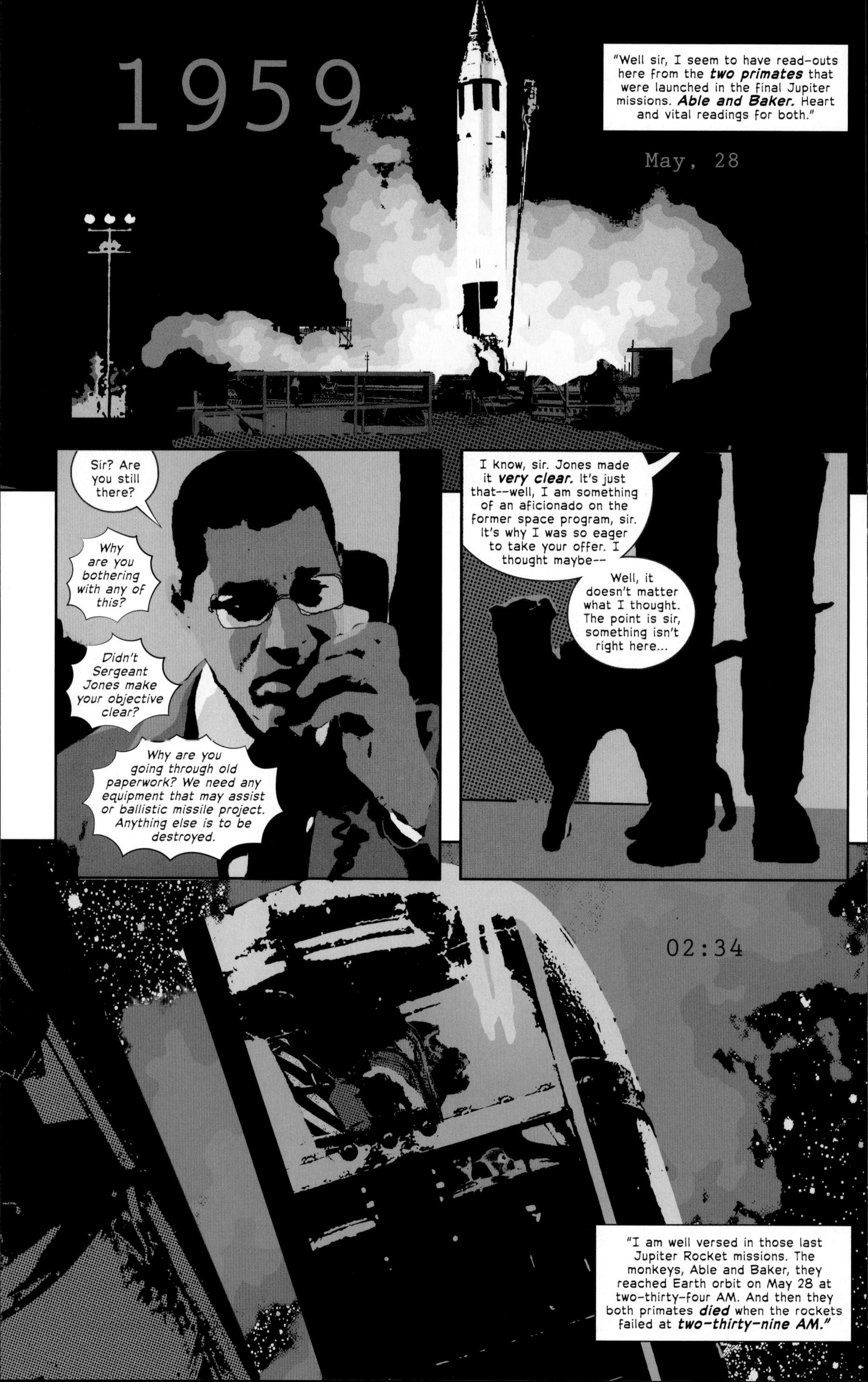
1959
"Well sir, I seem to have read-outs here from the **two primates** that were launched in the final Jupiter missions. ***Able and Baker.*** Heart and vital readings for both."
May, 28
Sir? Are you still there?
Why are you bothering with any of this?
Didn't Sergeant Jones make your objective clear?
Why are you going through old paperwork? We need any equipment that may assist or ballistic missile project. Anything else is to be destroyed.
I know, sir. Jones made it ***very clear.*** It's just that--well, I am something of an aficionado on the former space program, sir. It's why I was so eager to take your offer. I thought maybe--
Well, it doesn't matter what I thought. The point is sir, something isn't right here...
02:34
"I am well versed in those last Jupiter Rocket missions. The monkeys, Able and Baker, they reached Earth orbit on May 28 at two-thirty-four AM. And then they both primates ***died*** when the rockets failed at ***two-thirty-nine AM.***"

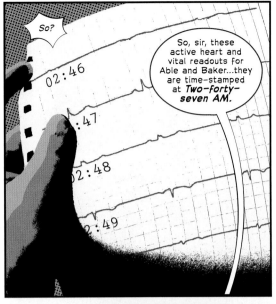

So?

So, sir, these active heart and vital readouts for Able and Baker...they are time-stamped at *Two-forty-seven AM.*

02:46
:47
02:48
2:49

That would be eight minutes *after they died,* sir.

I mean, this mission, and the deaths of those animals, well that was the reason we *shuttered the space program,* sir. Shouldn't we at least--

--Click

General?

02:52
02:53
02:54
02:55

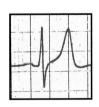

02:35

What's happening?!

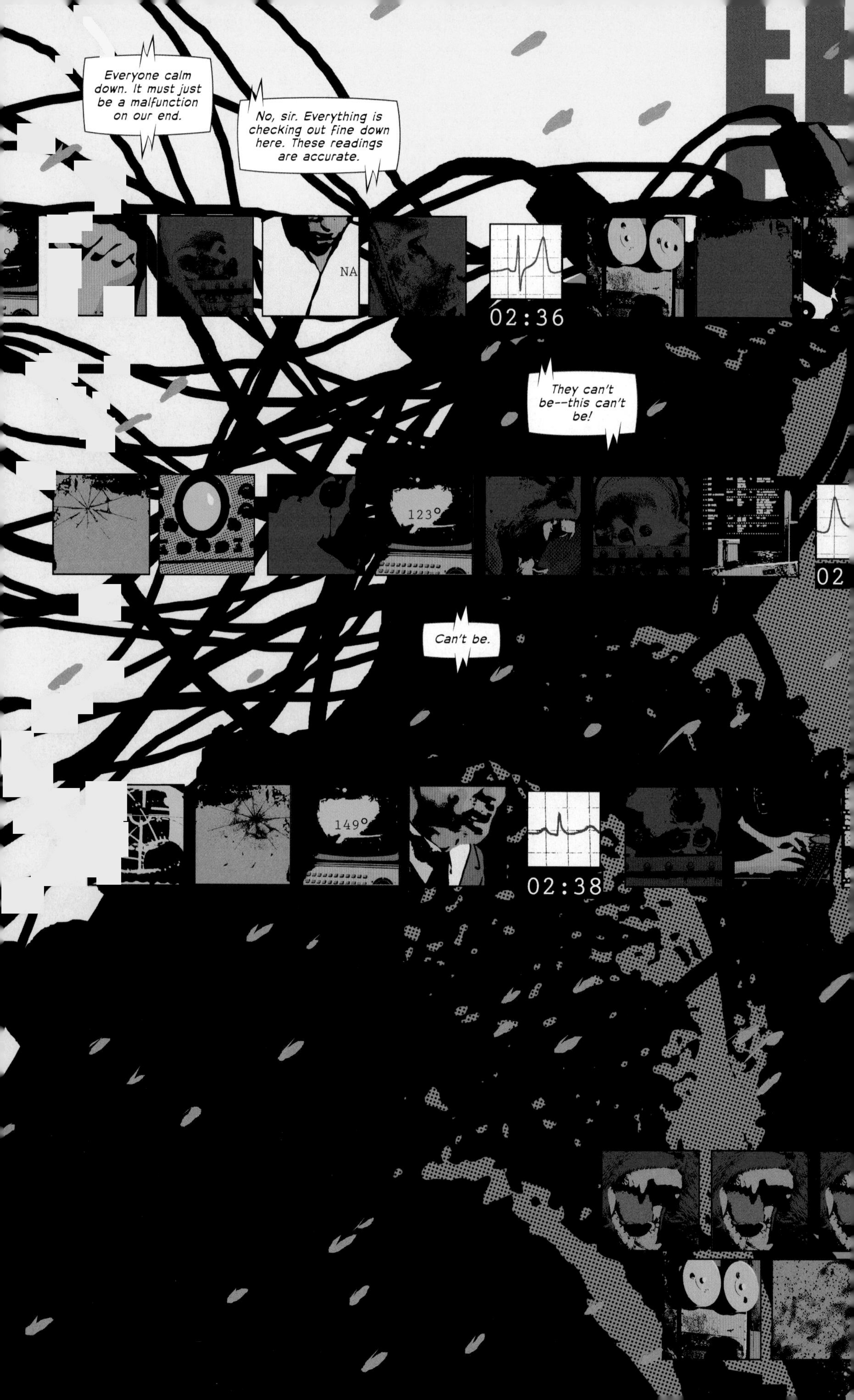
Everyone calm down. It must just be a malfunction on our end.
No, sir. Everything is checking out fine down here. These readings are accurate.
NA
02:36
They can't be--this can't be!
123°
02
Can't be.
149°
02:38

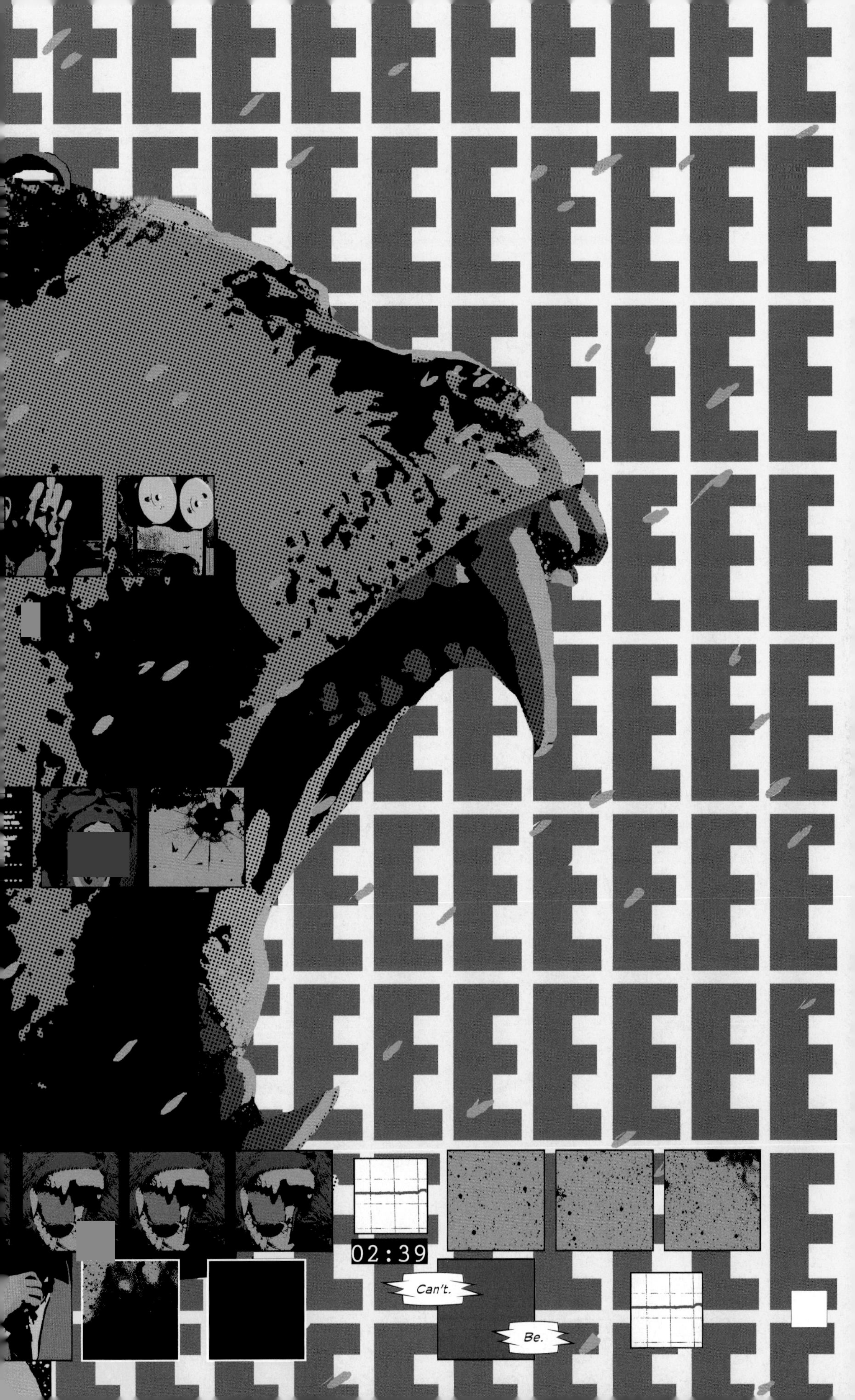
02:39
Can't.
Be.

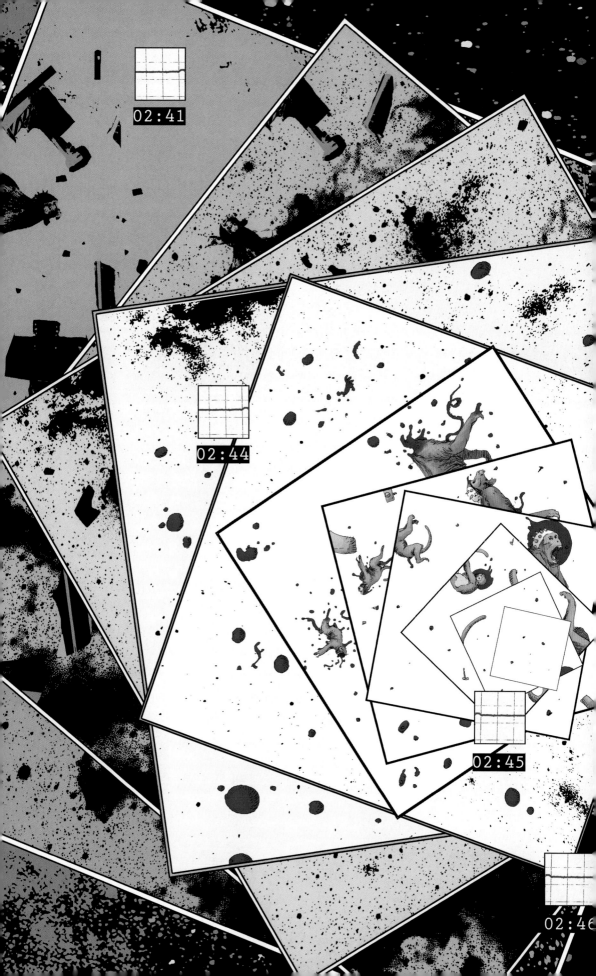

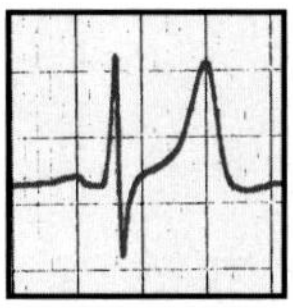

02:47

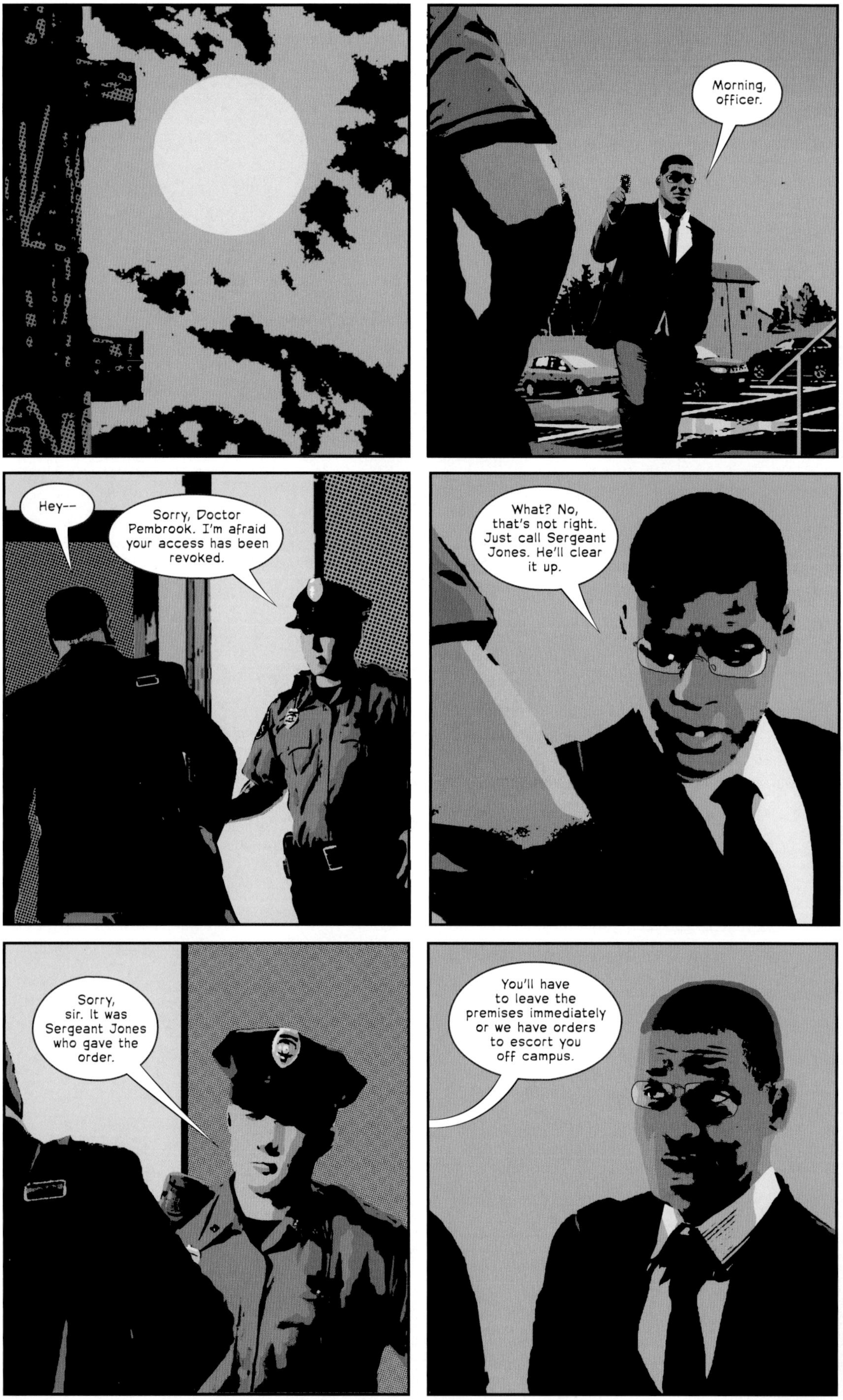
Morning, officer.
Hey--
Sorry, Doctor Pembrook. I'm afraid your access has been revoked.
What? No, that's not right. Just call Sergeant Jones. He'll clear it up.
Sorry, sir. It was Sergeant Jones who gave the order.
You'll have to leave the premises immediately or we have orders to escort you off campus.

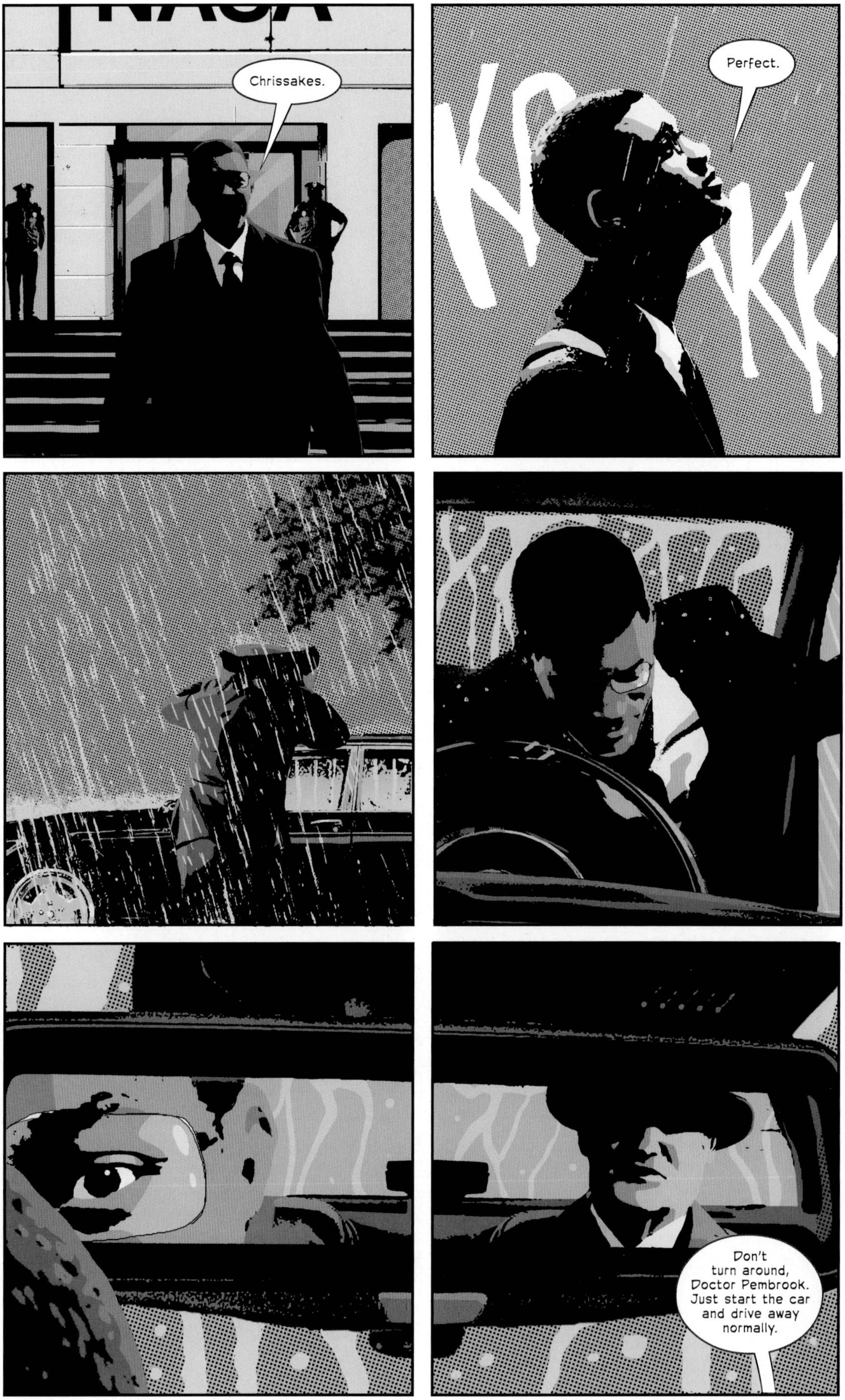
Chrissakes.
Perfect.
Don't turn around, Doctor Pembrook. Just start the car and drive away normally.

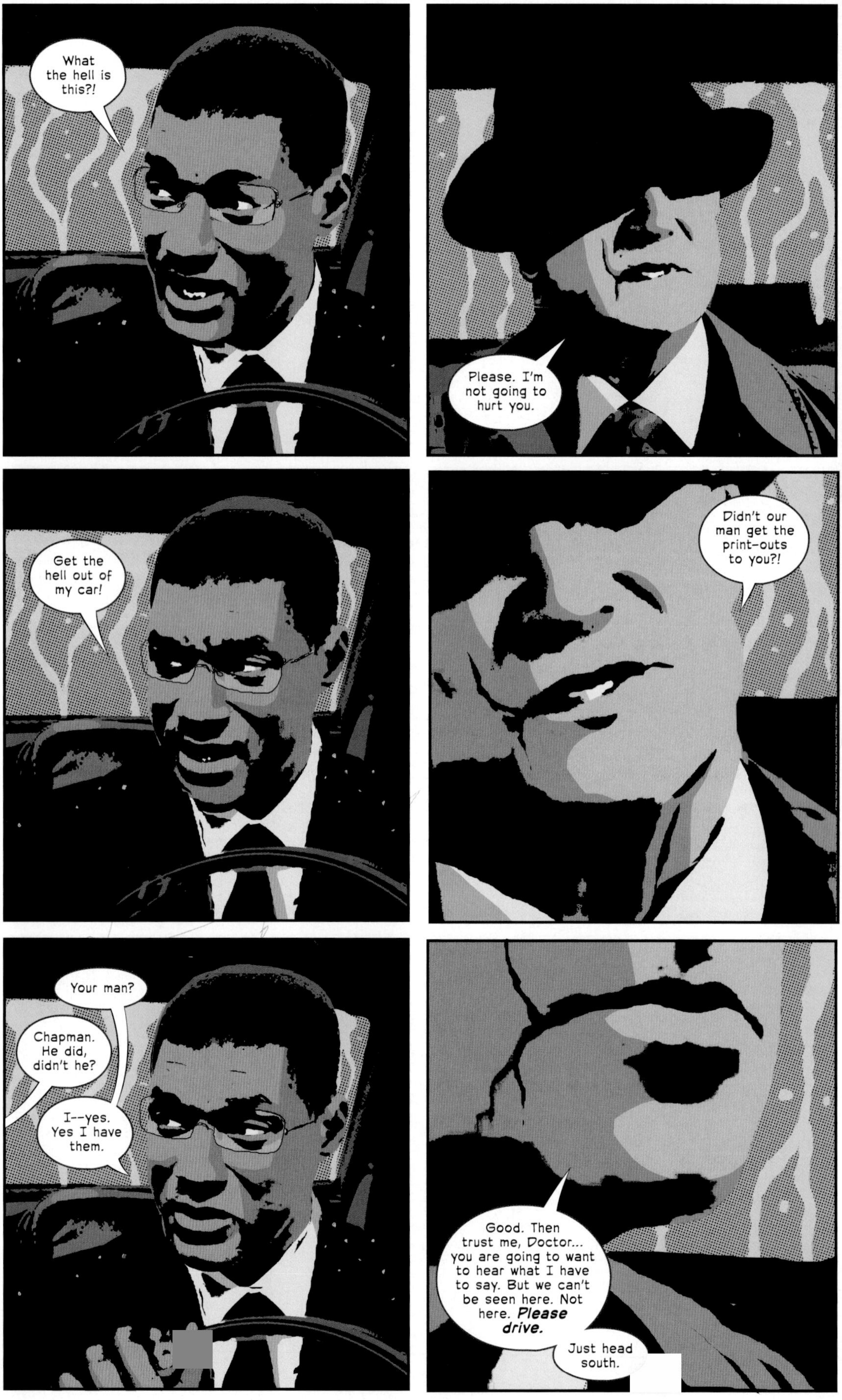
What the hell is this?!
Please. I'm not going to hurt you.
Get the hell out of my car!
Didn't our man get the print-outs to you?!
Your man?
Chapman. He did, didn't he?
I--yes. Yes I have them.
Good. Then trust me, Doctor... you are going to want to hear what I have to say. But we can't be seen here. Not here. *Please drive.*
Just head south.

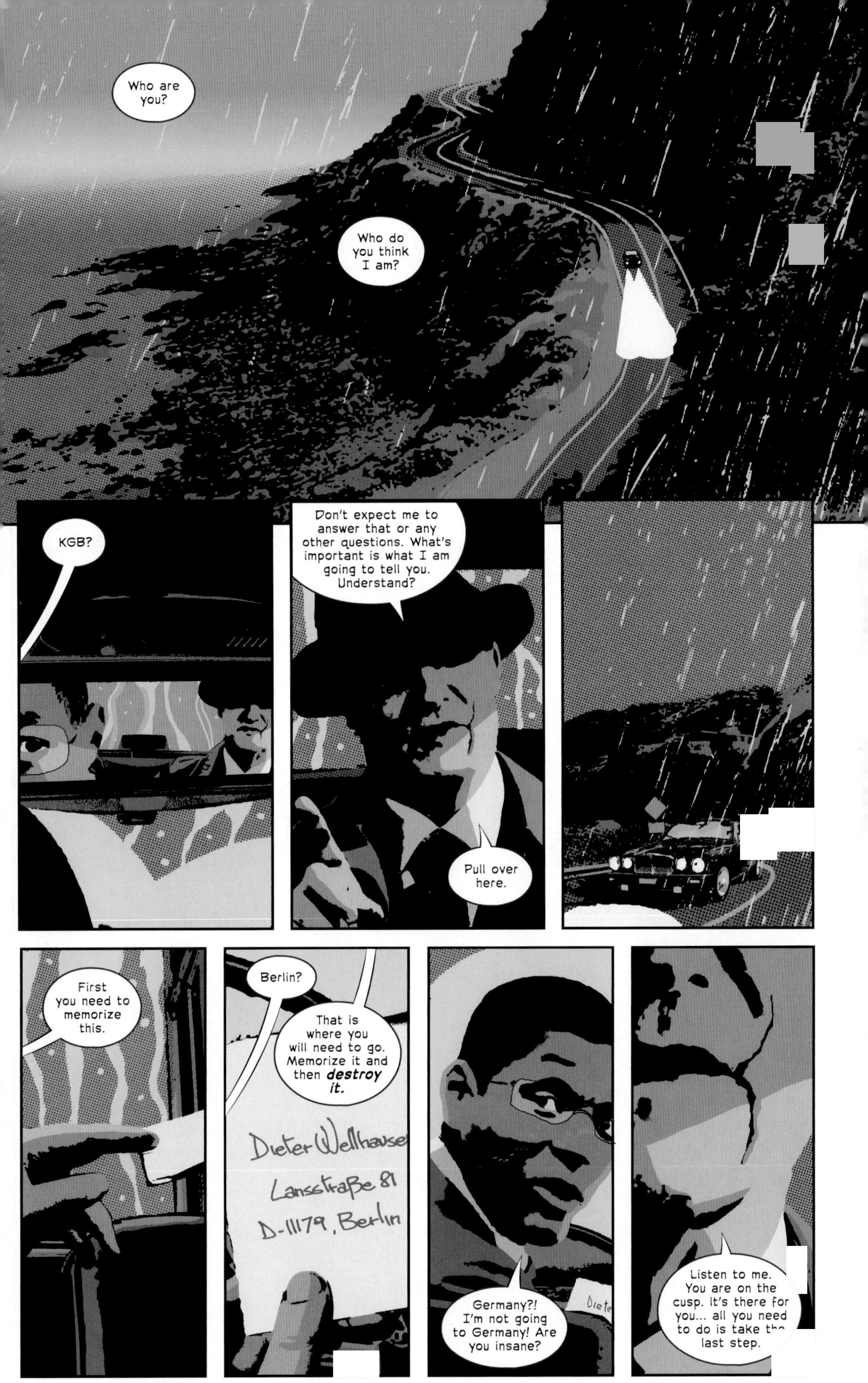
Who are you?
Who do you think I am?
KGB?
Don't expect me to answer that or any other questions. What's important is what I am going to tell you. Understand?
Pull over here.
First you need to memorize this.
Berlin?
That is where you will need to go. Memorize it and then *destroy it.*
Dieter Wellhause
Lansstraße 81
D-11179, Berlin
Germany?! I'm not going to Germany! Are you insane?
Listen to me. You are on the cusp. It's there for you... all you need to do is take th
last step.

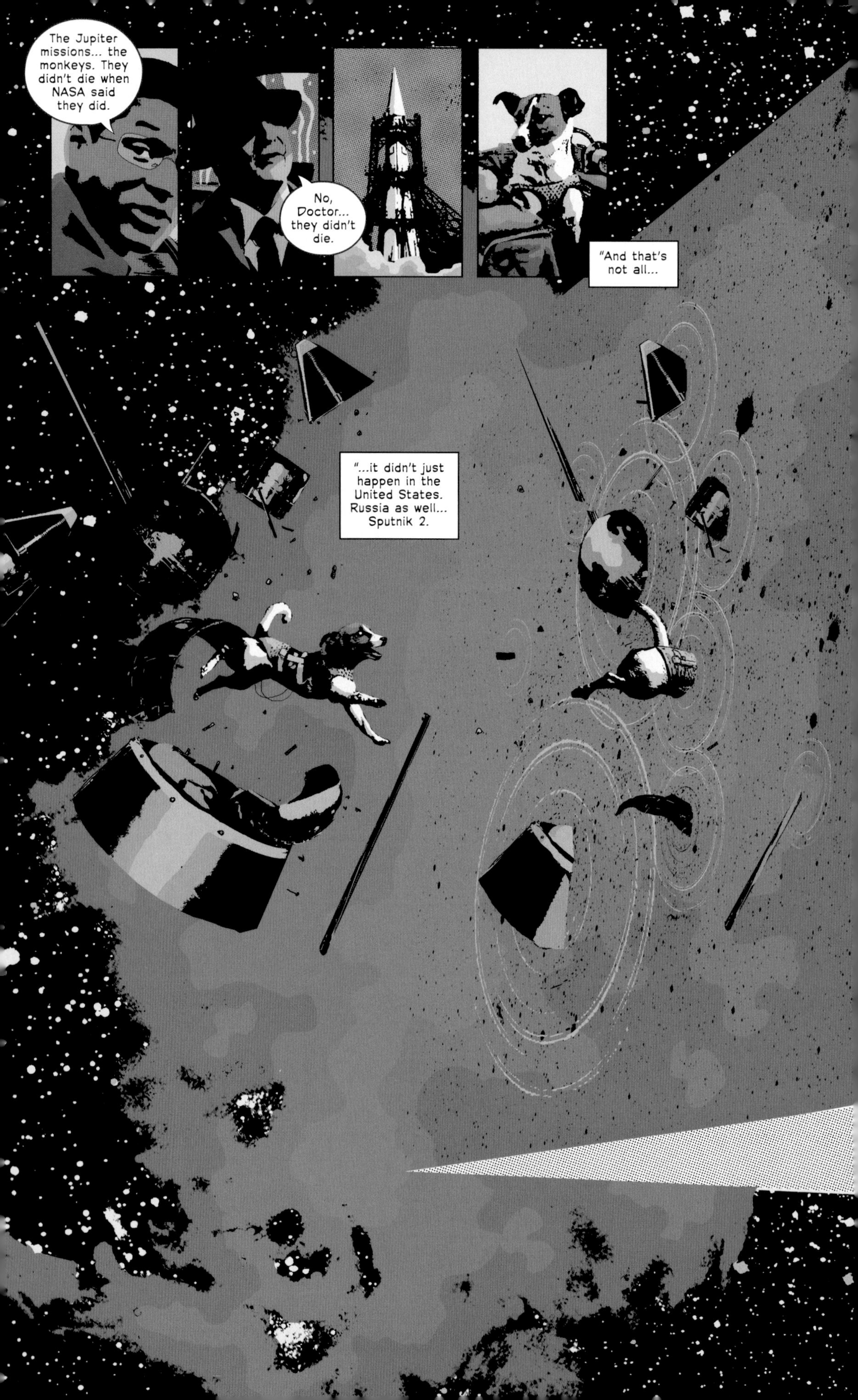
The Jupiter missions... the monkeys. They didn't die when NASA said they did.
No, Doctor... they didn't die.
"And that's not all...
"...it didn't just happen in the United States. Russia as well... Sputnik 2.

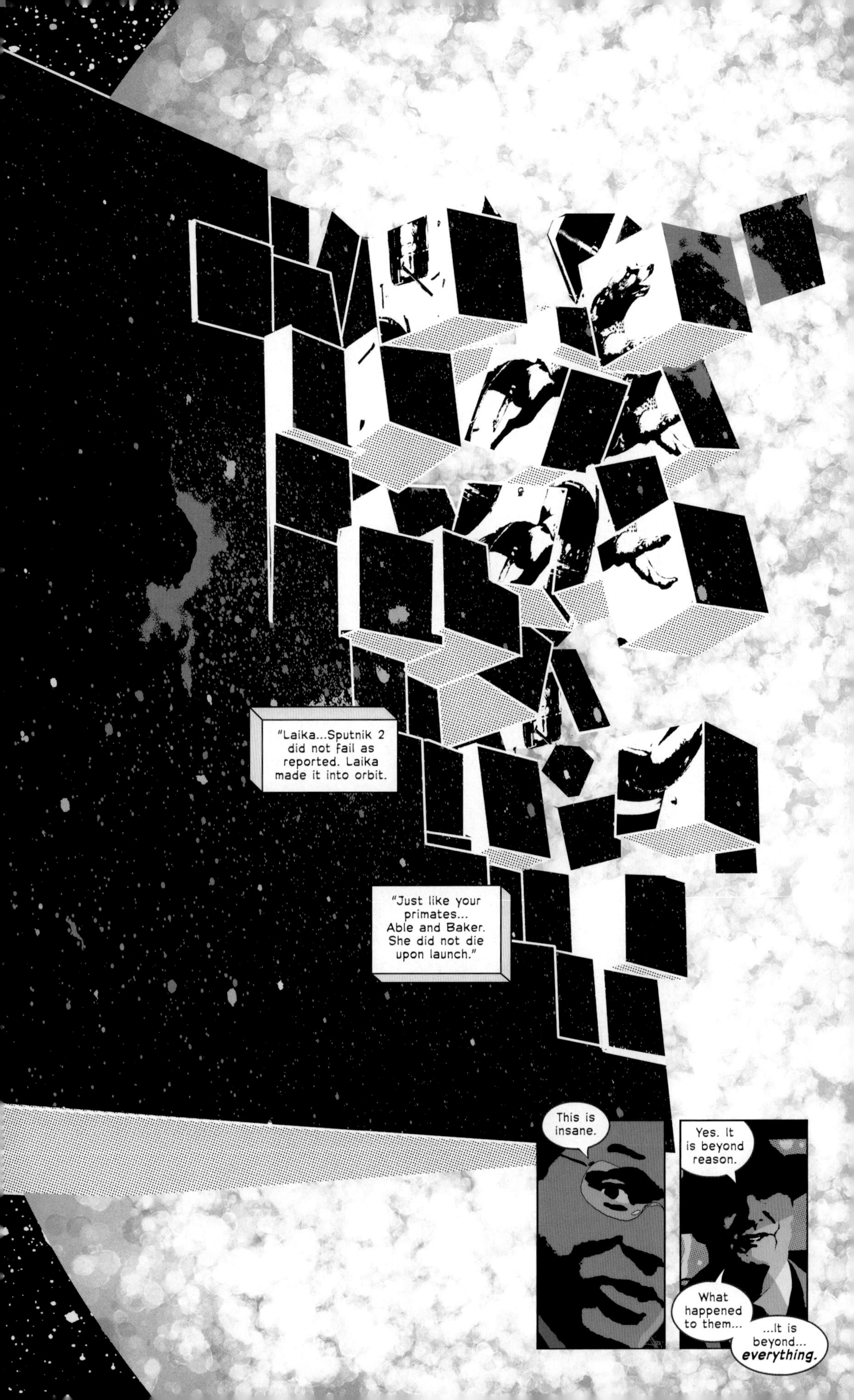
"Laika...Sputnik 2 did not fail as reported. Laika made it into orbit.
"Just like your primates... Able and Baker. She did not die upon launch."
This is insane.
Yes. It is beyond reason.
What happened to them...
...It is beyond... *everything.*

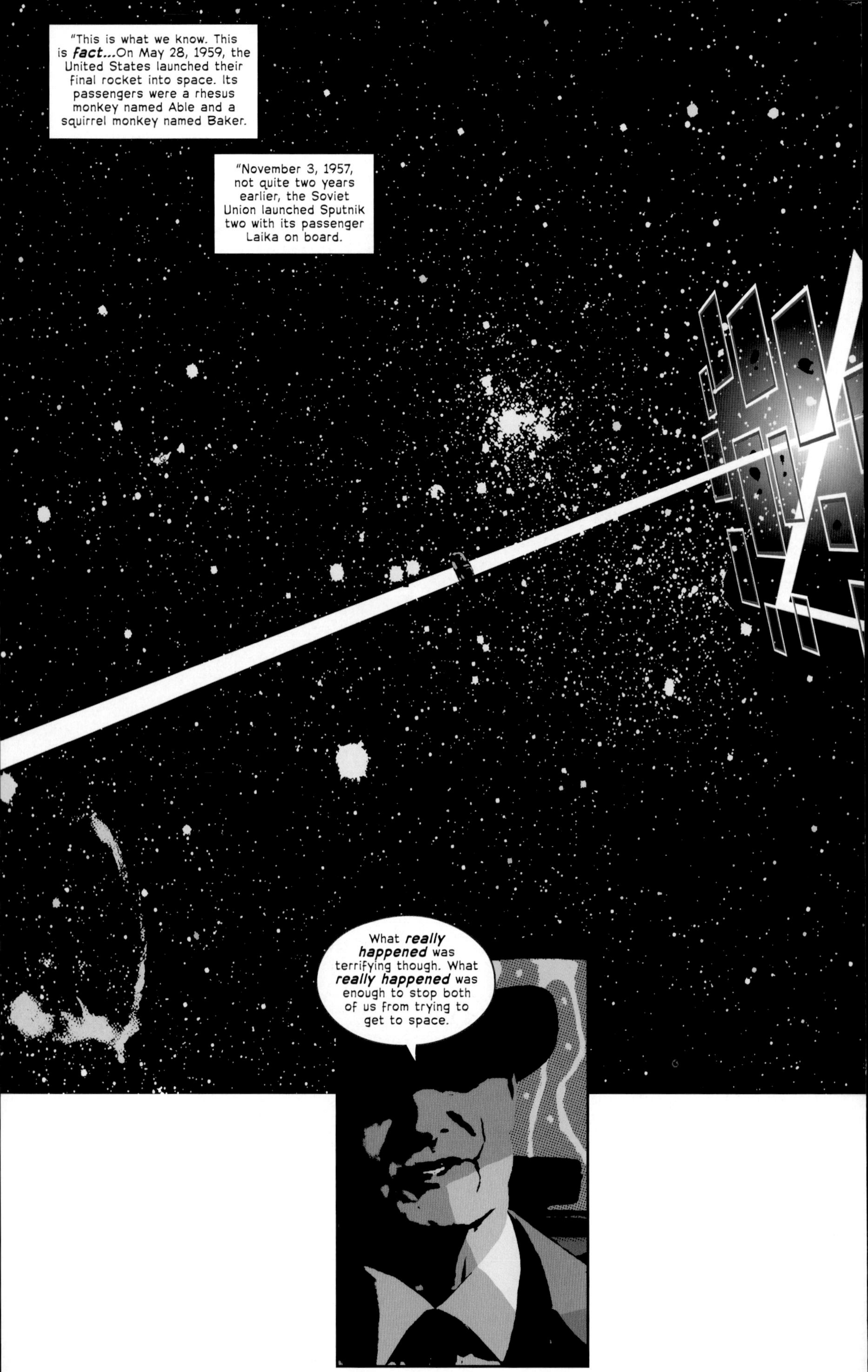
"This is what we know. This is *fact...*On May 28, 1959, the United States launched their final rocket into space. Its passengers were a rhesus monkey named Able and a squirrel monkey named Baker.
"November 3, 1957, not quite two years earlier, the Soviet Union launched Sputnik two with its passenger Laika on board.
What *really happened* was terrifying though. What *really happened* was enough to stop both of us from trying to get to space.

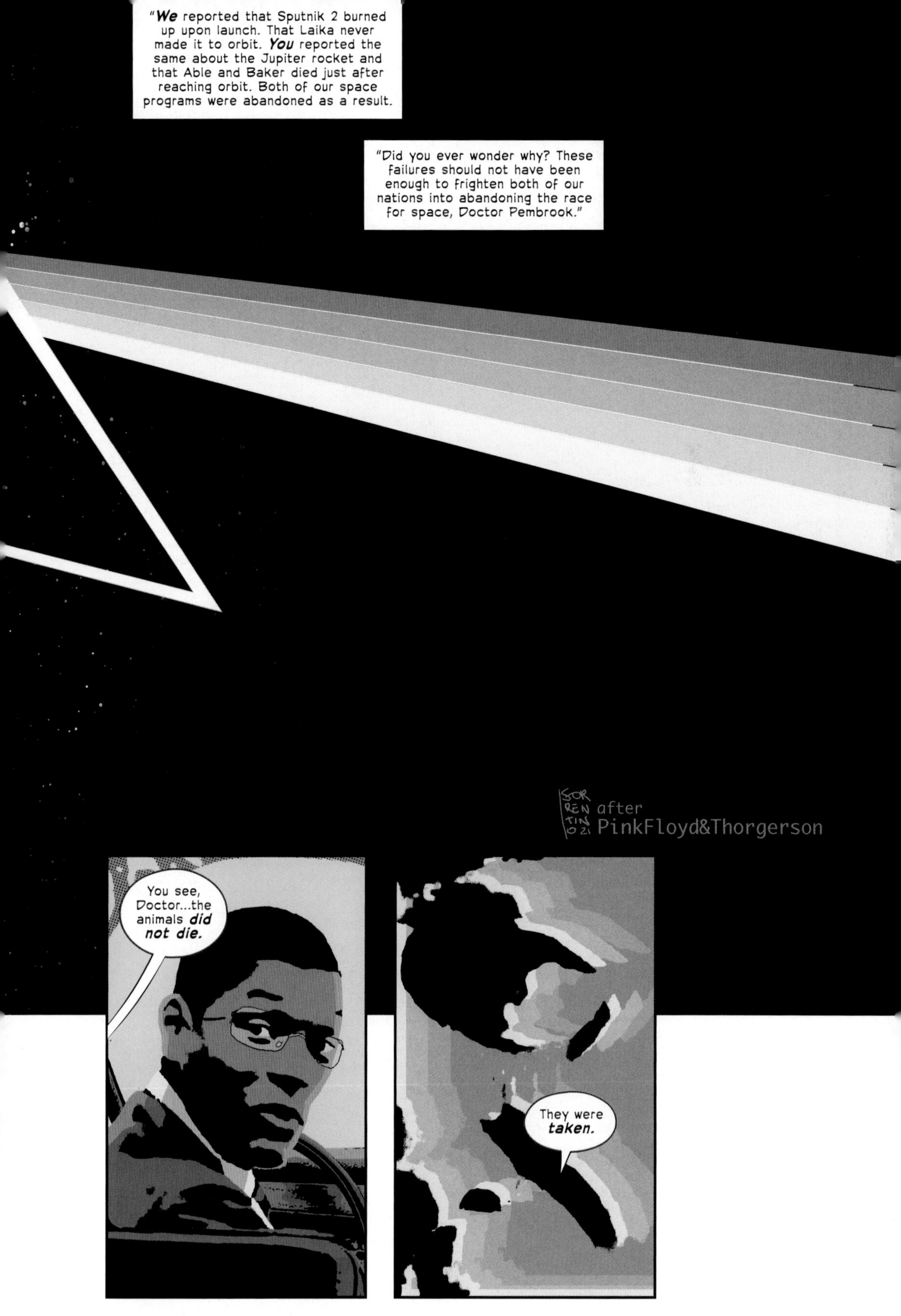
"We reported that Sputnik 2 burned up upon launch. That Laika never made it to orbit. You reported the same about the Jupiter rocket and that Able and Baker died just after reaching orbit. Both of our space programs were abandoned as a result.
"Did you ever wonder why? These failures should not have been enough to frighten both of our nations into abandoning the race for space, Doctor Pembrook."
after PinkFloyd&Thorgerson
You see, Doctor...the animals did not die.
They were taken.

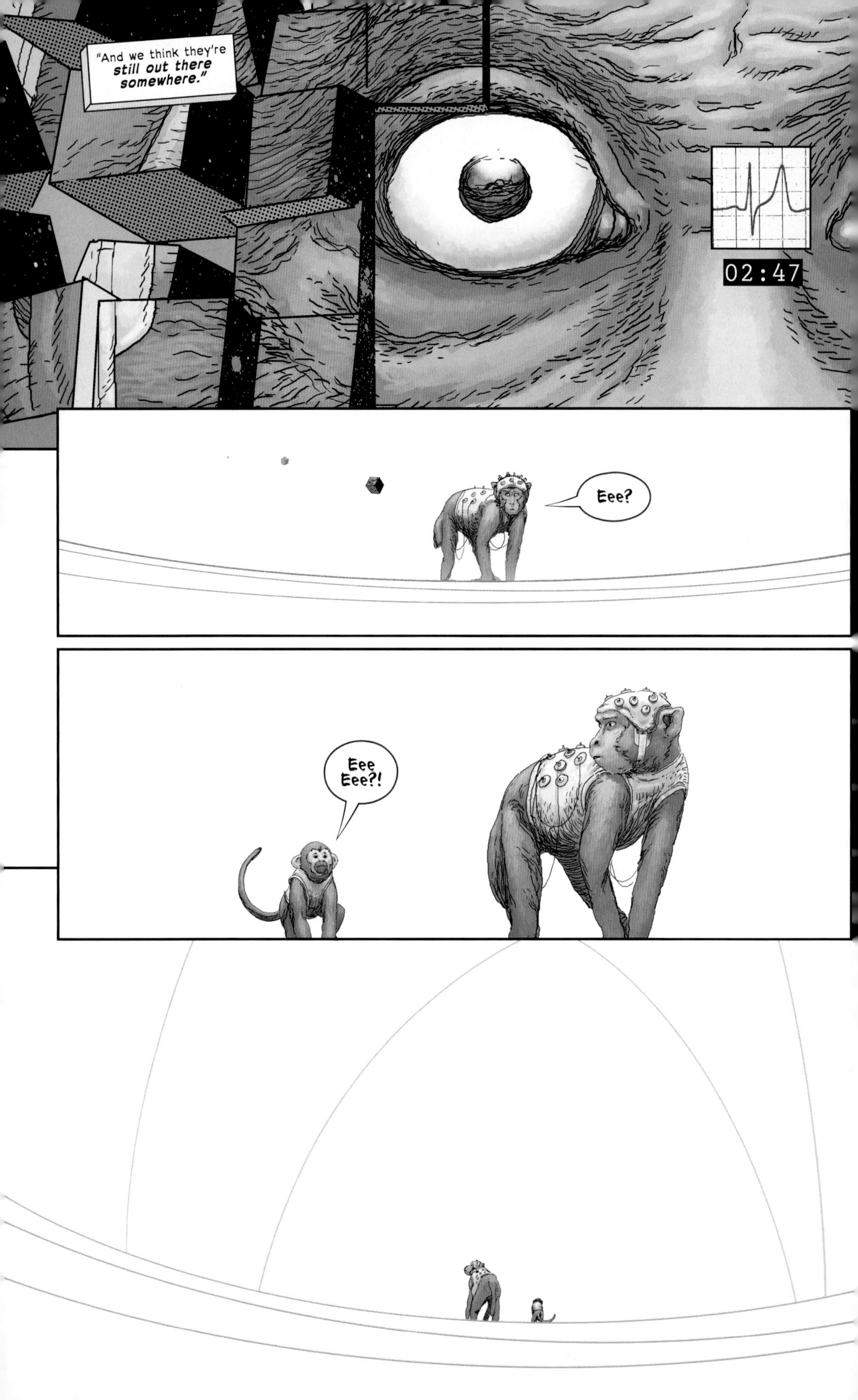
"And we think they're still out there somewhere."
02:47
Eee?
Eee Eee?!

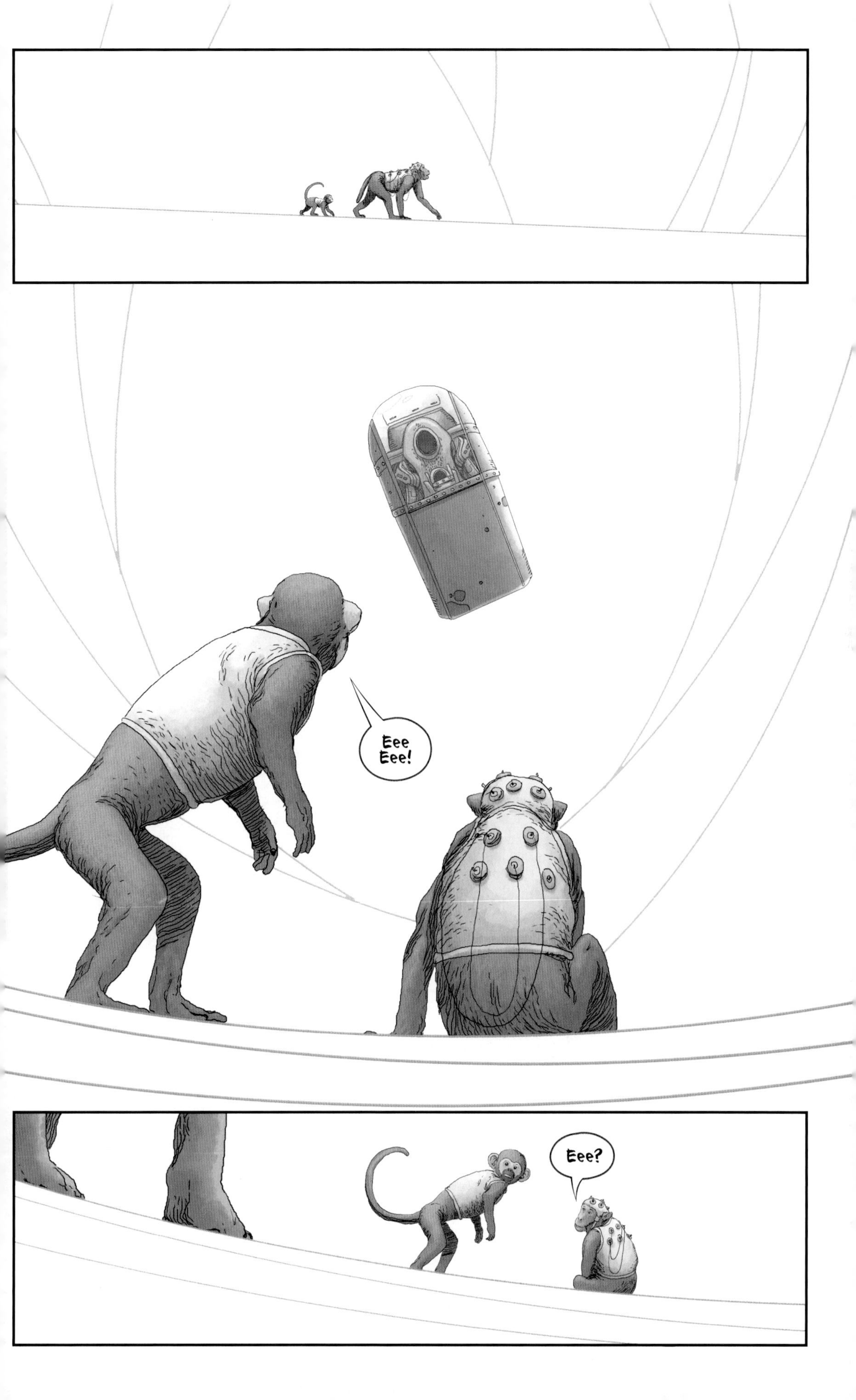
Eee
Eee!
Eee?

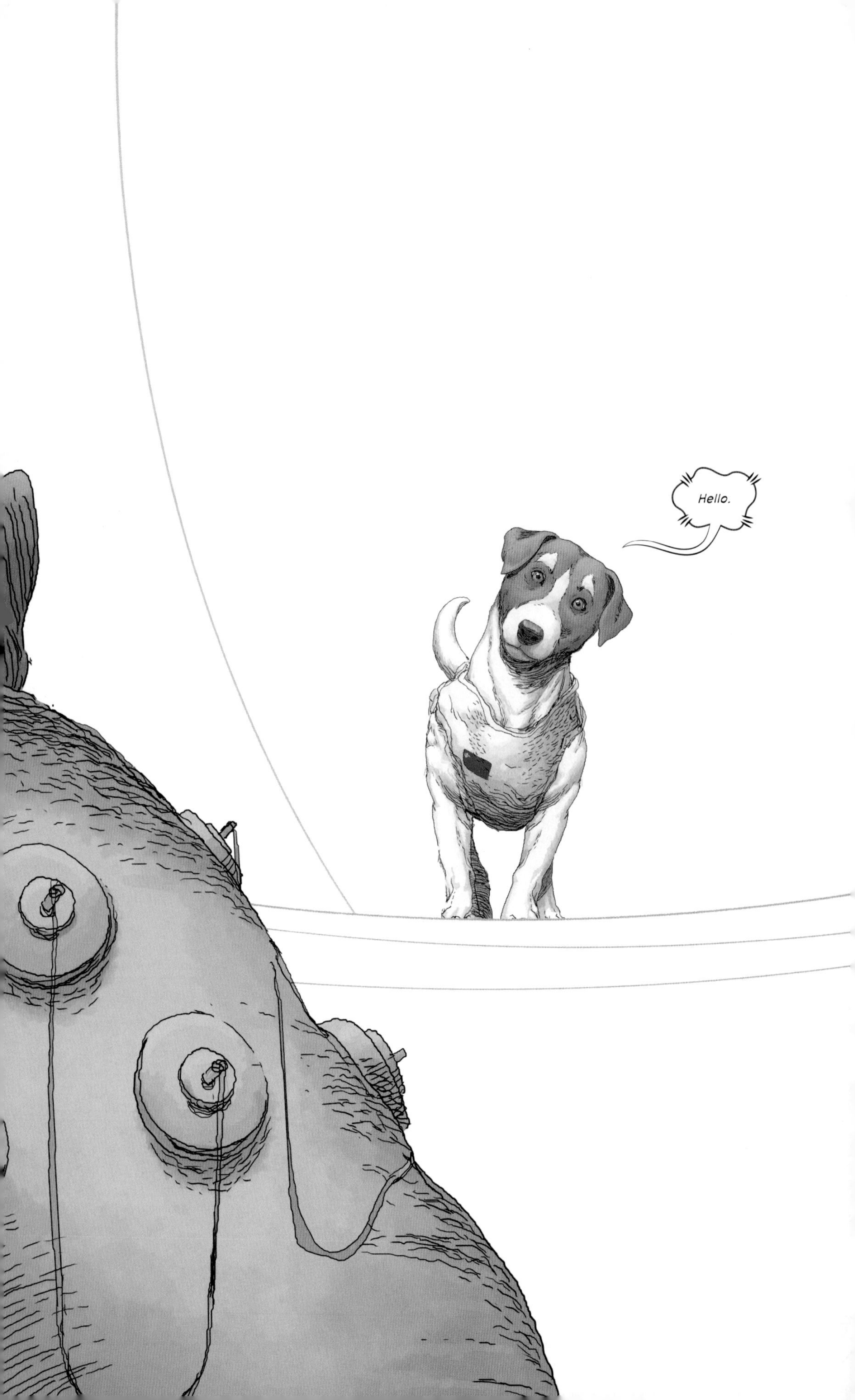
Hello.

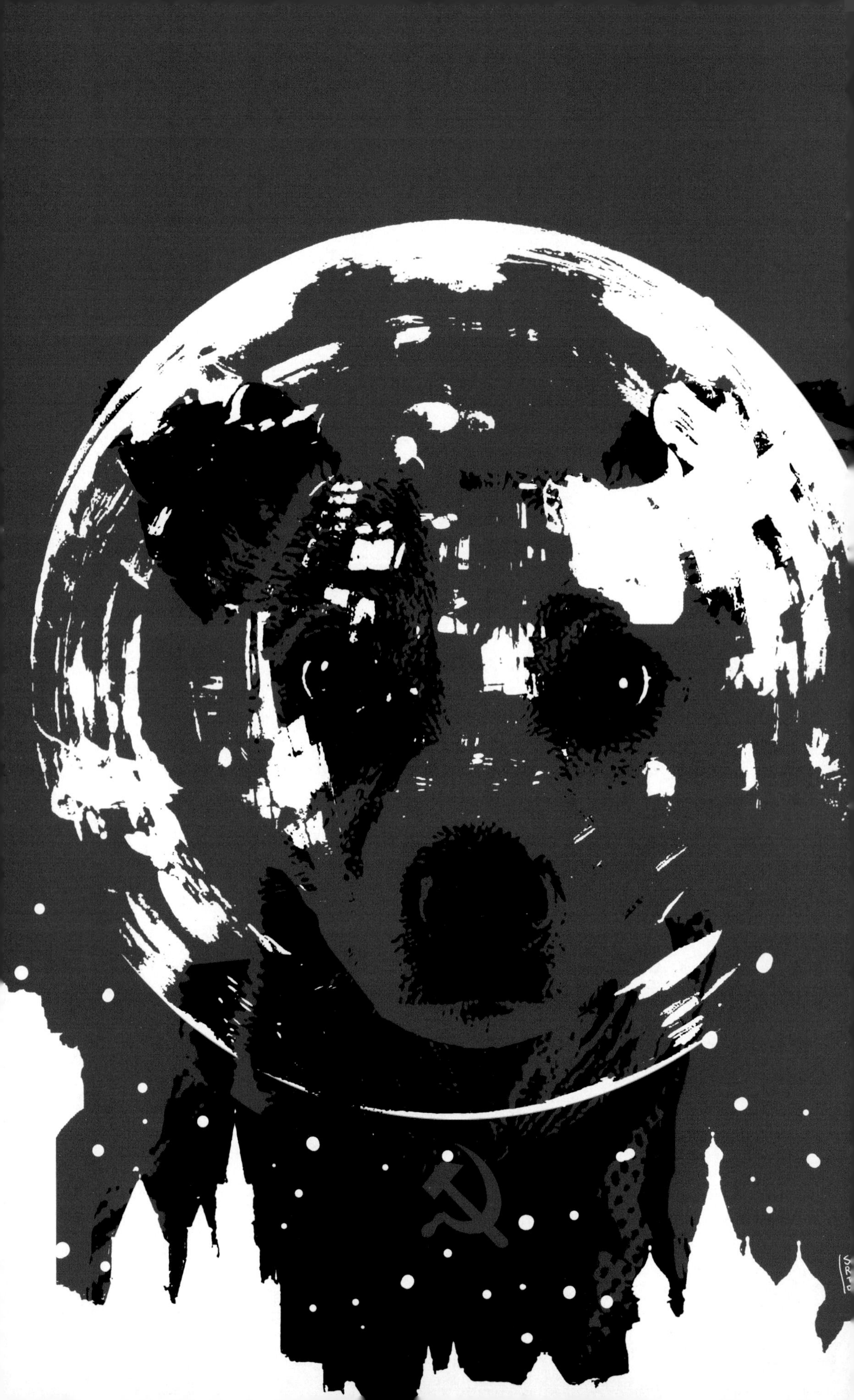

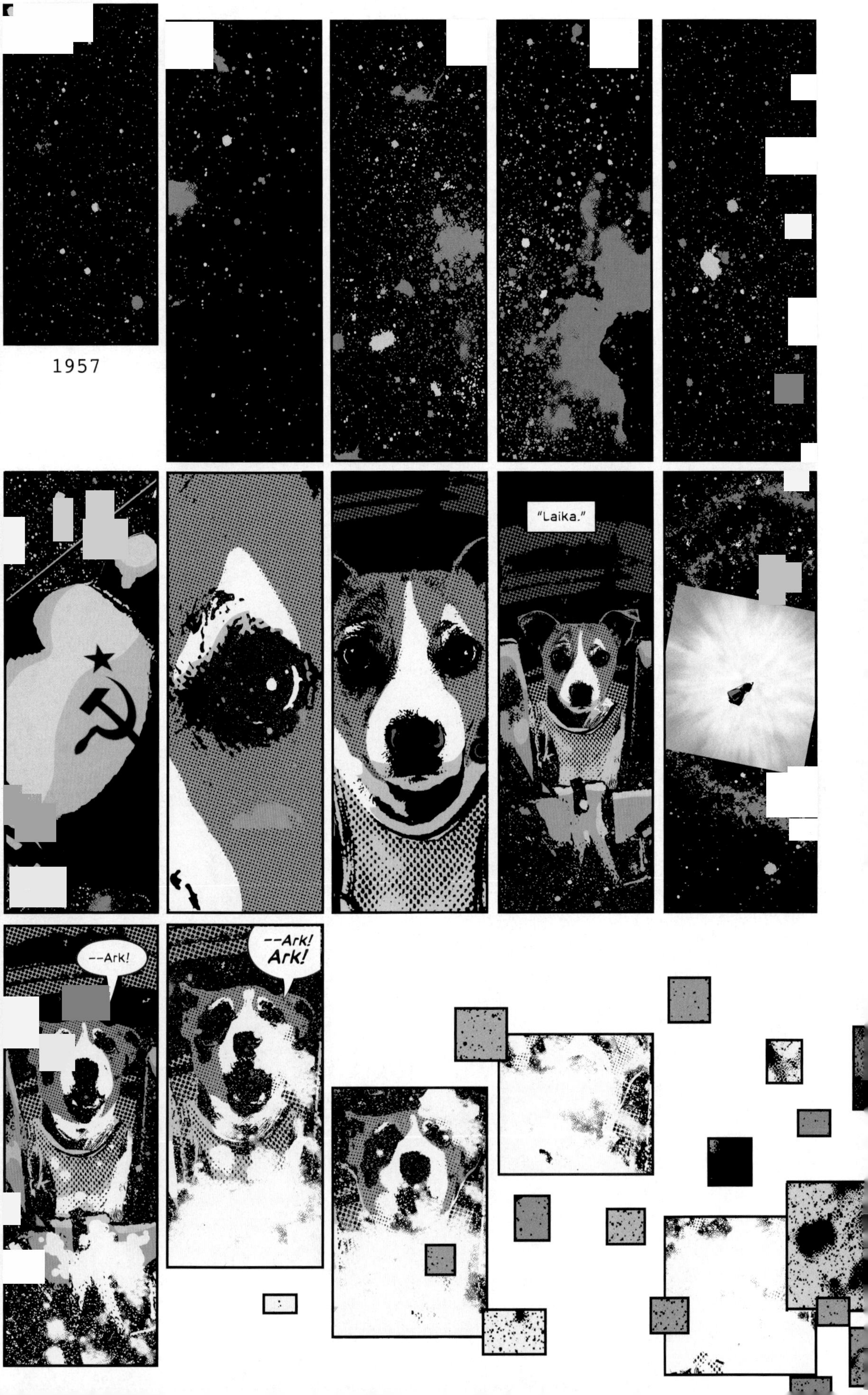
1957
"Laika."
--Ark!
--Ark! Ark!

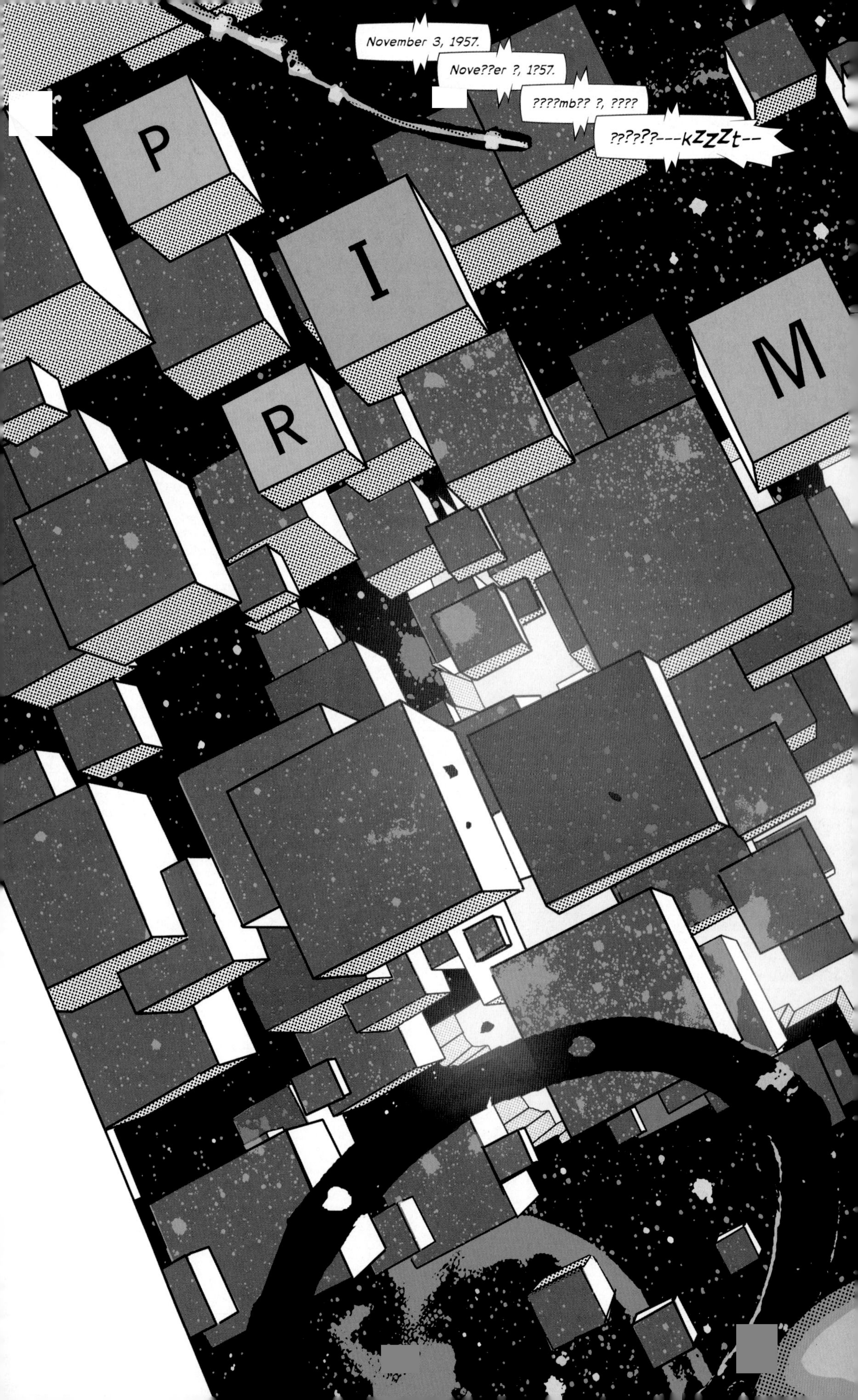
November 3, 1957.
Nove??er ?, 1?57.
????mb?? ?, ????
??????---kZZZt--
P
I
R
M

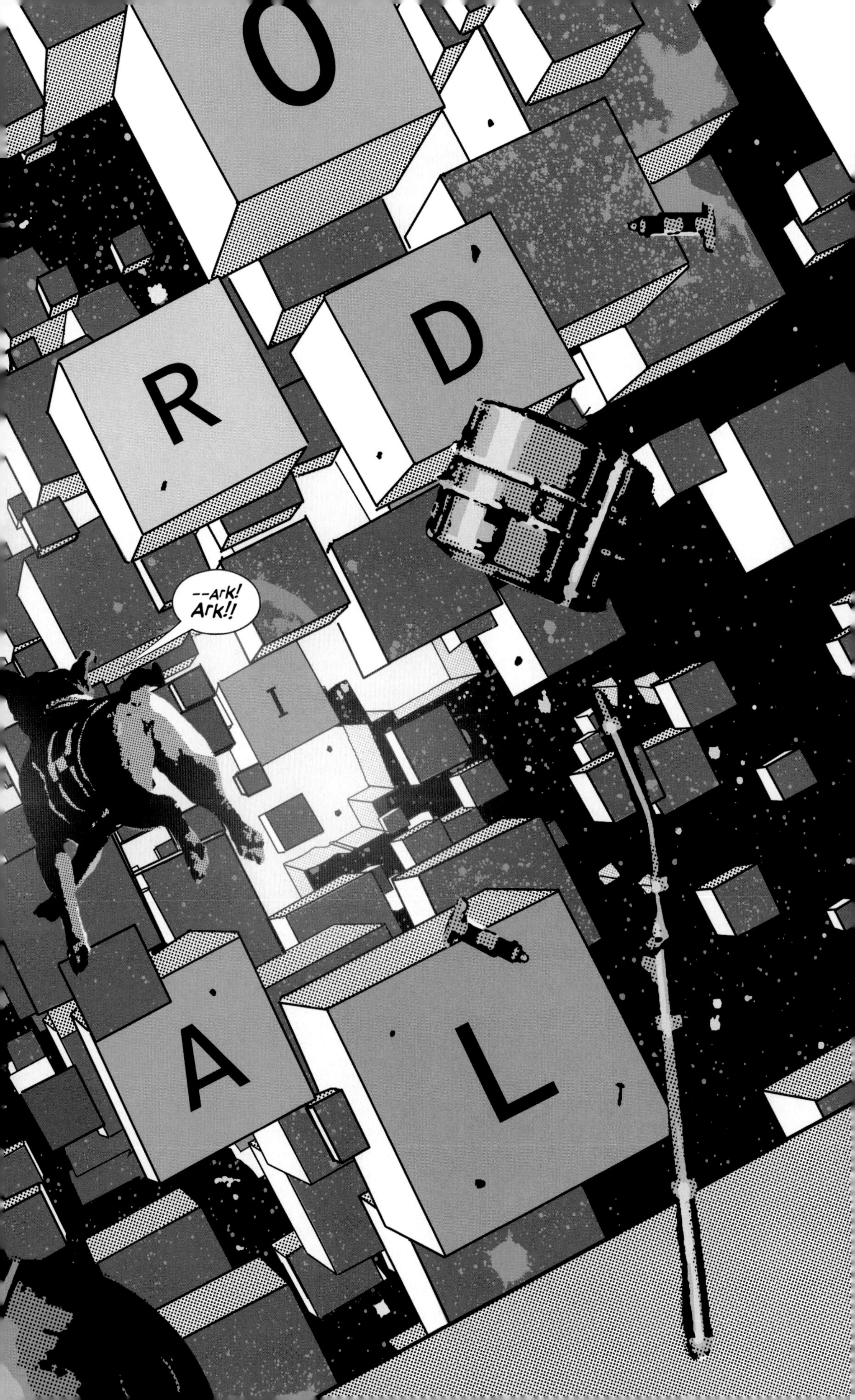
O
R
D
I
A
L
--Ark! Ark!!

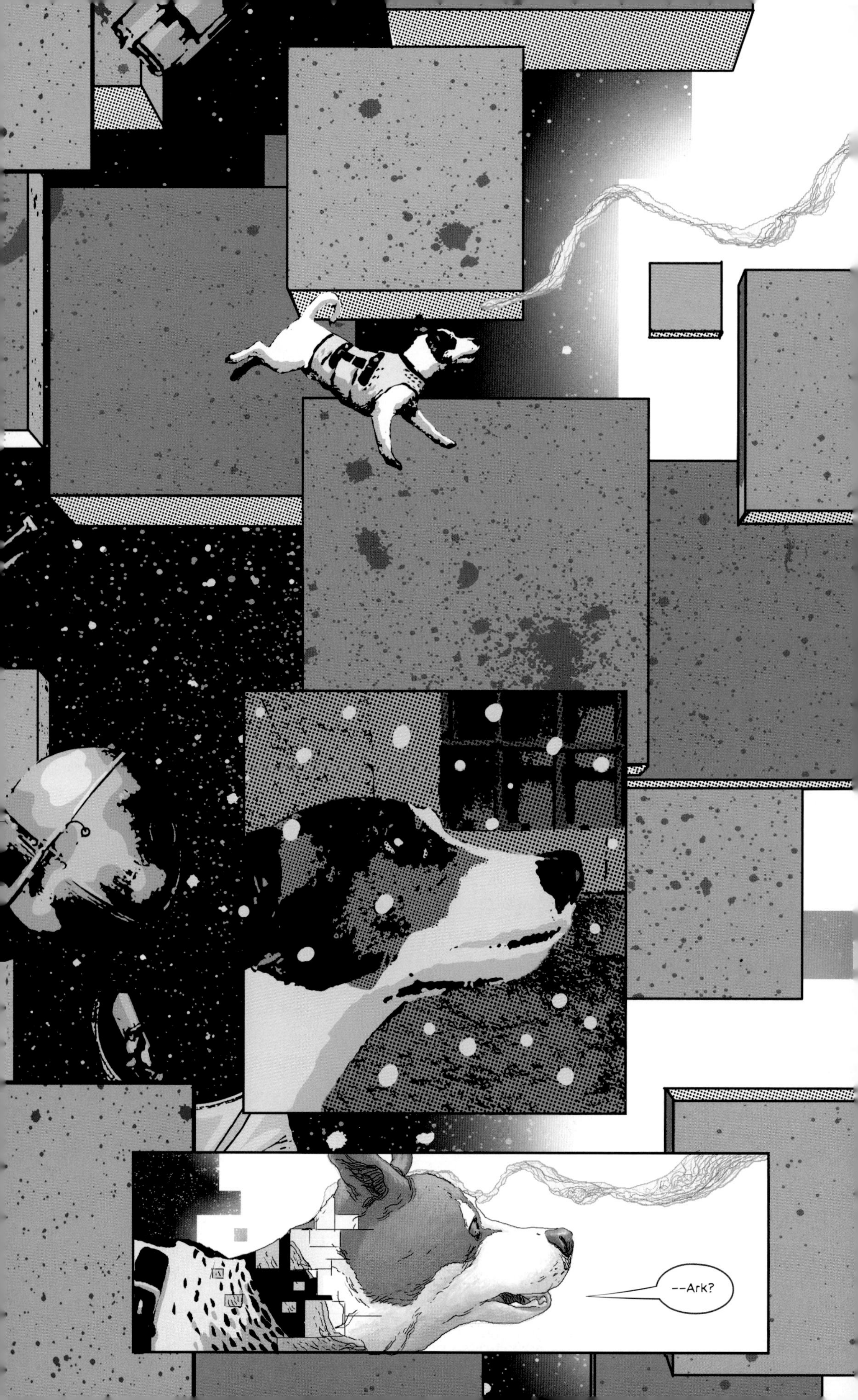
--Ark?

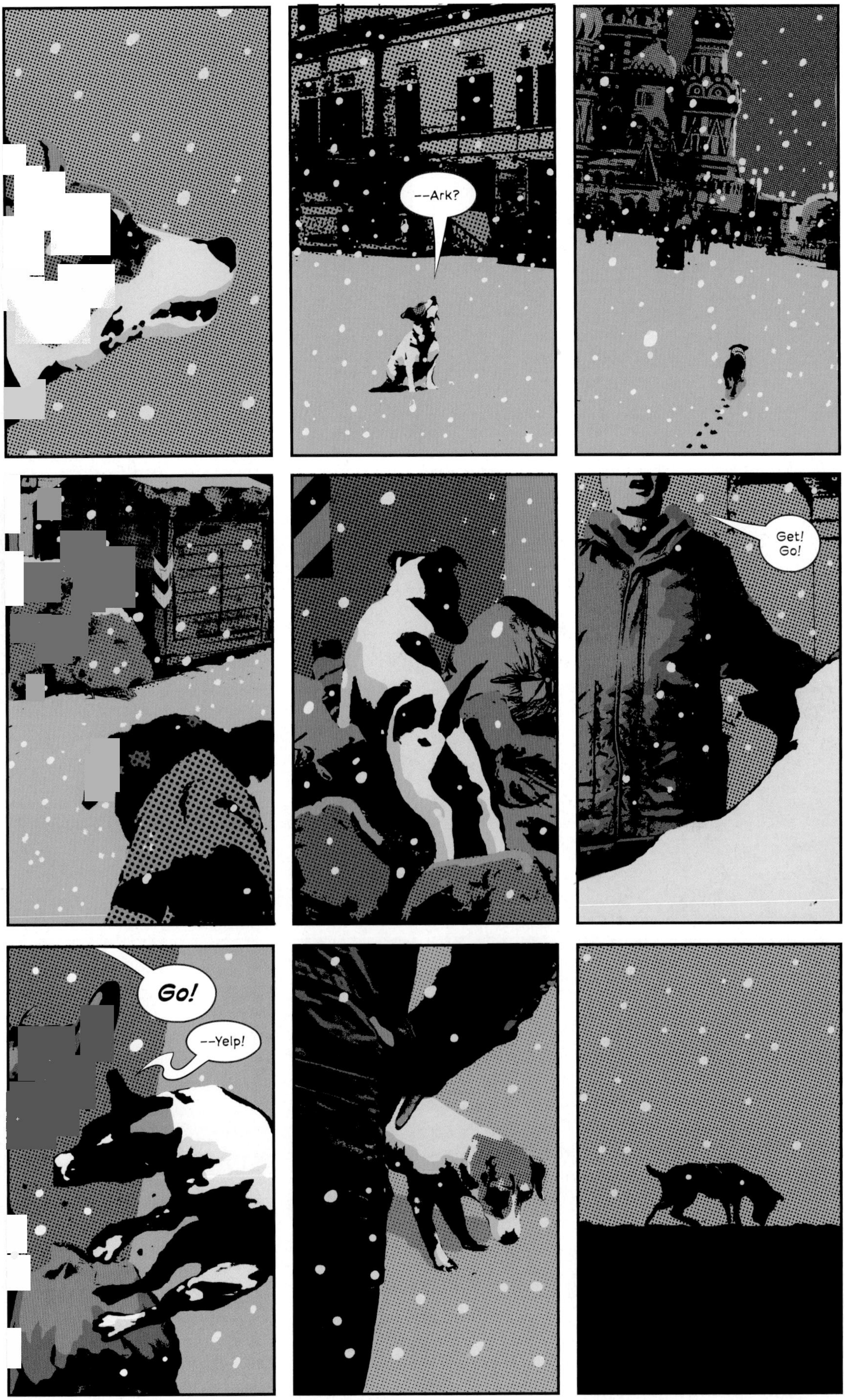
--Ark?
Get! Go!
Go!
--Yelp!

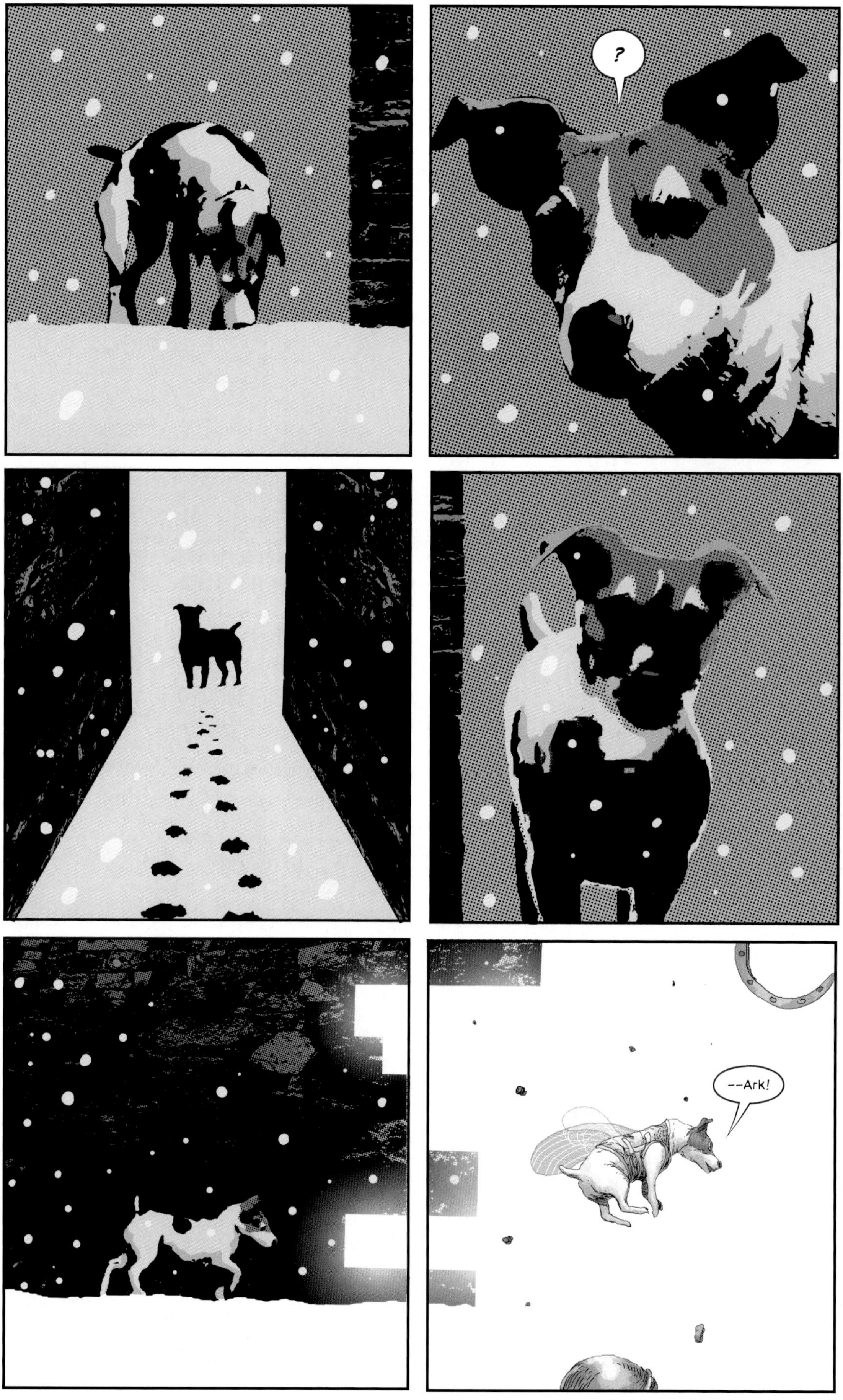
?
--Ark!

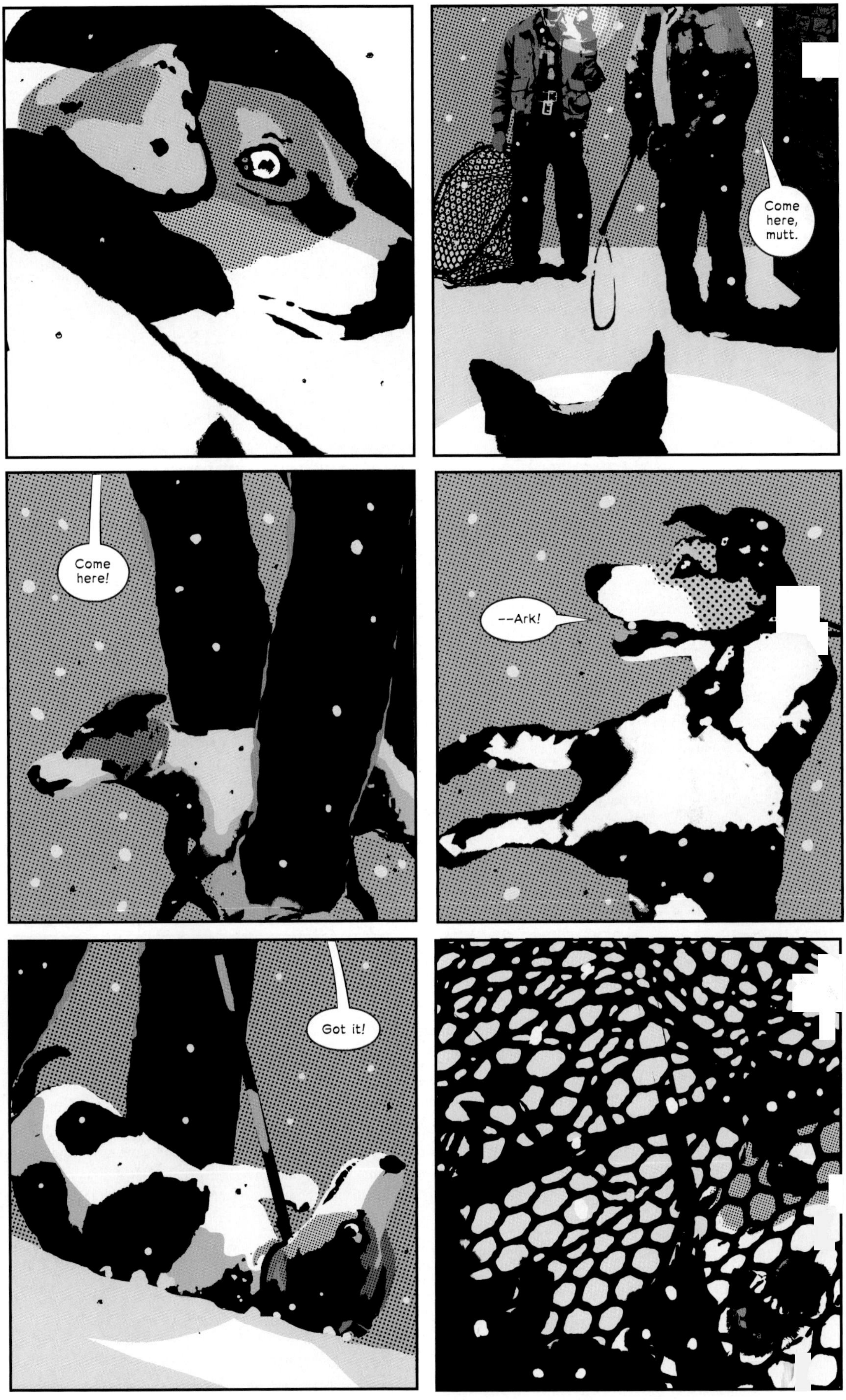
Come here, mutt.
Come here!
--Ark!
Got it!

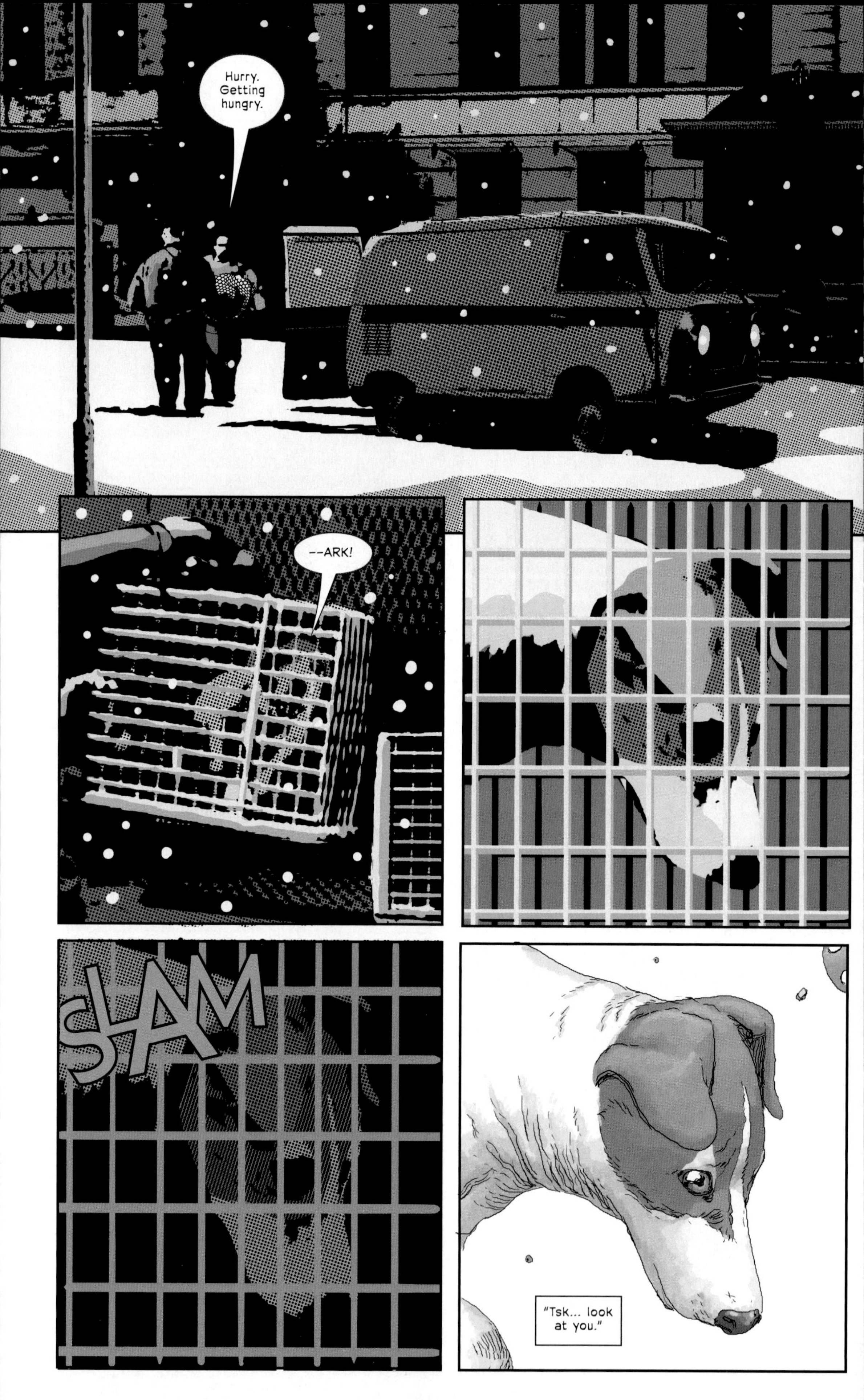
Hurry. Getting hungry.
--ARK!
SLAM
"Tsk... look at you."

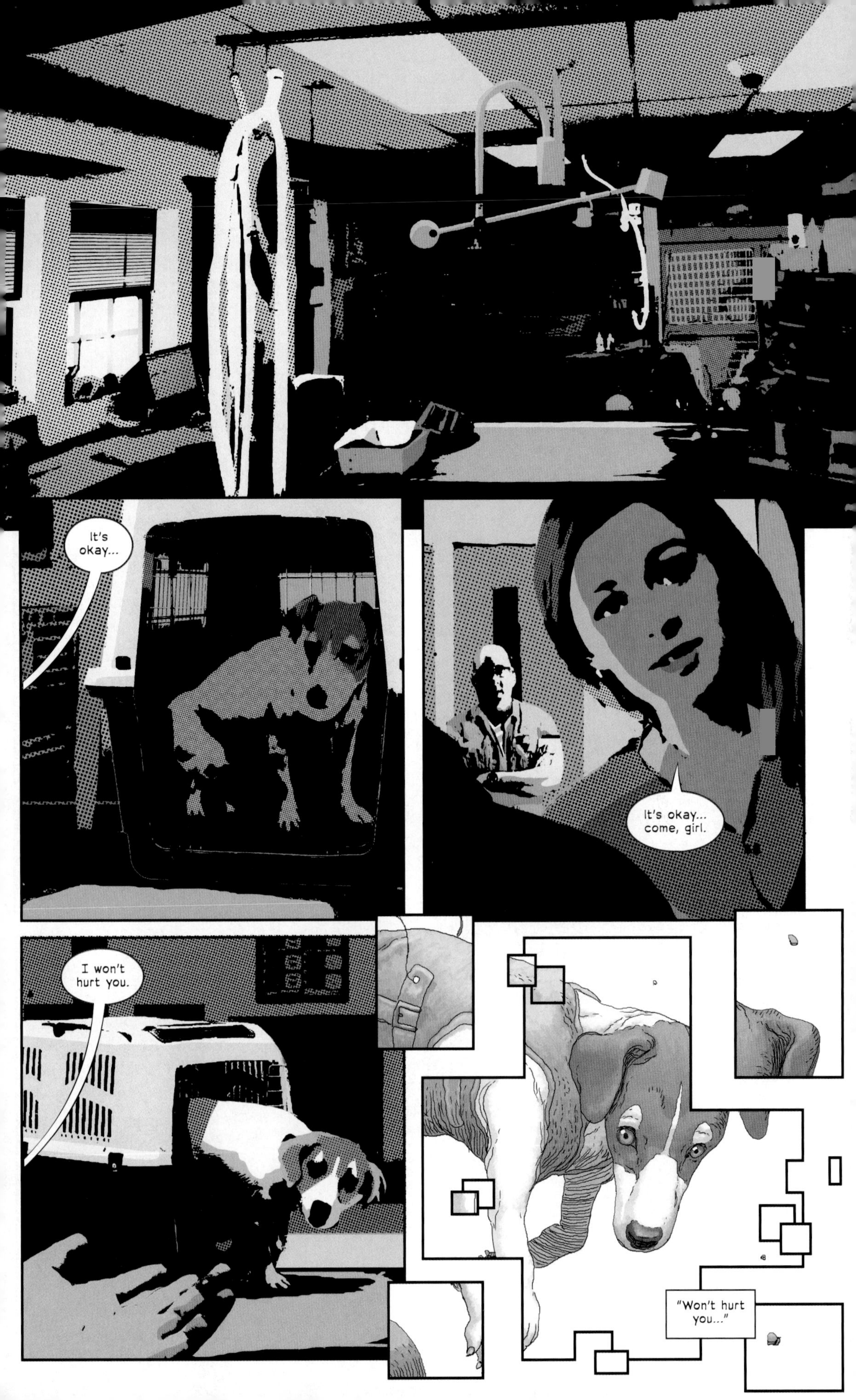
It's okay...
It's okay... come, girl.
I won't hurt you.
"Won't hurt you..."

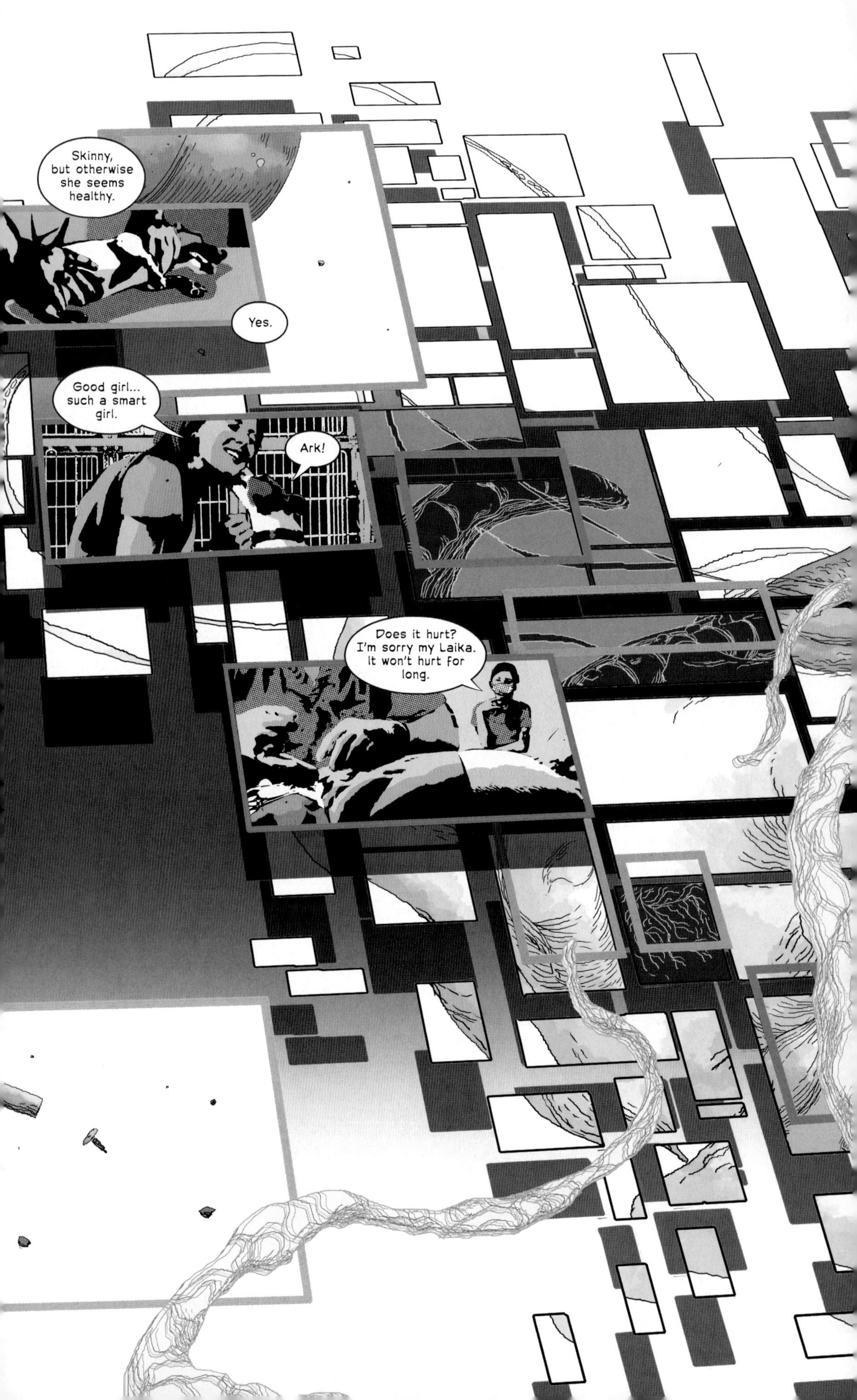
Skinny, but otherwise she seems healthy.
Yes.
Good girl... such a smart girl.
Ark!
Does it hurt? I'm sorry my Laika. It won't hurt for long.

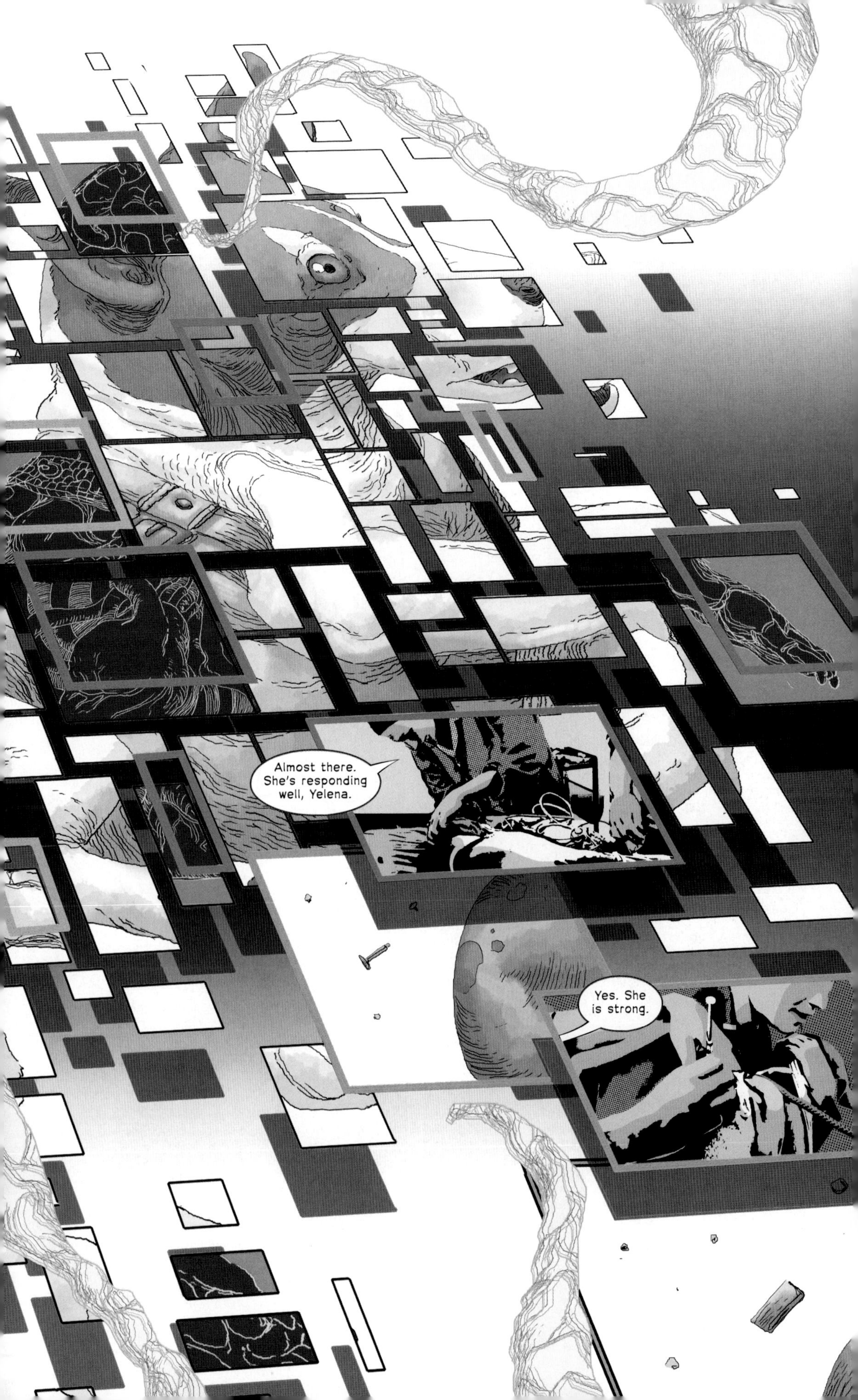
Almost there. She's responding well, Yelena.
Yes. She is strong.

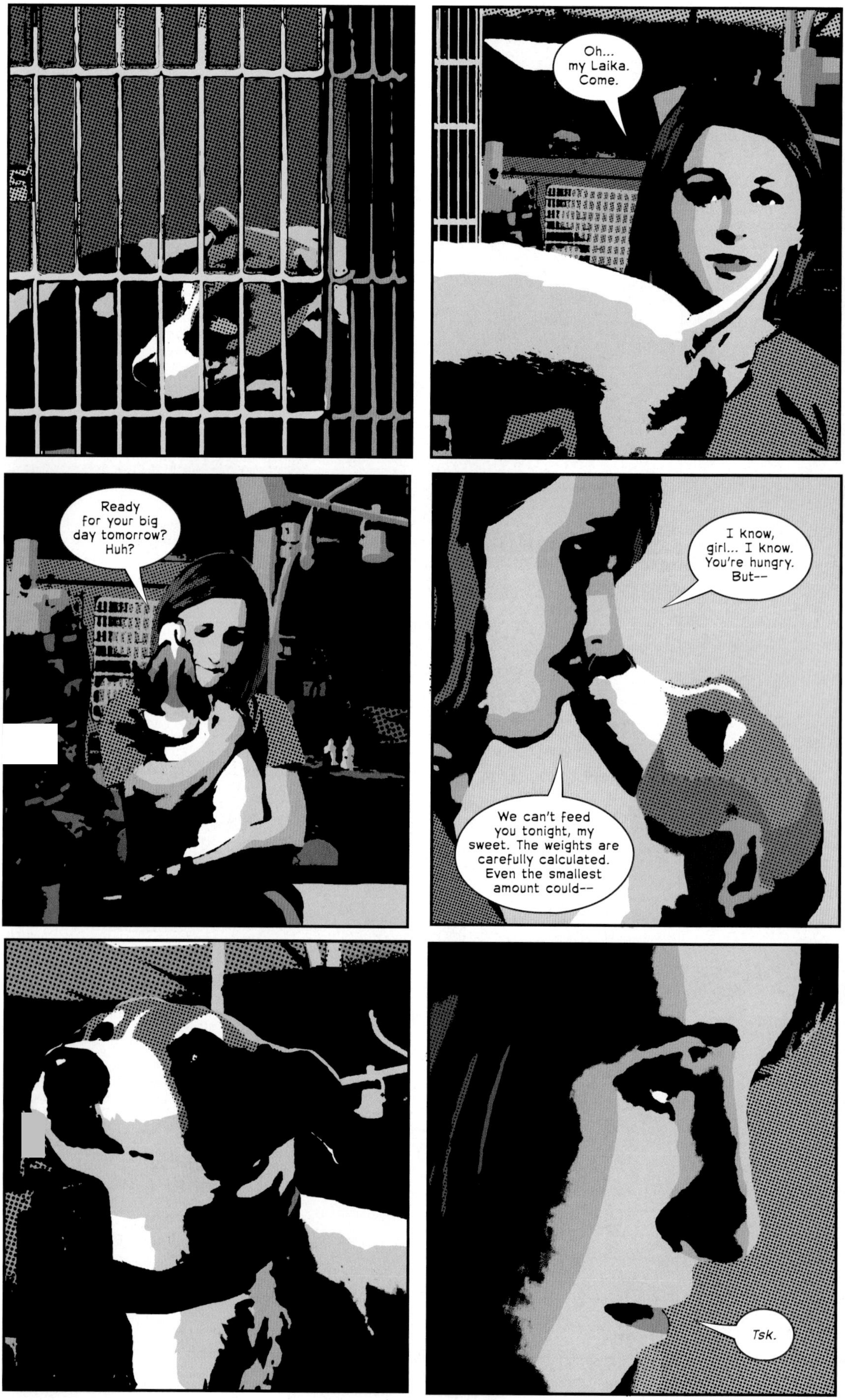
Oh... my Laika. Come.
Ready for your big day tomorrow? Huh?
I know, girl... I know. You're hungry. But--
We can't feed you tonight, my sweet. The weights are carefully calculated. Even the smallest amount could--
Tsk.

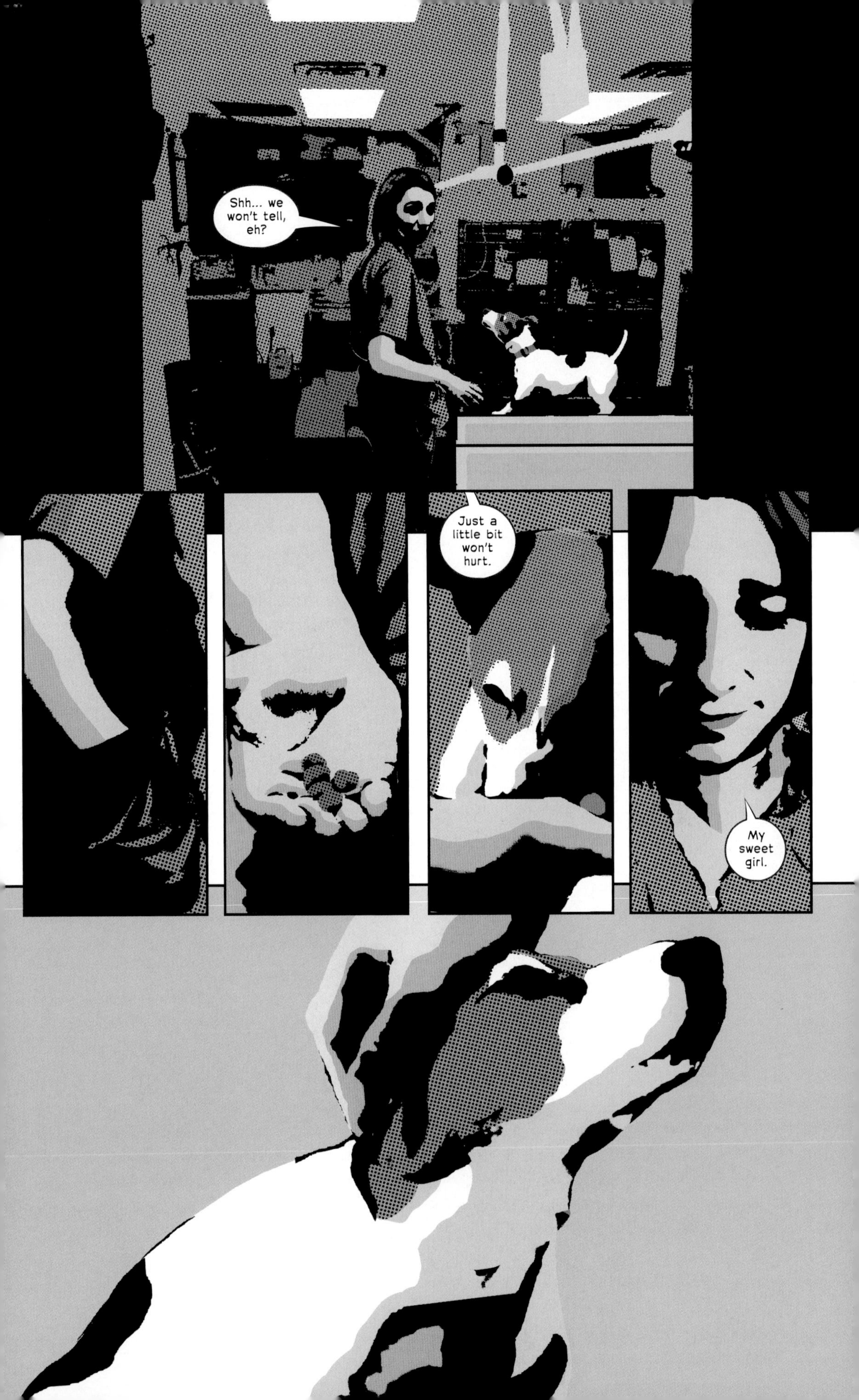
Shh... we won't tell, eh?
Just a little bit won't hurt.
My sweet girl.

Can be so lonely here.

But not like it will be up there, eh?

Up there you will be alone. All alone.

I will miss you.

"...miss you."

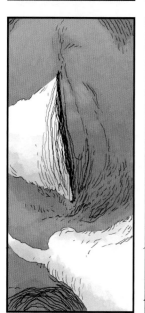

?

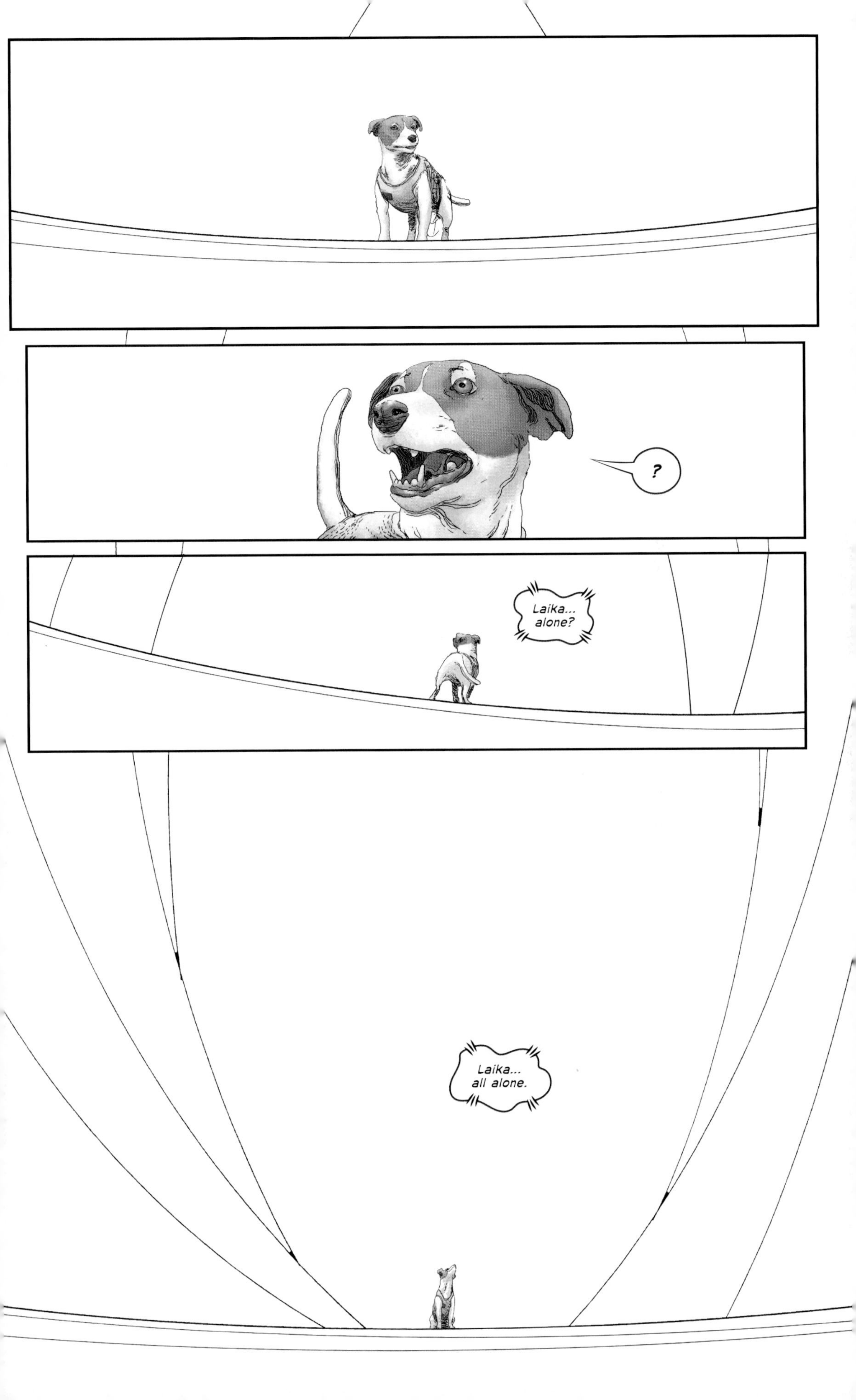
?
Laika... alone?
Laika... all alone.

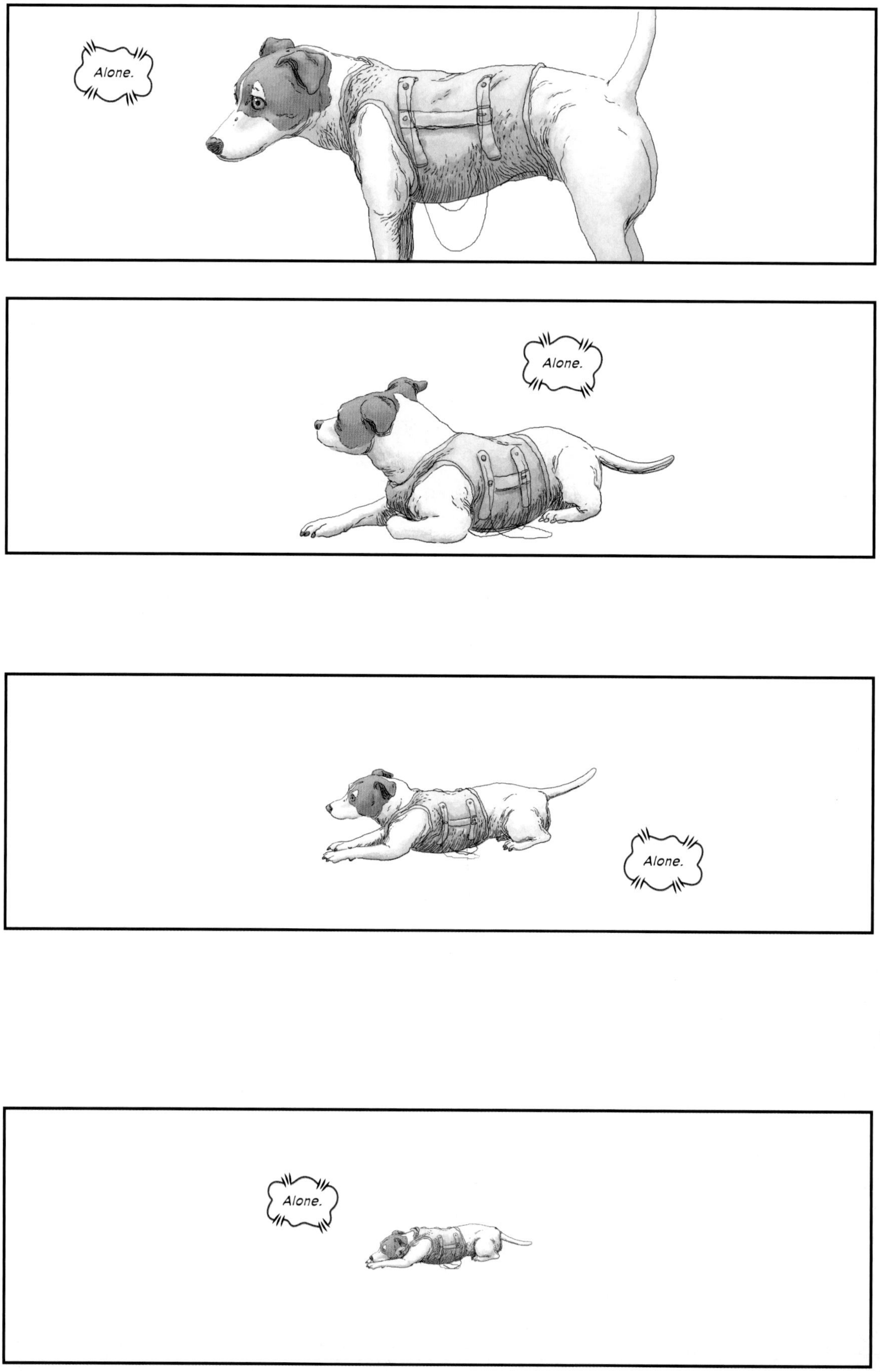
Alone.
Alone.
Alone.
Alone.

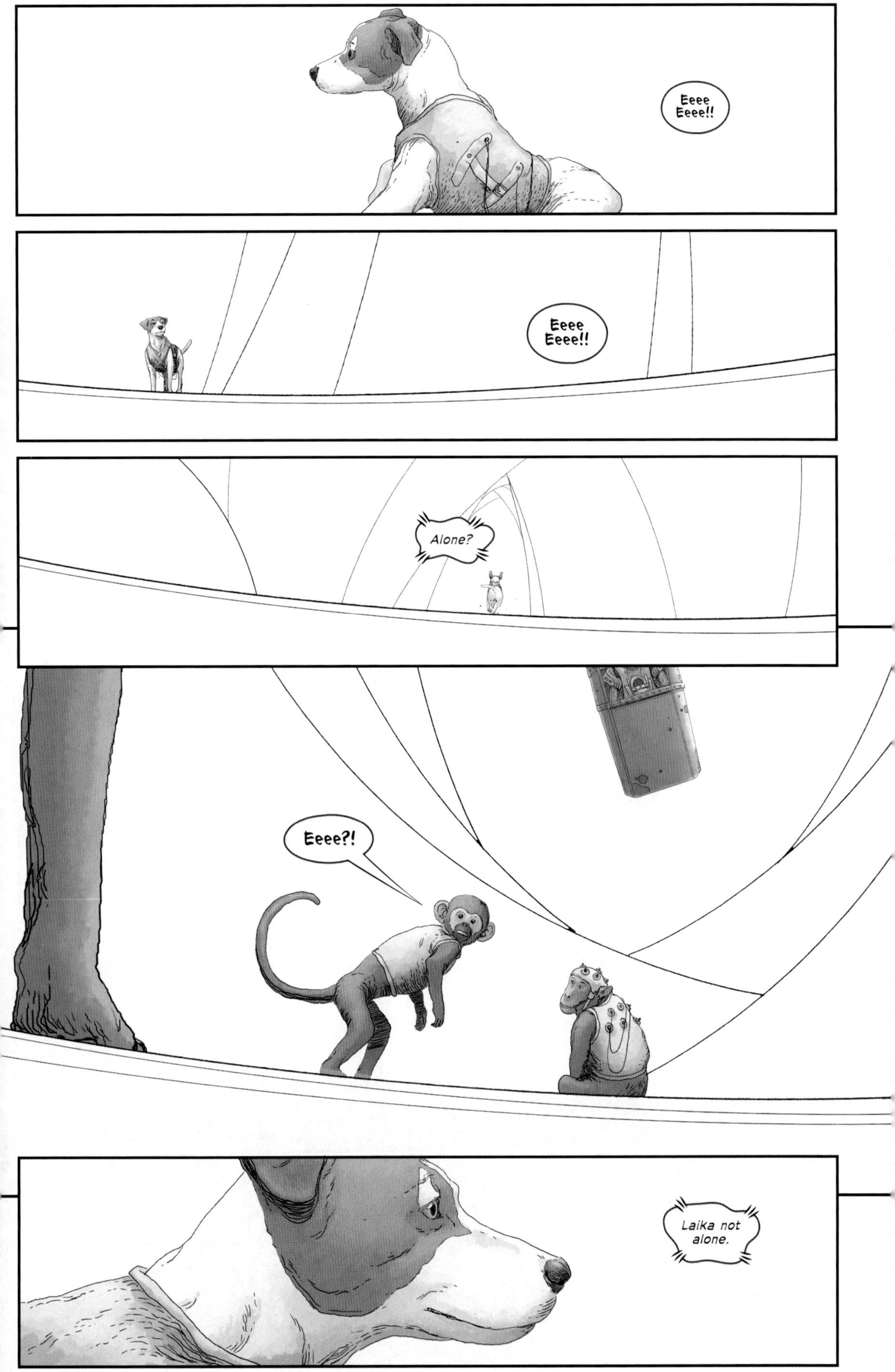
Eeee Eeee!!
Eeee Eeee!!
Alone?
Eeee?!
Laika not alone.

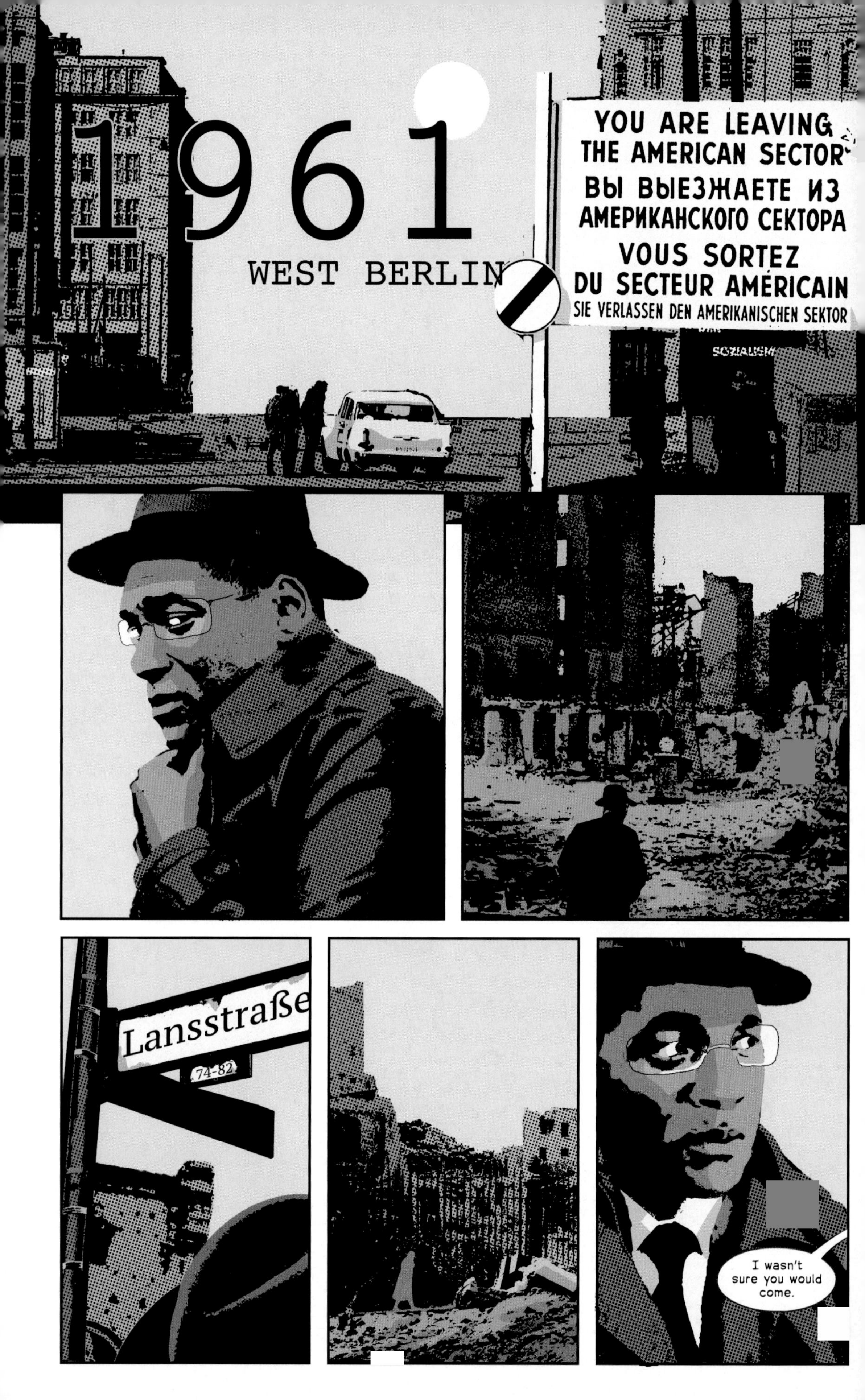
1961
WEST BERLIN
YOU ARE LEAVING
THE AMERICAN SECTOR
ВЫ ВЫЕЗЖАЕТЕ ИЗ
АМЕРИКАНСКОГО СЕКТОРА
VOUS SORTEZ
DU SECTEUR AMÉRICAIN
SIE VERLASSEN DEN AMERIKANISCHEN SEKTOR
Lansstraße
74-82
I wasn't sure you would come.

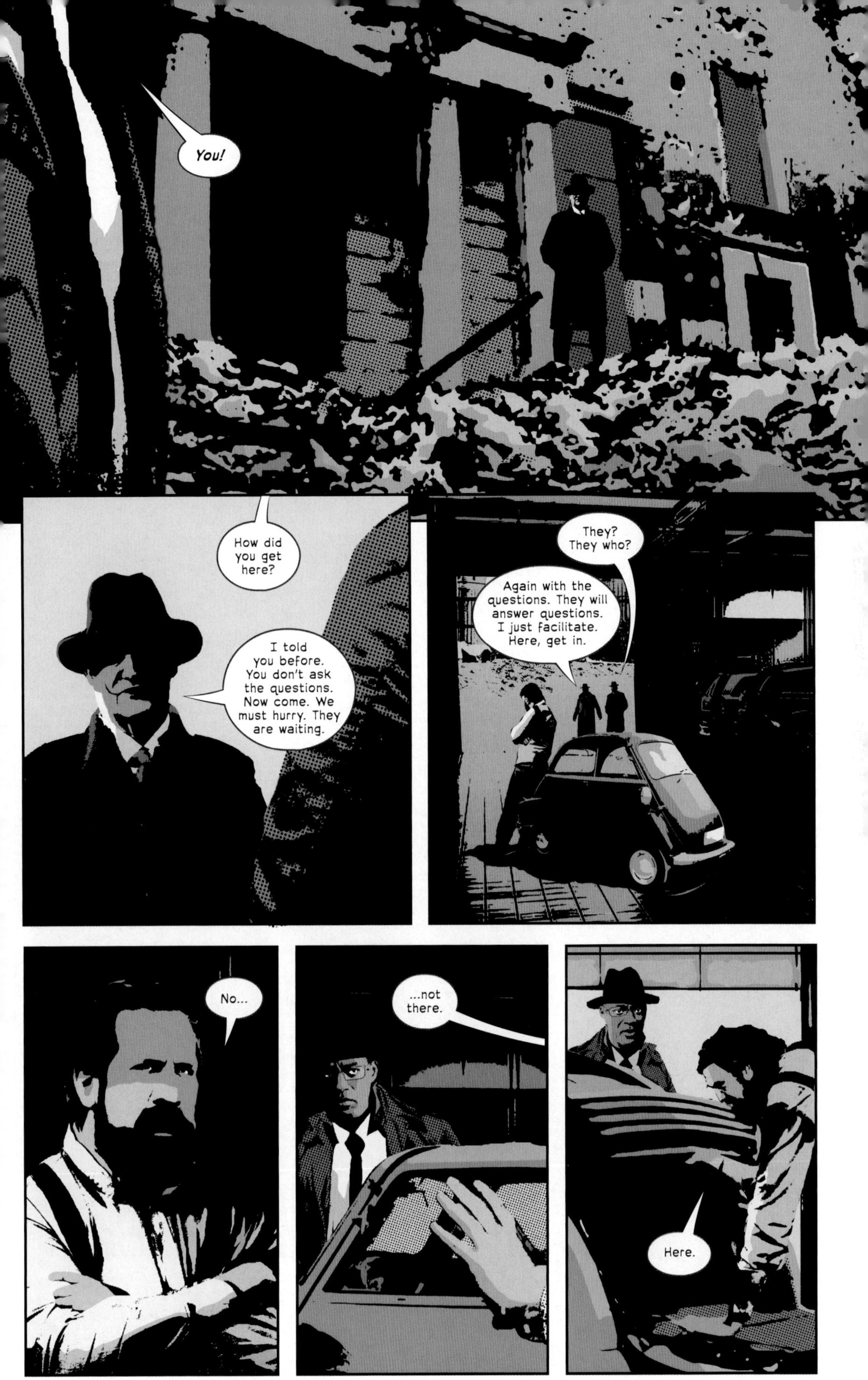
You!
How did you get here?
I told you before. You don't ask the questions. Now come. We must hurry. They are waiting.
They? They who?
Again with the questions. They will answer questions. I just facilitate. Here, get in.
No...
...not there.
Here.

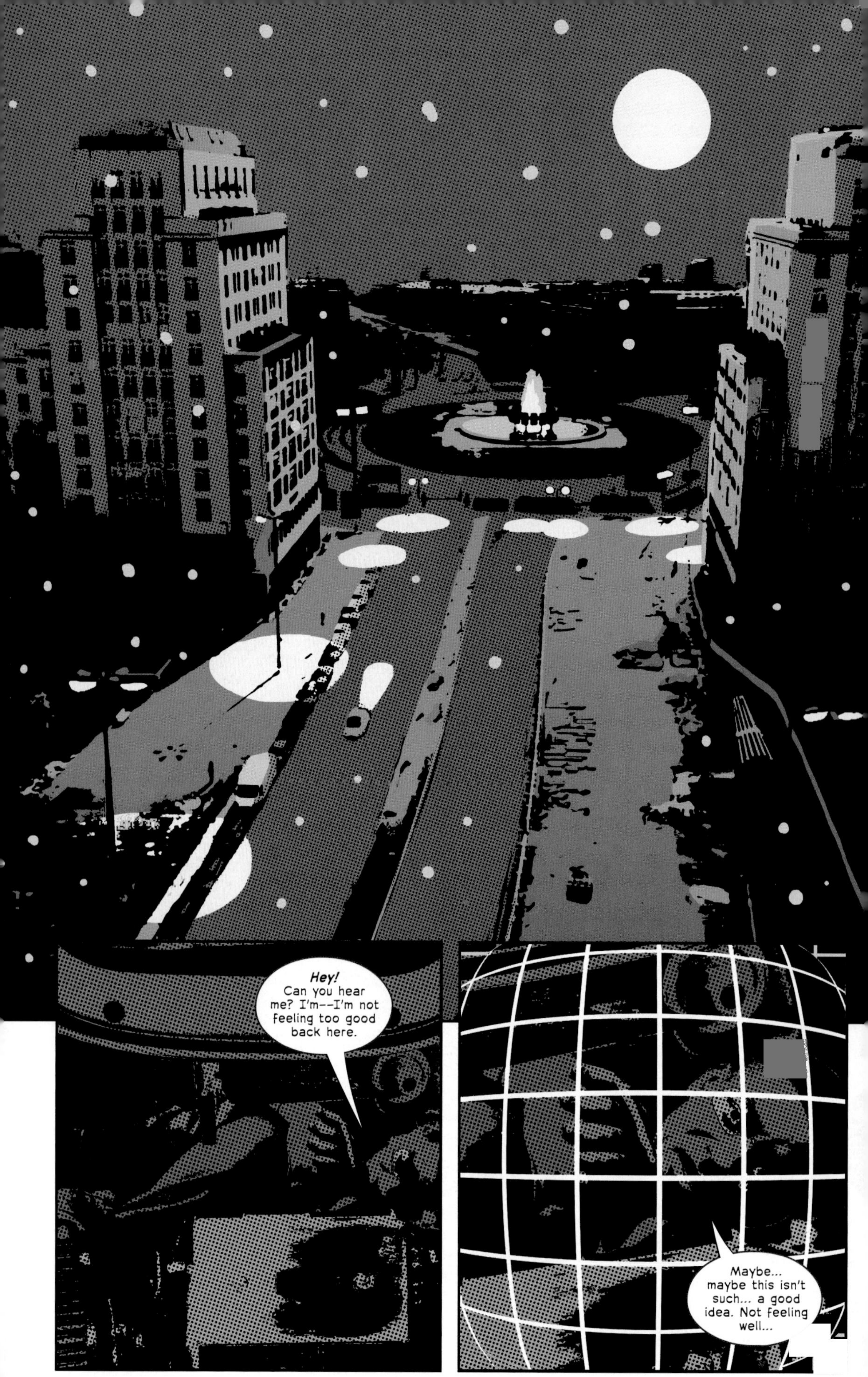
Hey! Can you hear me? I'm--I'm not feeling too good back here.
Maybe... maybe this isn't such... a good idea. Not feeling well...

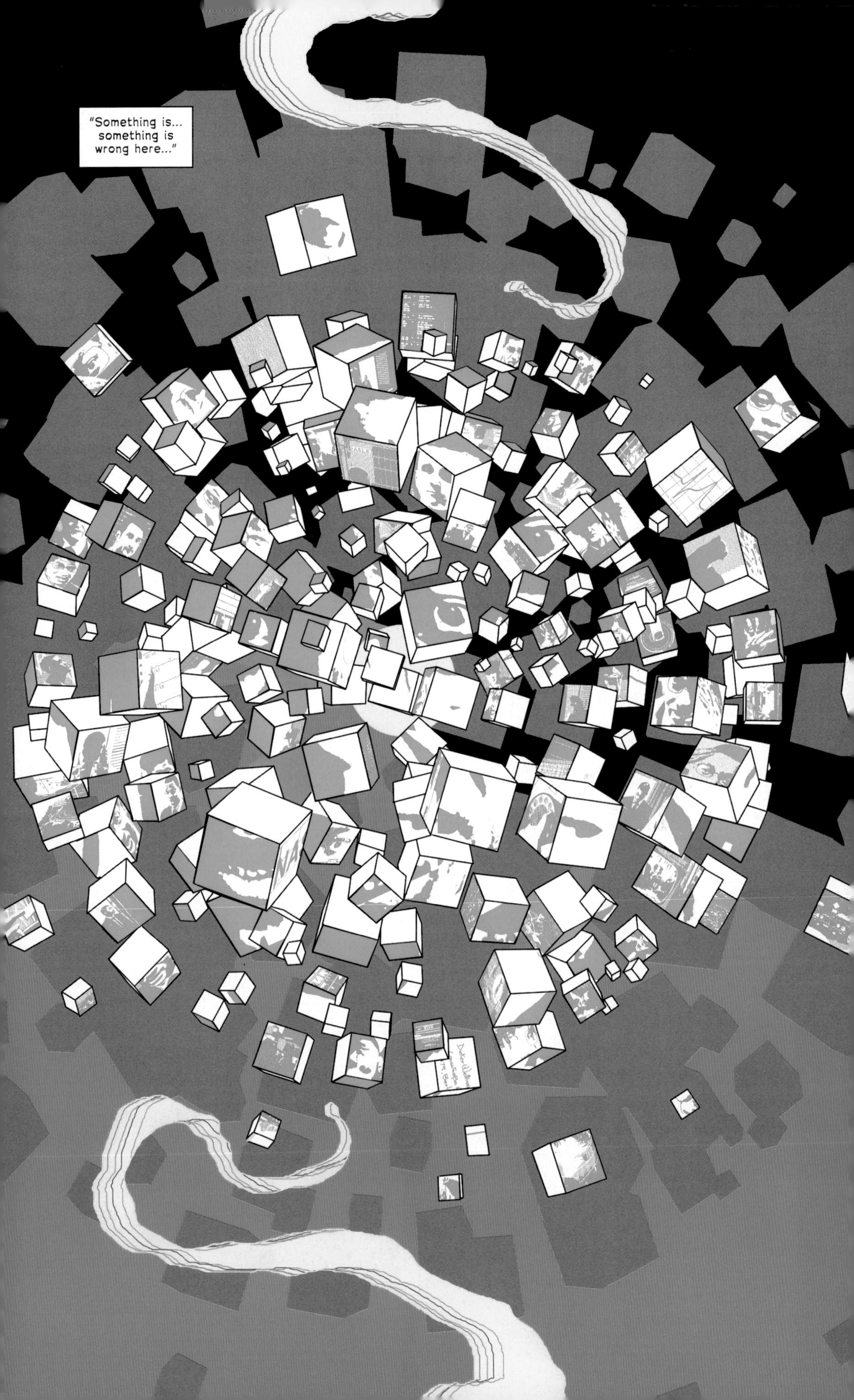
"Something is... something is wrong here..."

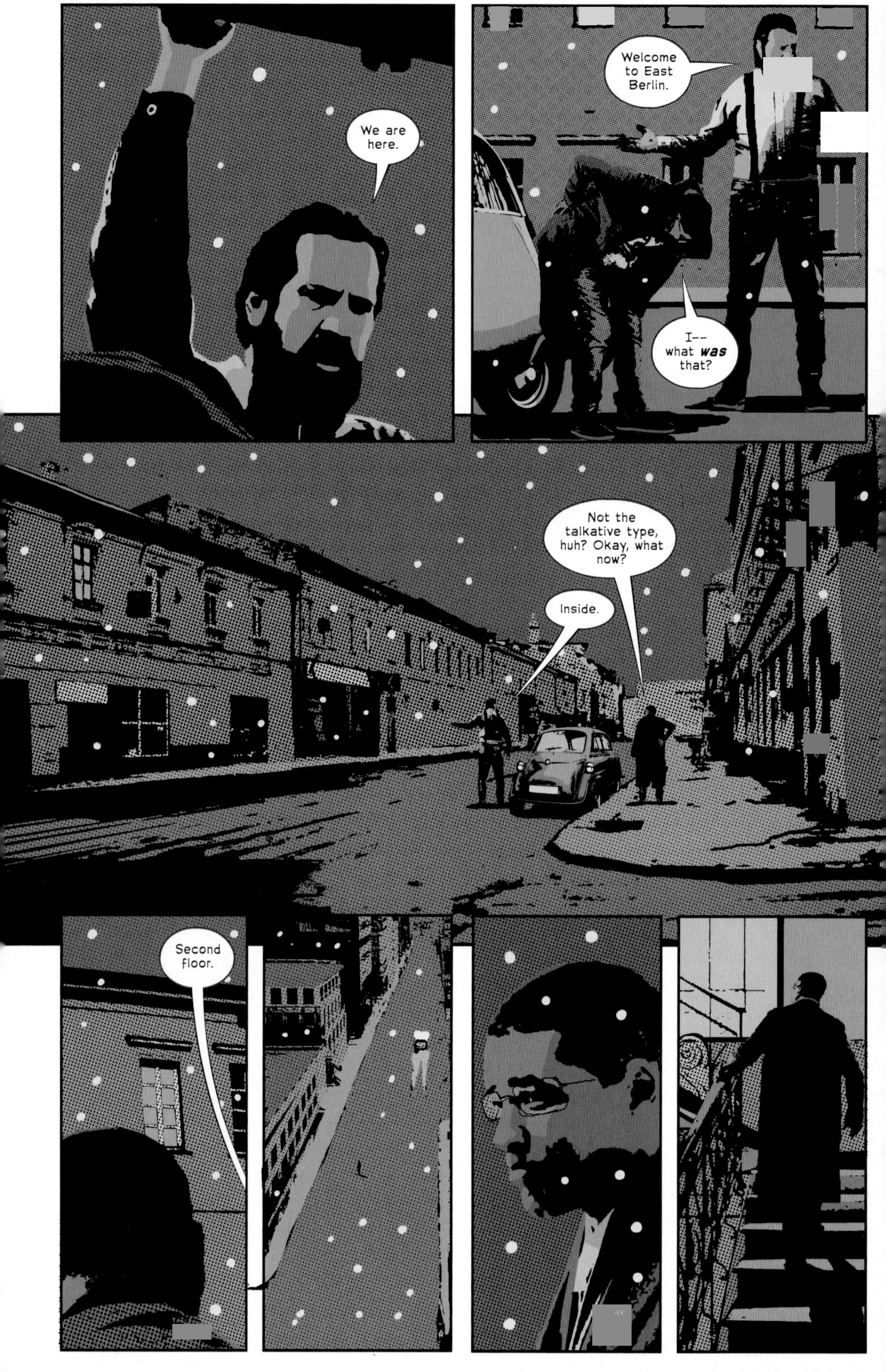
We are here.
Welcome to East Berlin.
I-- what *was* that?
Not the talkative type, huh? Okay, what now?
Inside.
Second floor.

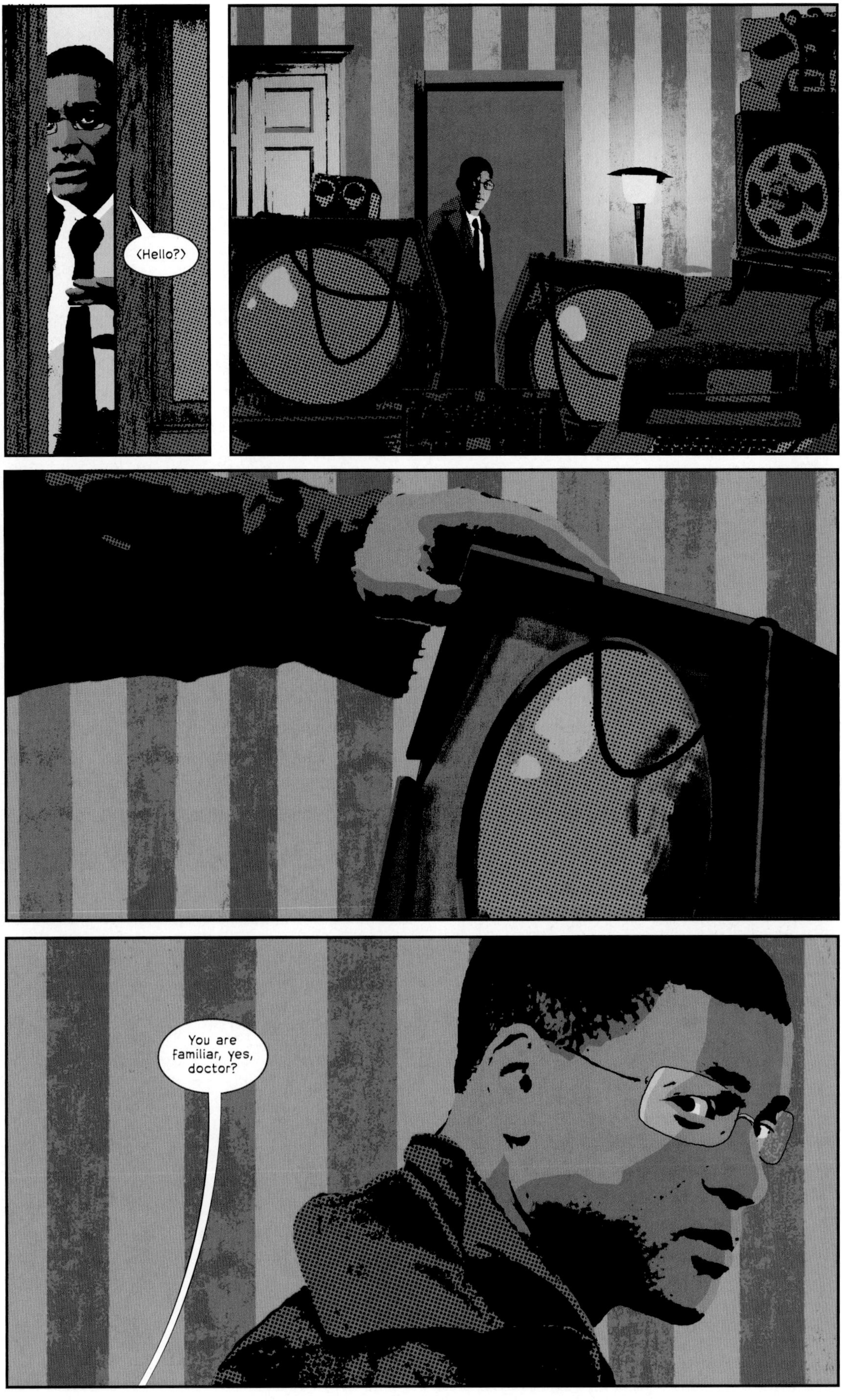
⟨Hello?⟩
You are familiar, yes, doctor?

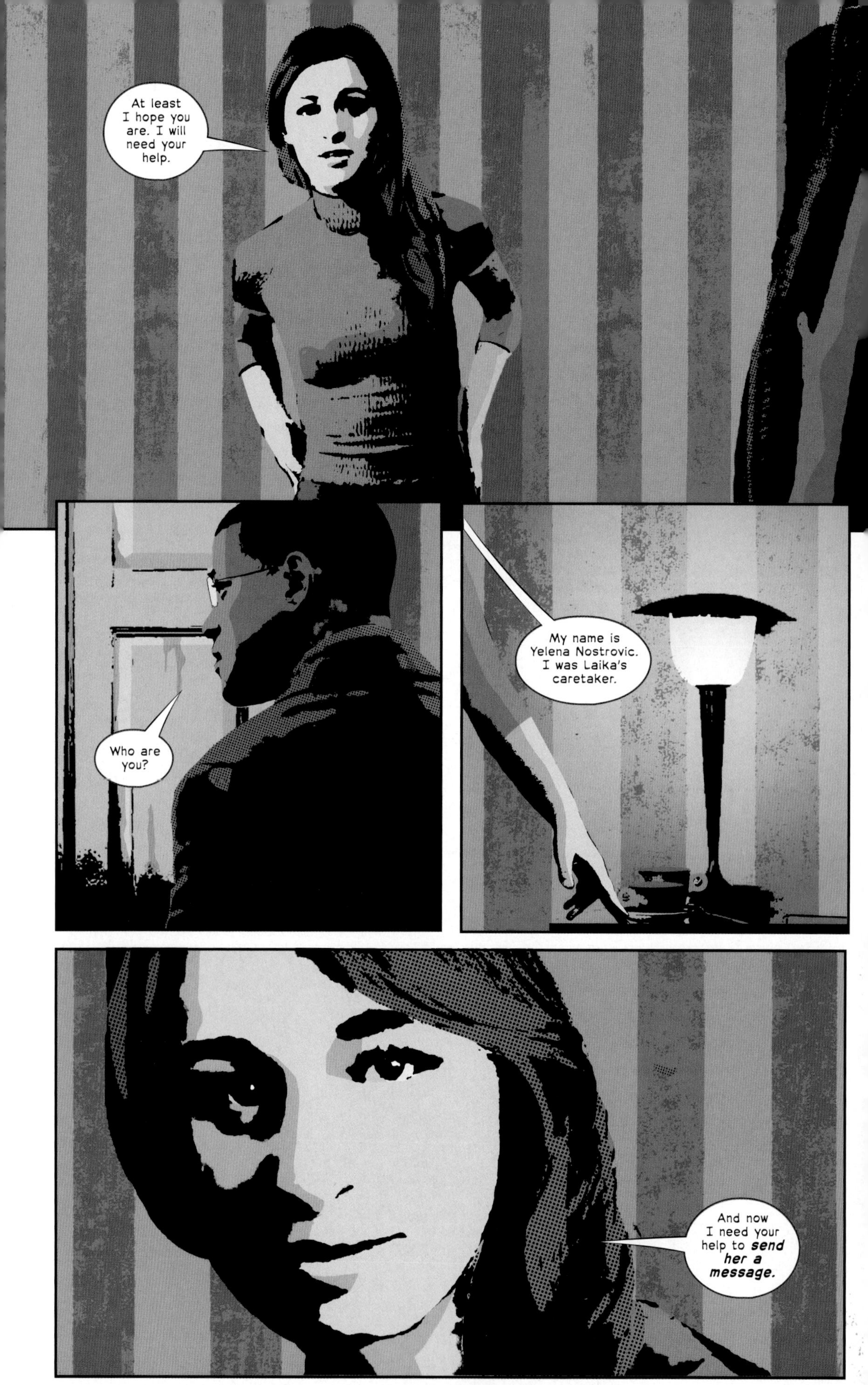
At least I hope you are. I will need your help.
Who are you?
My name is Yelena Nostrovic. I was Laika's caretaker.
And now I need your help to ***send her a message.***

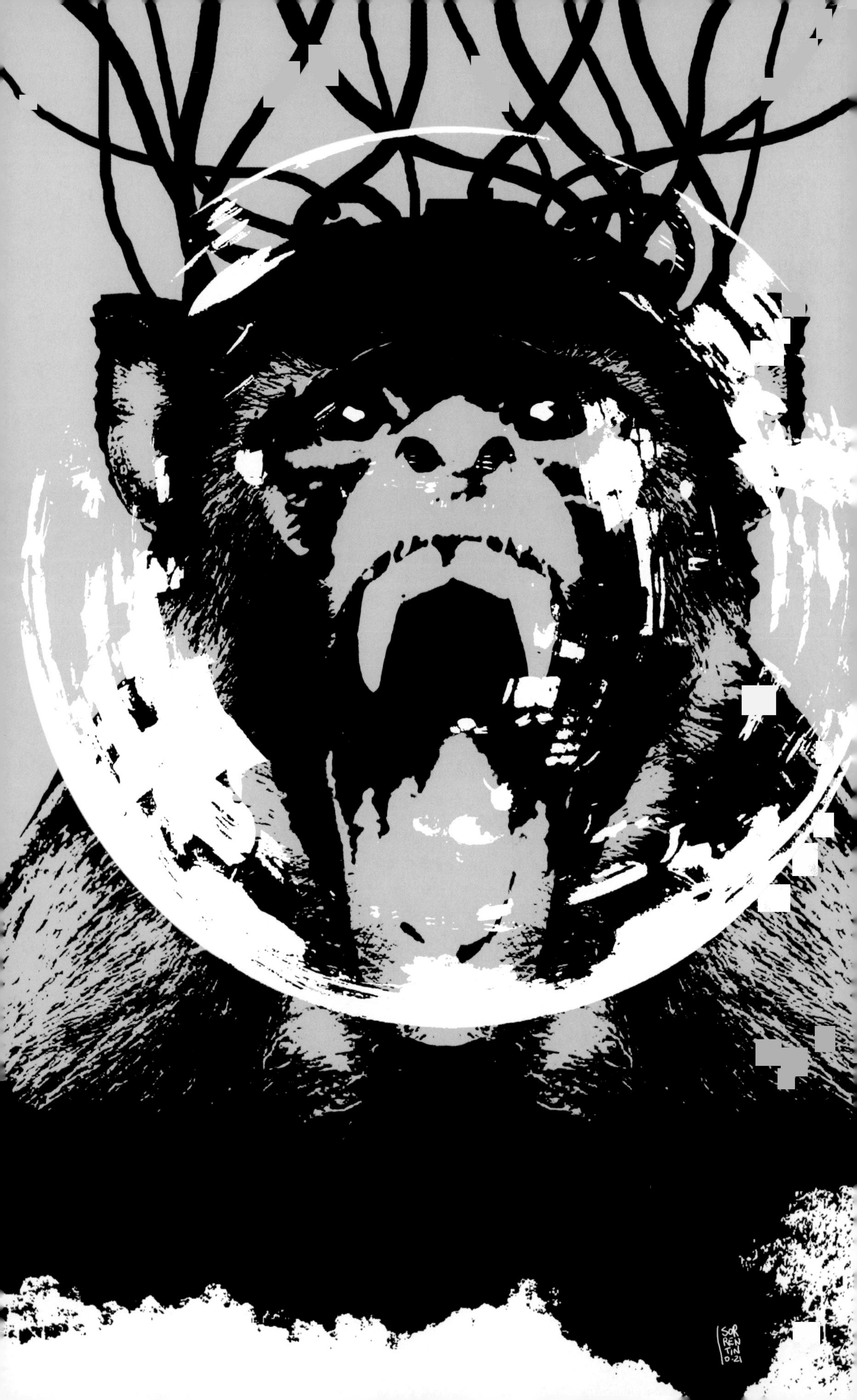
SOR
REN
TIN
O·21

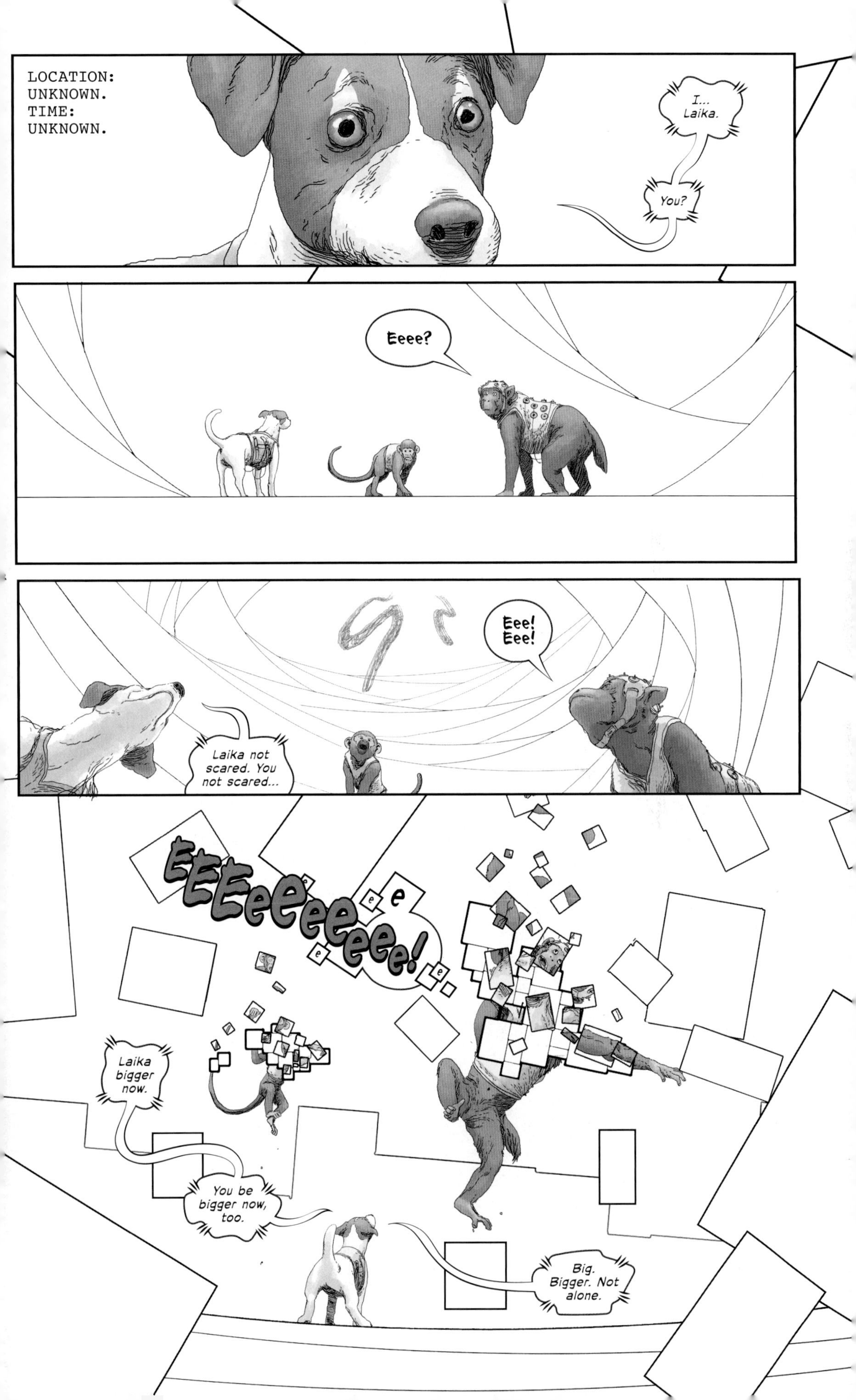
LOCATION:
UNKNOWN.
TIME:
UNKNOWN.
I... Laika.
You?
Eeee?
Eee! Eee!
Laika not scared. You not scared...
EEEeeeeeeee!
e
e
e
e
e
Laika bigger now.
You be bigger now, too.
Big. Bigger. Not alone.

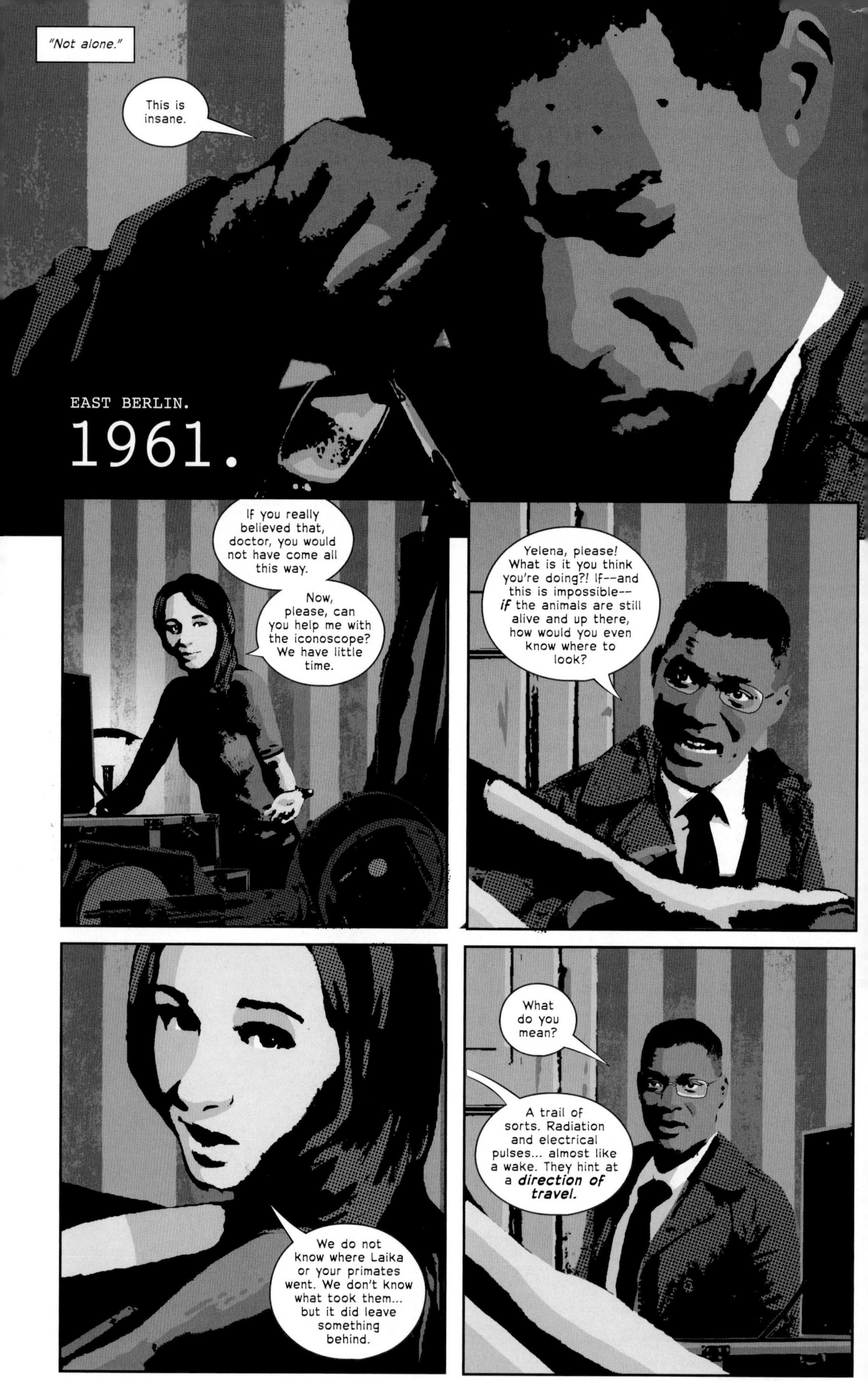
"Not alone."
This is insane.
EAST BERLIN.
1961.
If you really believed that, doctor, you would not have come all this way.
Now, please, can you help me with the iconoscope? We have little time.
Yelena, please! What is it you think you're doing?! If--and this is impossible--*if* the animals are still alive and up there, how would you even know where to look?
We do not know where Laika or your primates went. We don't know what took them... but it did leave something behind.
What do you mean?
A trail of sorts. Radiation and electrical pulses... almost like a wake. They hint at a ***direction of travel.***

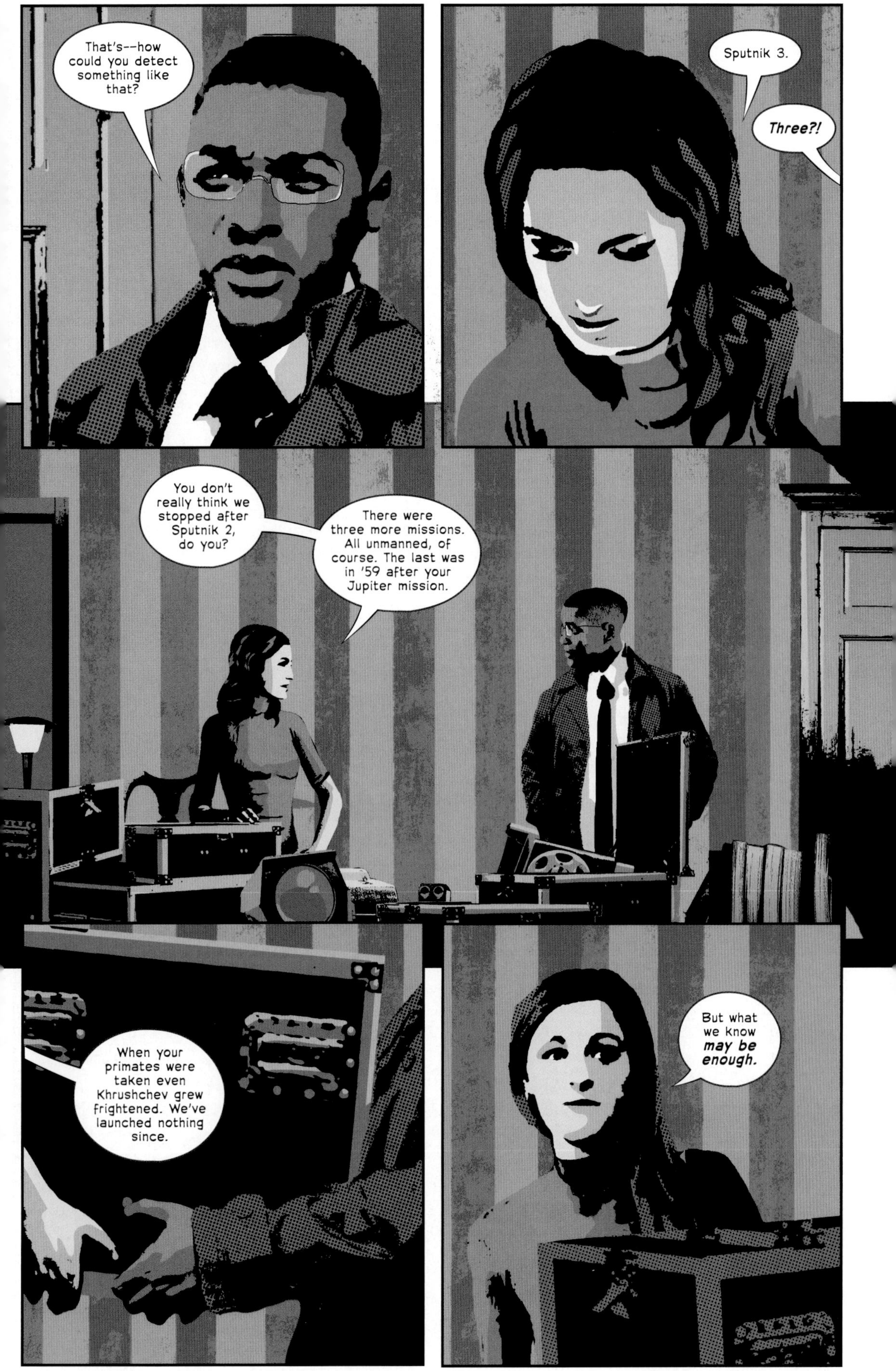
That's--how could you detect something like that?
Sputnik 3.
Three?!
You don't really think we stopped after Sputnik 2, do you?
There were three more missions. All unmanned, of course. The last was in '59 after your Jupiter mission.
When your primates were taken even Khrushchev grew frightened. We've launched nothing since.
But what we know *may be enough.*

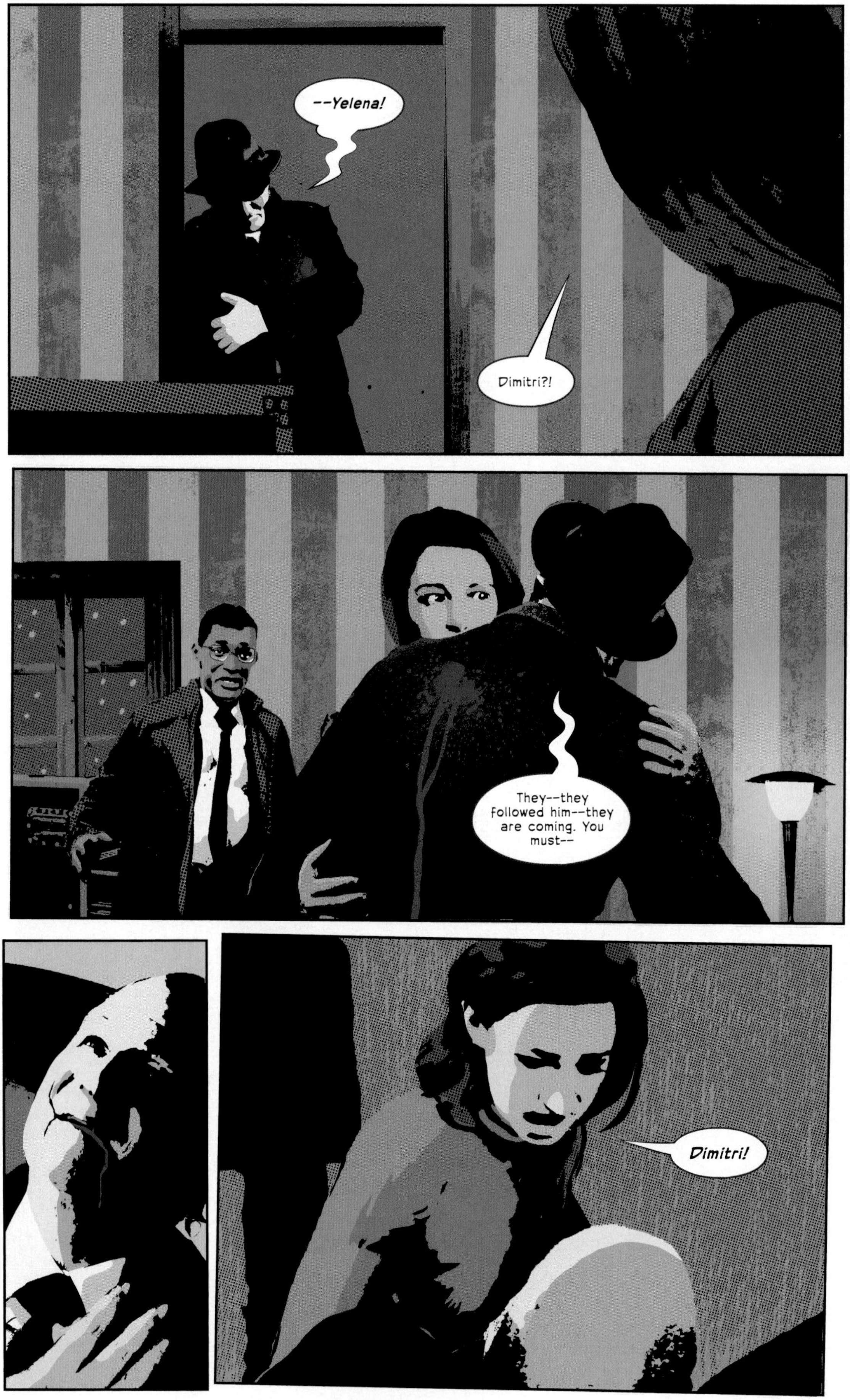
--Yelena!
Dimitri?!
They--they followed him--they are coming. You must--
Dimitri!

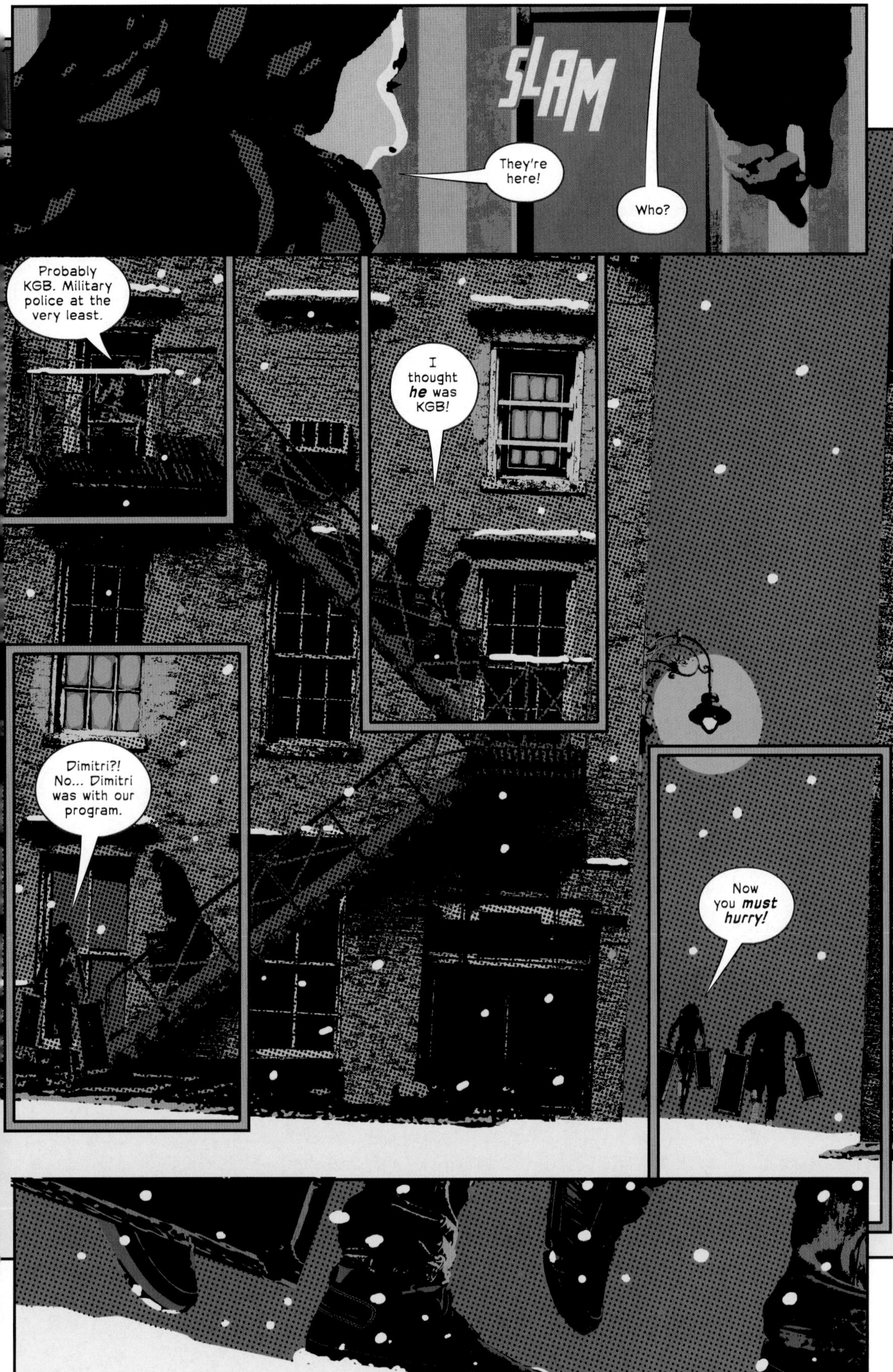
SLAM
They're here!
Who?
Probably KGB. Military police at the very least.
I thought *he* was KGB!
Dimitri?! No... Dimitri was with our program.
Now you *must* hurry!

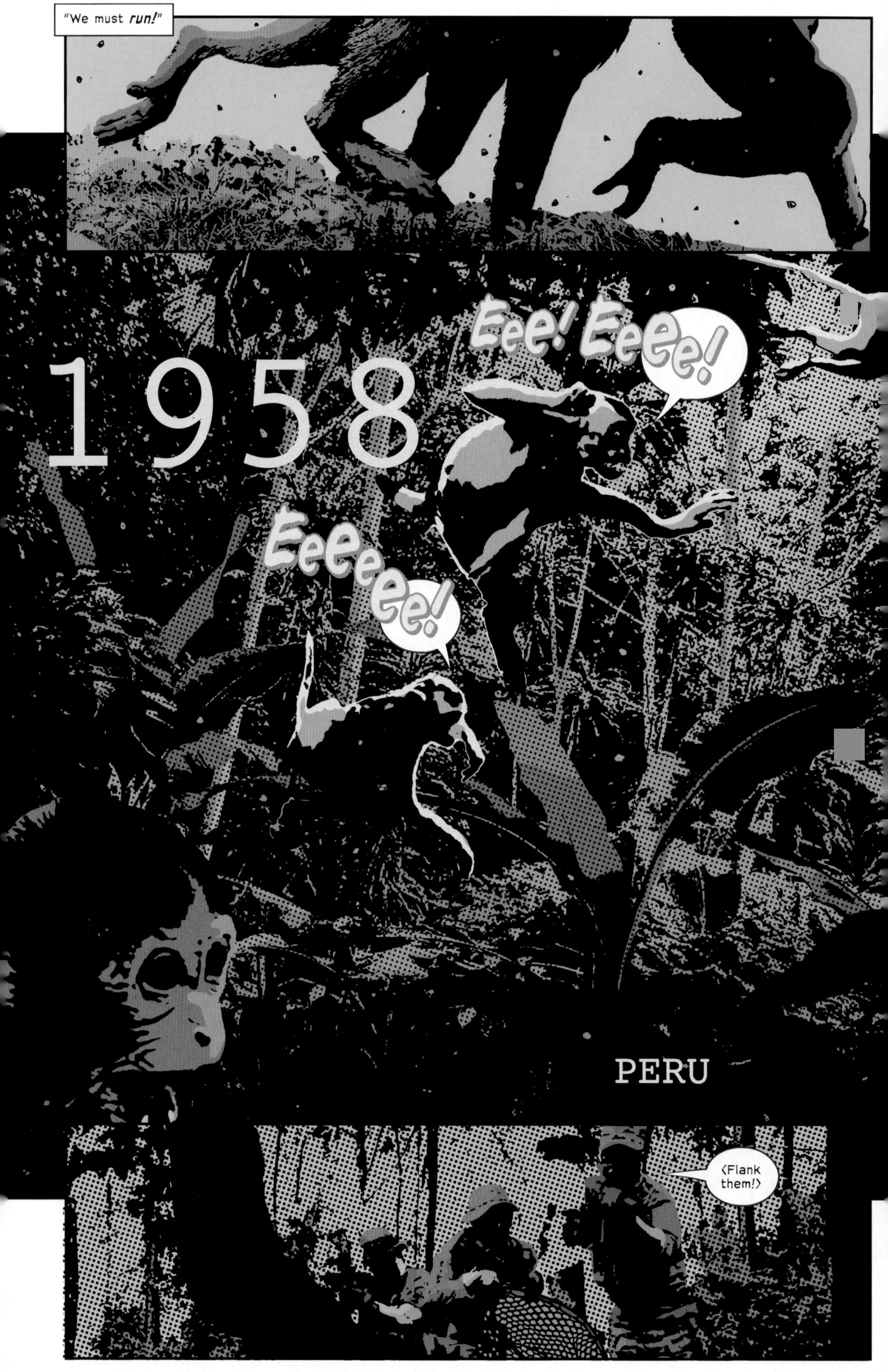
"We must run!"
1958
Eee! Eeeee!
Eeeeeee!
PERU
‹Flank them!›

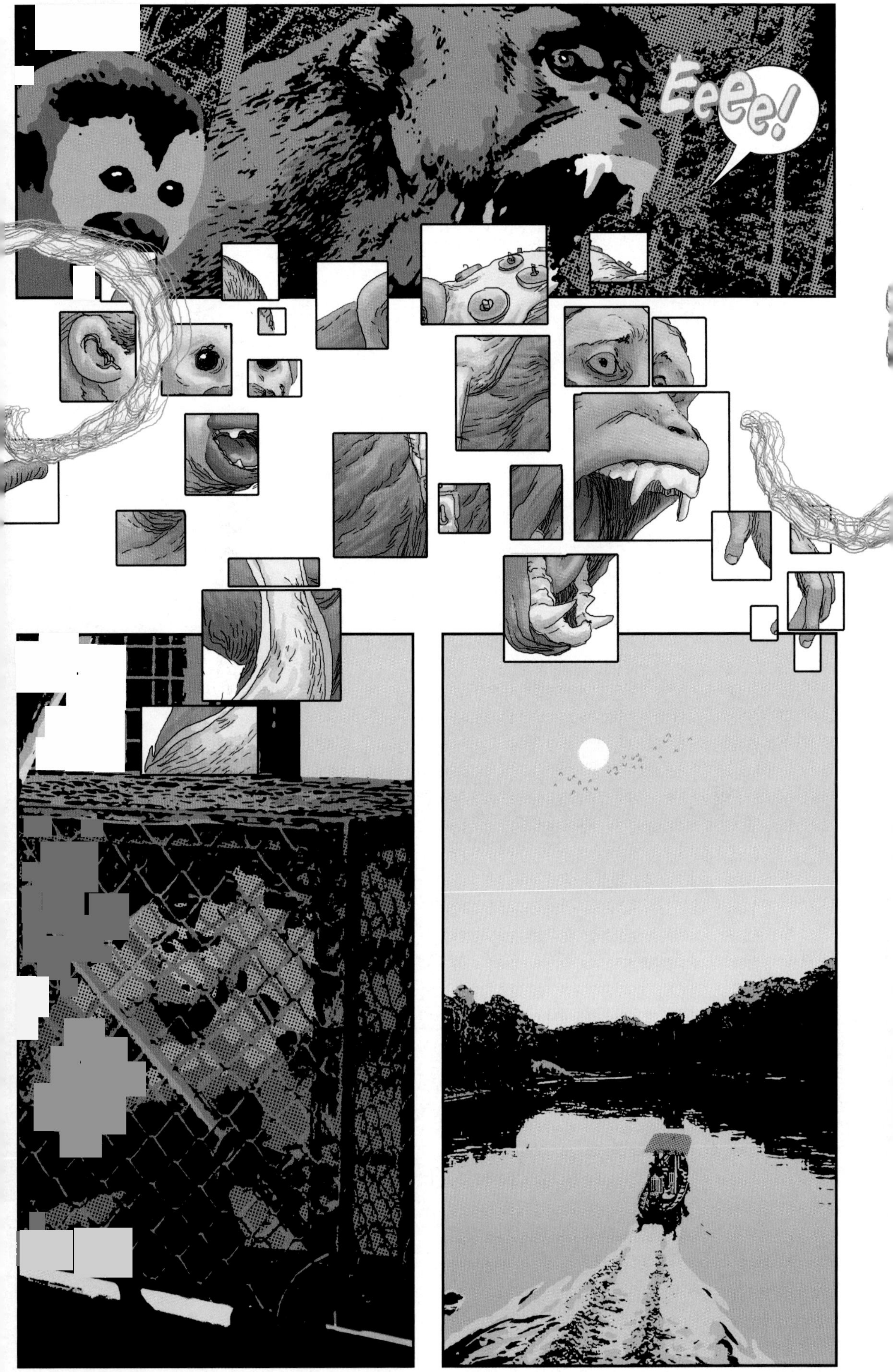
Eeee!

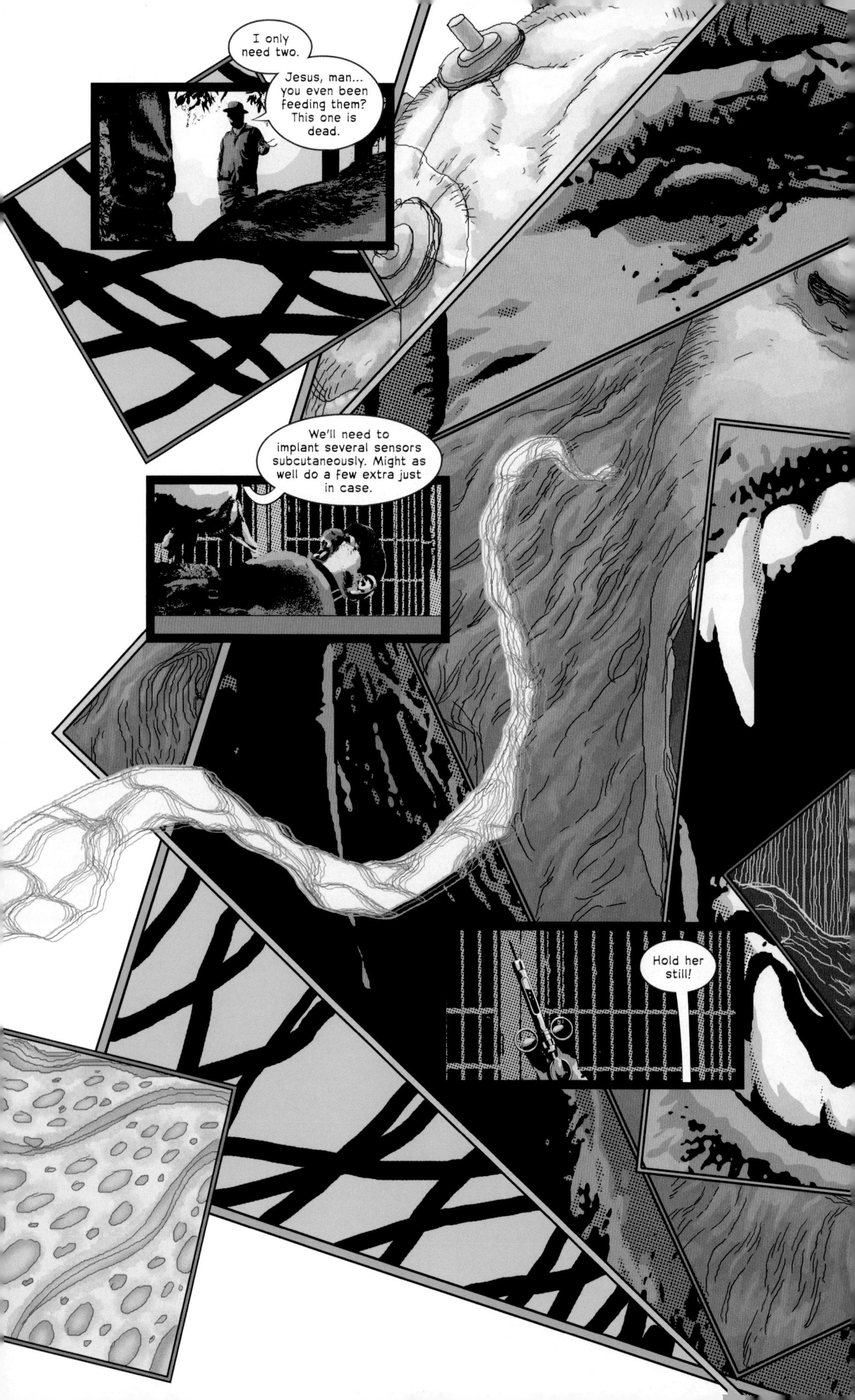

I only need two.
Jesus, man... you even been feeding them? This one is dead.
We'll need to implant several sensors subcutaneously. Might as well do a few extra just in case.
Hold her still!

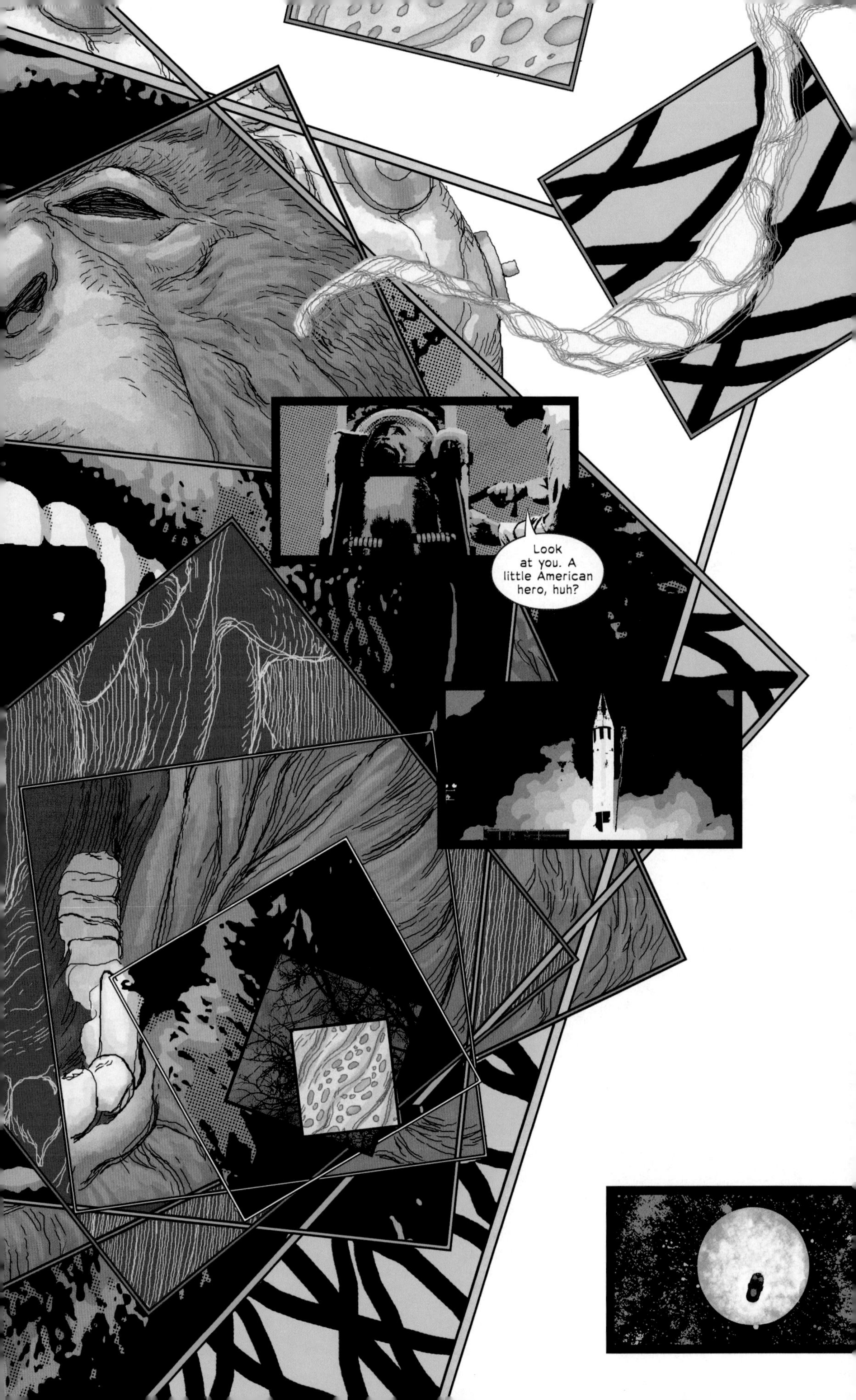
Look at you. A little American hero, huh?

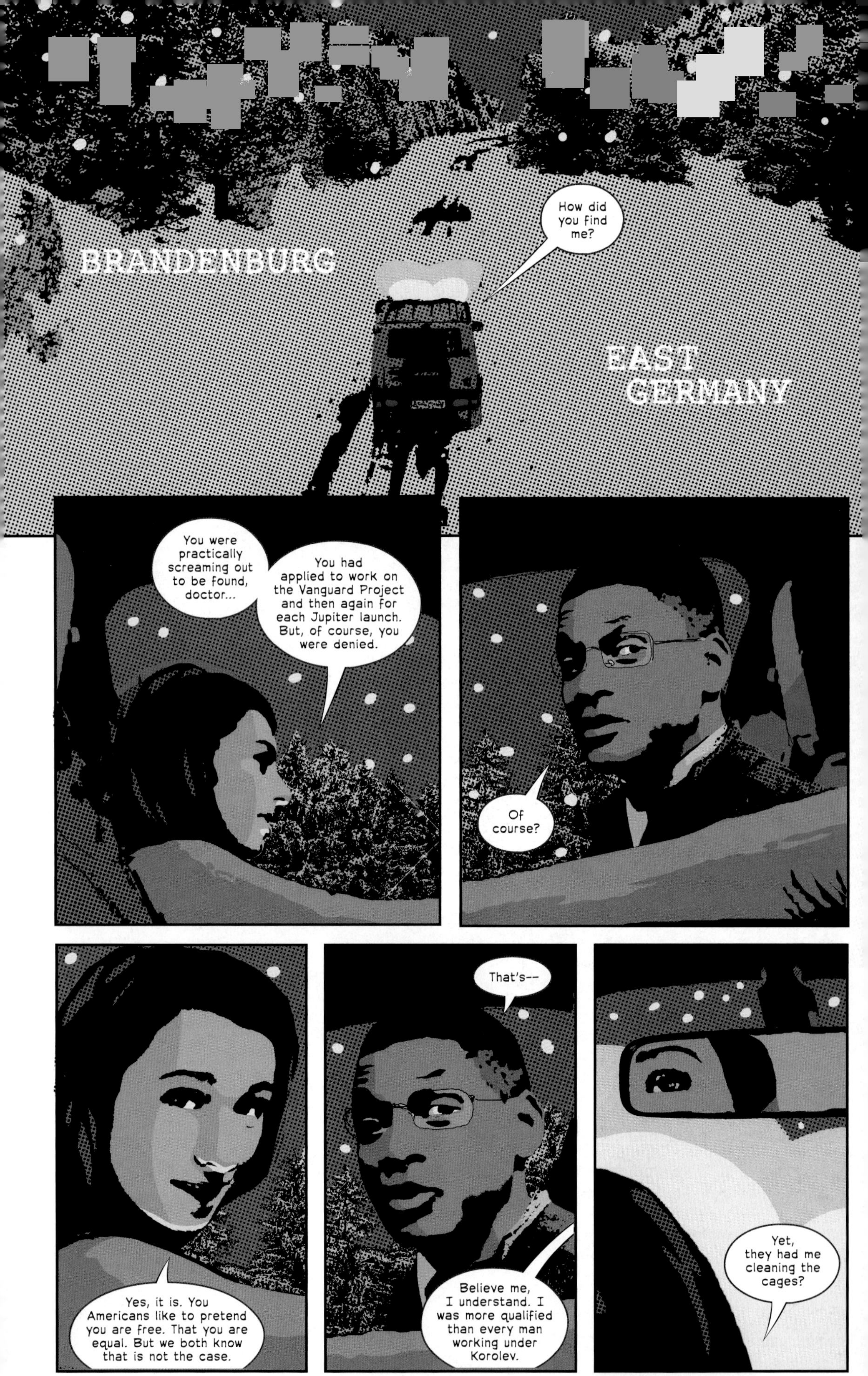
BRANDENBURG
EAST GERMANY
How did you find me?
You were practically screaming out to be found, doctor...
You had applied to work on the Vanguard Project and then again for each Jupiter launch. But, of course, you were denied.
Of course?
Yes, it is. You Americans like to pretend you are free. That you are equal. But we both know that is not the case.
That's--
Believe me, I understand. I was more qualified than every man working under Korolev.
Yet, they had me cleaning the cages?

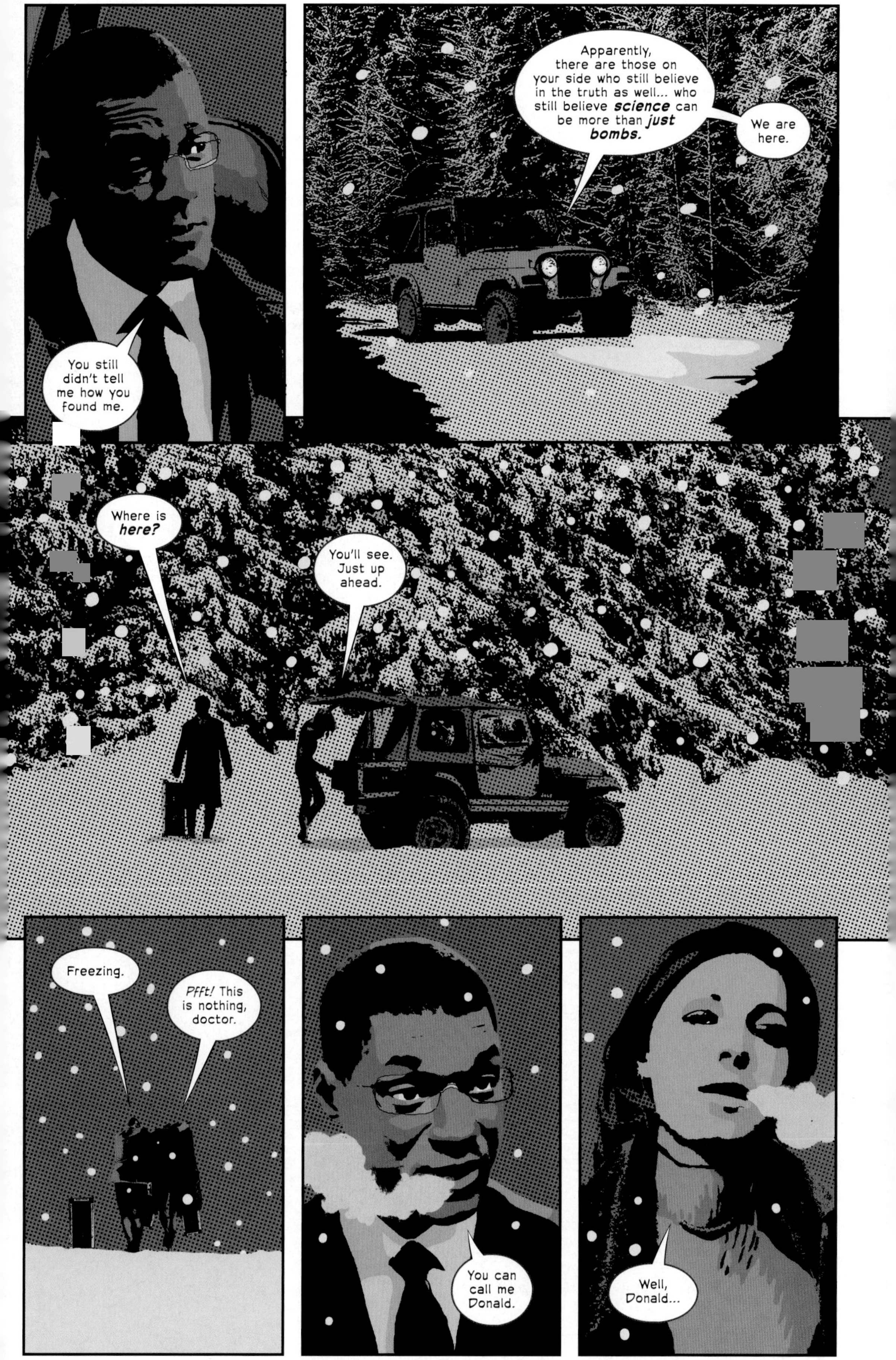
You still didn't tell me how you found me.
Apparently, there are those on your side who still believe in the truth as well... who still believe **science** can be more than ***just* bombs.**
We are here.
Where is ***here?***
You'll see. Just up ahead.
Freezing.
Pfft! This is nothing, doctor.
You can call me Donald.
Well, Donald...

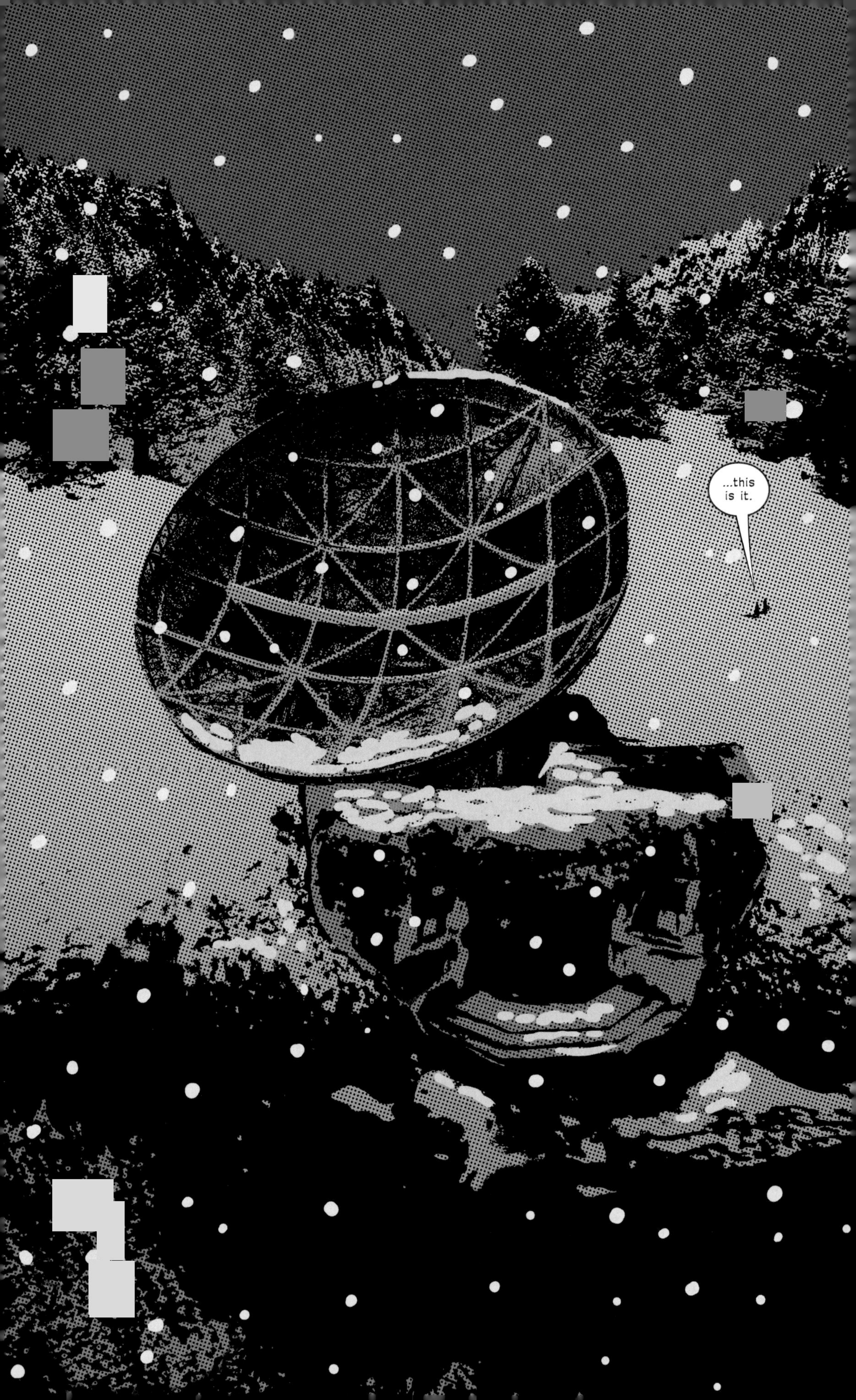
...this is it.

What is this place?

It was a Nazi installation. Von Braun used it during the V2 trials. It was decommissioned soon after, and when we arrived, Korolev moved everything to Kazakhstan.

I pray the generator will still work.

Still has some gas. Not sure if it's any good or how long it will last.

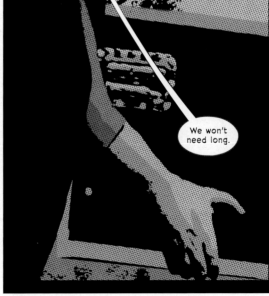

We won't need long.

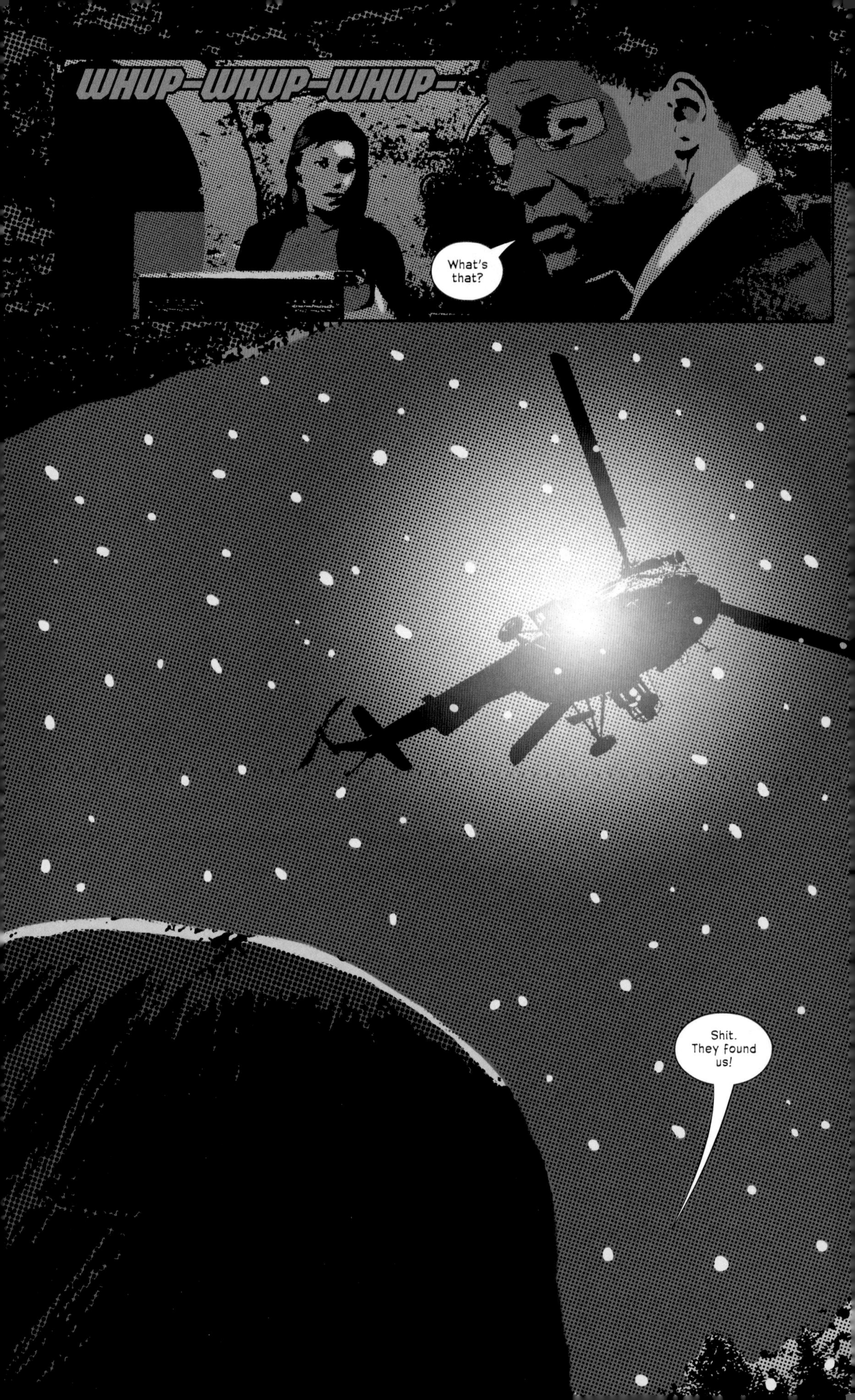
WHUP-WHUP-WHUP-
What's that?
Shit. They found us!

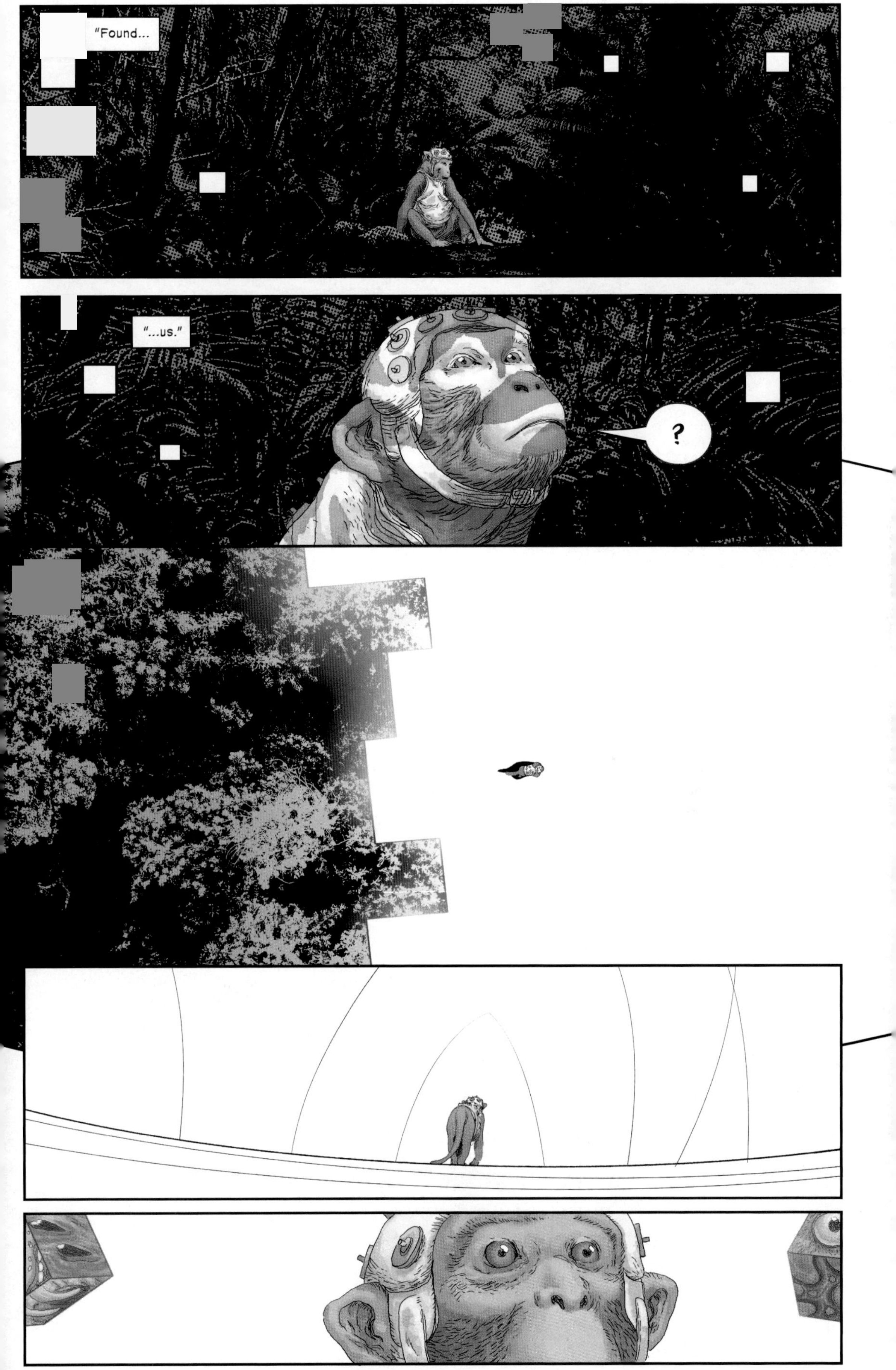
"Found...
"...us."
?

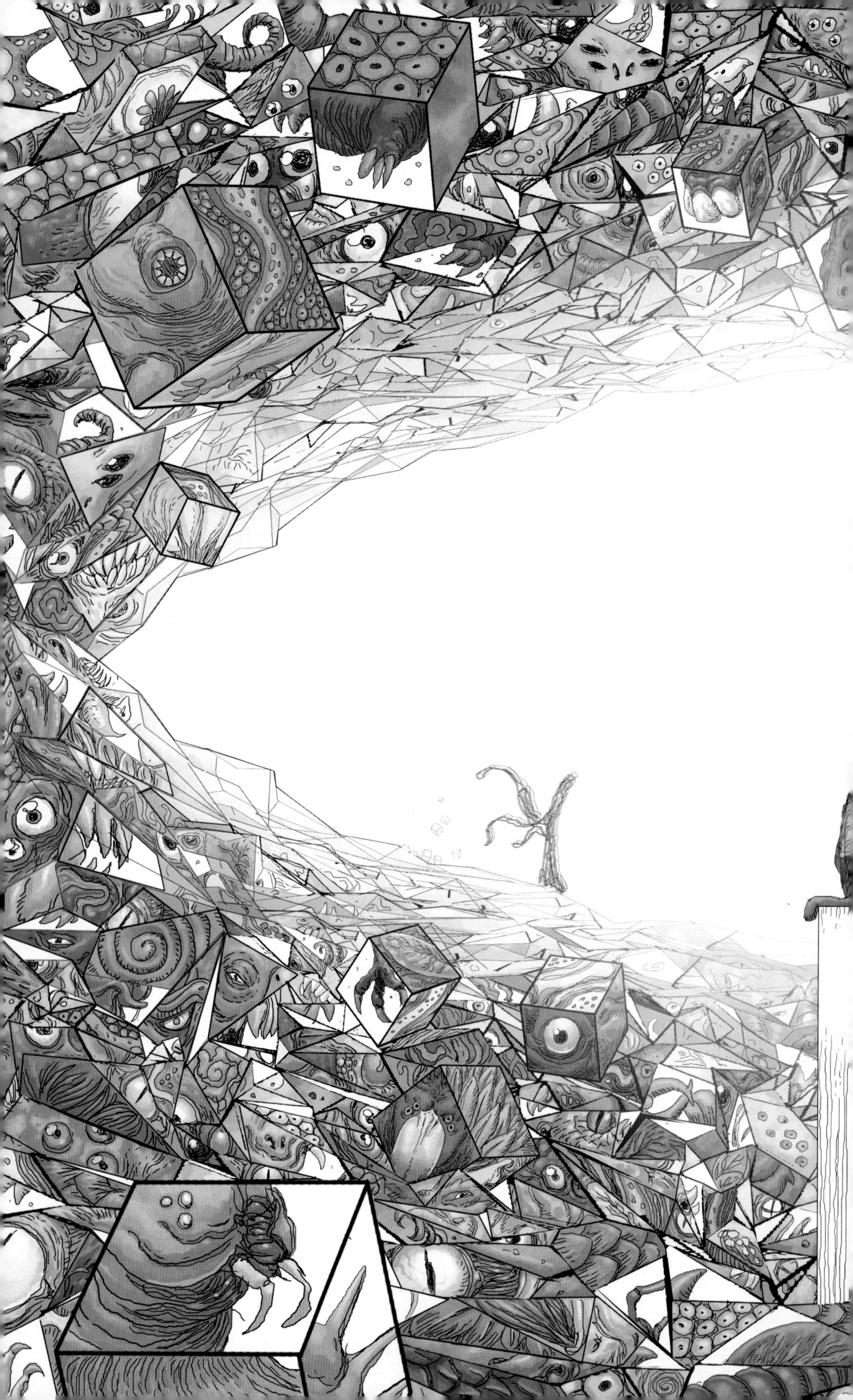

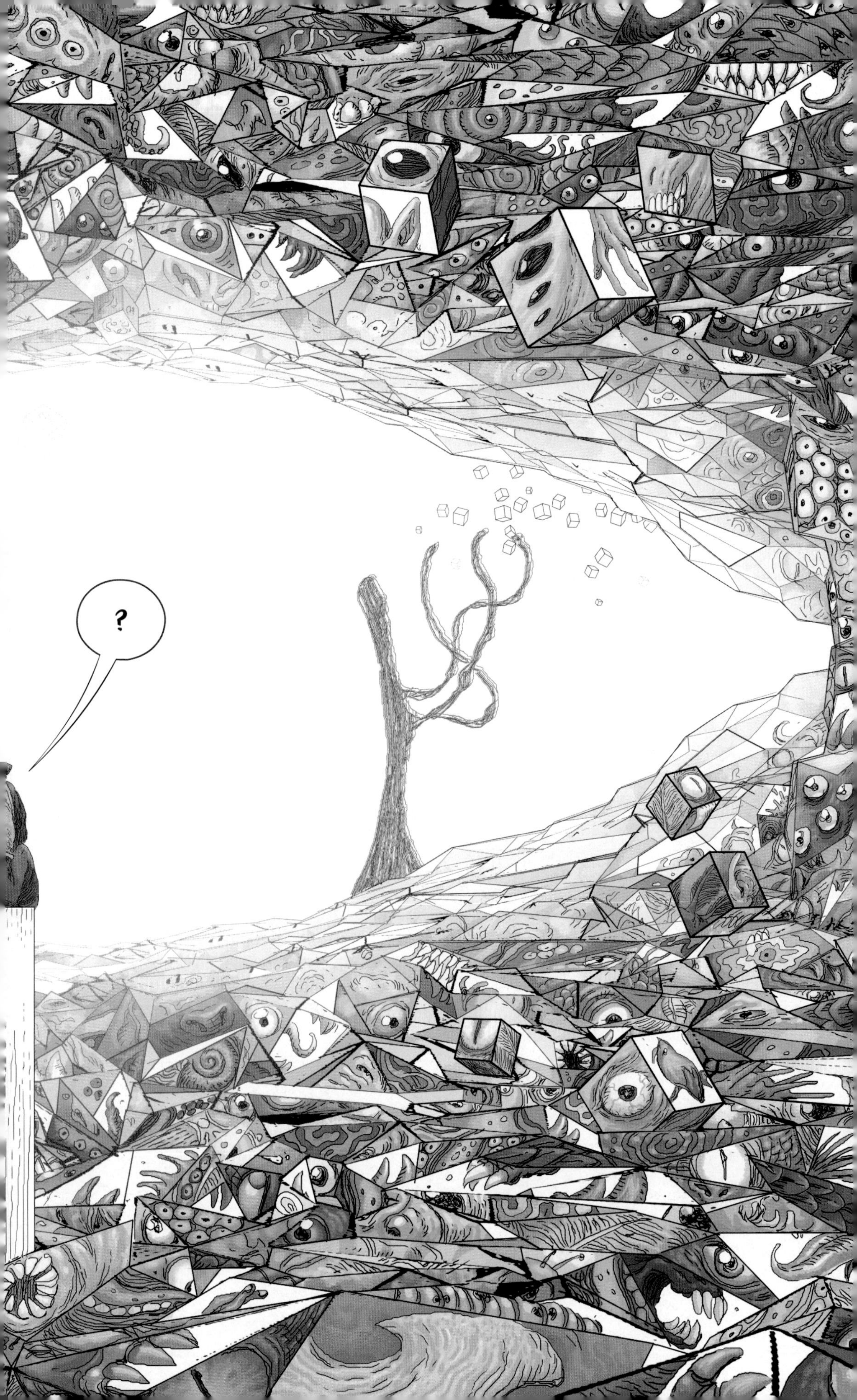
?

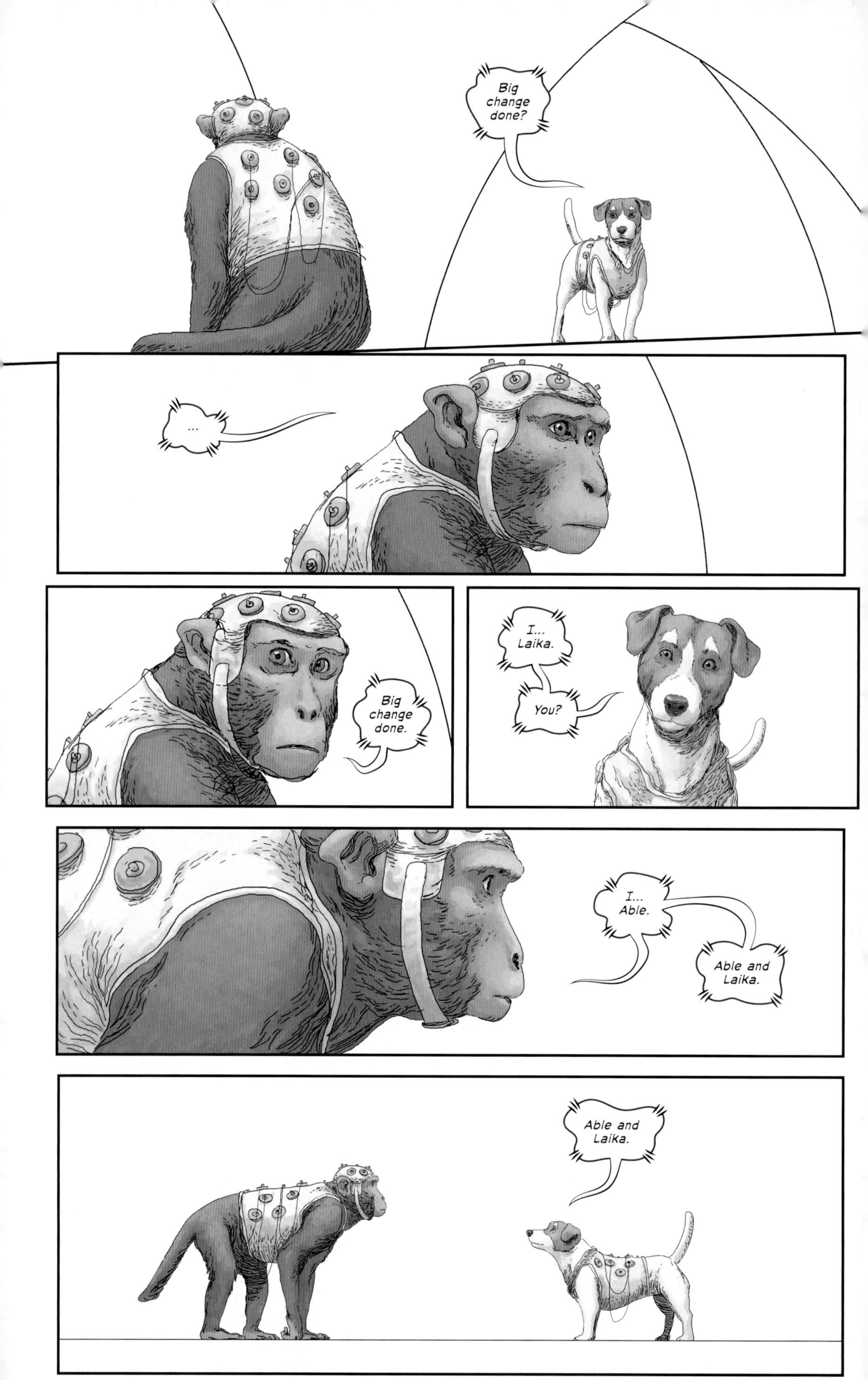
Big change done?
...
Big change done.
I... Laika.
You?
I... Able.
Able and Laika.
Able and Laika.

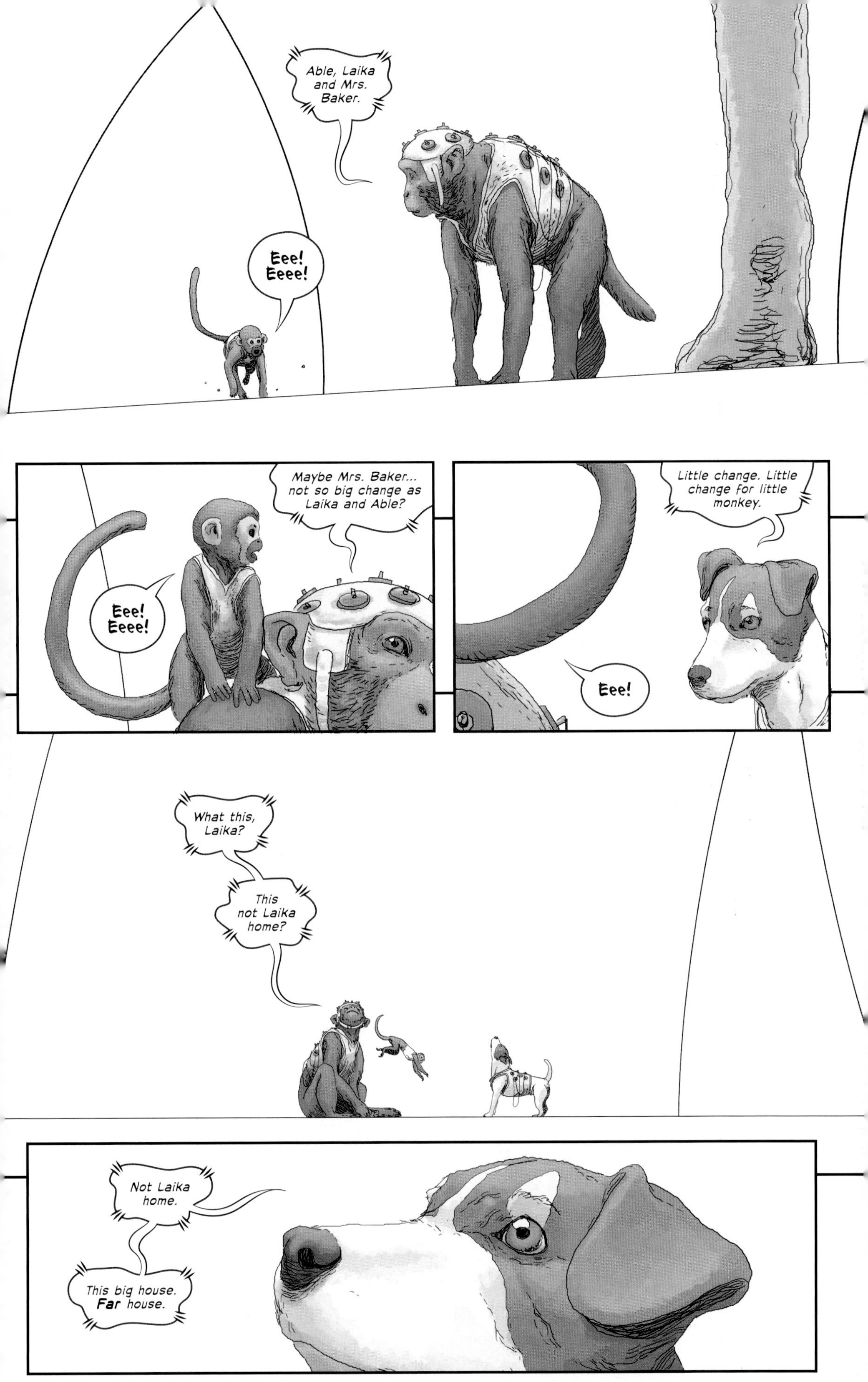

Able, Laika and Mrs. Baker.
Eee! Eeee!
Maybe Mrs. Baker... not so big change as Laika and Able?
Eee! Eeee!
Little change. Little change for little monkey.
Eee!
What this, Laika?
This not Laika home?
Not Laika home.
This big house. **Far** house.

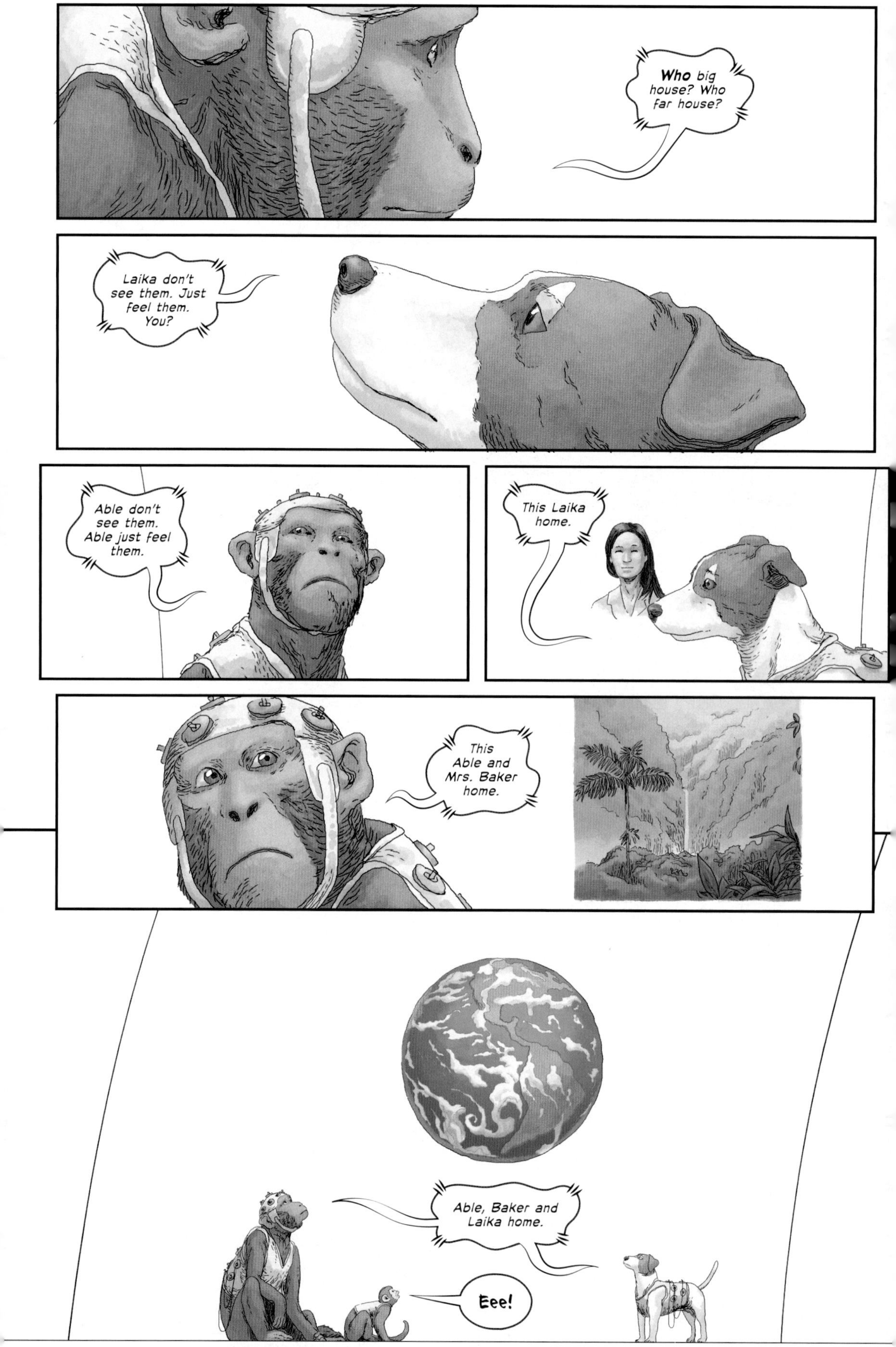
Who big house? Who far house?
Laika don't see them. Just feel them. You?
Able don't see them. Able just feel them.
This Laika home.
This Able and Mrs. Baker home.
Able, Baker and Laika home.
Eee!

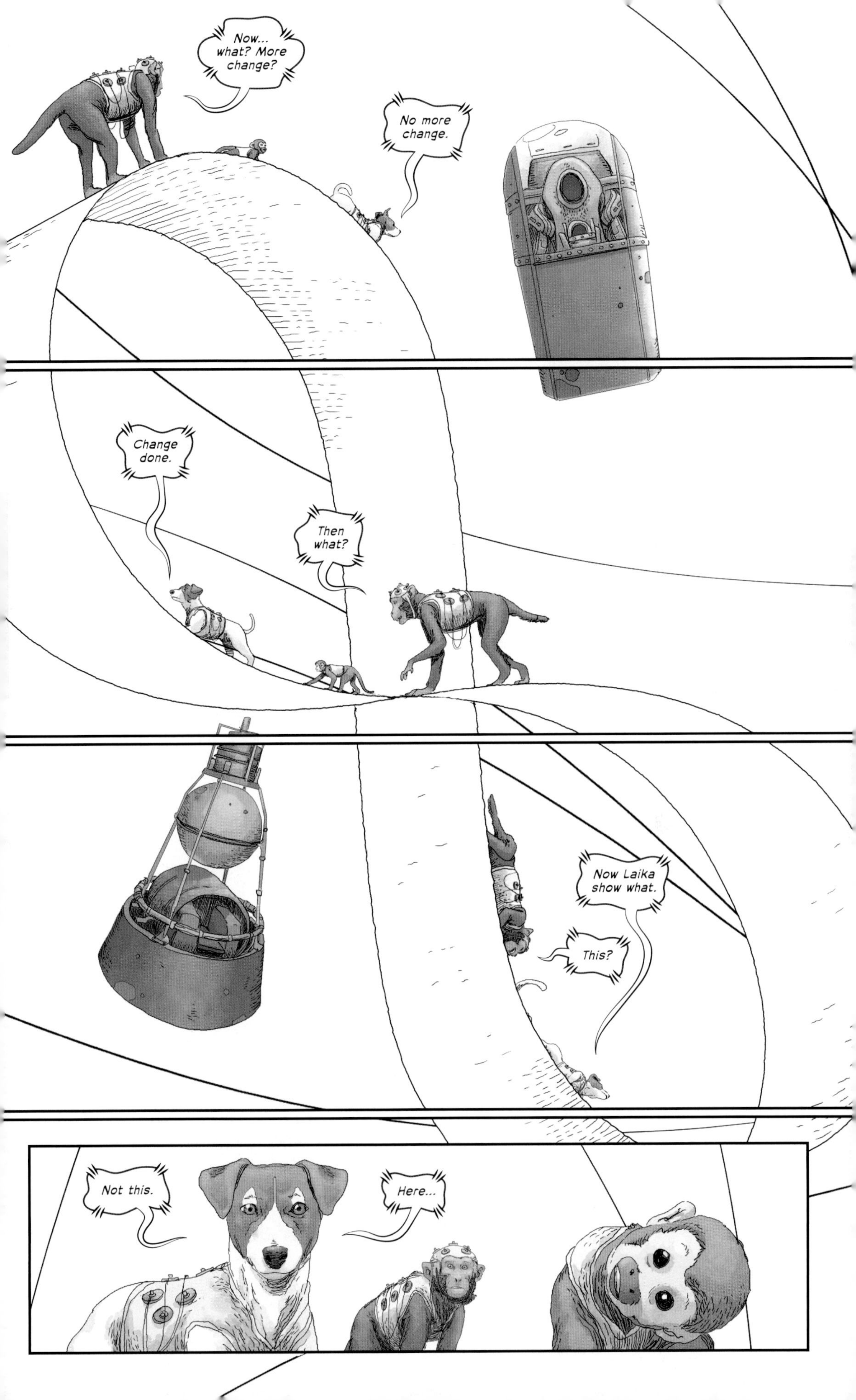
Now... what? More change?
No more change.
Change done.
Then what?
Now Laika show what.
This?
Not this.
Here...

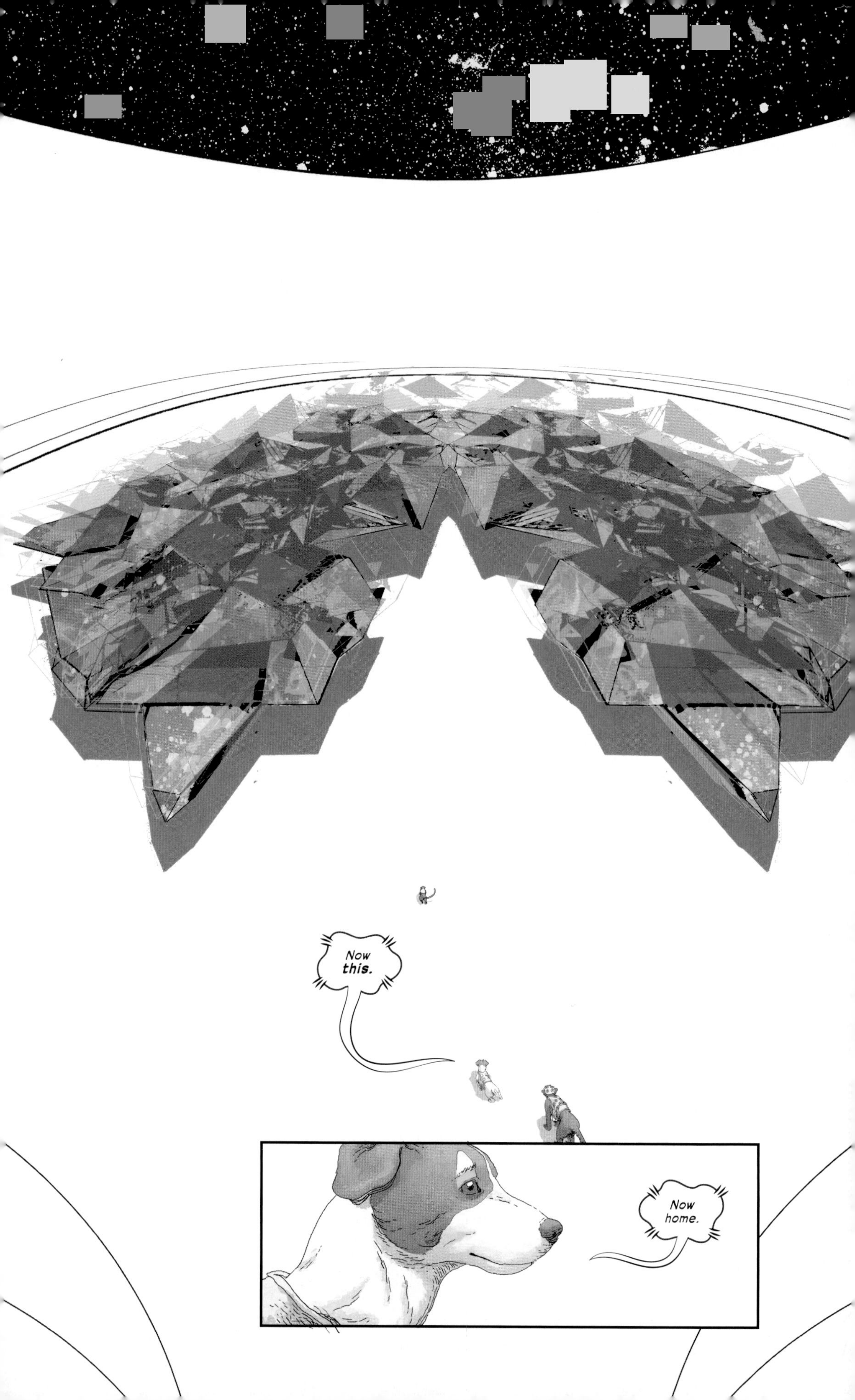
Now this.
Now home.

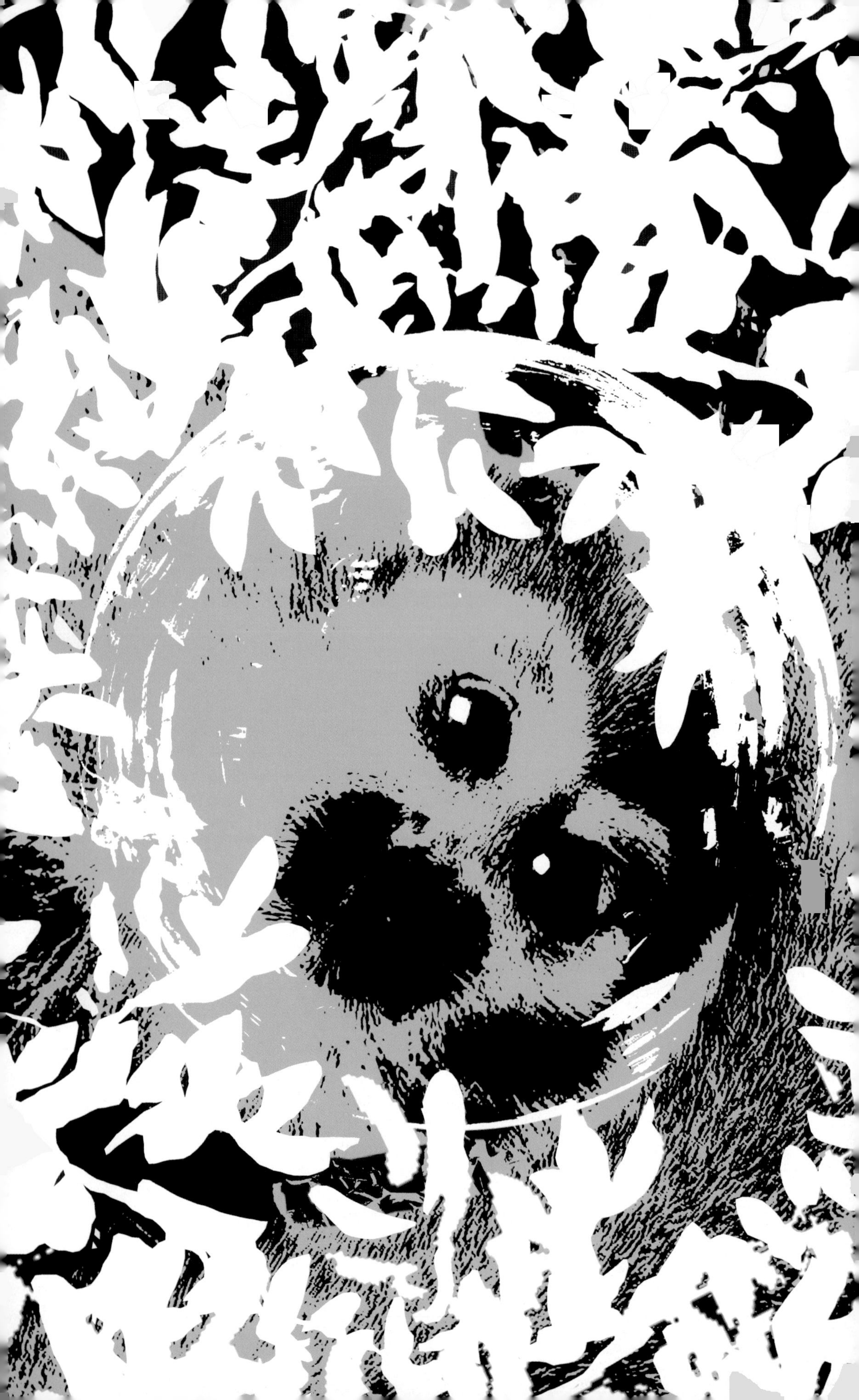

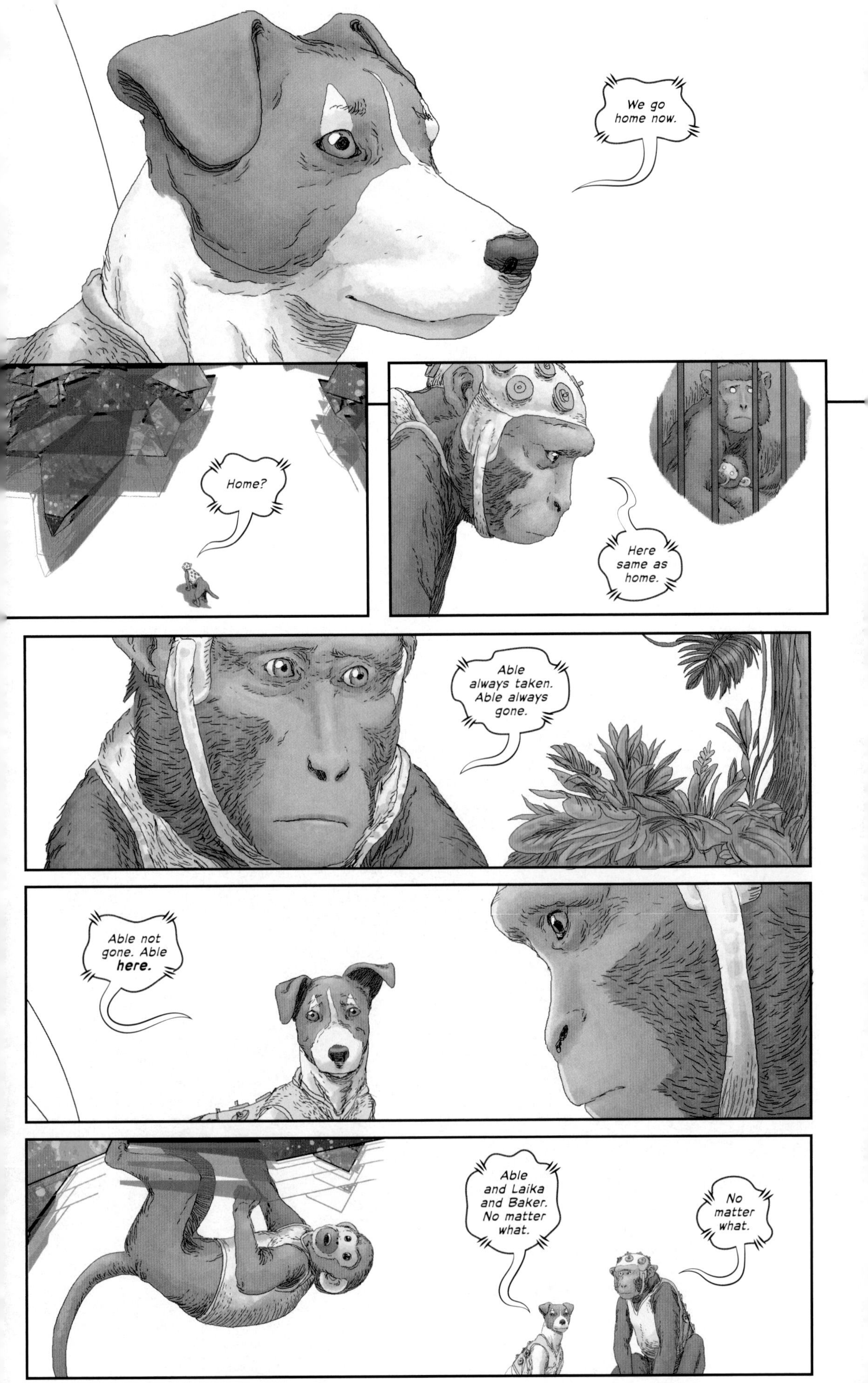
We go home now.
Home?
Here same as home.
Able always taken. Able always gone.
Able not gone. Able **here.**
Able and Laika and Baker. No matter what.
No matter what.

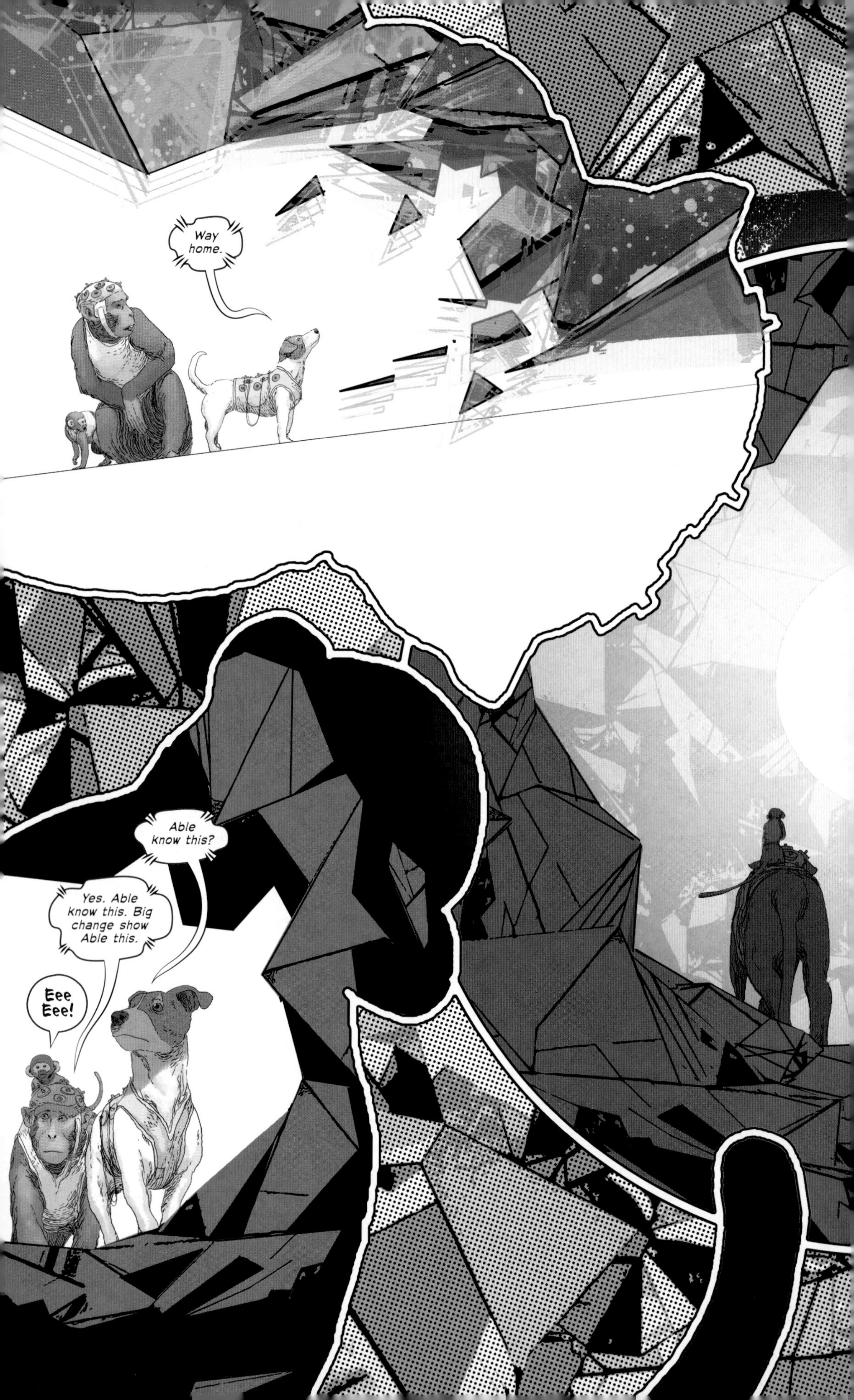
Way home.
Able know this?
Yes. Able know this. Big change show Able this.
Eee Eee!

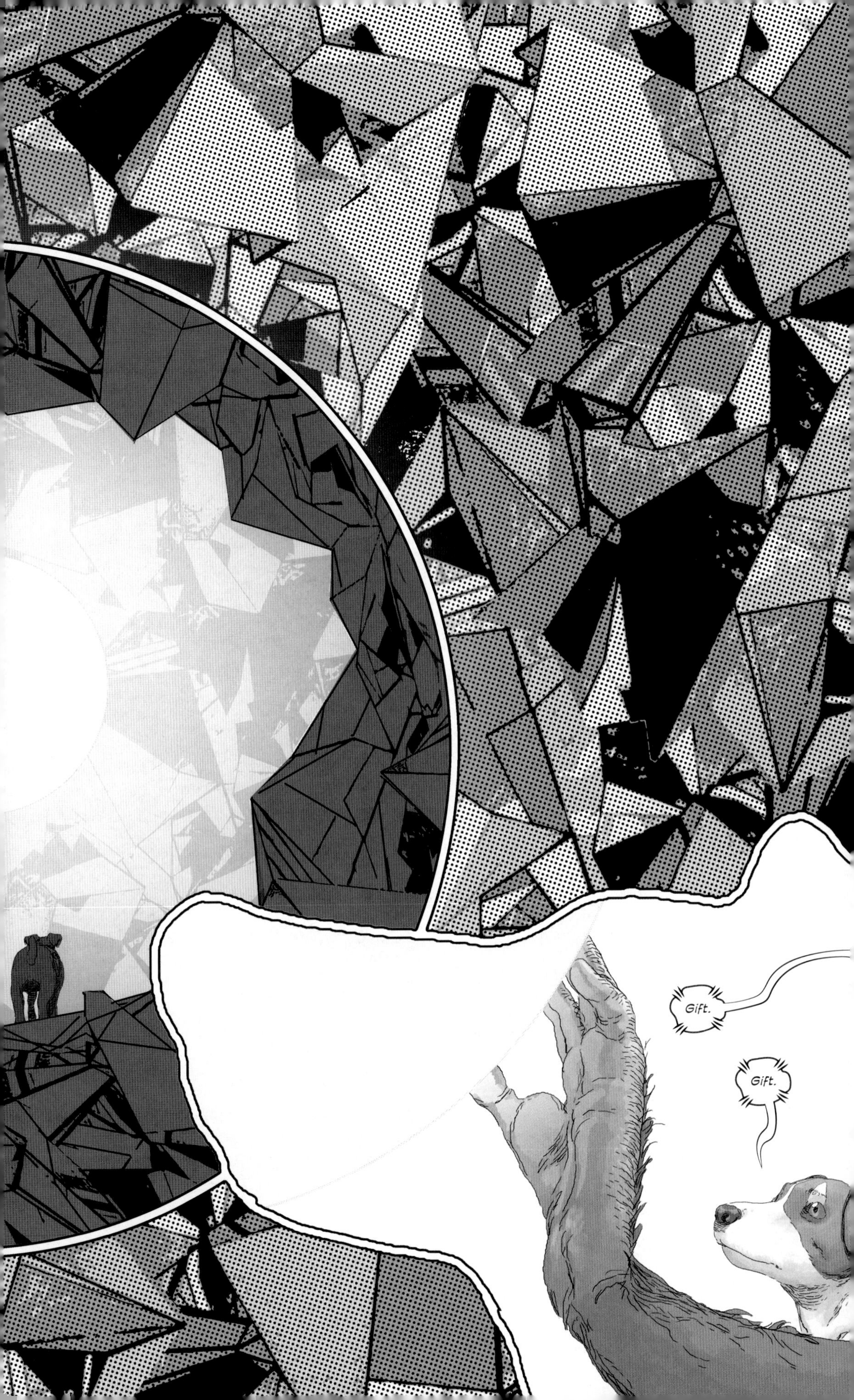
Gift.
Gift.

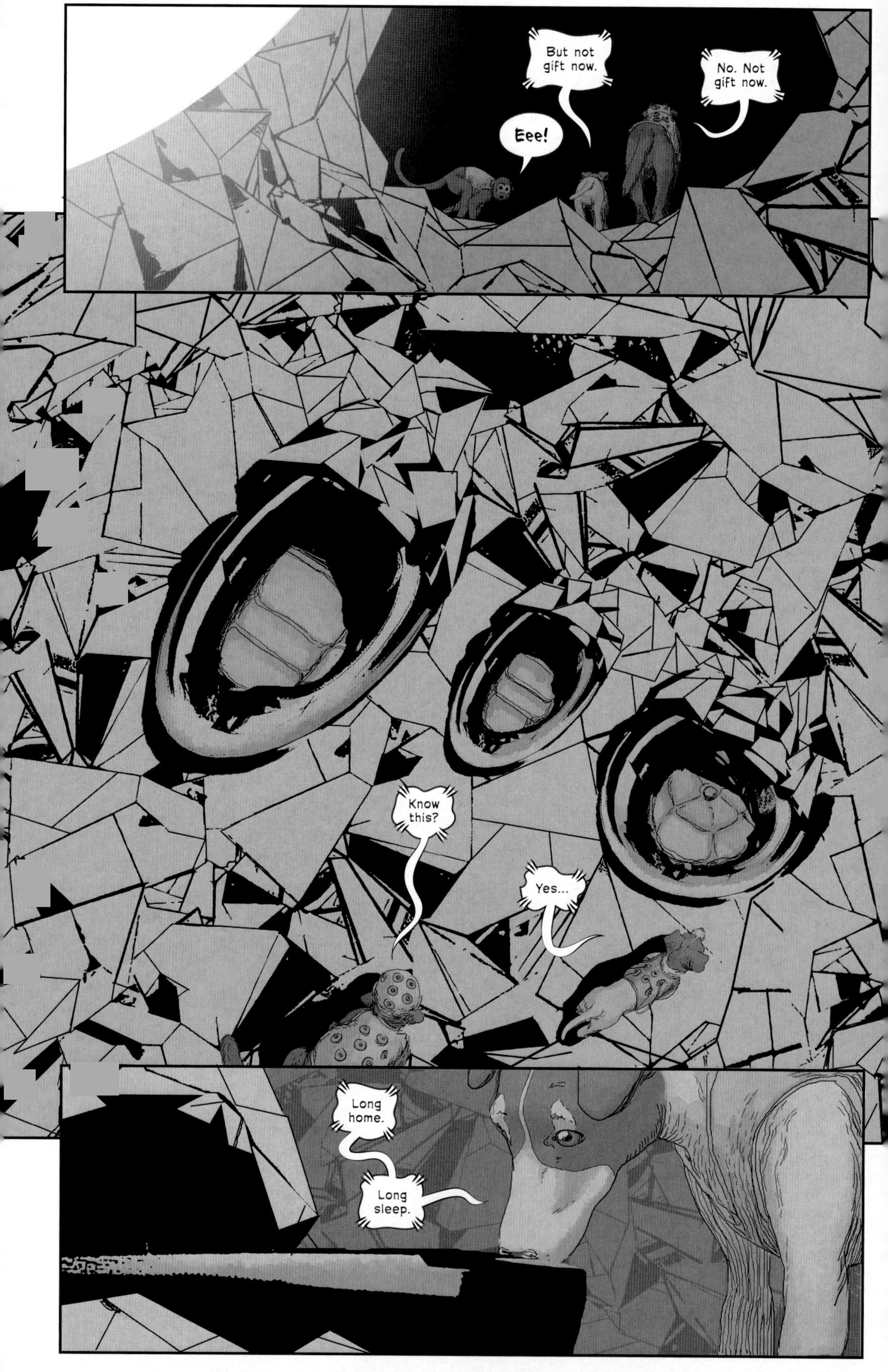

Eee!
But not gift now.
No. Not gift now.
Know this?
Yes...
Long home.
Long sleep.

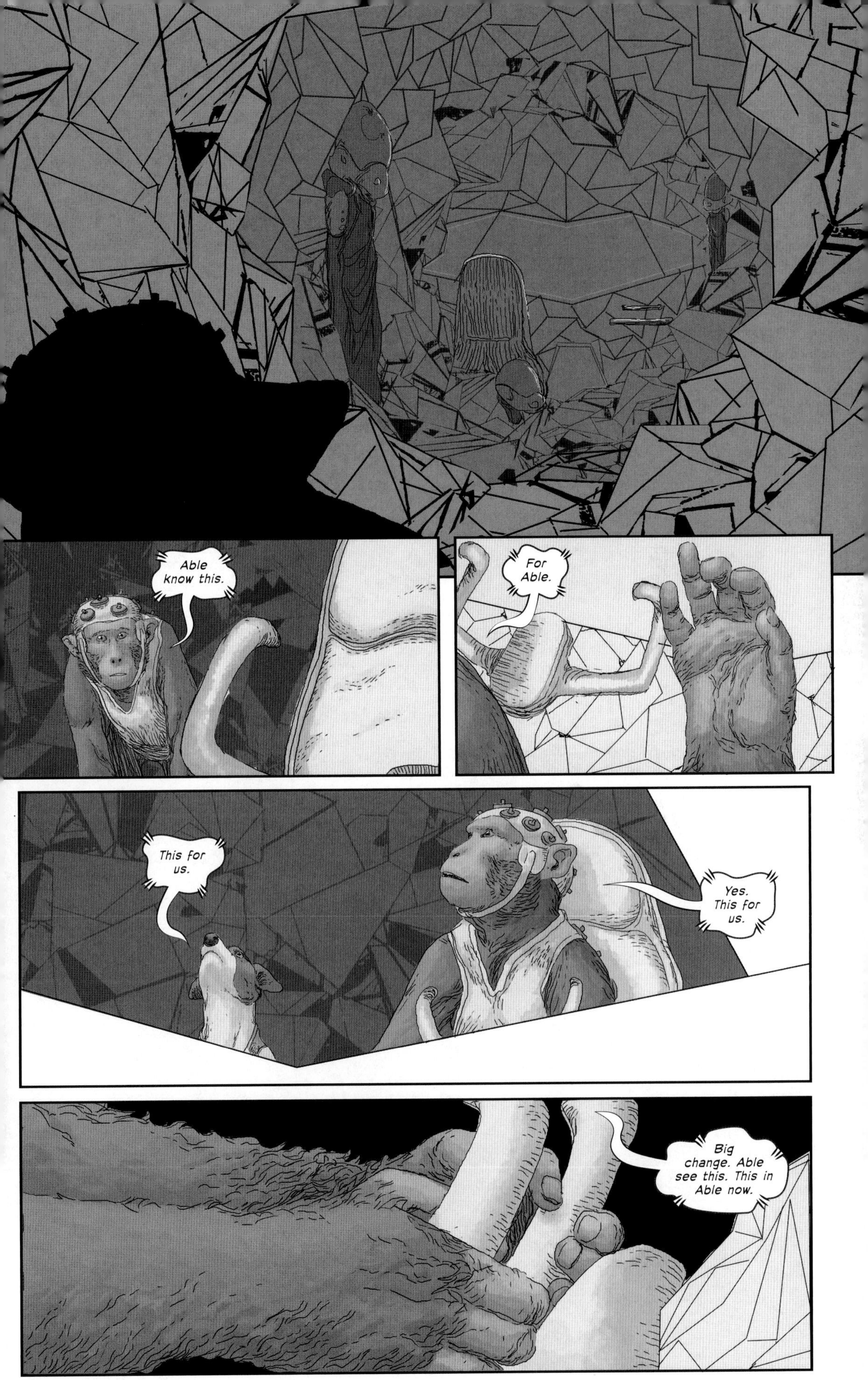
Able know this.
For Able.
This for us.
Yes. This for us.
Big change. Able see this. This in Able now.

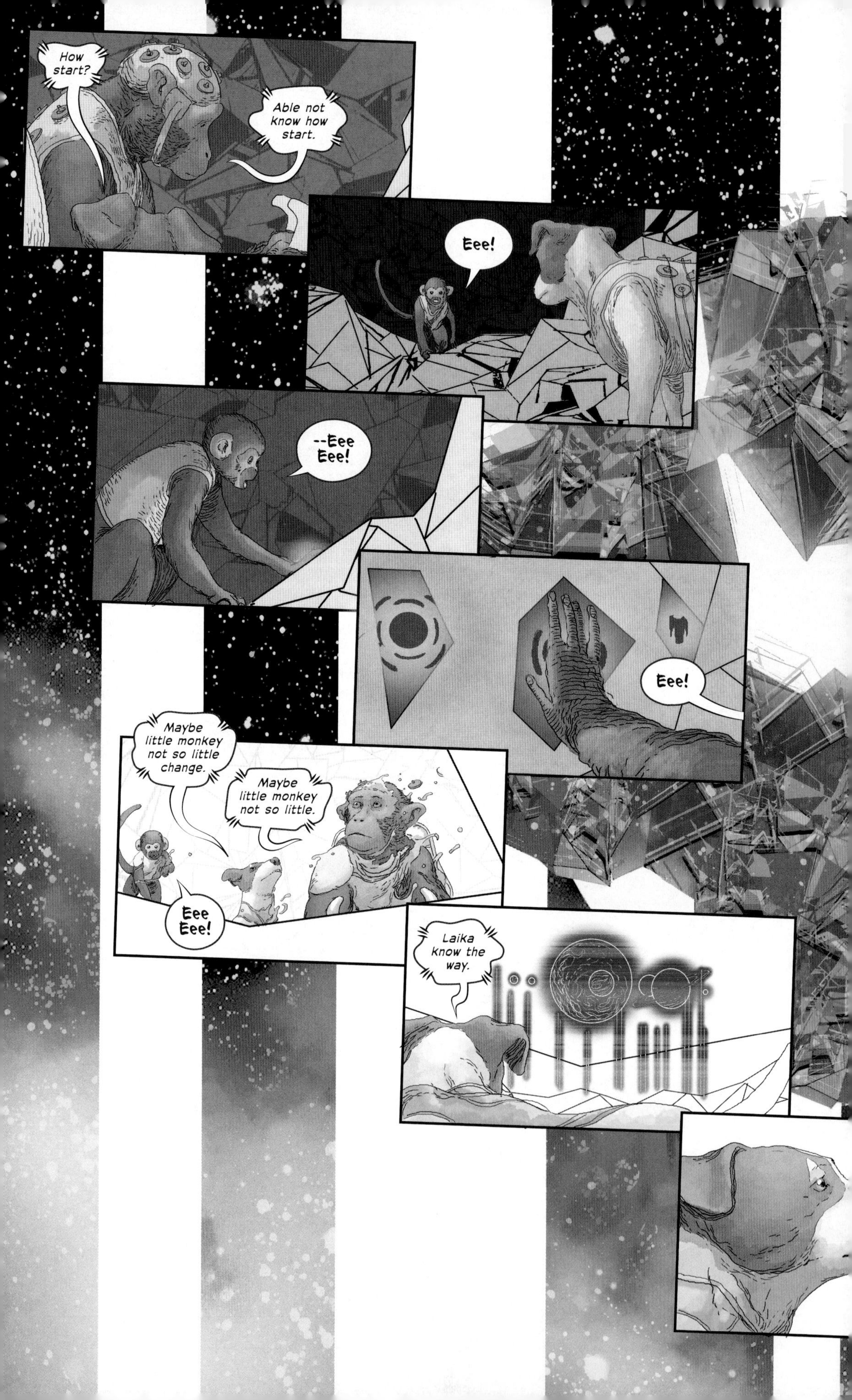
How start?
Able not know how start.
Eee!
--Eee Eee!
Eee!
Maybe little monkey not so little change.
Maybe little monkey not so little.
Eee Eee!
Laika know the way.

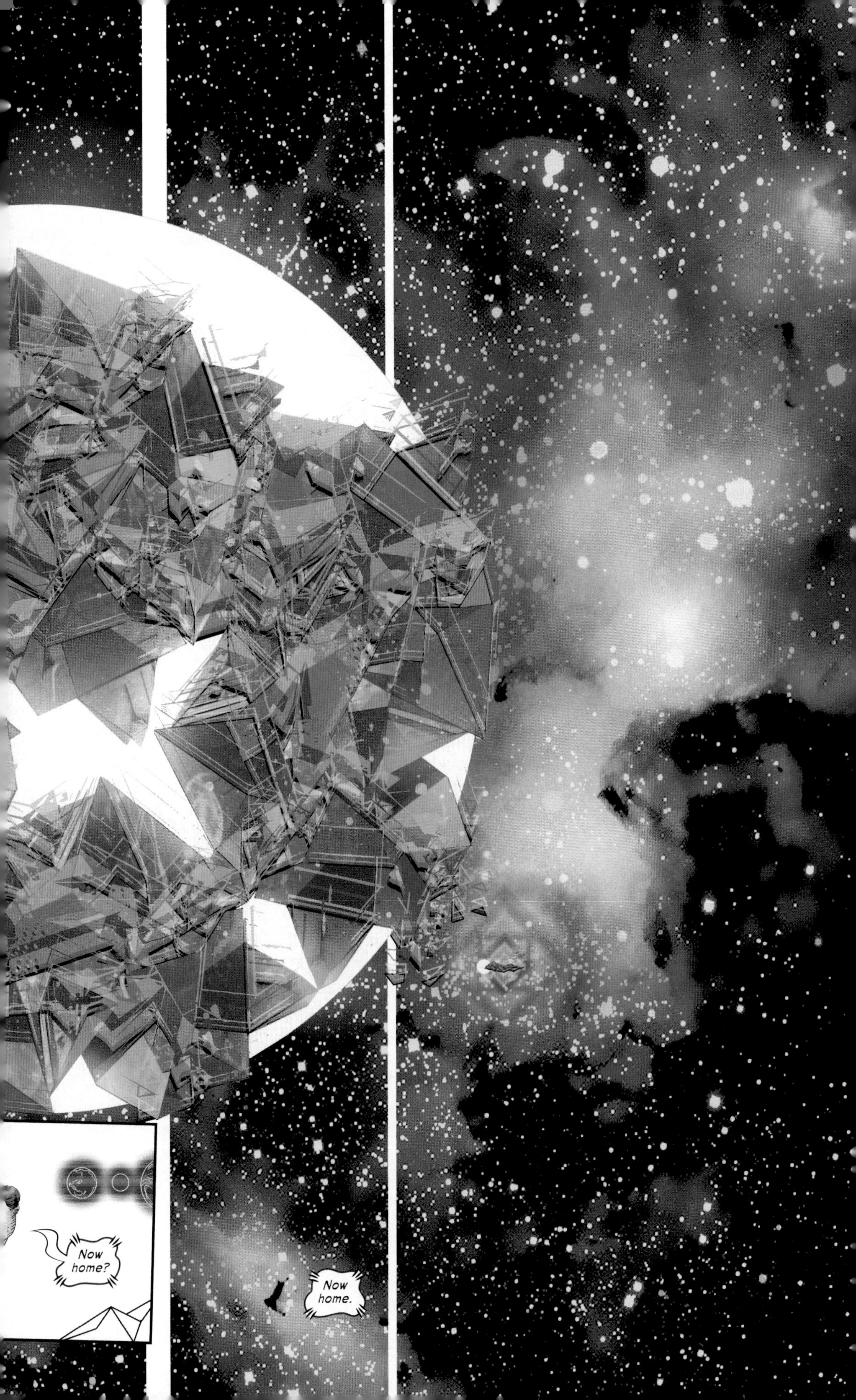
Now home?
Now home.

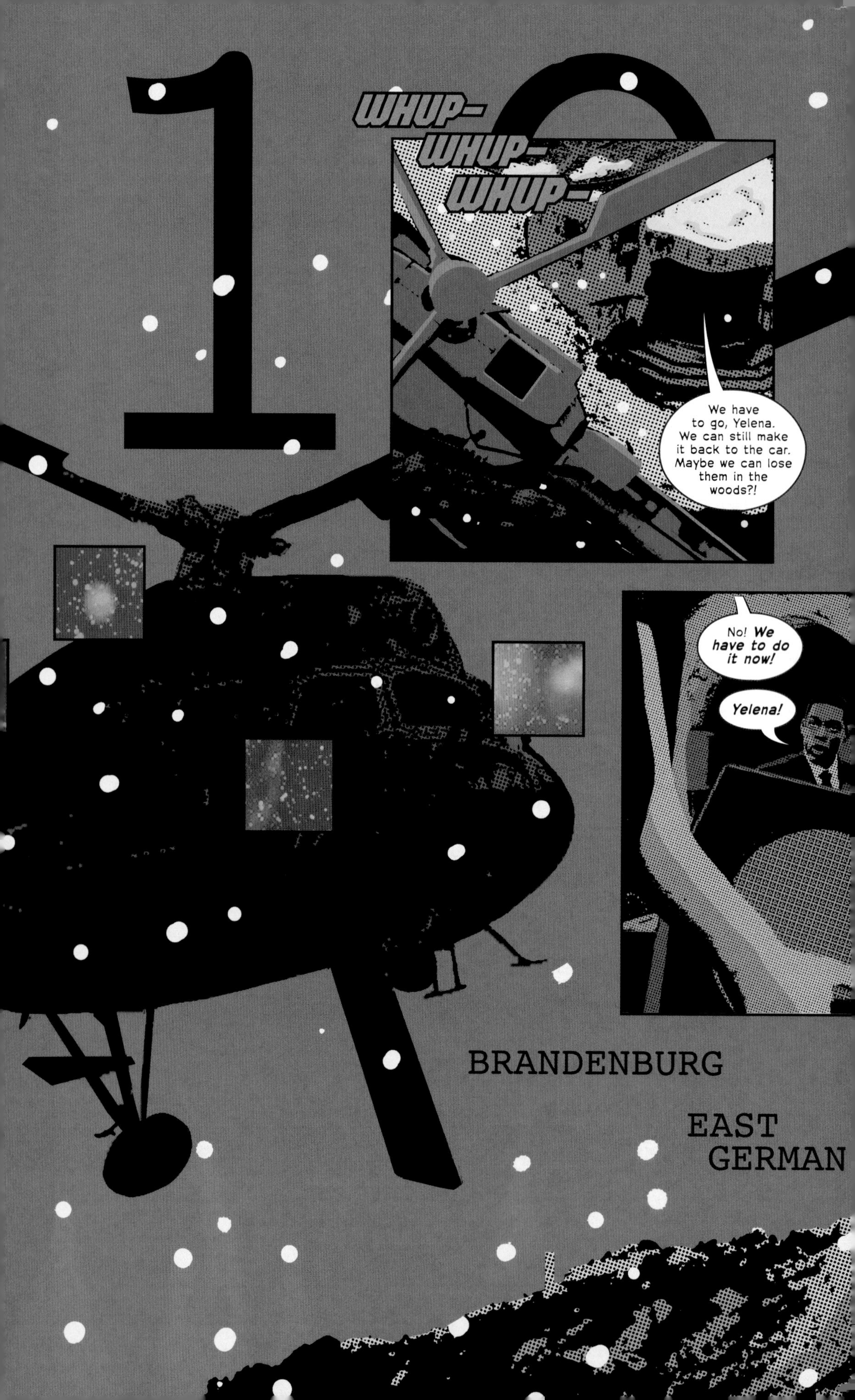

10
WHUP-
WHUP-
WHUP-
We have to go, Yelena. We can still make it back to the car. Maybe we can lose them in the woods?!
No! We have to do it now!
Yelena!
BRANDENBURG
EAST GERMAN

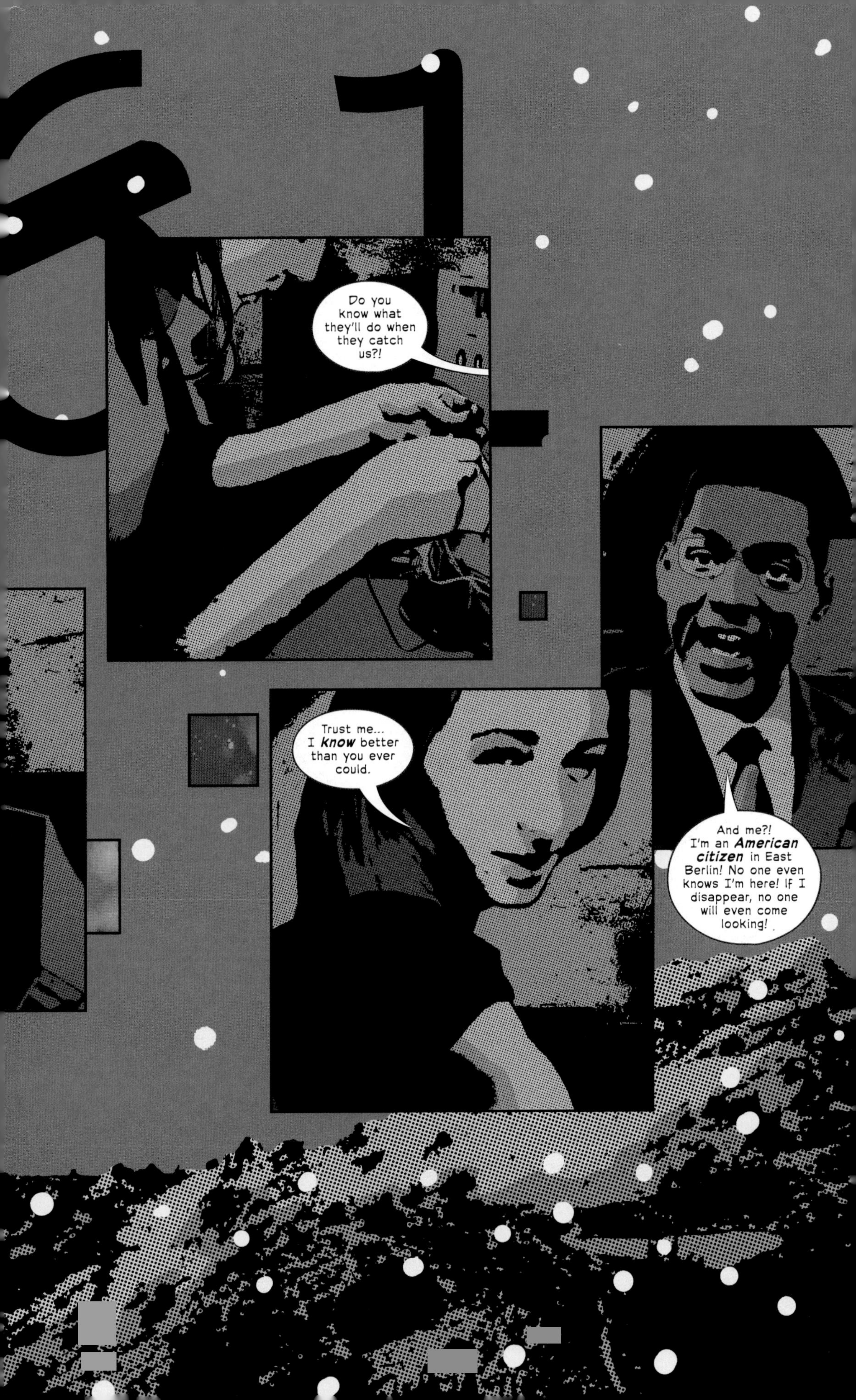
Do you know what they'll do when they catch us?!
Trust me... I *know* better than you ever could.
And me?! I'm an ***American citizen*** in East Berlin! No one even knows I'm here! If I disappear, no one will even come looking!

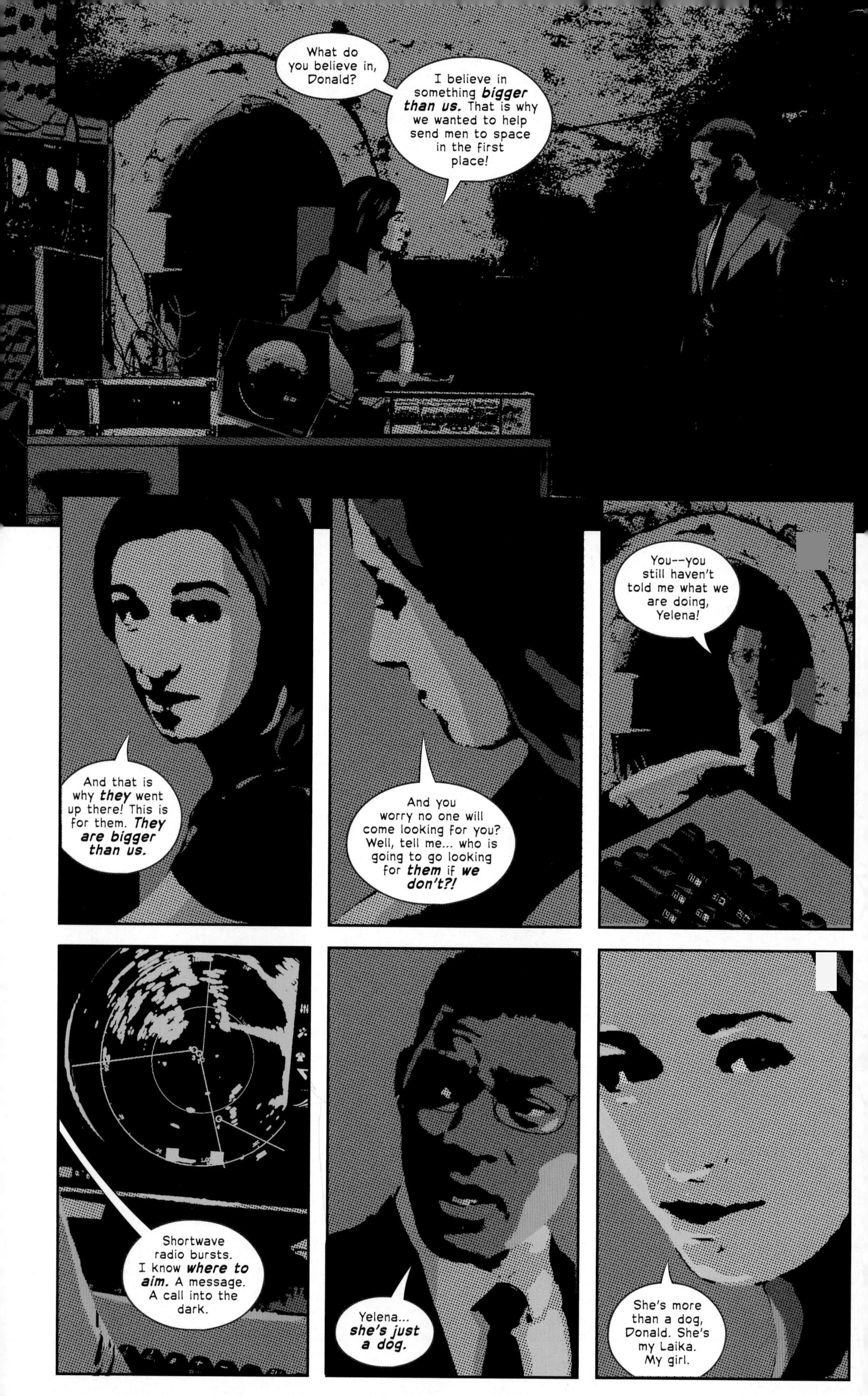
What do you believe in, Donald?
I believe in something bigger than us. That is why we wanted to help send men to space in the first place!
And that is why they went up there! This is for them. They are bigger than us.
And you worry no one will come looking for you? Well, tell me... who is going to go looking for them if we don't?!
You--you still haven't told me what we are doing, Yelena!
Shortwave radio bursts. I know where to aim. A message. A call into the dark.
Yelena... she's just a dog.
She's more than a dog, Donald. She's my Laika. My girl.

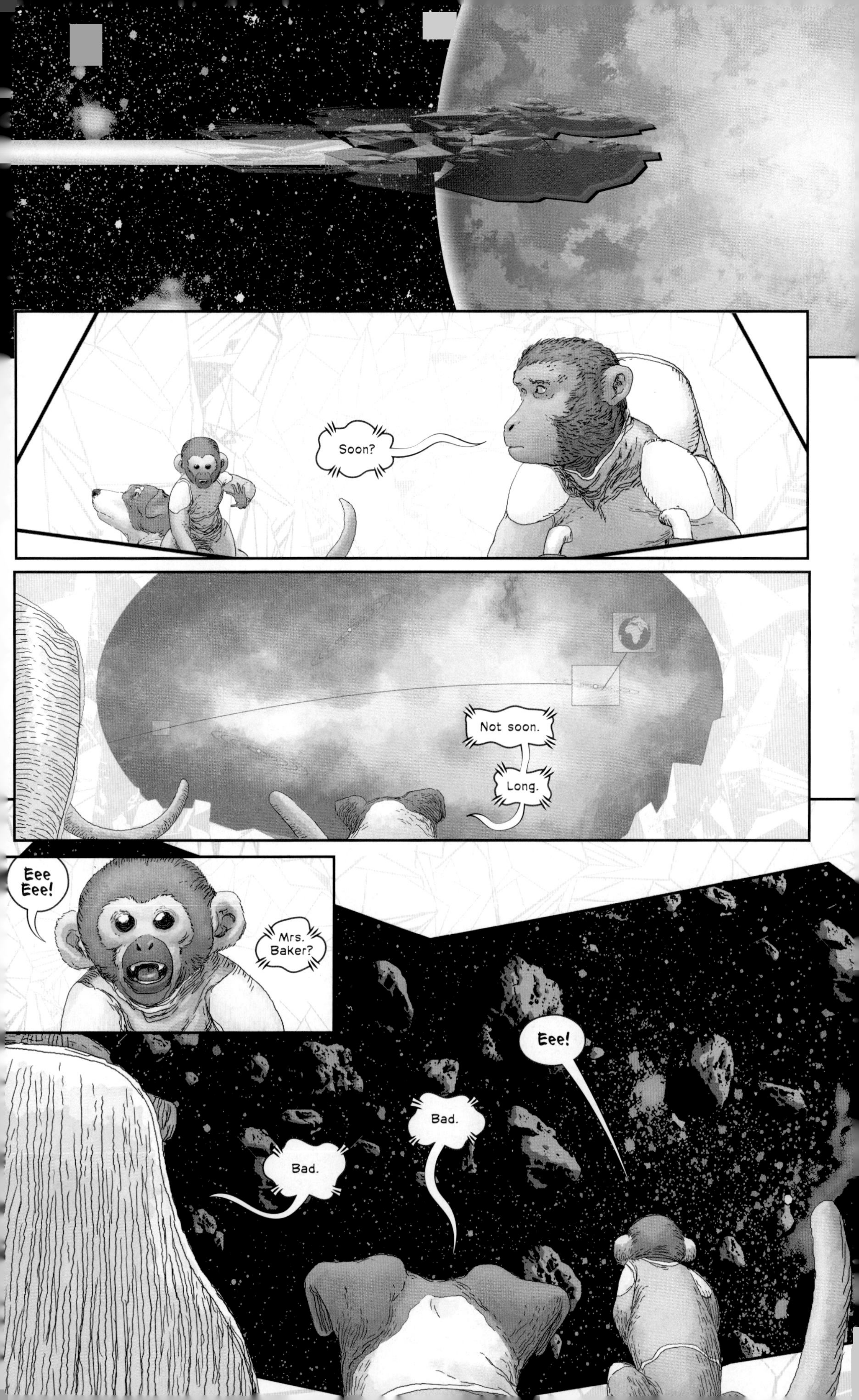
Soon?
Not soon.
Long.
Eee
Eee!
Mrs.
Baker?
Eee!
Bad.
Bad.

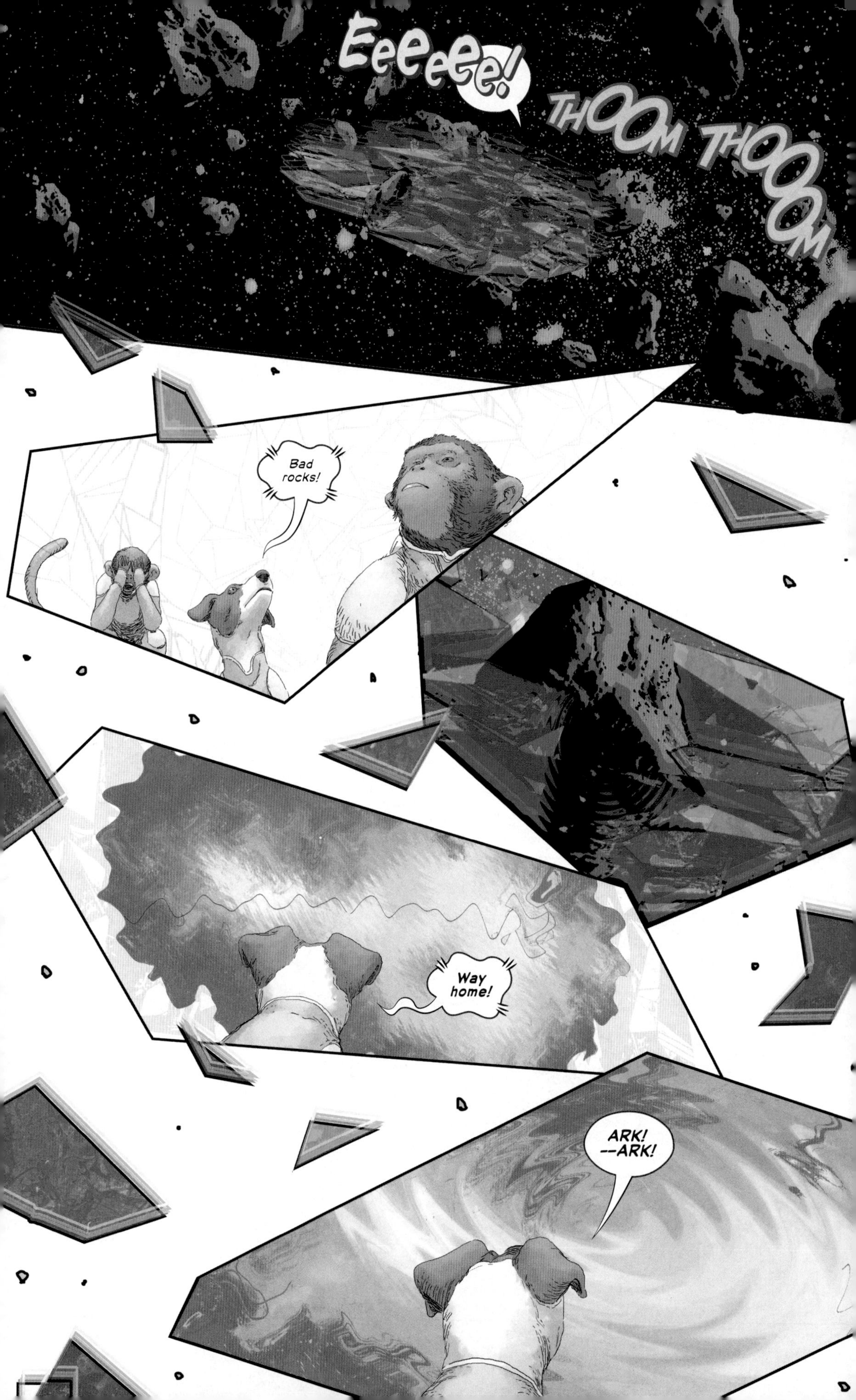
Eeeeee!
THOOM THOOOM
Bad rocks!
Way home!
ARK! --ARK!

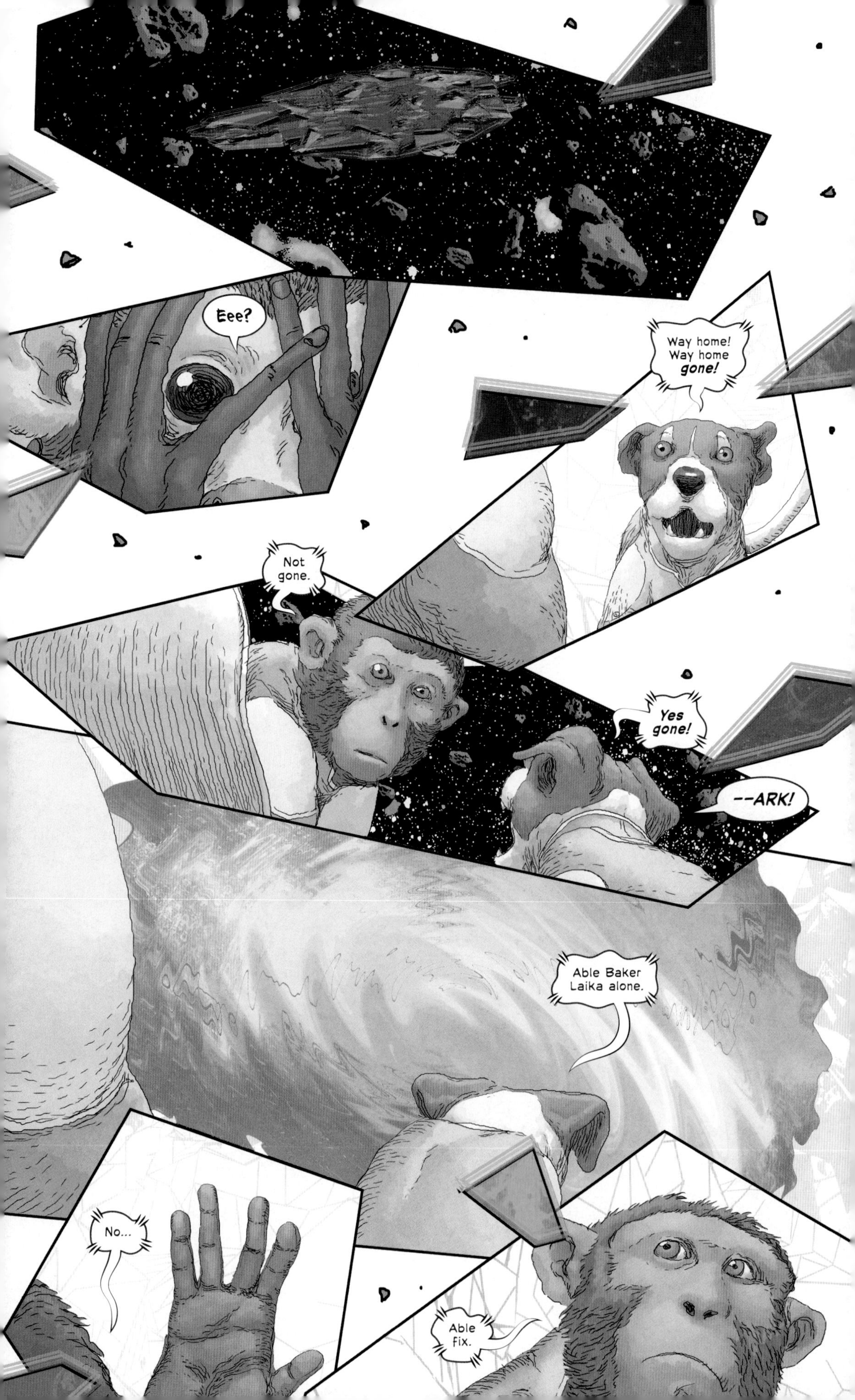
Eee?
Way home! Way home gone!
Not gone.
Yes gone!
--ARK!
Able Baker Laika alone.
No...
Able fix.

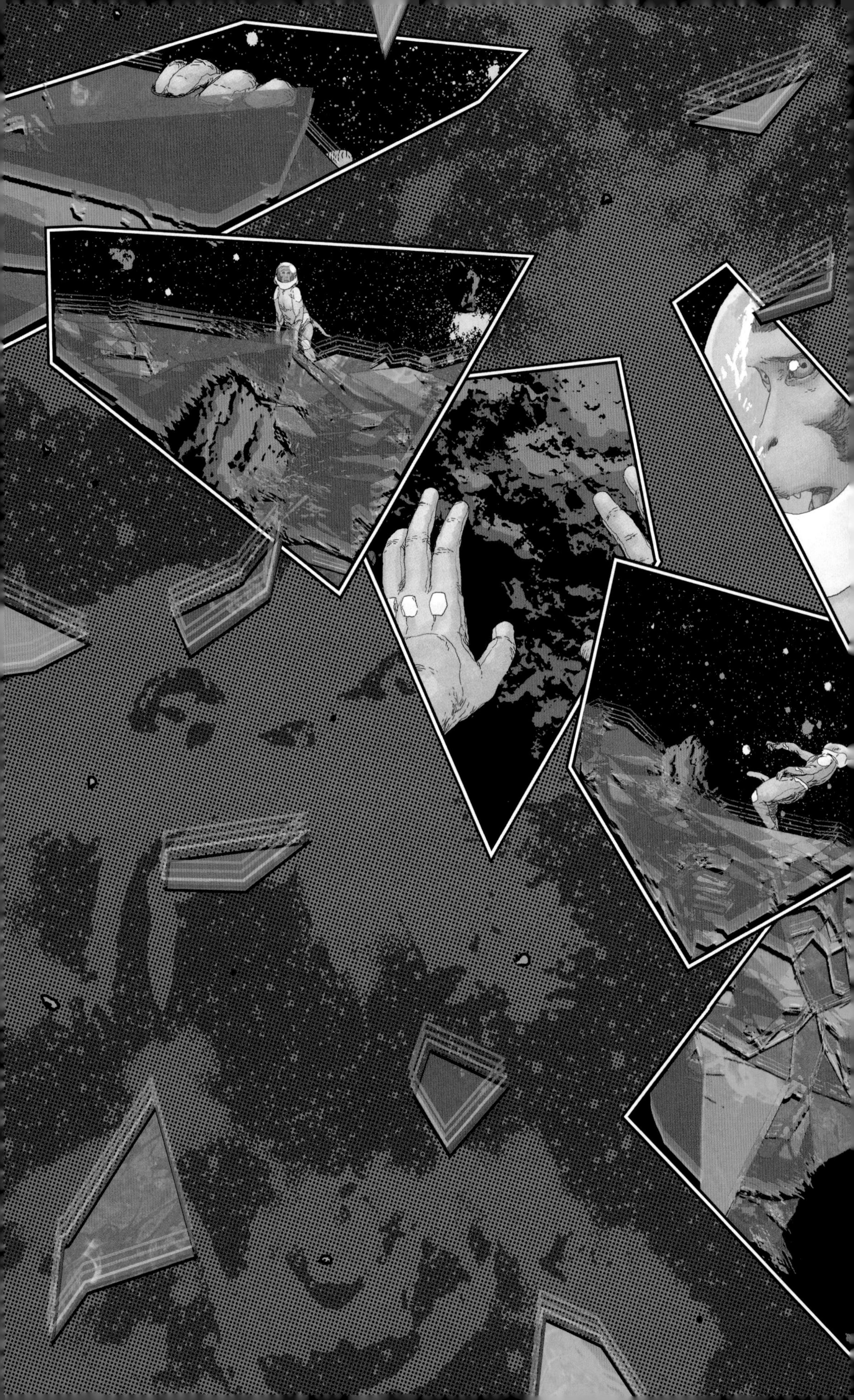

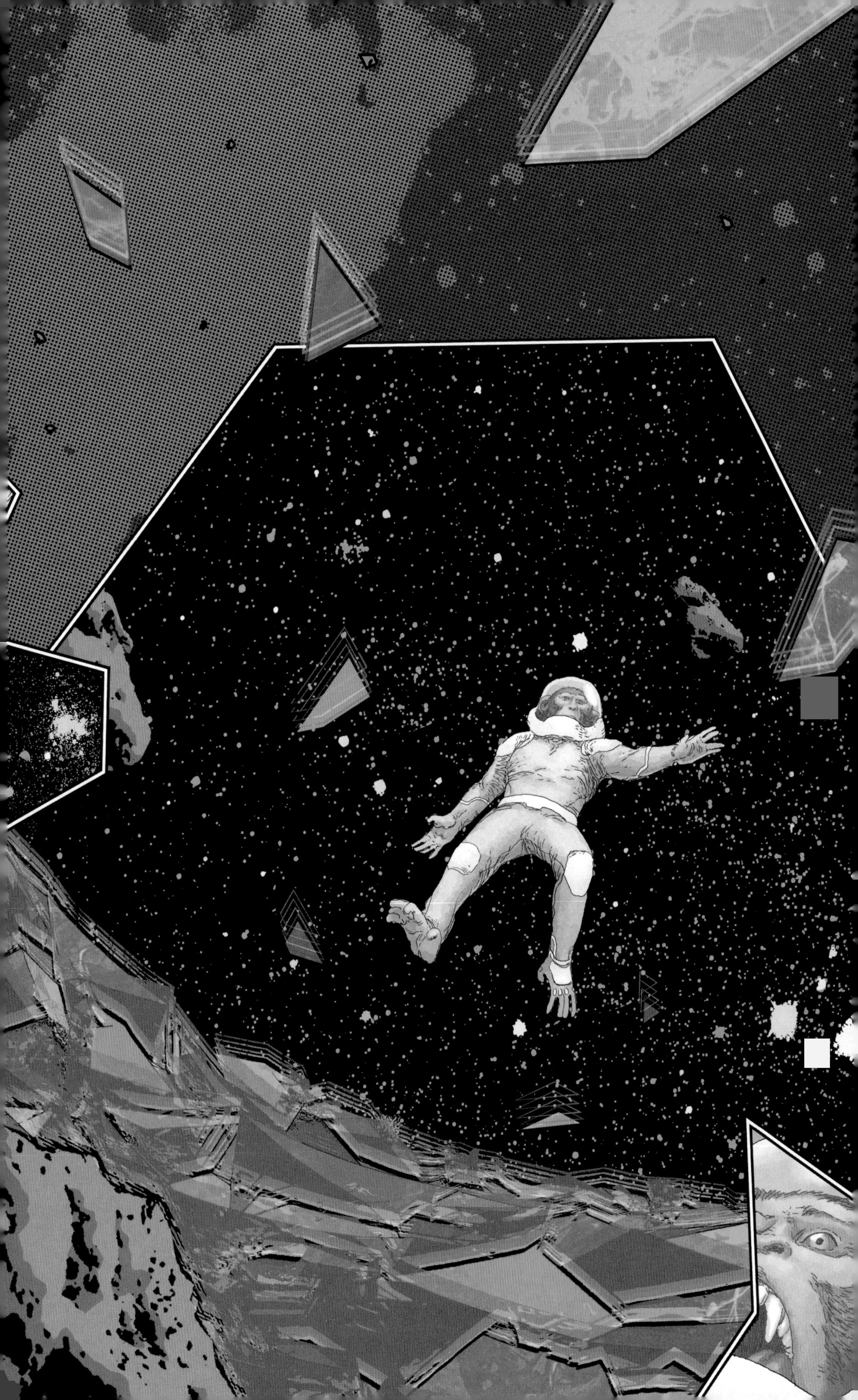

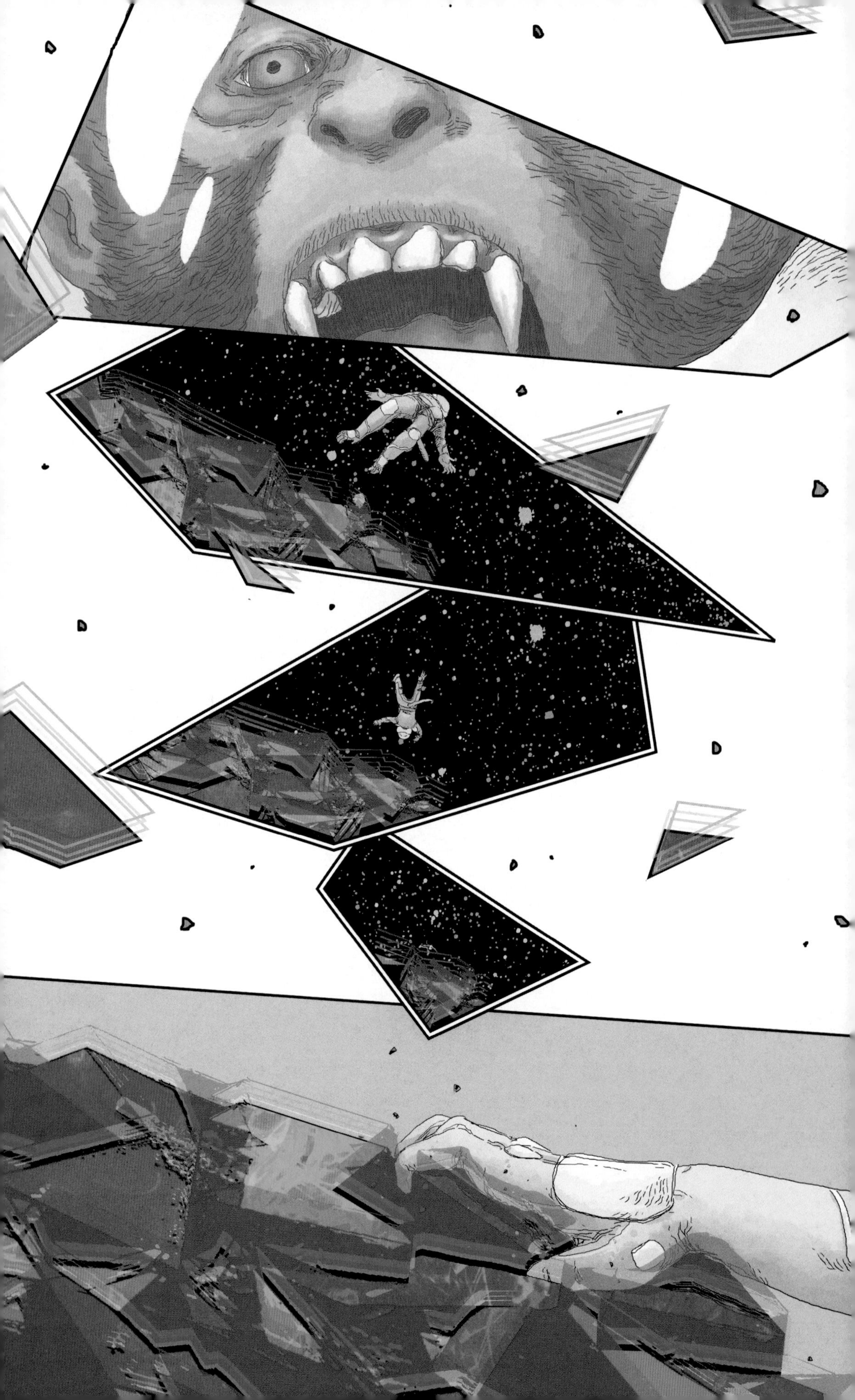

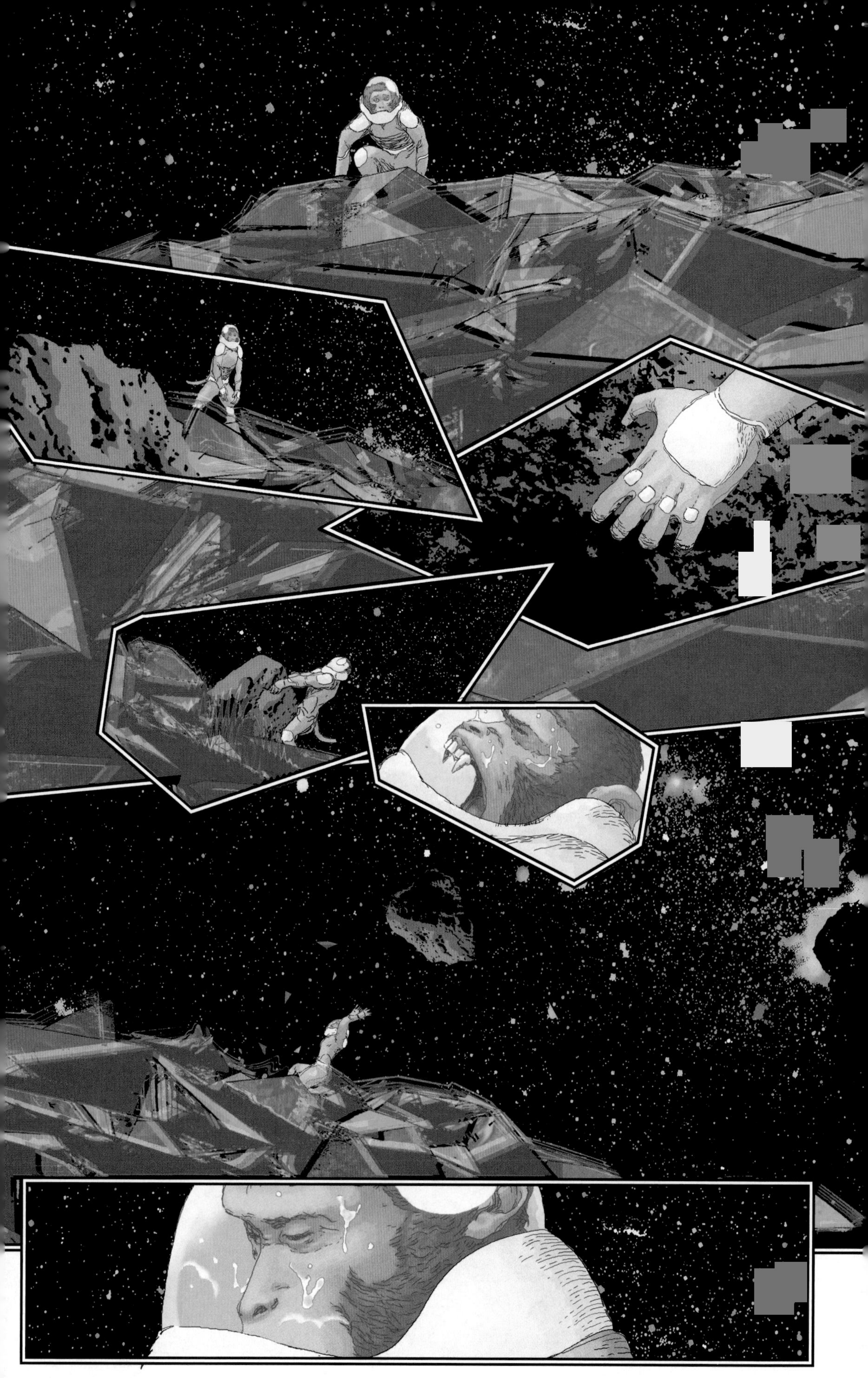

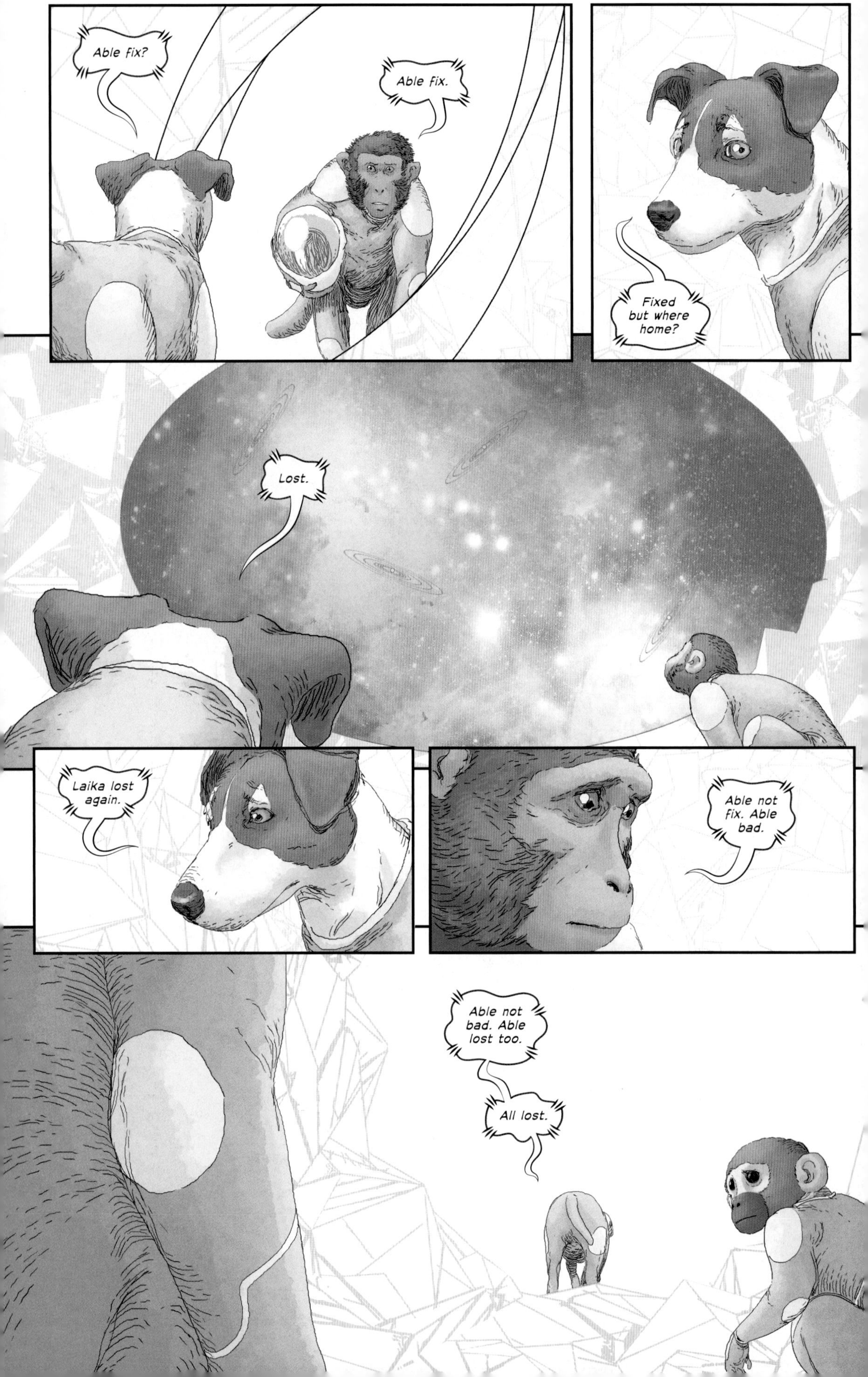
Able fix?
Able fix.
Fixed but where home?
Lost.
Laika lost again.
Able not fix. Able bad.
Able not bad. Able lost too.
All lost.

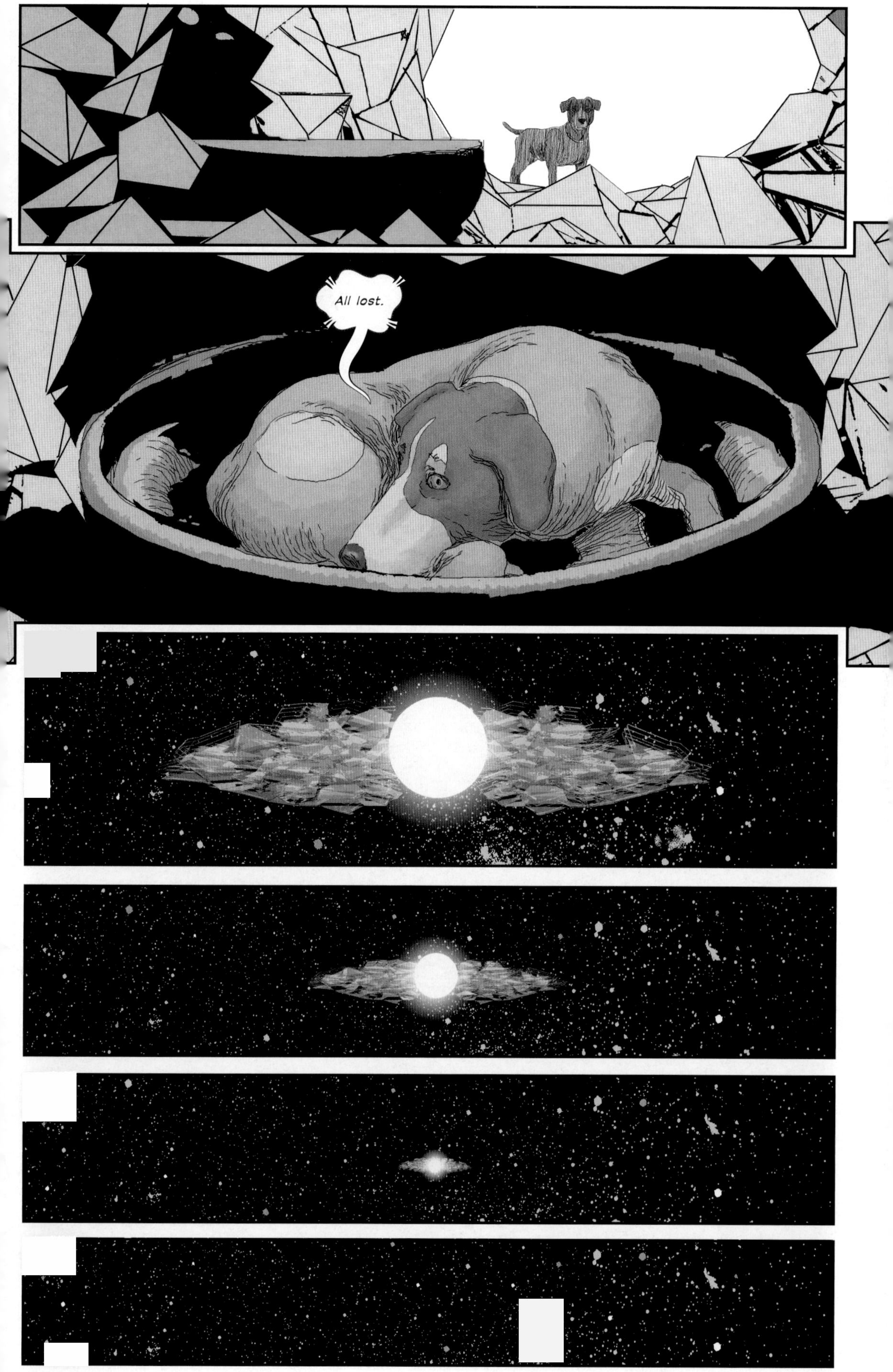
All lost.

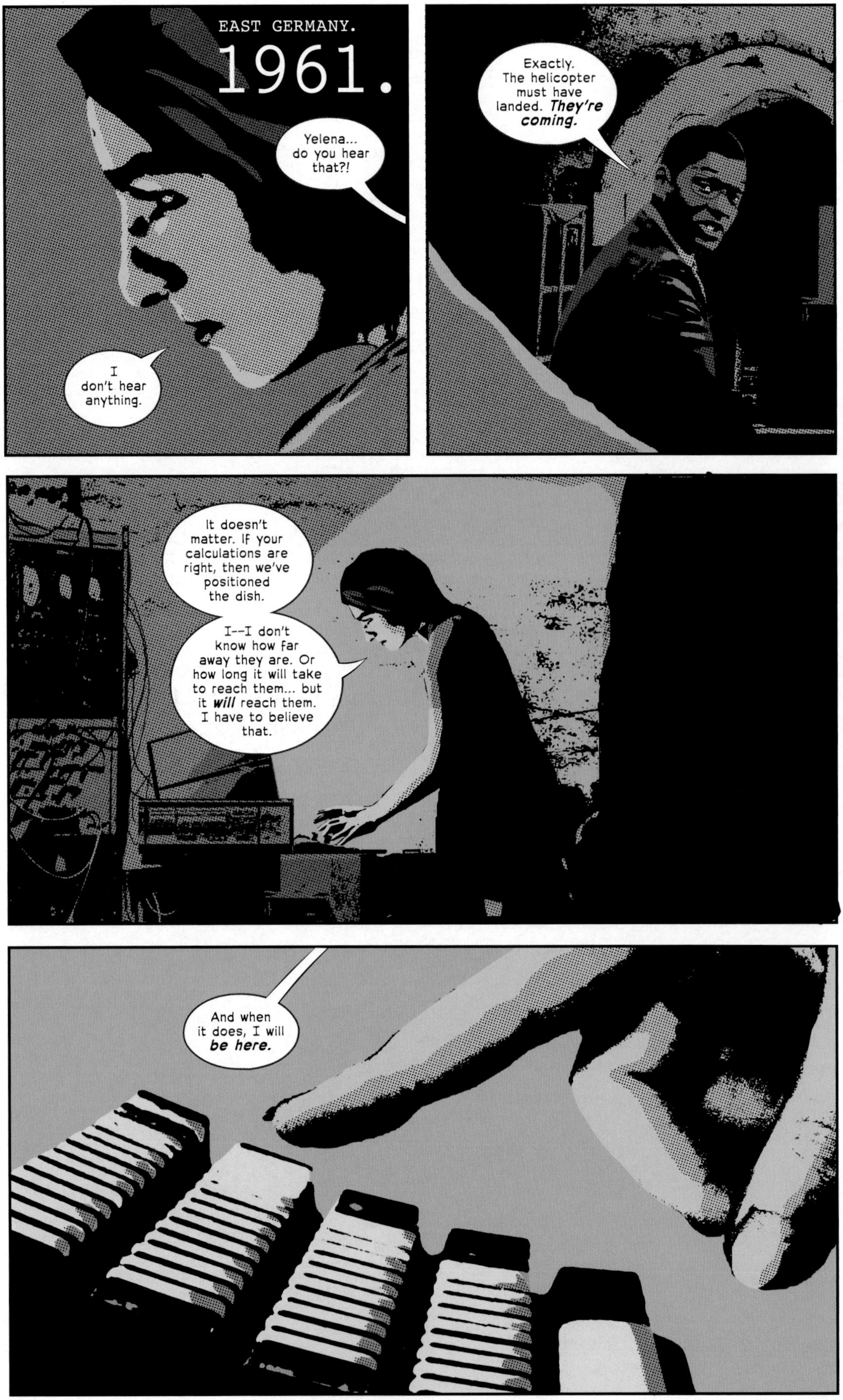
EAST GERMANY.
1961.
Yelena... do you hear that?!
I don't hear anything.
Exactly. The helicopter must have landed. *They're coming.*
It doesn't matter. If your calculations are right, then we've positioned the dish.
I--I don't know how far away they are. Or how long it will take to reach them... but it *will* reach them. I have to believe that.
And when it does, I will *be here.*

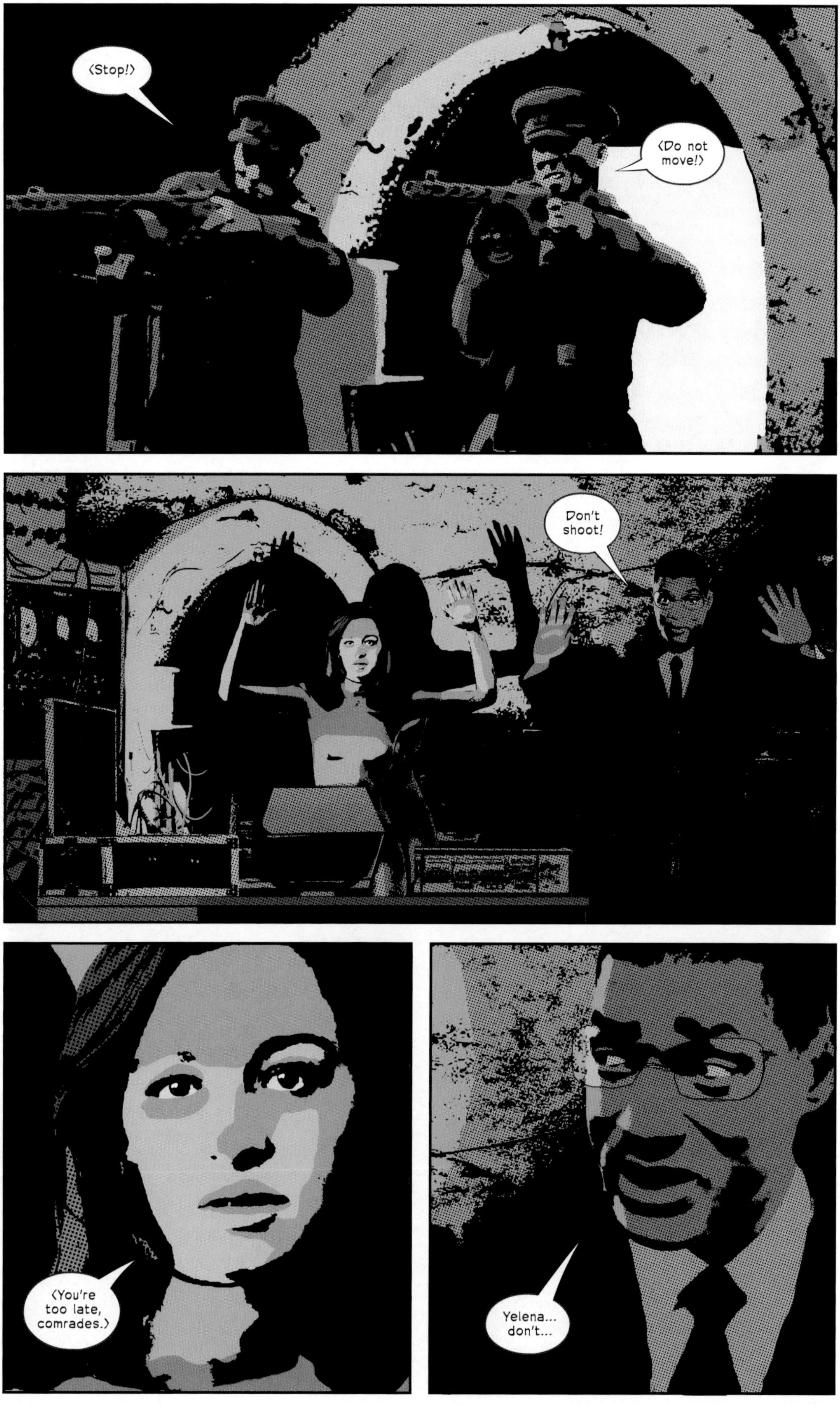
‹Stop!›
‹Do not move!›
Don't shoot!
‹You're too late, comrades.›
Yelena... don't...

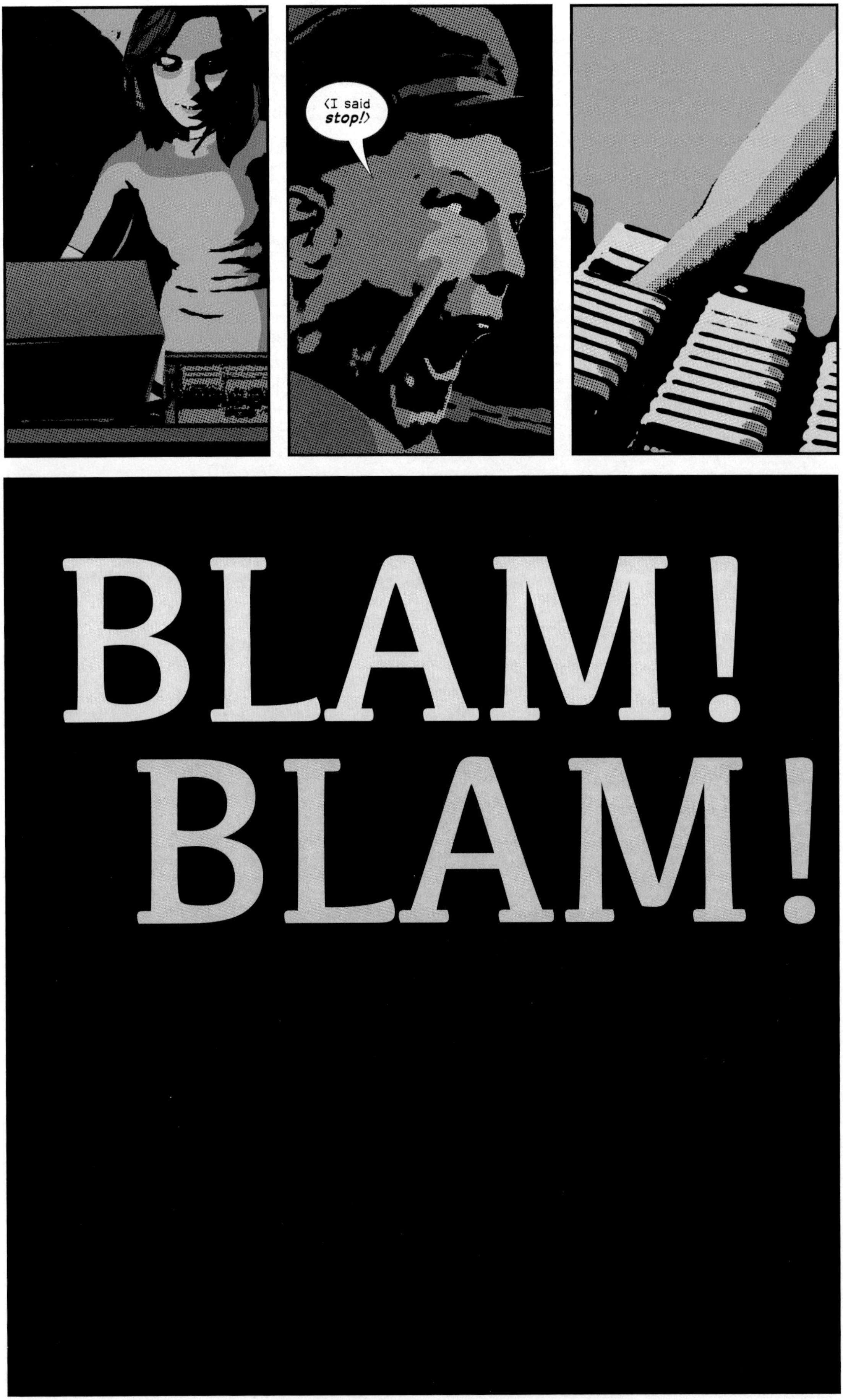

‹I said *stop!*›
BLAM! BLAM!

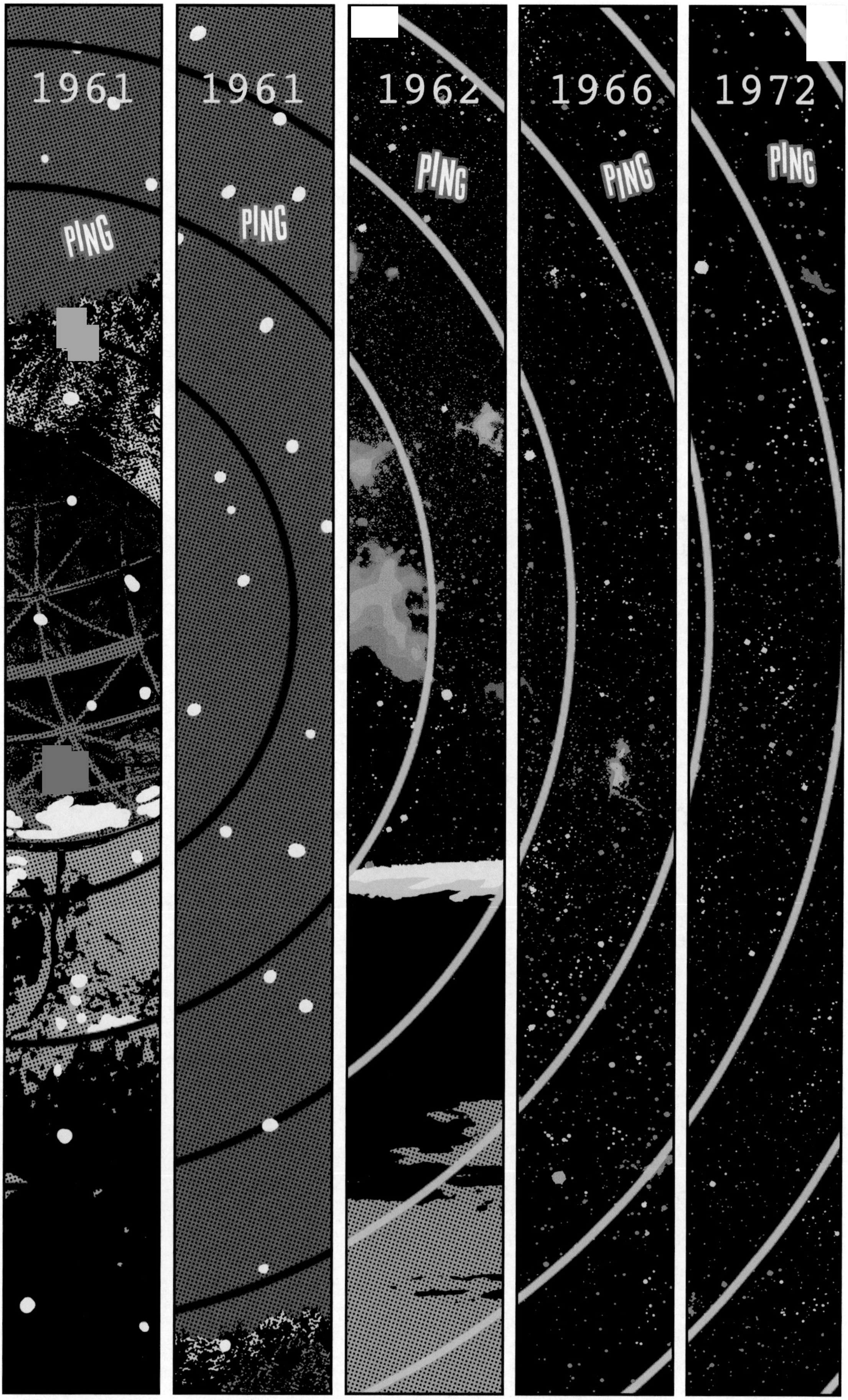
1961
PING
1961
PING
1962
PING
1966
PING
1972
PING

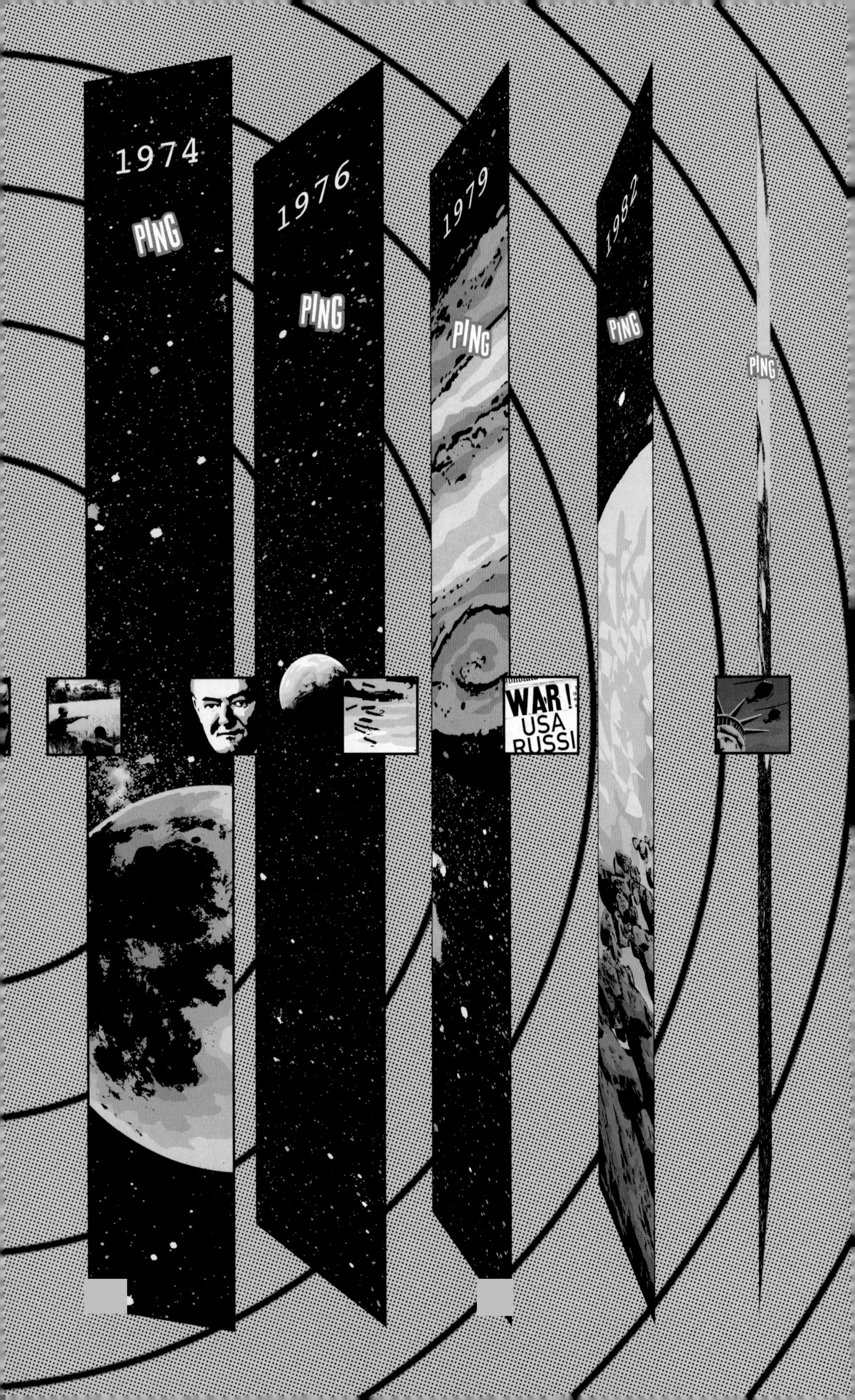
1974
PING
1976
PING
1979
PING
WAR!
USA
RUSSI
1982
PING
PING

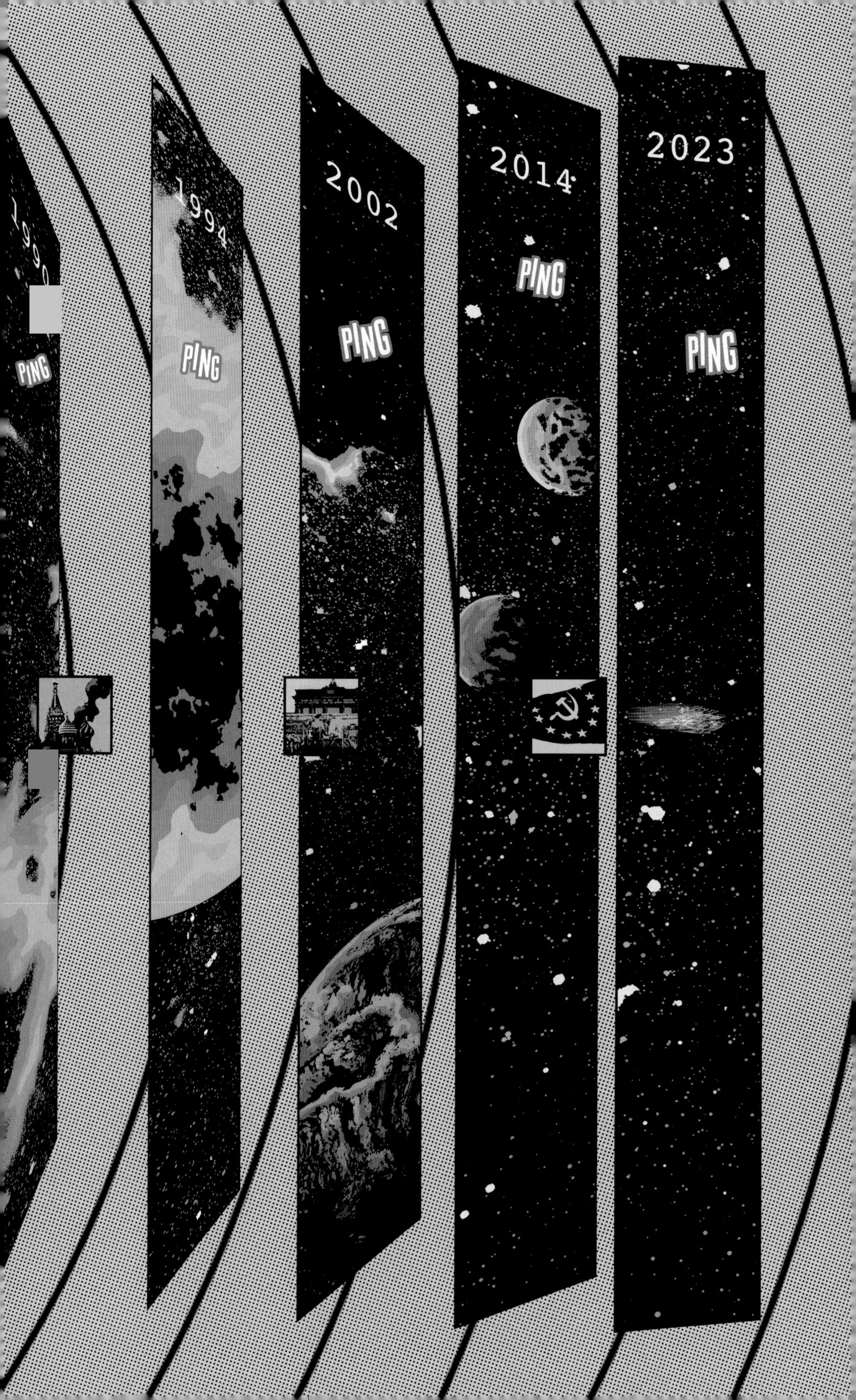

1990
PING
1994
PING
2002
PING
2014
PING
2023
PING

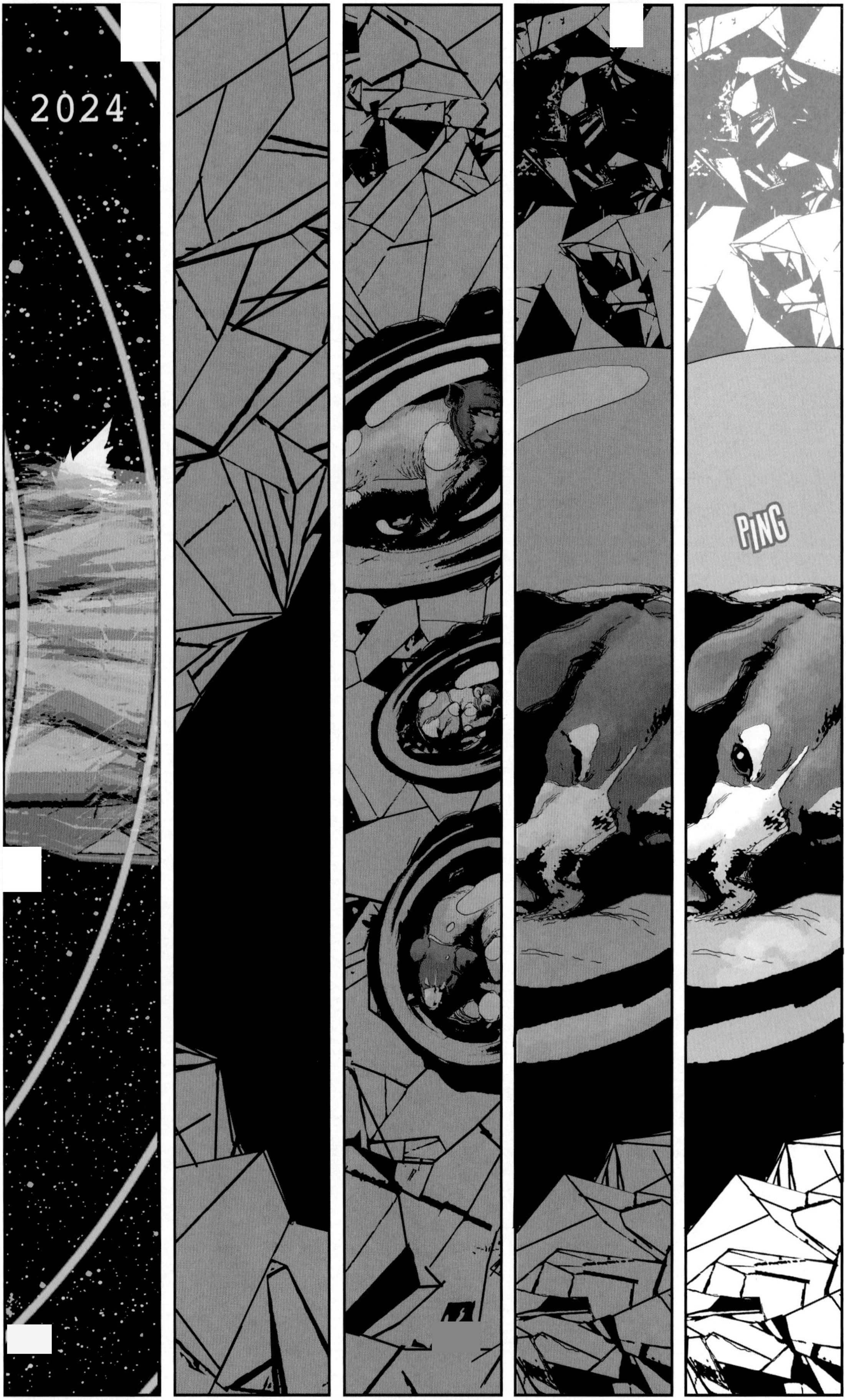
2024
PING

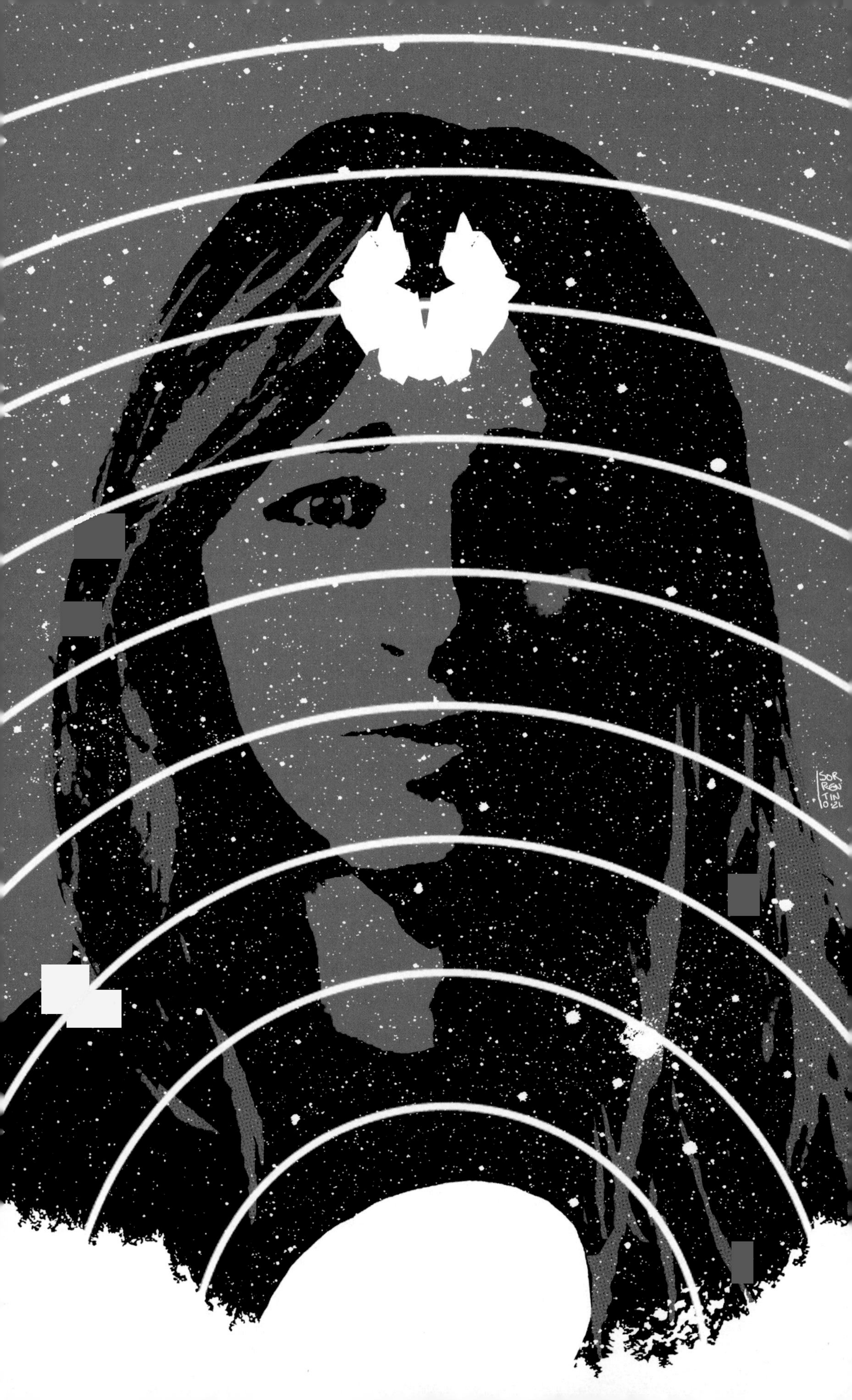

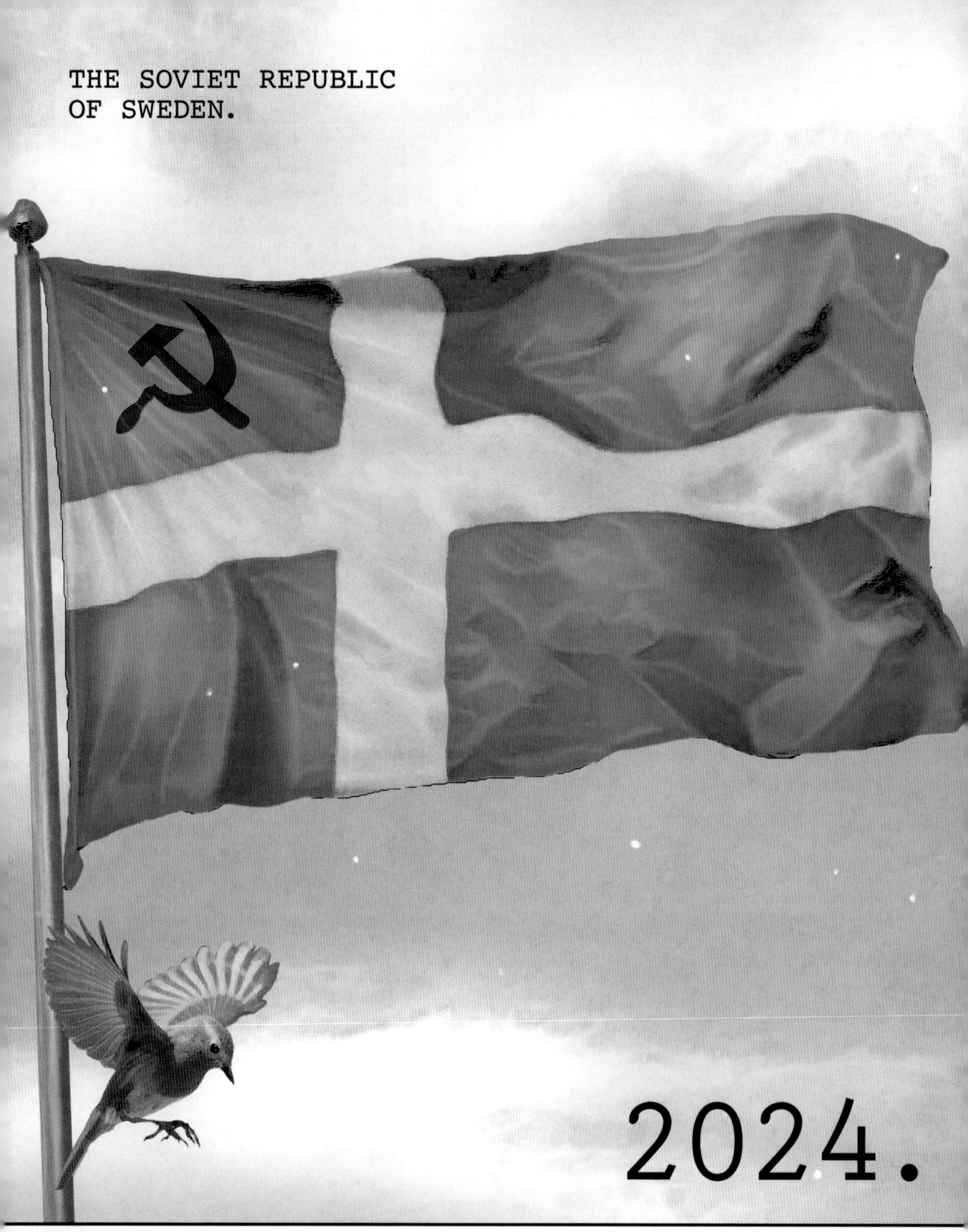
THE SOVIET REPUBLIC
OF SWEDEN.
2024.

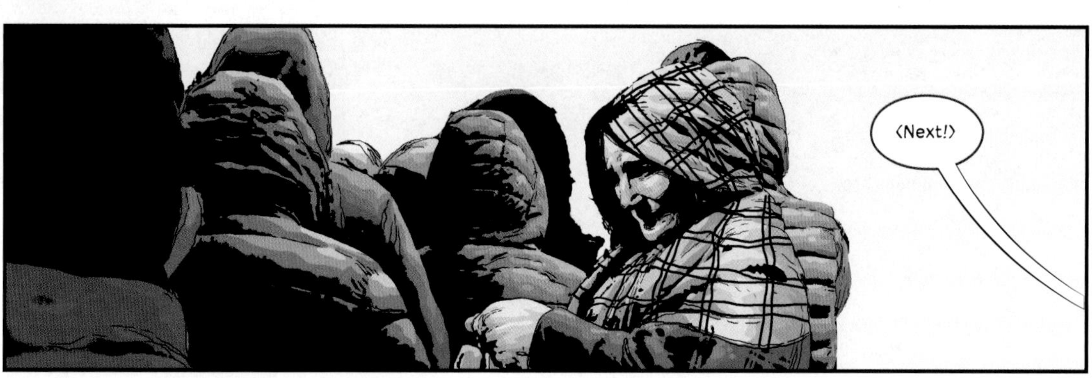
⟨Next!⟩

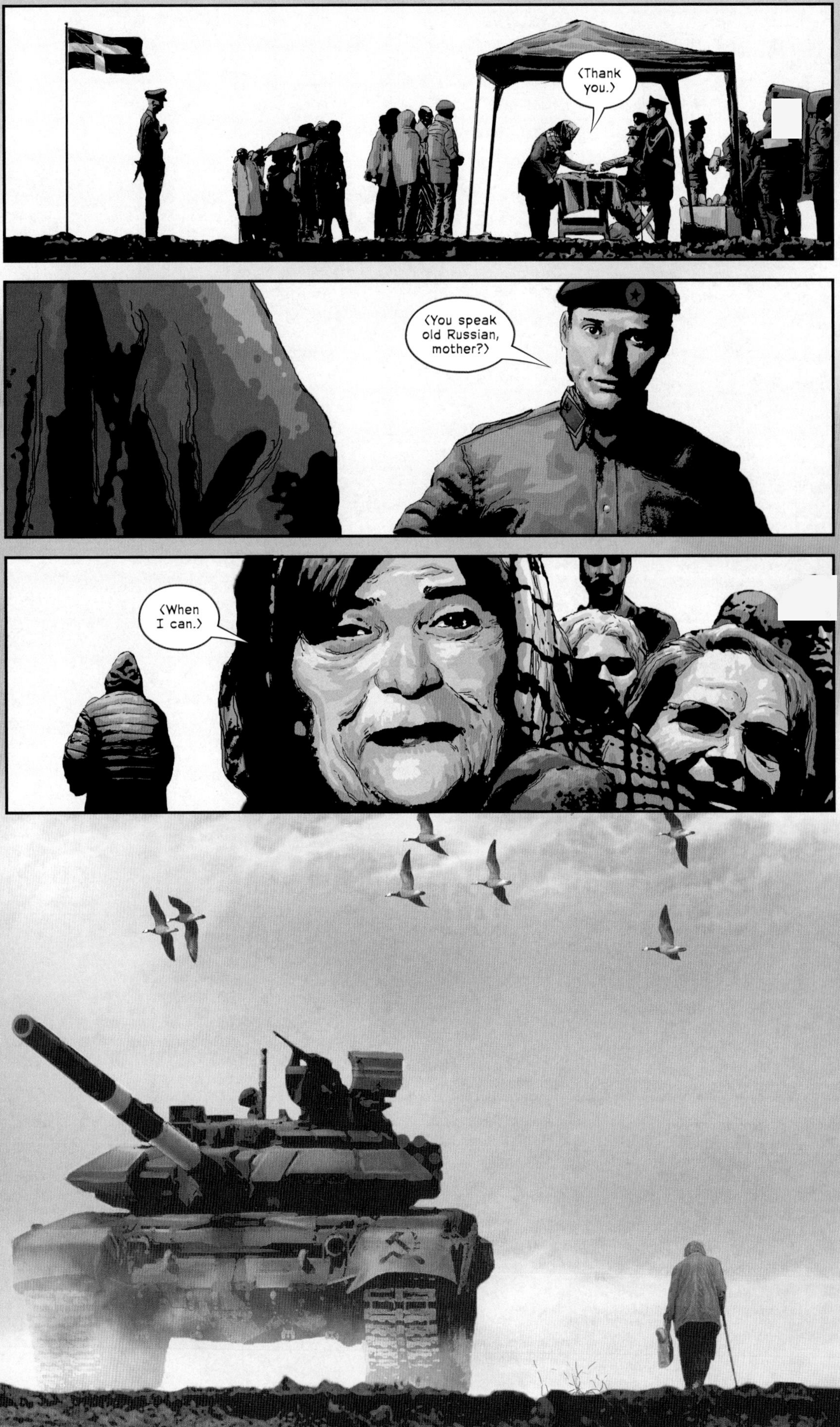
⟨Thank you.⟩
⟨You speak old Russian, mother?⟩
⟨When I can.⟩

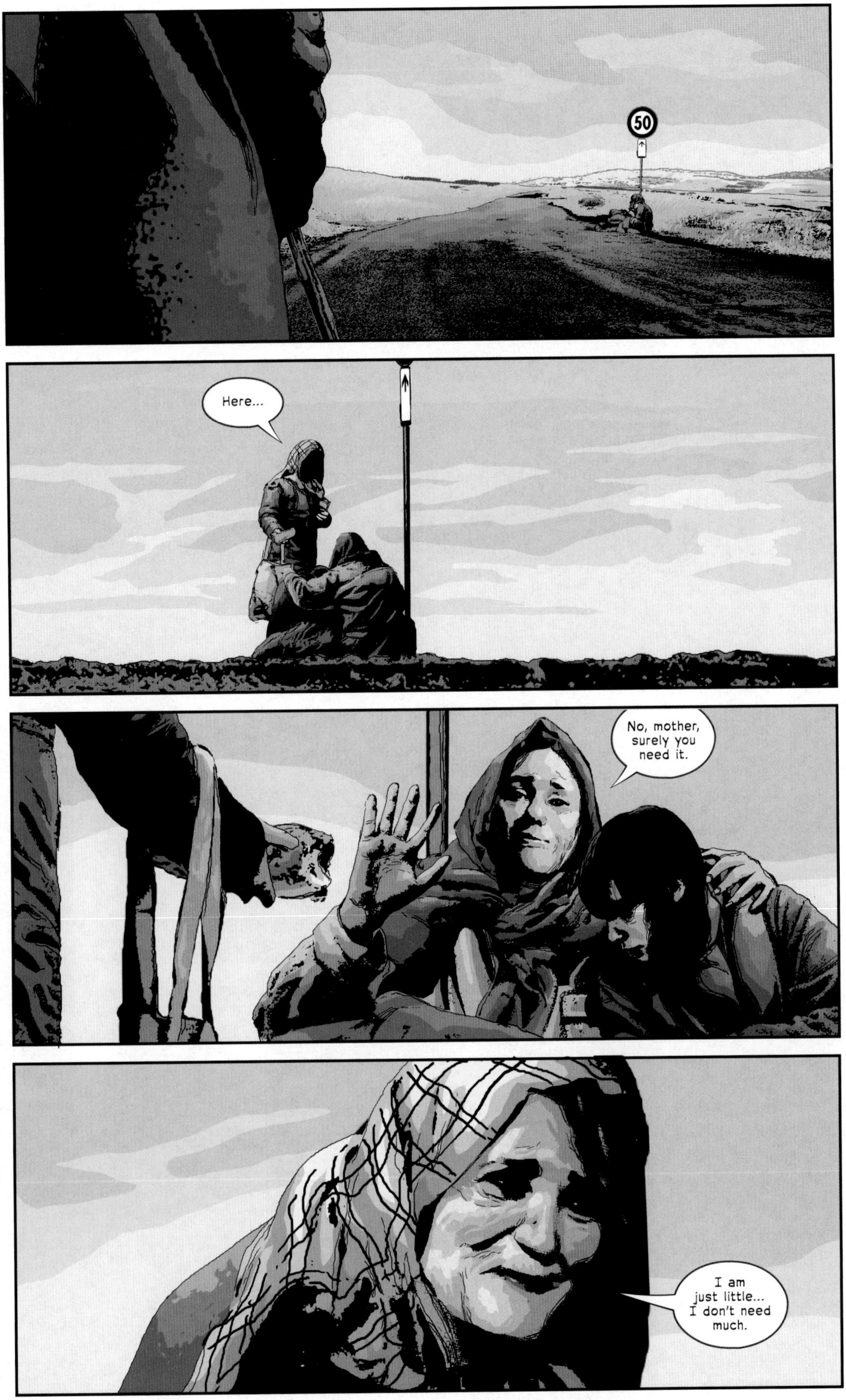
50
Here...
No, mother, surely you need it.
I am just little... I don't need much.

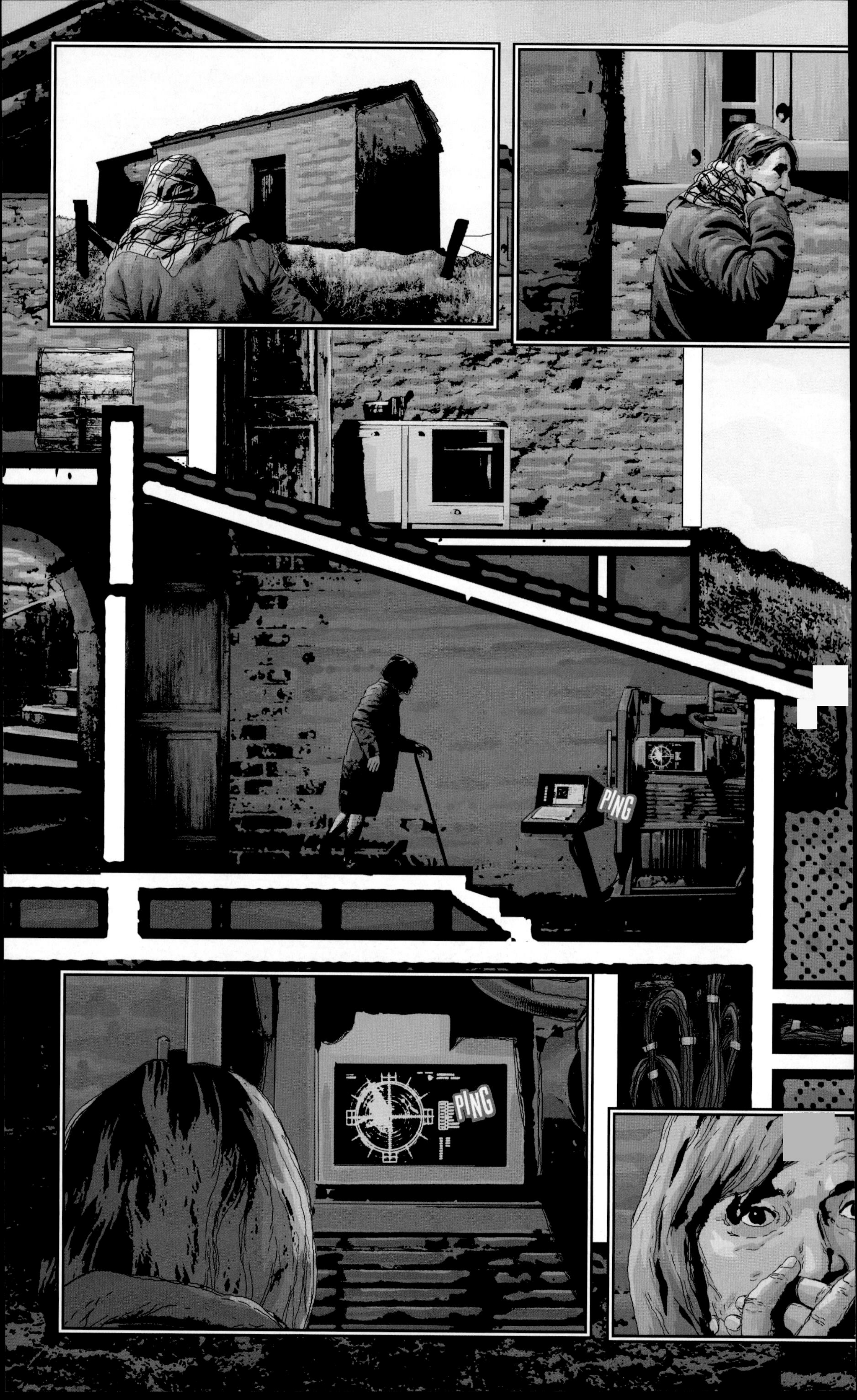
PING
PING

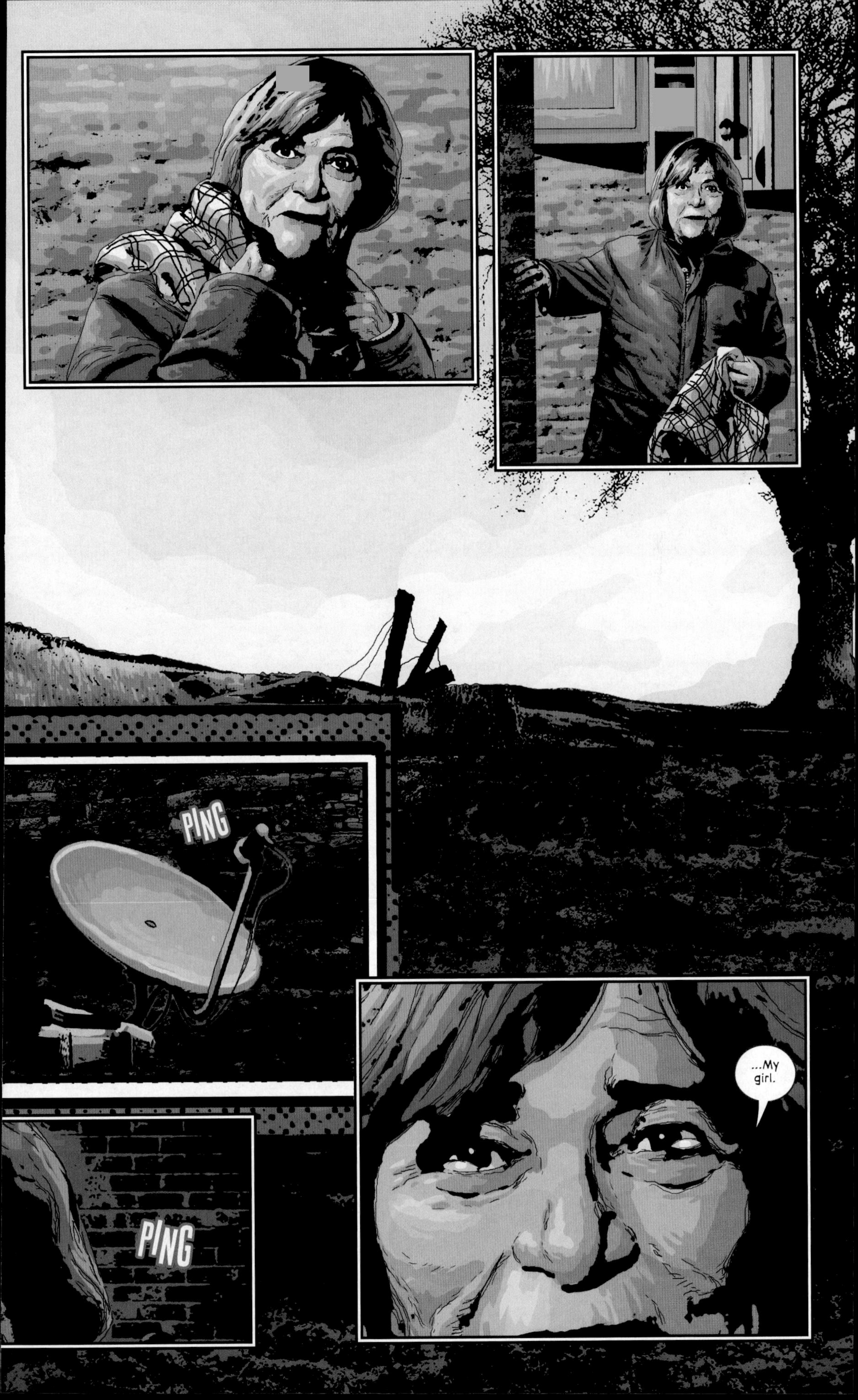
PING
PING
...My girl.

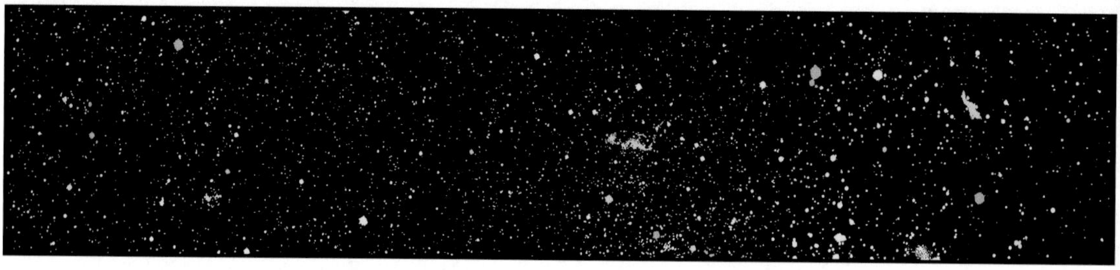
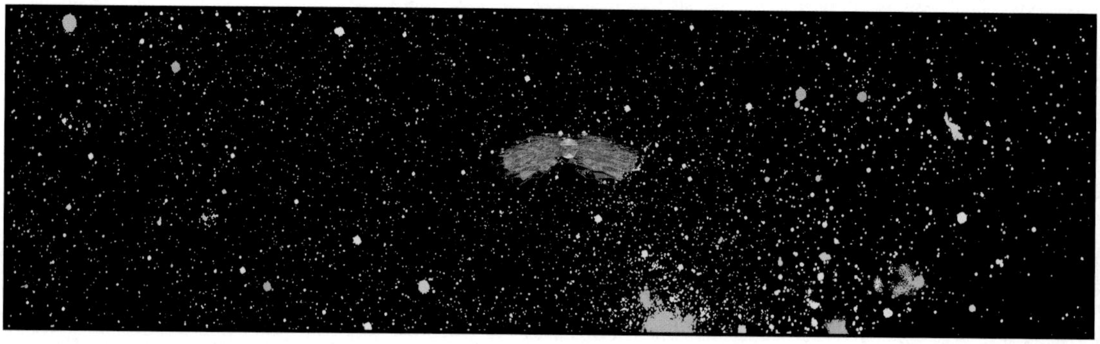
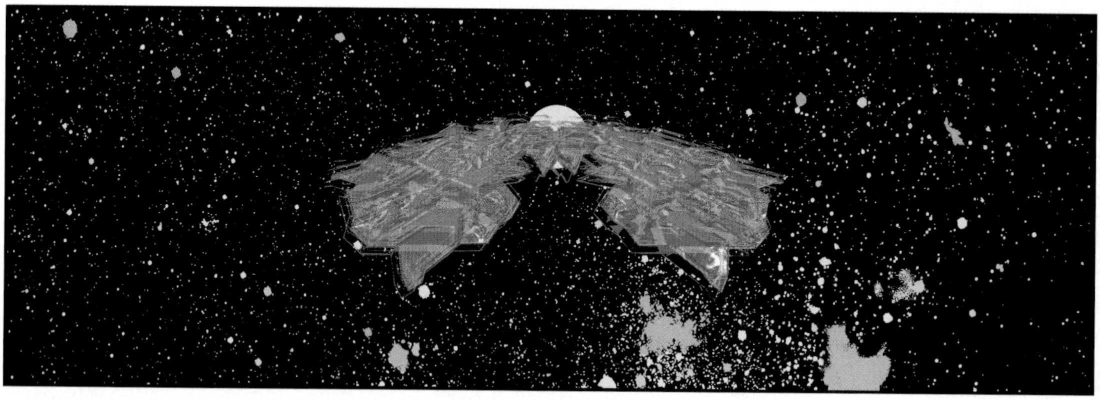
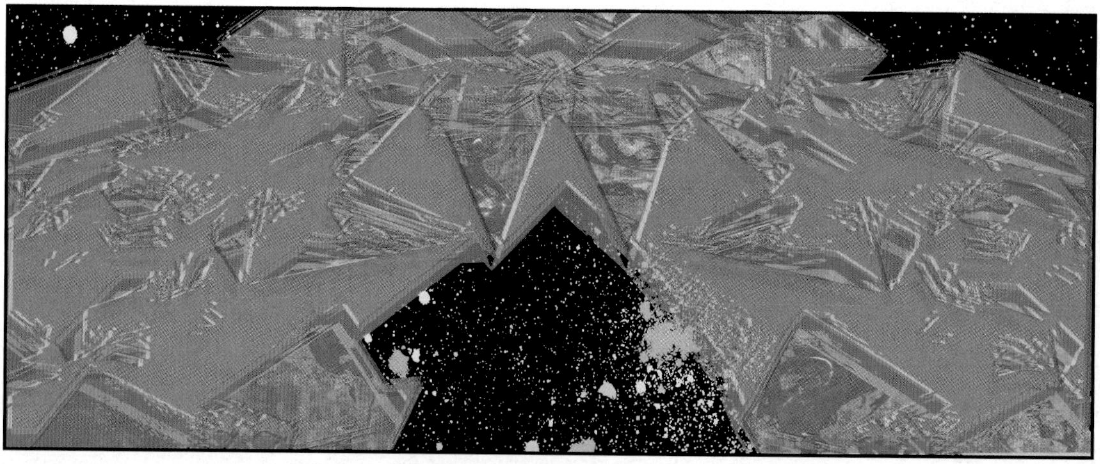

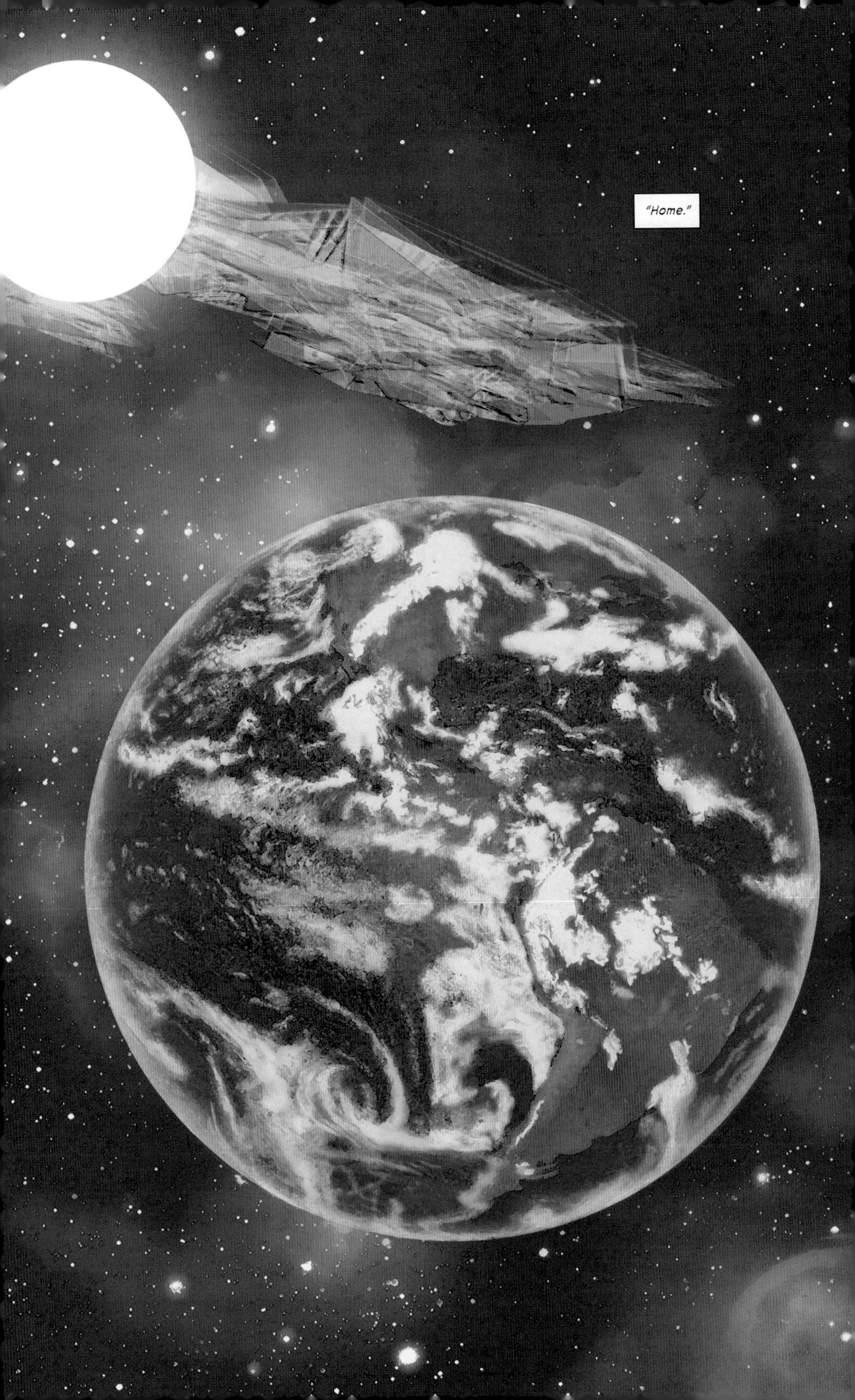
"Home."

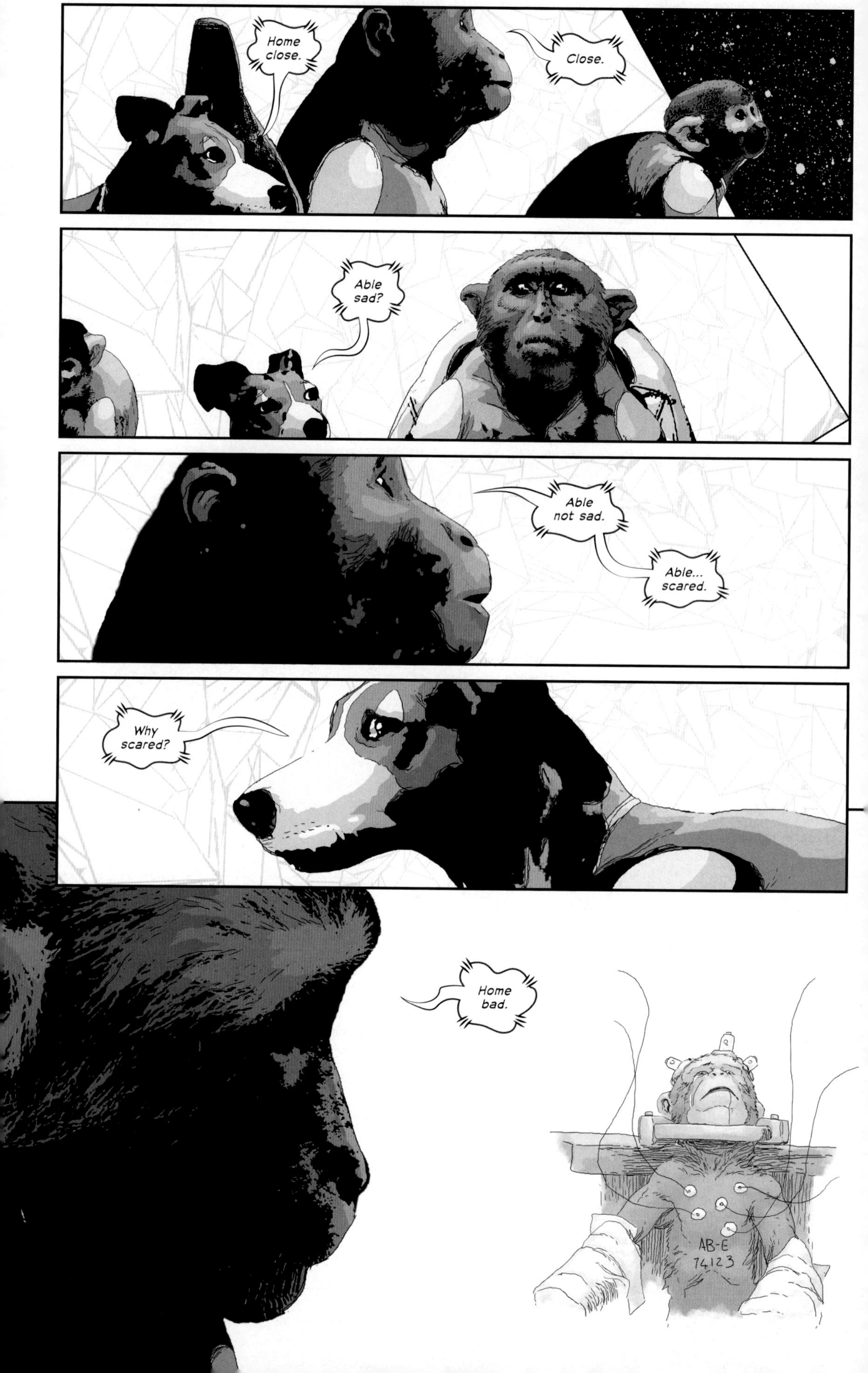
Home close.
Close.
Able sad?
Able not sad.
Able... scared.
Why scared?
Home bad.
AB-E 74123

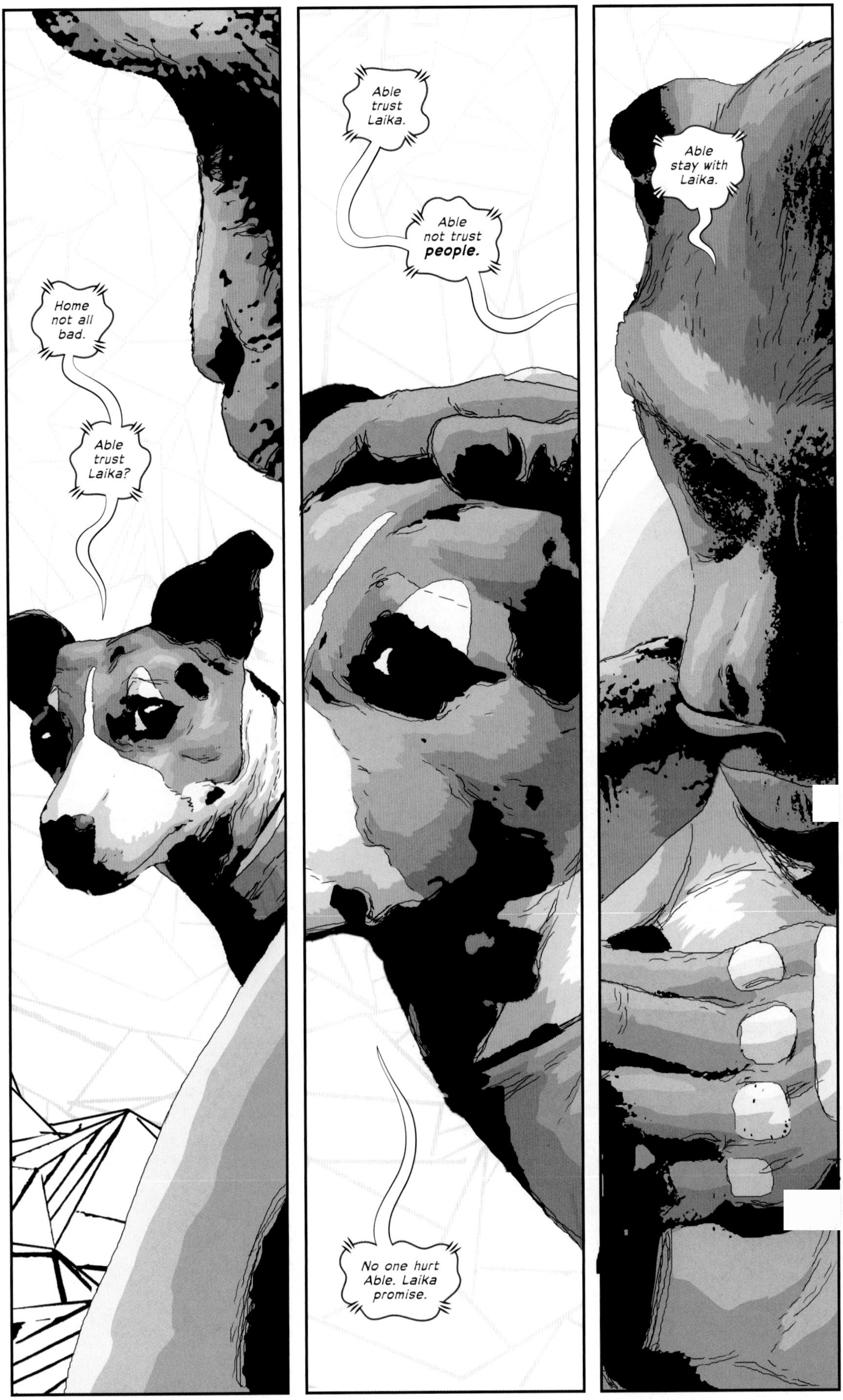
Home not all bad.
Able trust Laika?
Able trust Laika.
Able not trust **people.**
No one hurt Able. Laika promise.
Able stay with Laika.

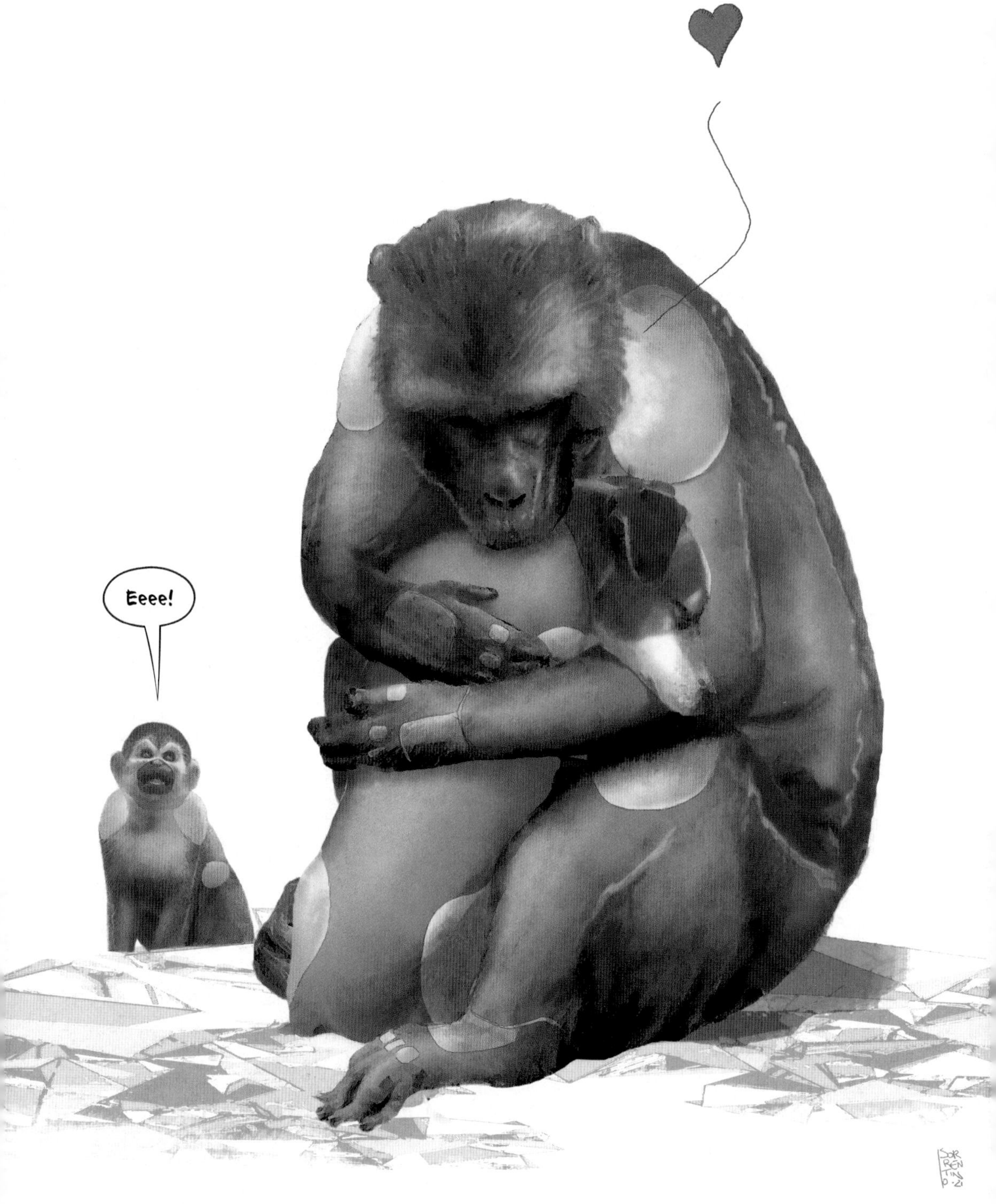
Eeee!

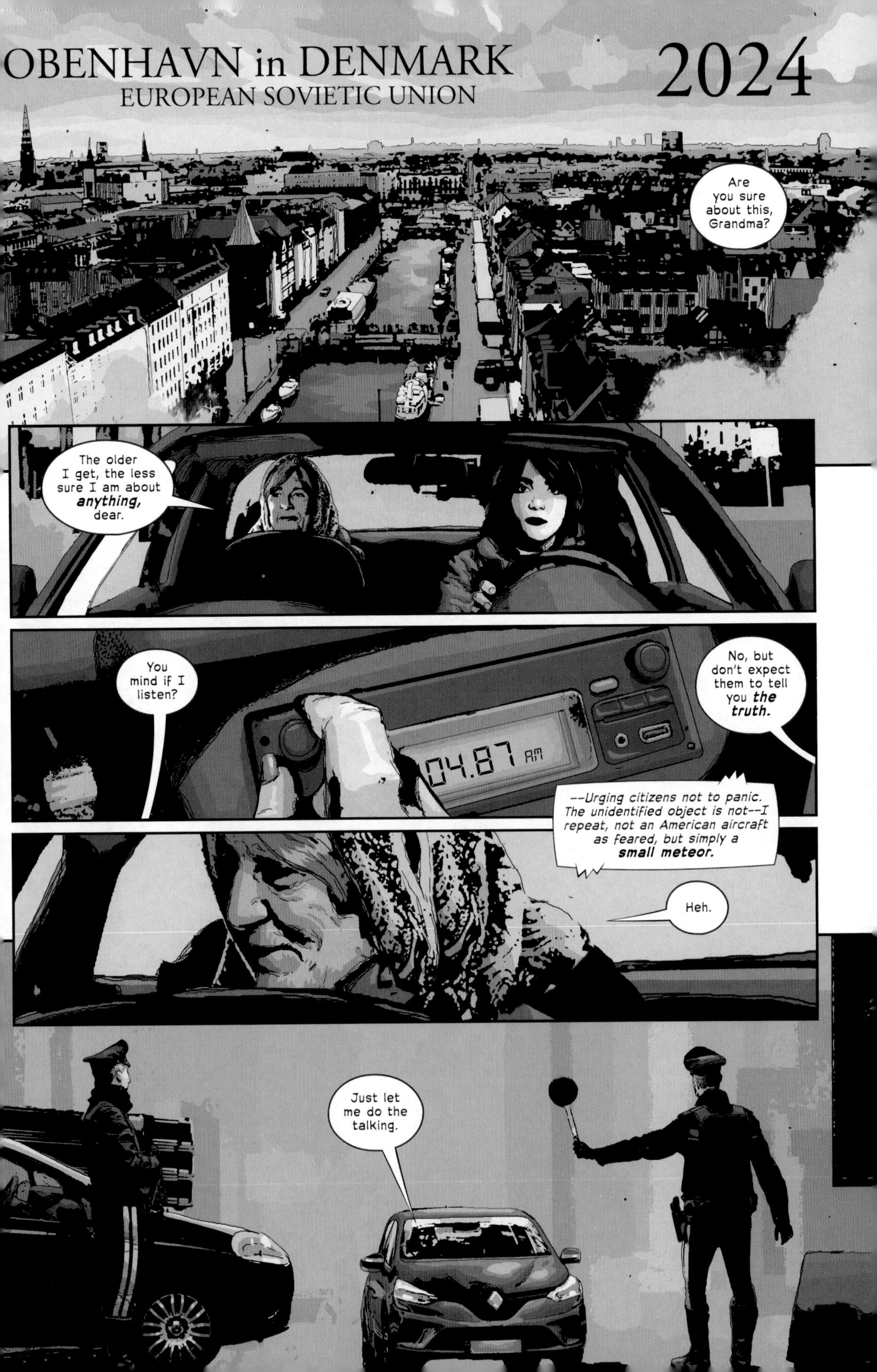
OBENHAVN in DENMARK
EUROPEAN SOVIETIC UNION
2024
Are you sure about this, Grandma?
The older I get, the less sure I am about ***anything,*** dear.
You mind if I listen?
No, but don't expect them to tell you ***the truth.***
04.87 AM
*--Urging citizens not to panic. The unidentified object is not--I repeat, not an American aircraft as feared, but simply a **small meteor.***
Heh.
Just let me do the talking.

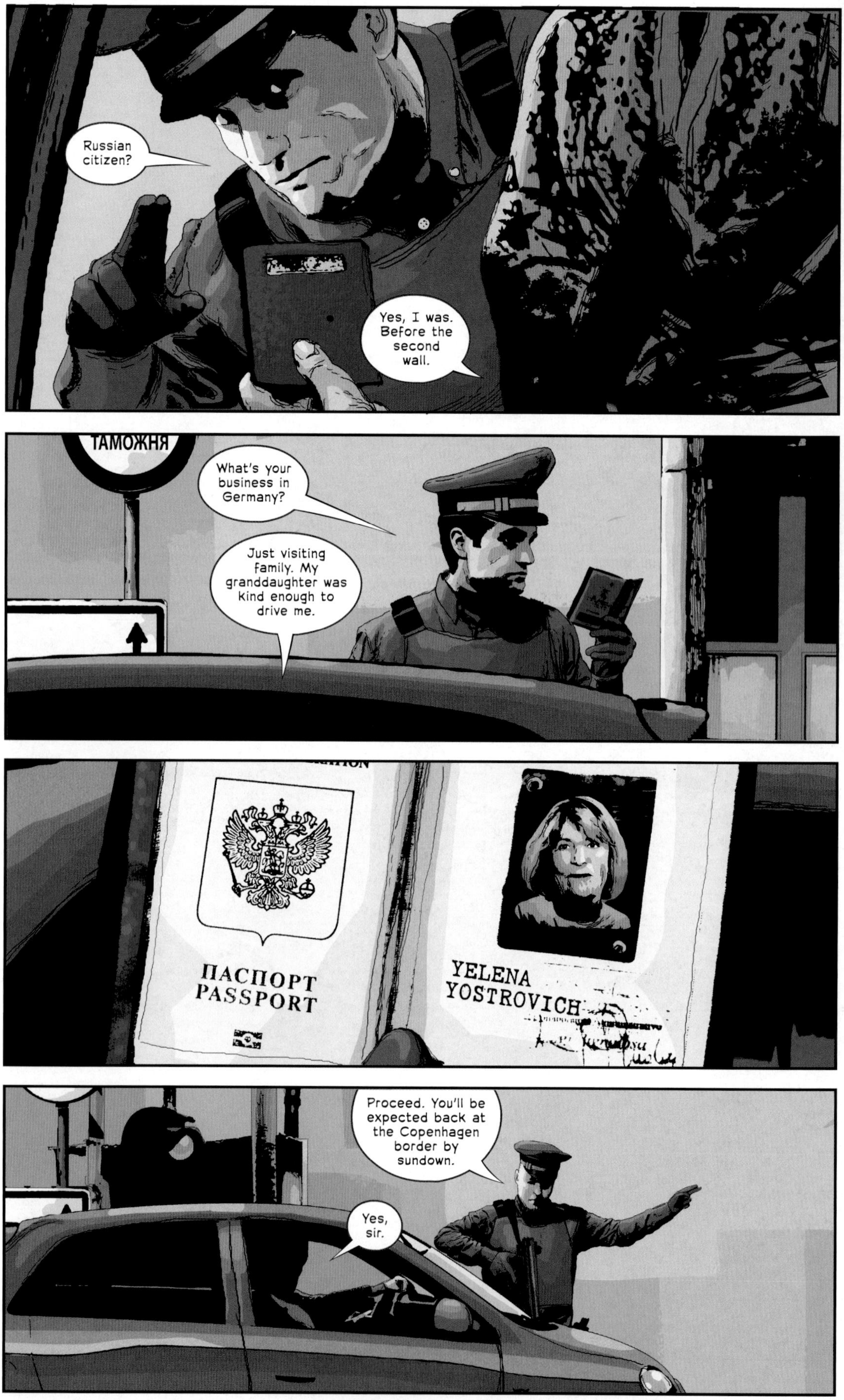
Russian citizen?
Yes, I was. Before the second wall.
ТАМОЖНЯ
What's your business in Germany?
Just visiting family. My granddaughter was kind enough to drive me.
ПАСПОРТ
PASSPORT
YELENA YOSTROVICH
Proceed. You'll be expected back at the Copenhagen border by sundown.
Yes, sir.

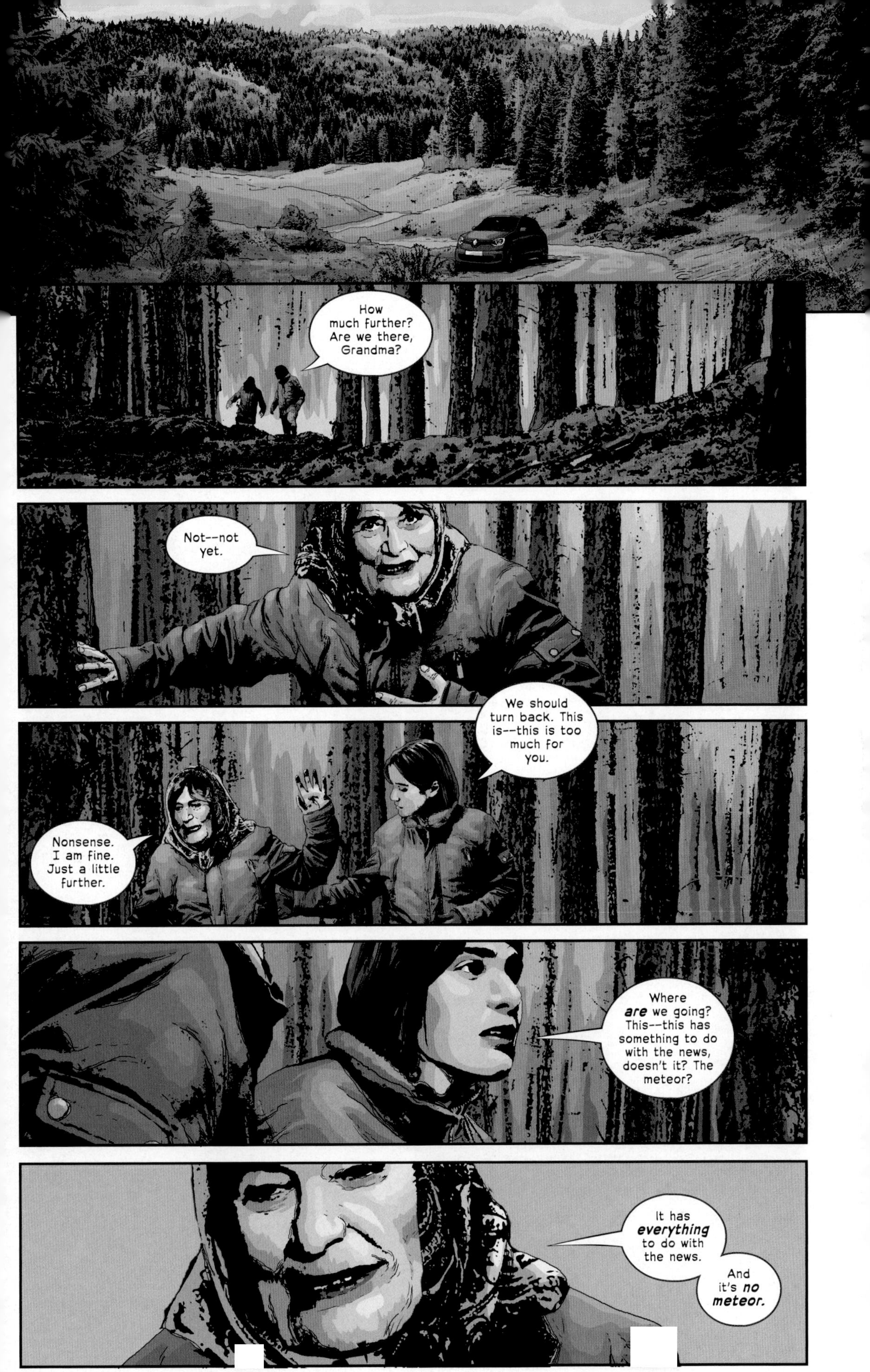
How much further? Are we there, Grandma?
Not--not yet.
We should turn back. This is--this is too much for you.
Nonsense. I am fine. Just a little further.
Where *are* we going? This--this has something to do with the news, doesn't it? The meteor?
It has *everything* to do with the news.
And it's *no meteor.*

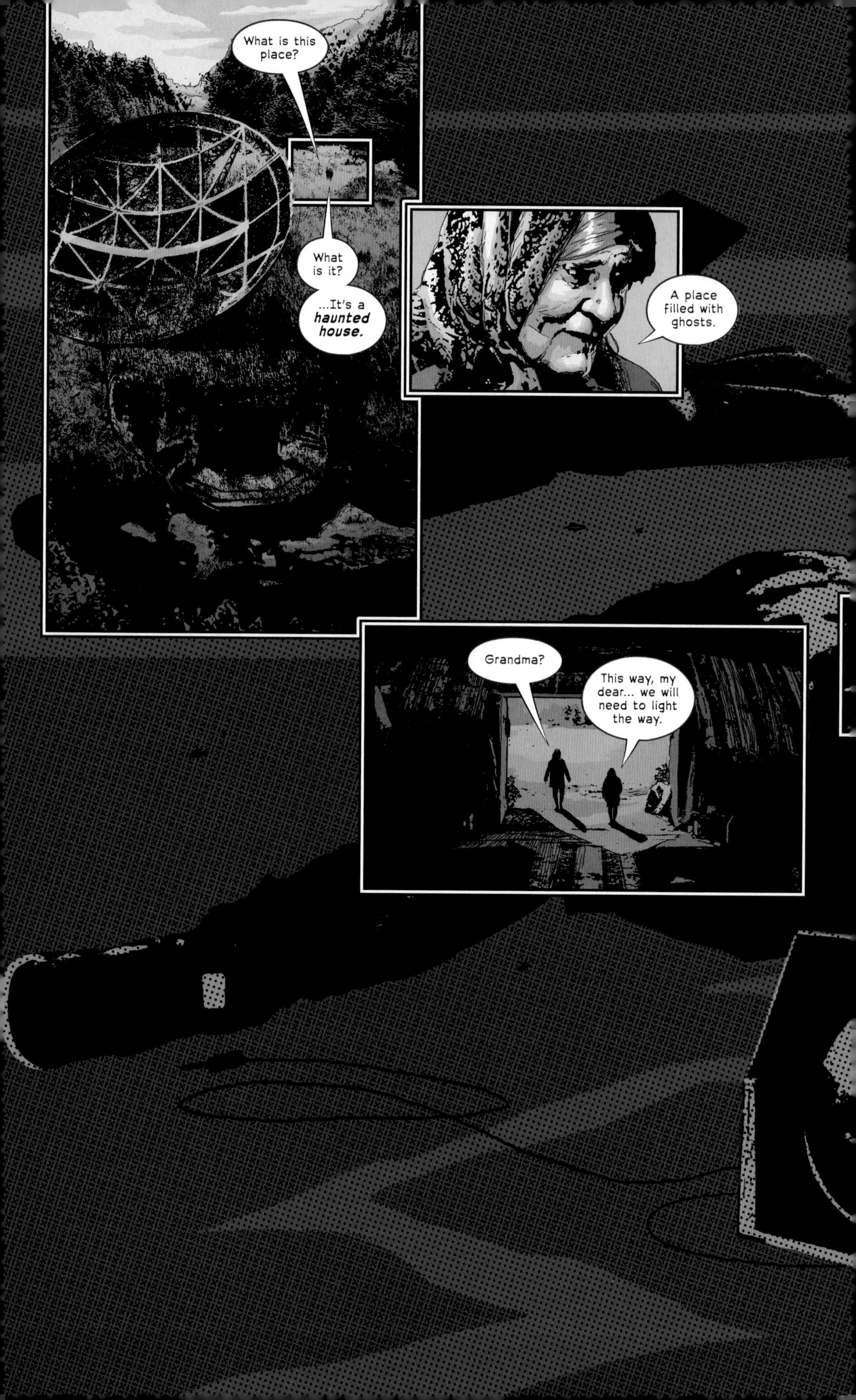
What is this place?
What is it?
...It's a *haunted house.*
A place filled with ghosts.
Grandma?
This way, my dear... we will need to light the way.

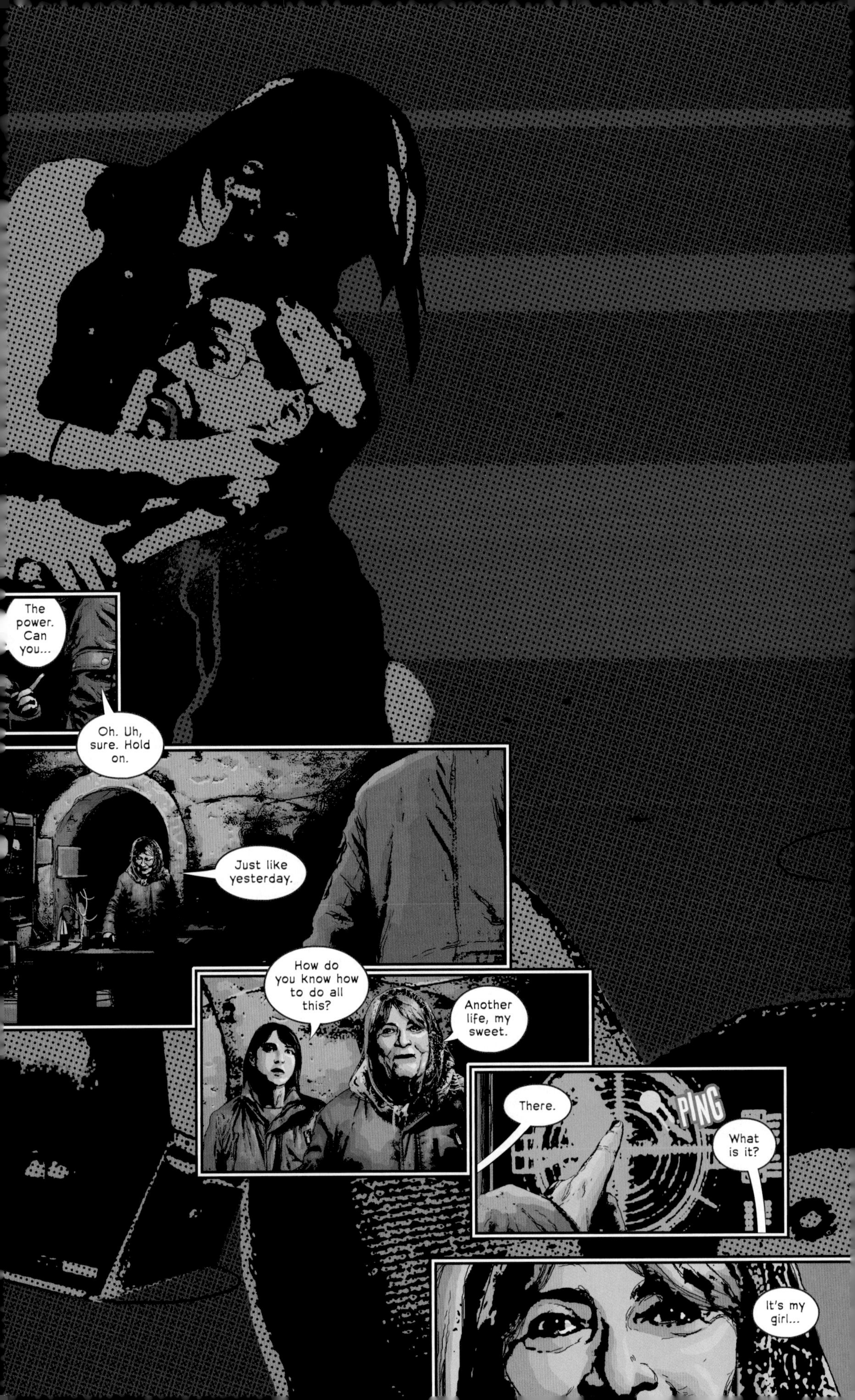
The power. Can you...
Oh. Uh, sure. Hold on.
Just like yesterday.
How do you know how to do all this?
Another life, my sweet.
There.
PING
What is it?
It's my girl...

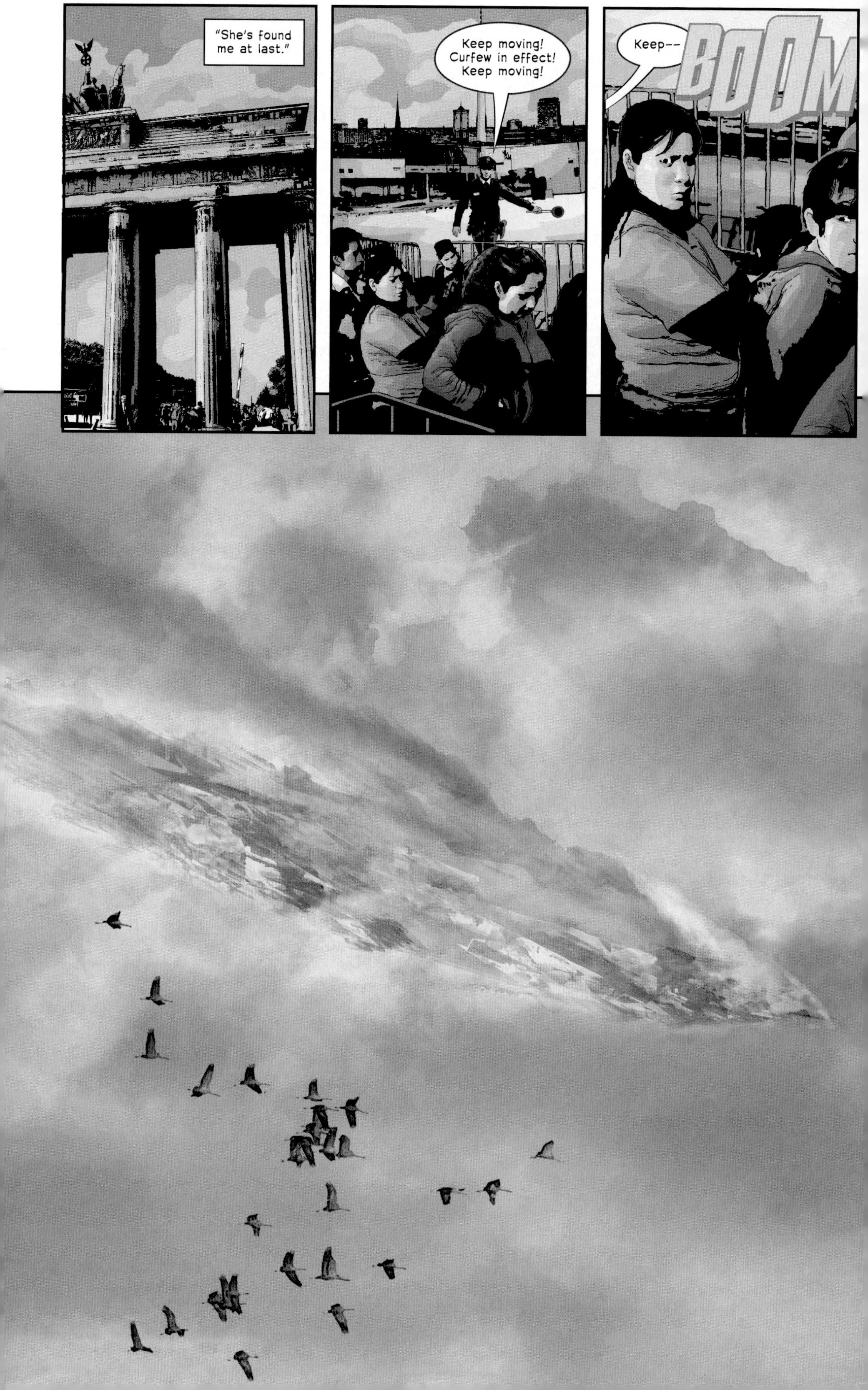
"She's found me at last."
Keep moving! Curfew in effect! Keep moving!
Keep--
BOOM

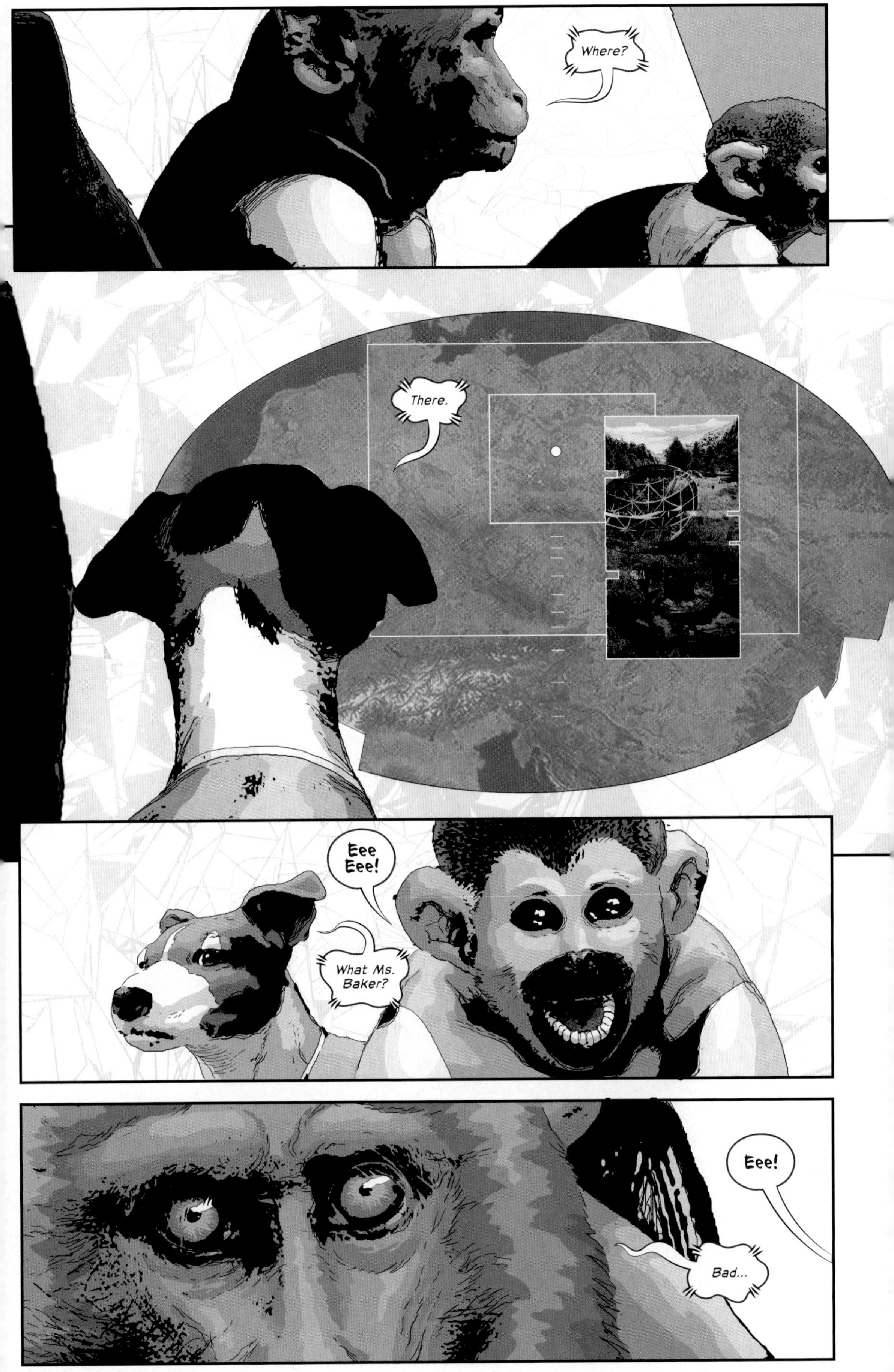
Where?
There.
Eee Eee!
What Ms. Baker?
Eee!
Bad...

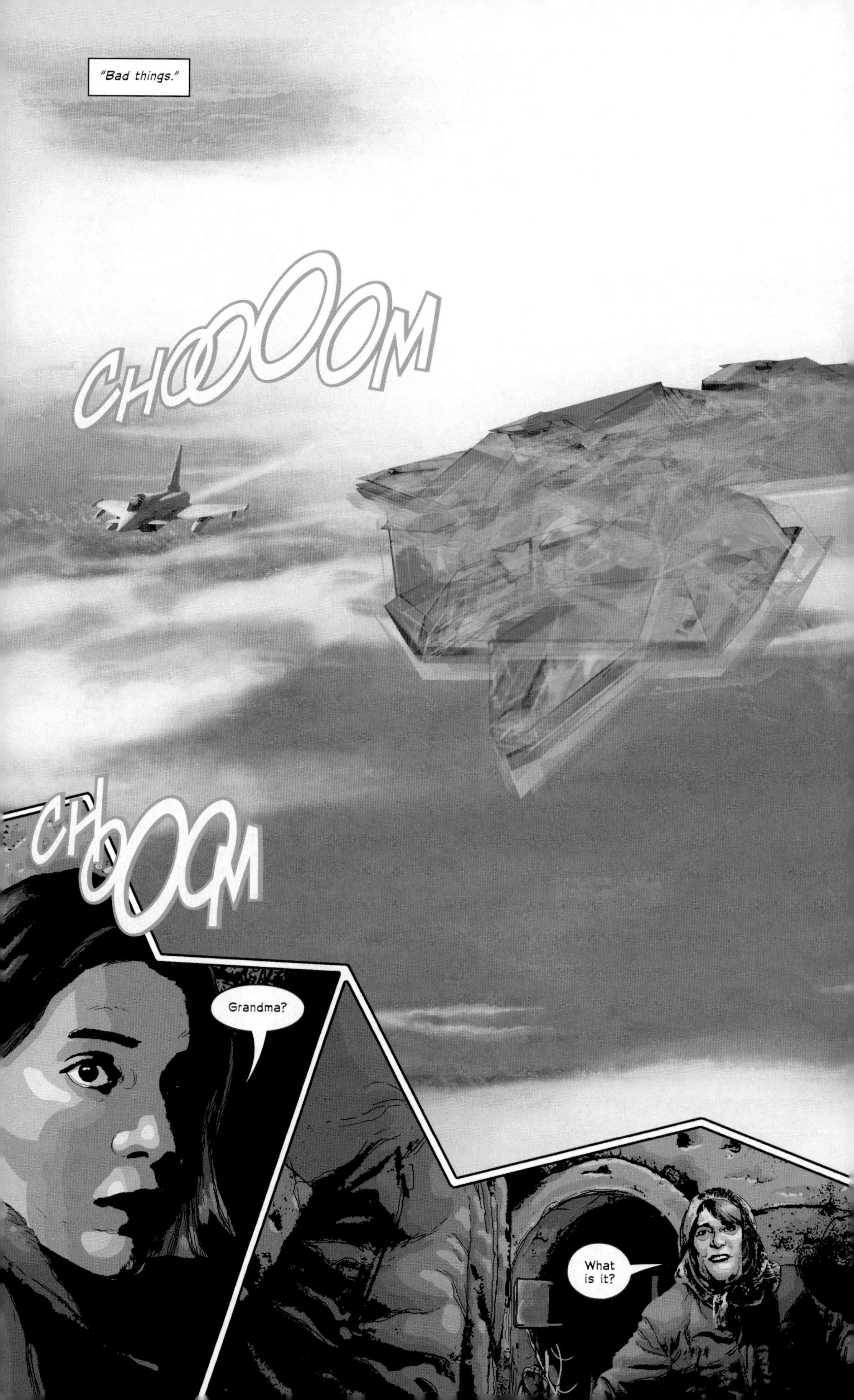
"Bad things."
CHOOOOM
CHOOOM
Grandma?
What is it?

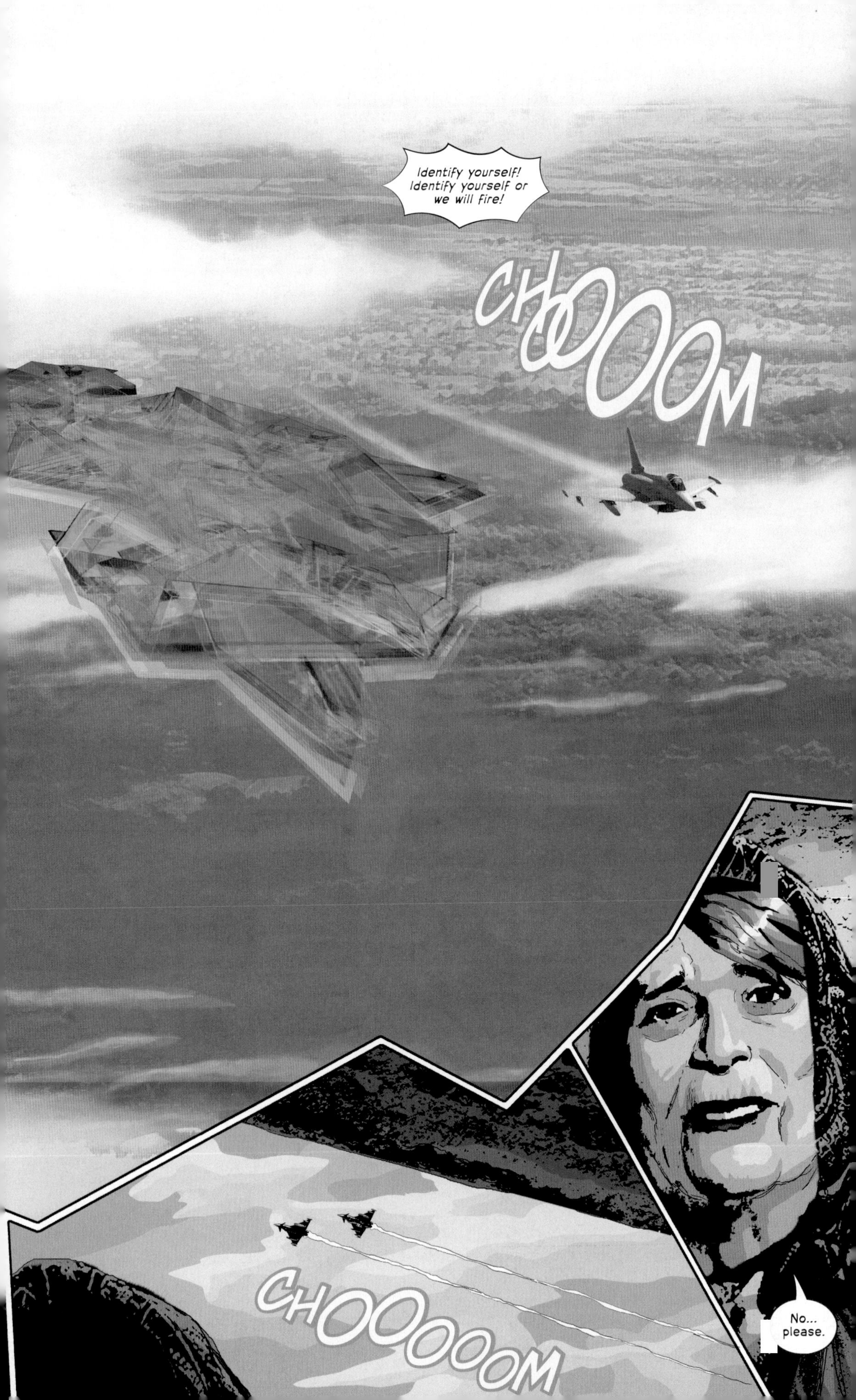
Identify yourself! Identify yourself or we will fire!
CHOOOOM
CHOOOOOM
No... please.

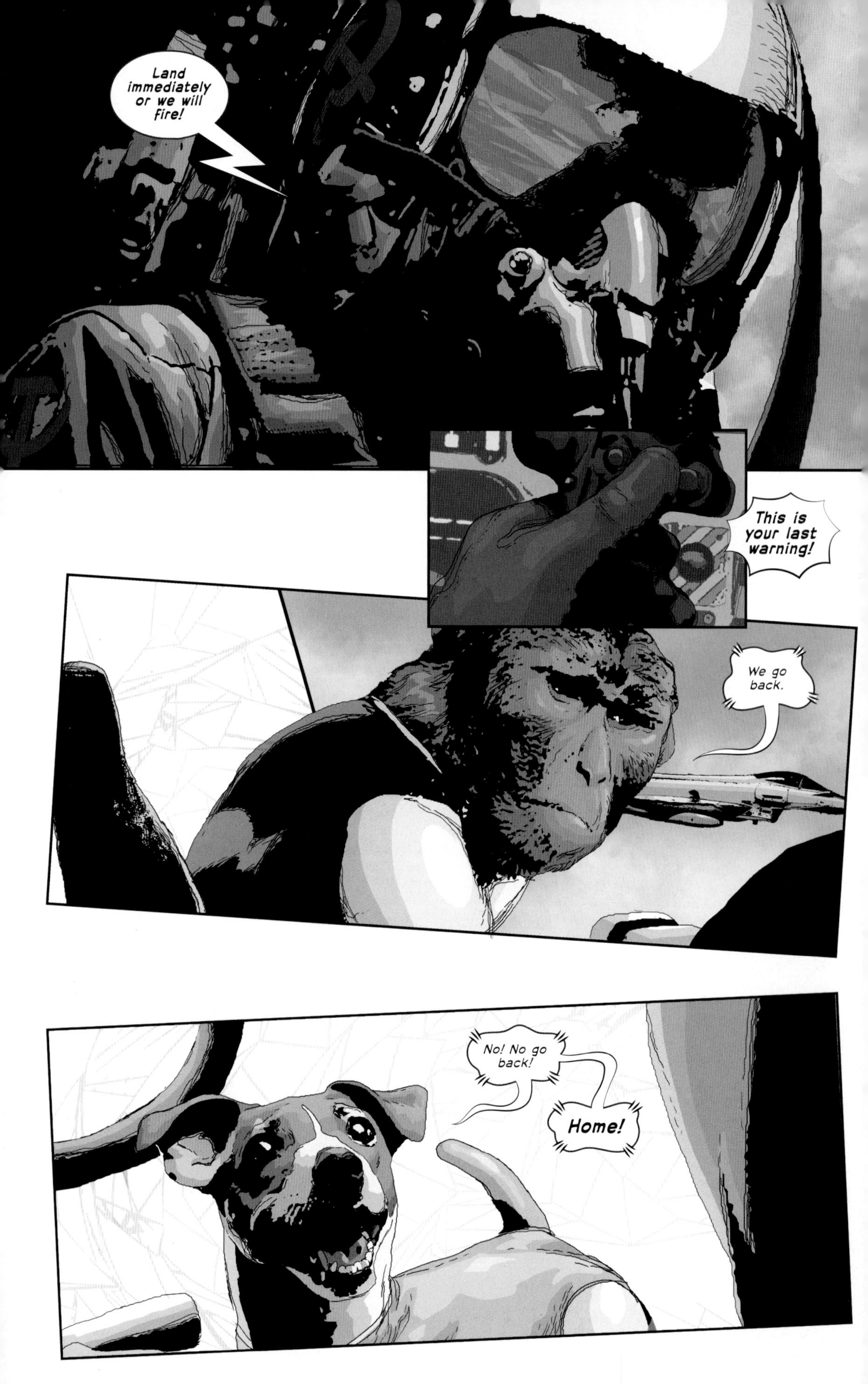
Land immediately or we will fire!
This is your last warning!
We go back.
No! No go back!
Home!

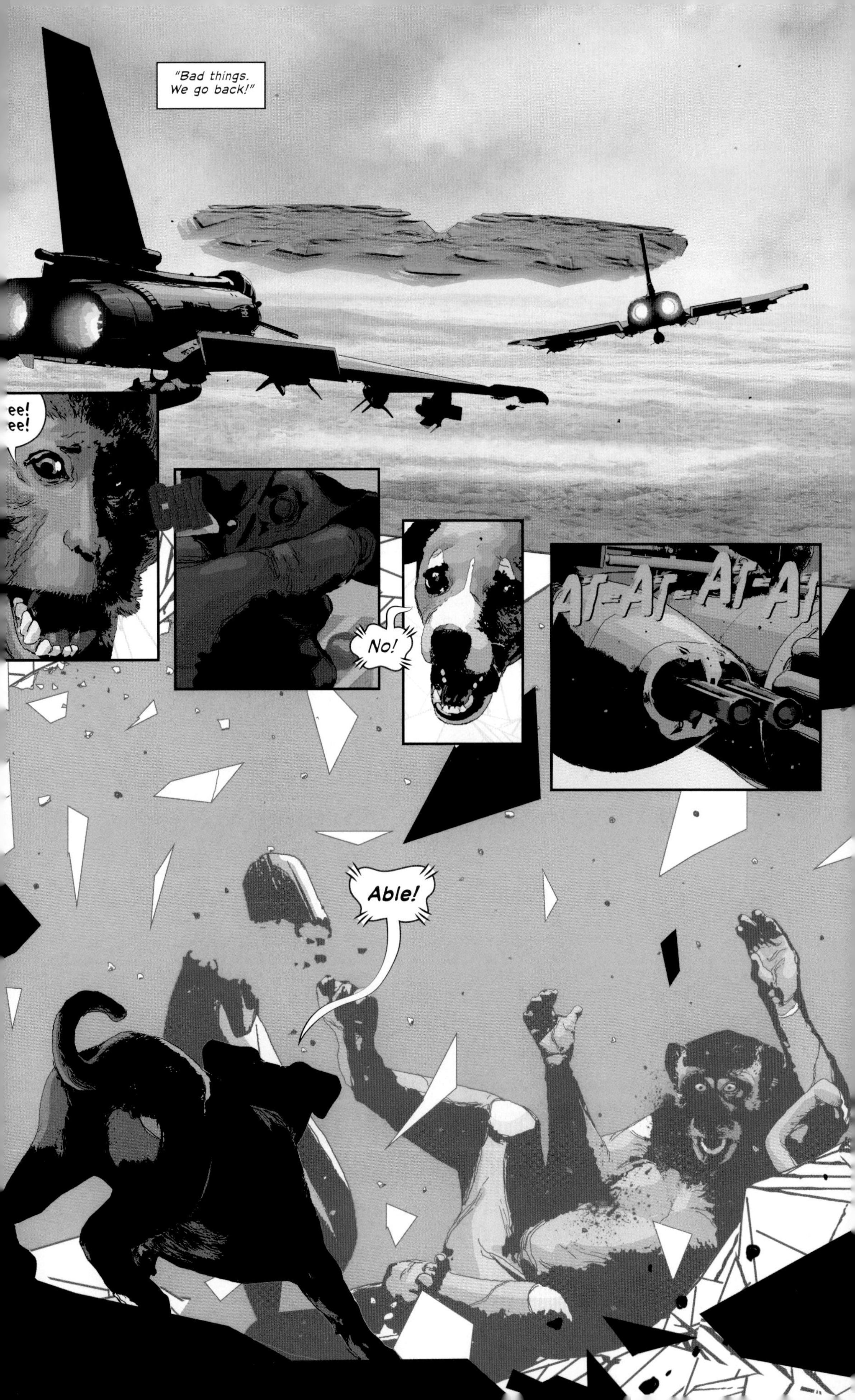
"Bad things. We go back!"
ee!
ee!
No!
Able!

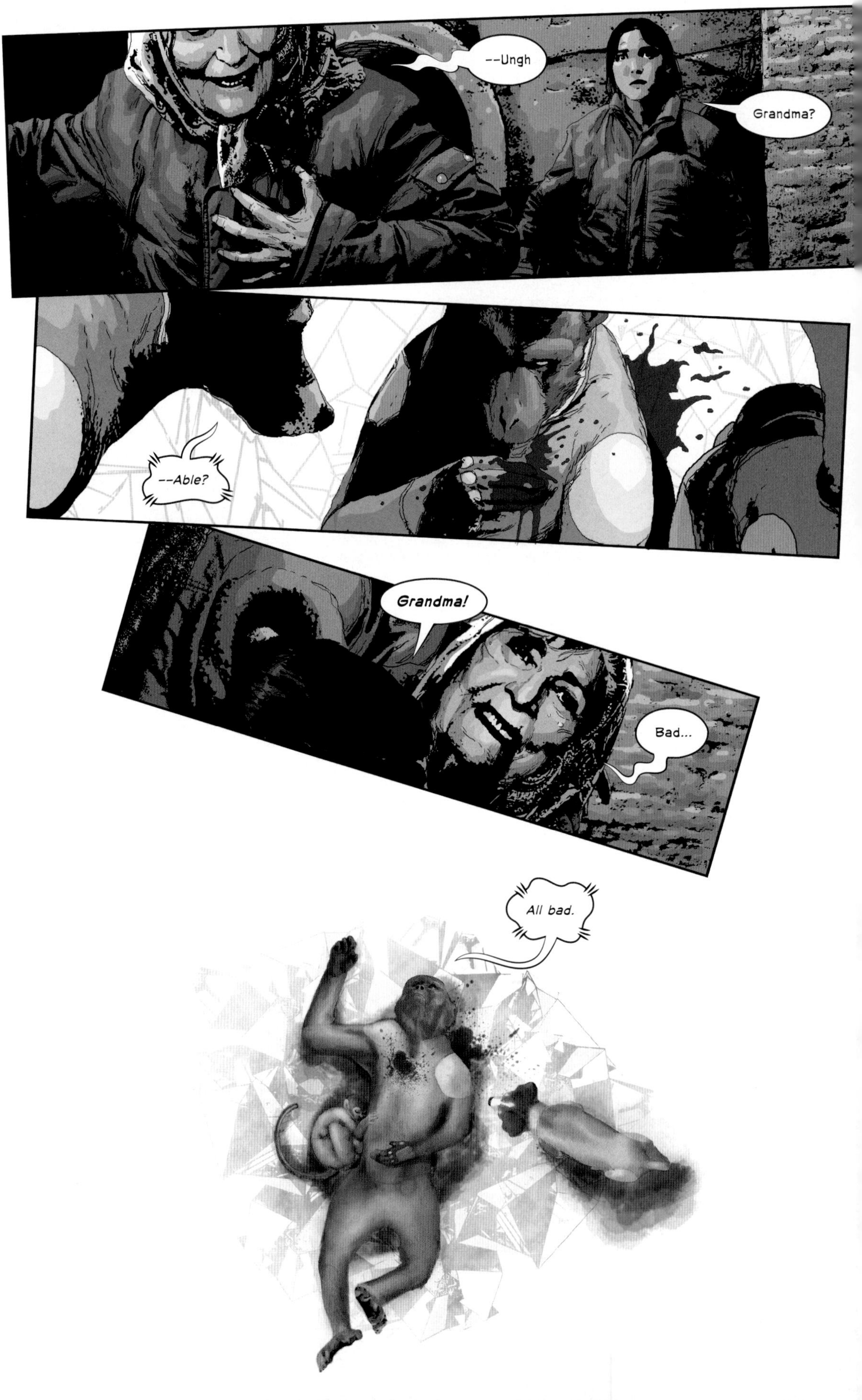
--Ungh
Grandma?
--Able?
Grandma!
Bad...
All bad.

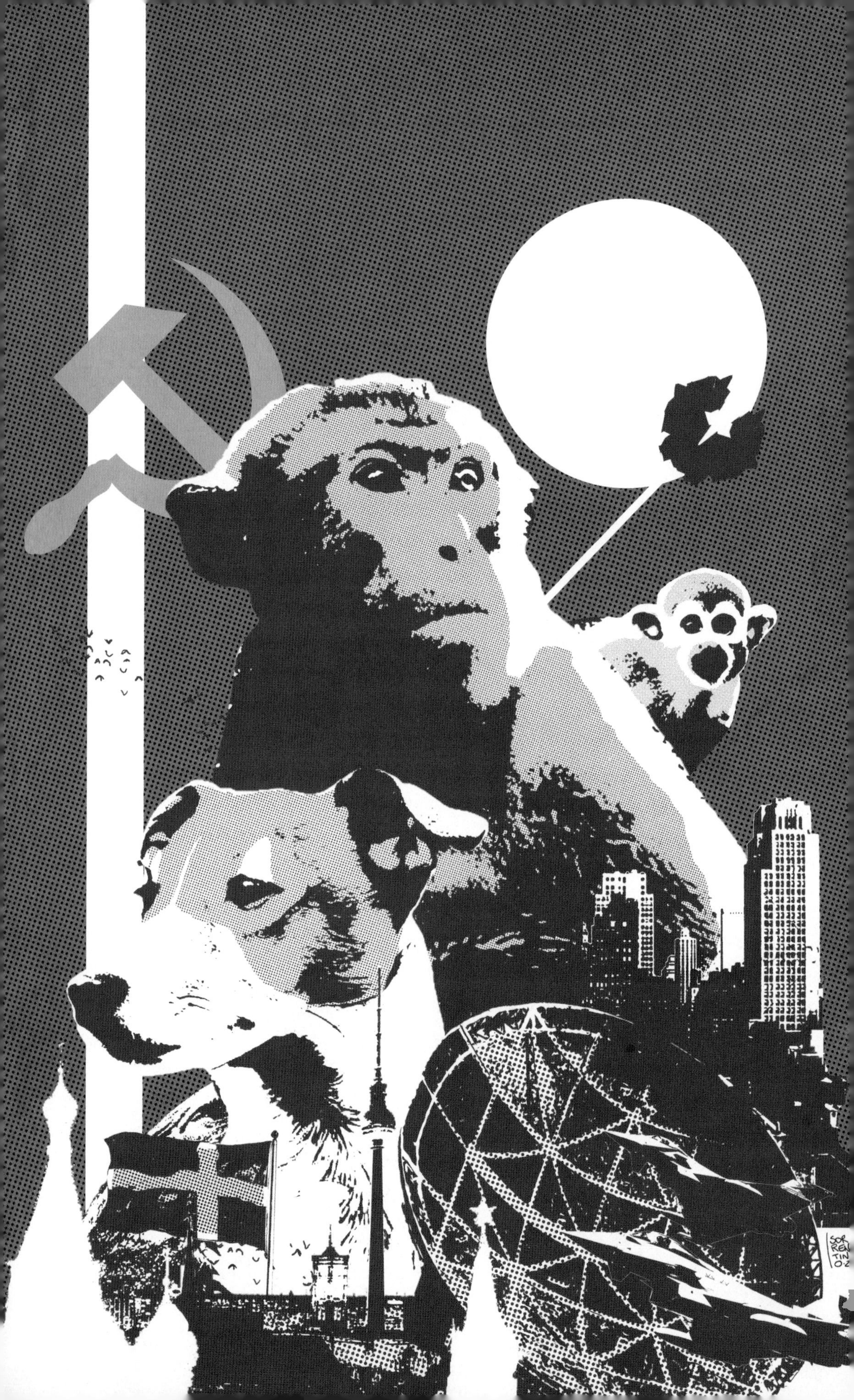

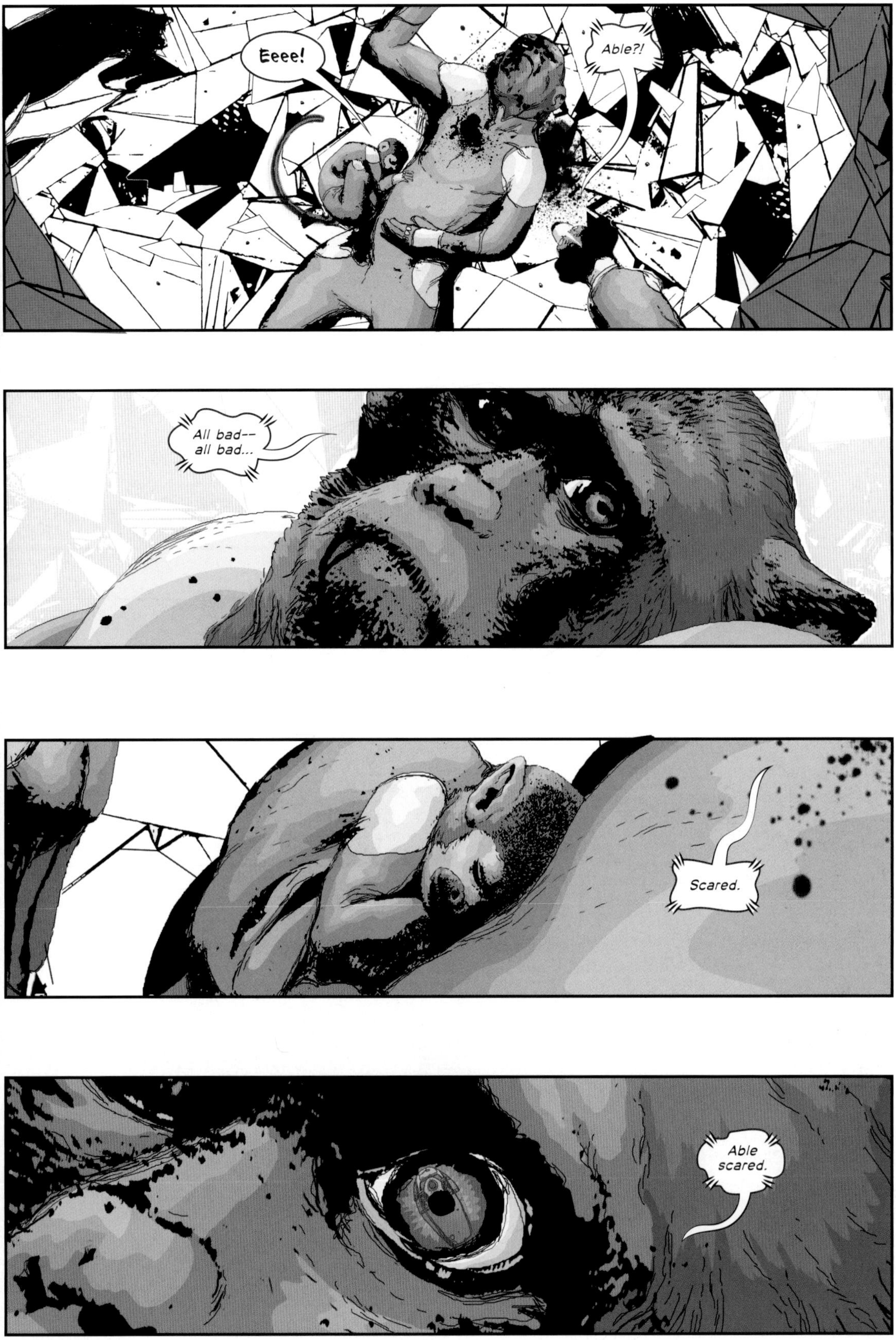
Eeee!
Able?!
All bad--
all bad...
Scared.
Able
scared.

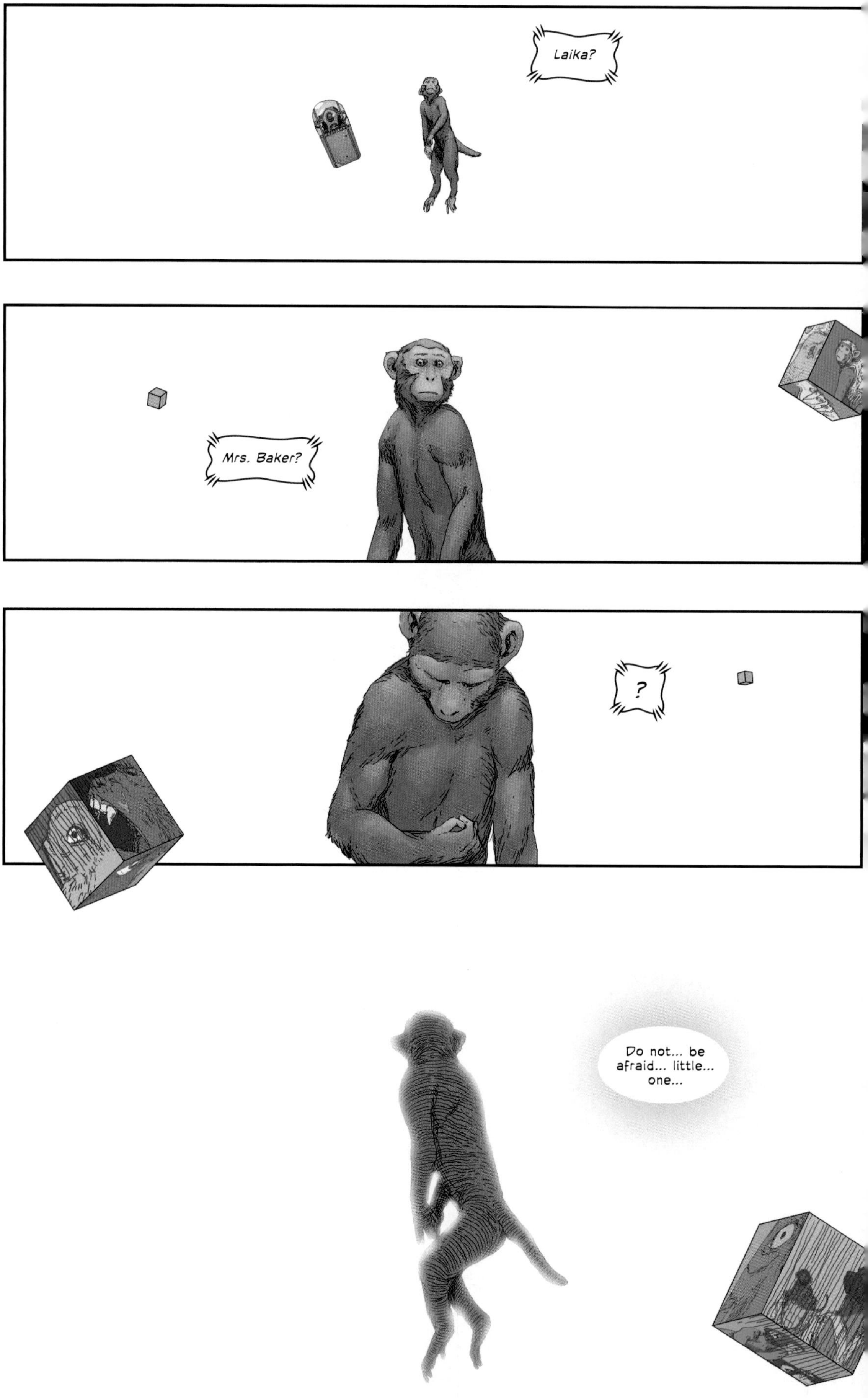
Laika?
Mrs. Baker?
?
Do not... be afraid... little... one...

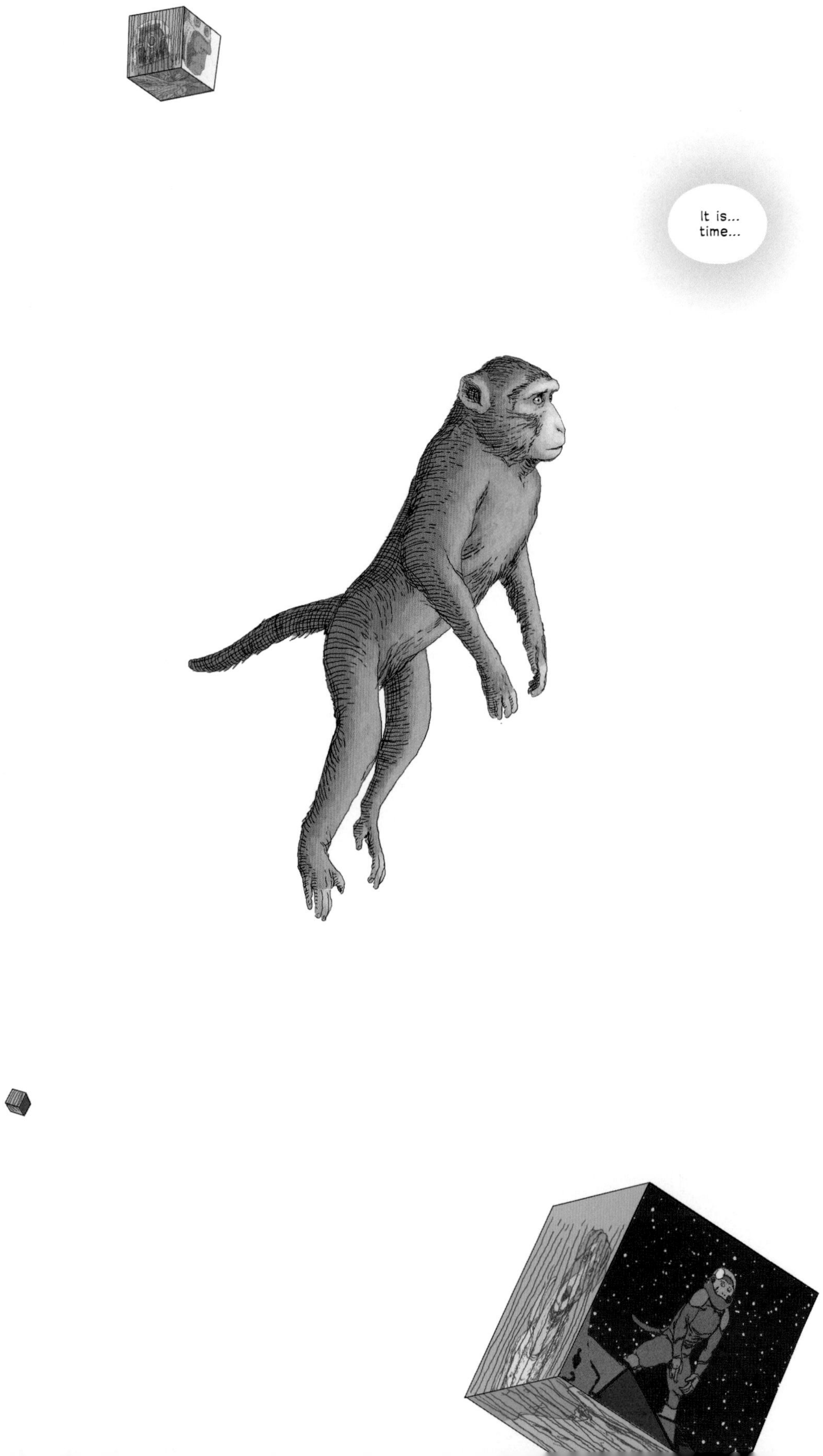
It is... time...

Able... Able ending?
Not ending...
Nothing... ends...
Change... there is... only change.

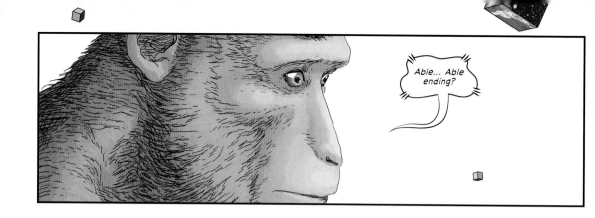

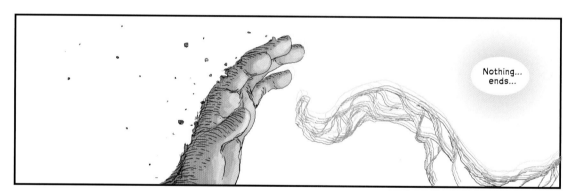

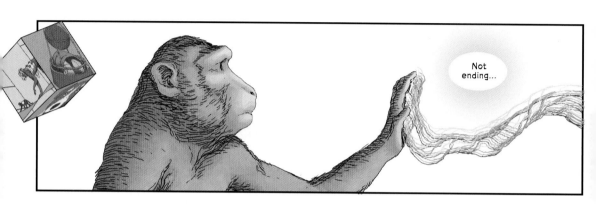

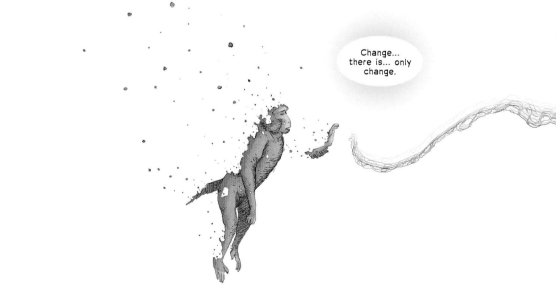

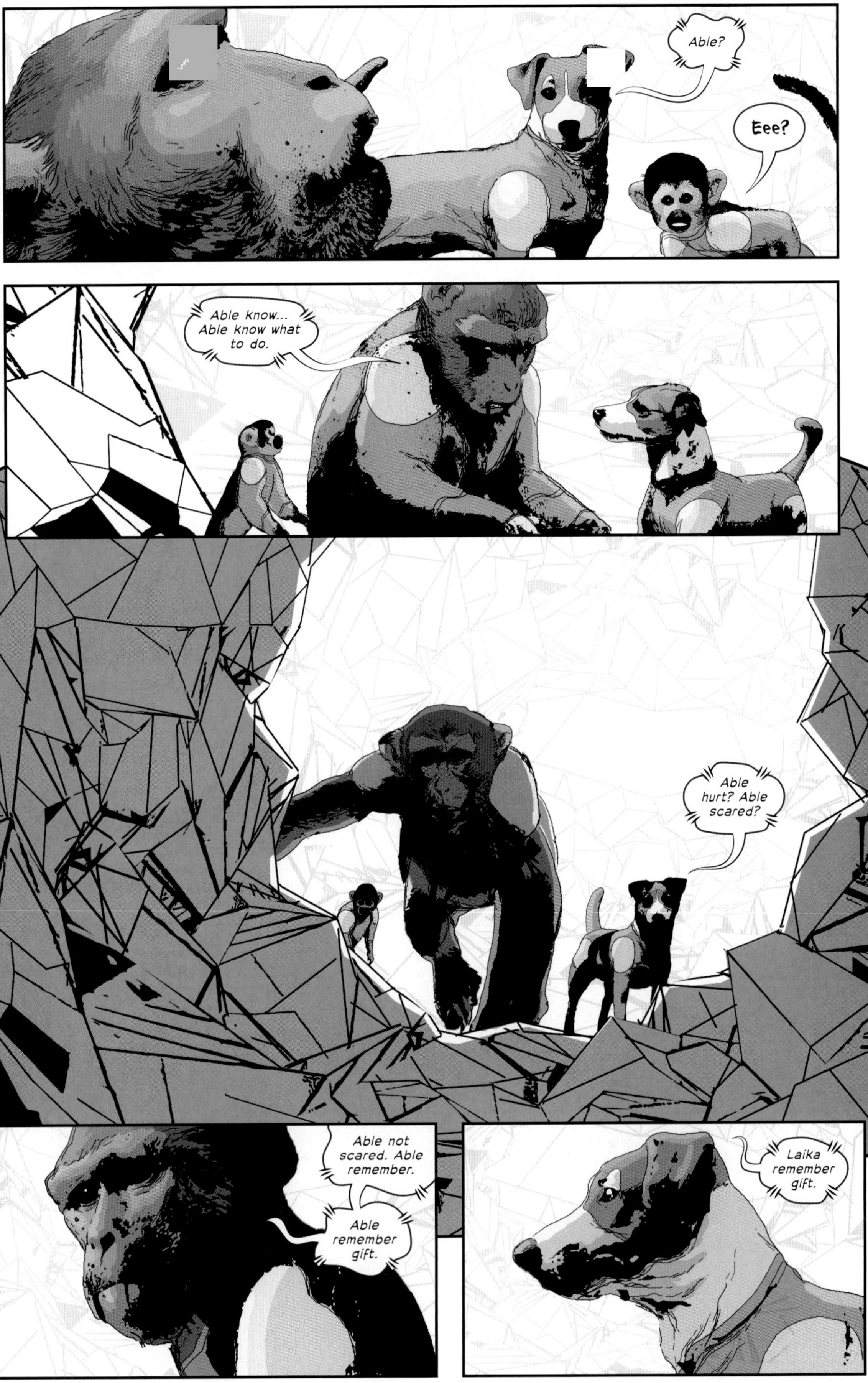
Able?
Eee?
Able know... Able know what to do.
Able hurt? Able scared?
Able not scared. Able remember.
Able remember gift.
Laika remember gift.

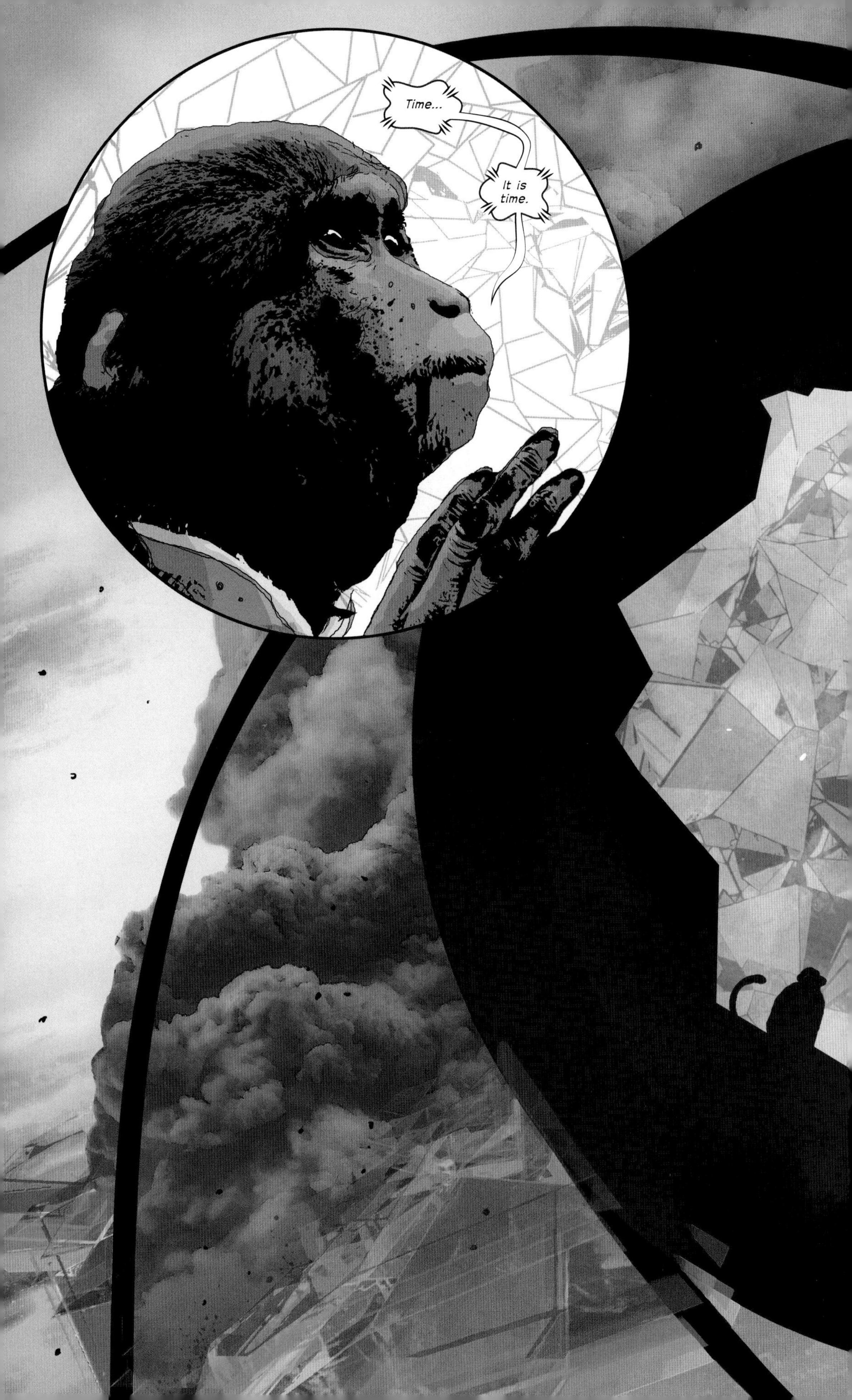
Time...
It is time.

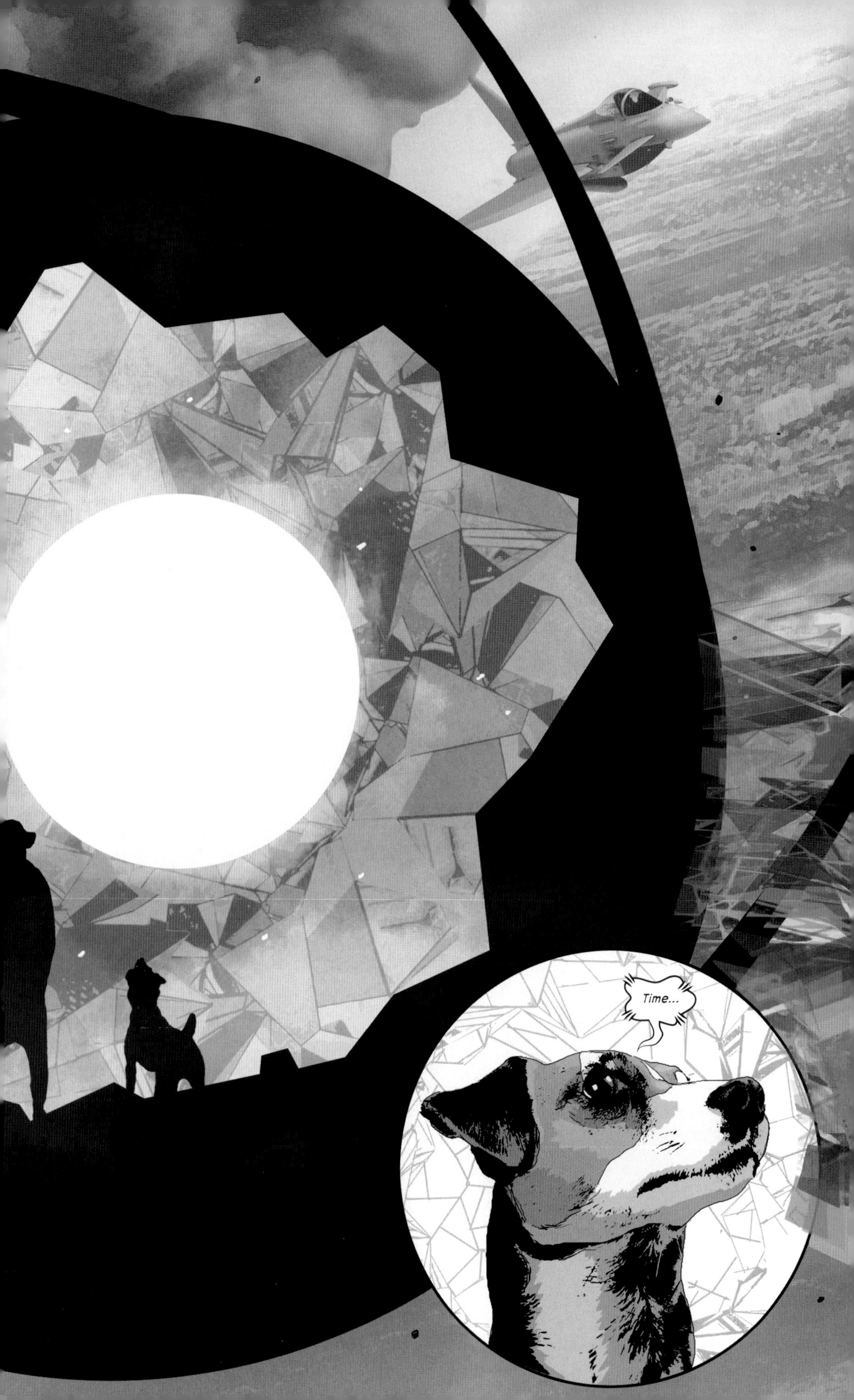
Time...

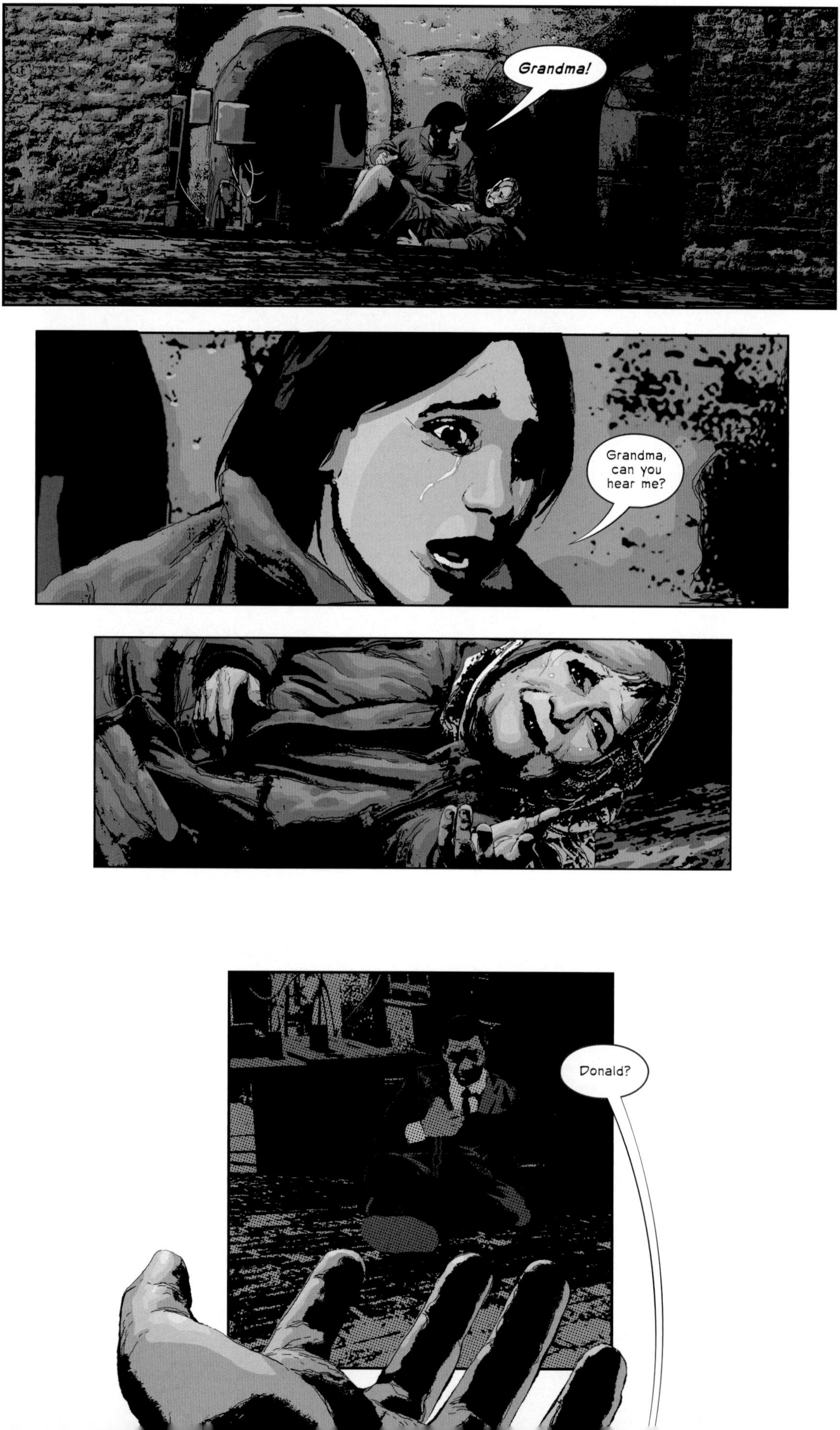
Grandma!
Grandma, can you hear me?
Donald?

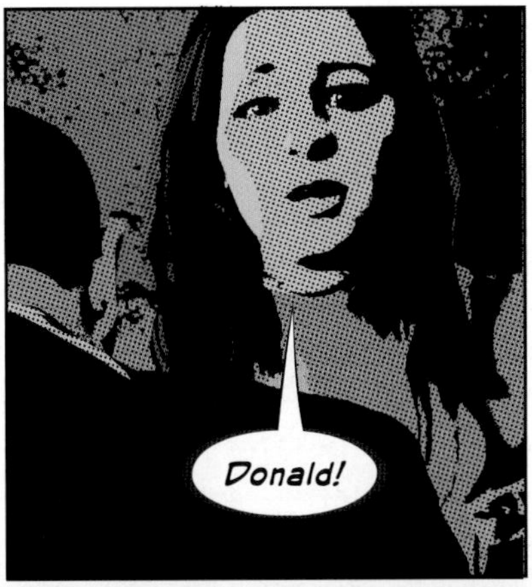
Donald!

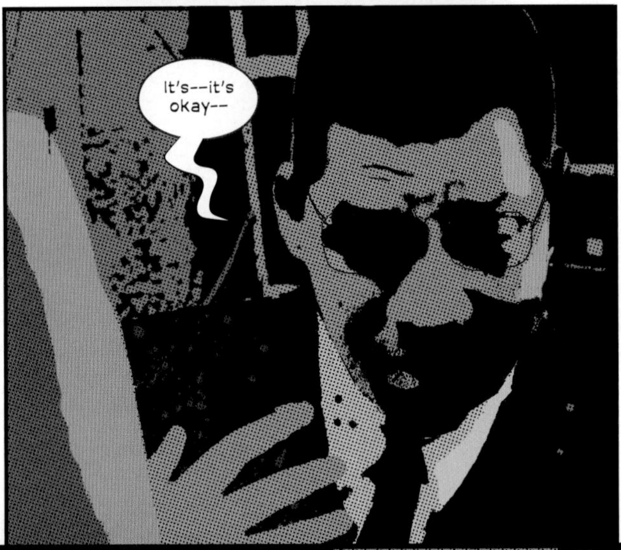
It's--it's okay--

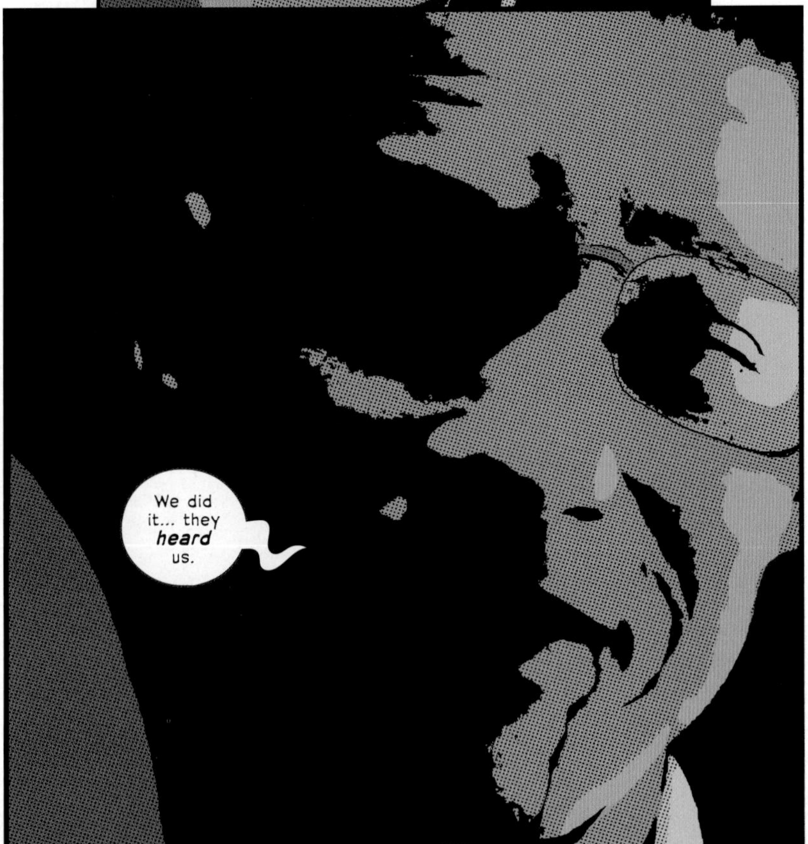
We did it... they *heard* us.

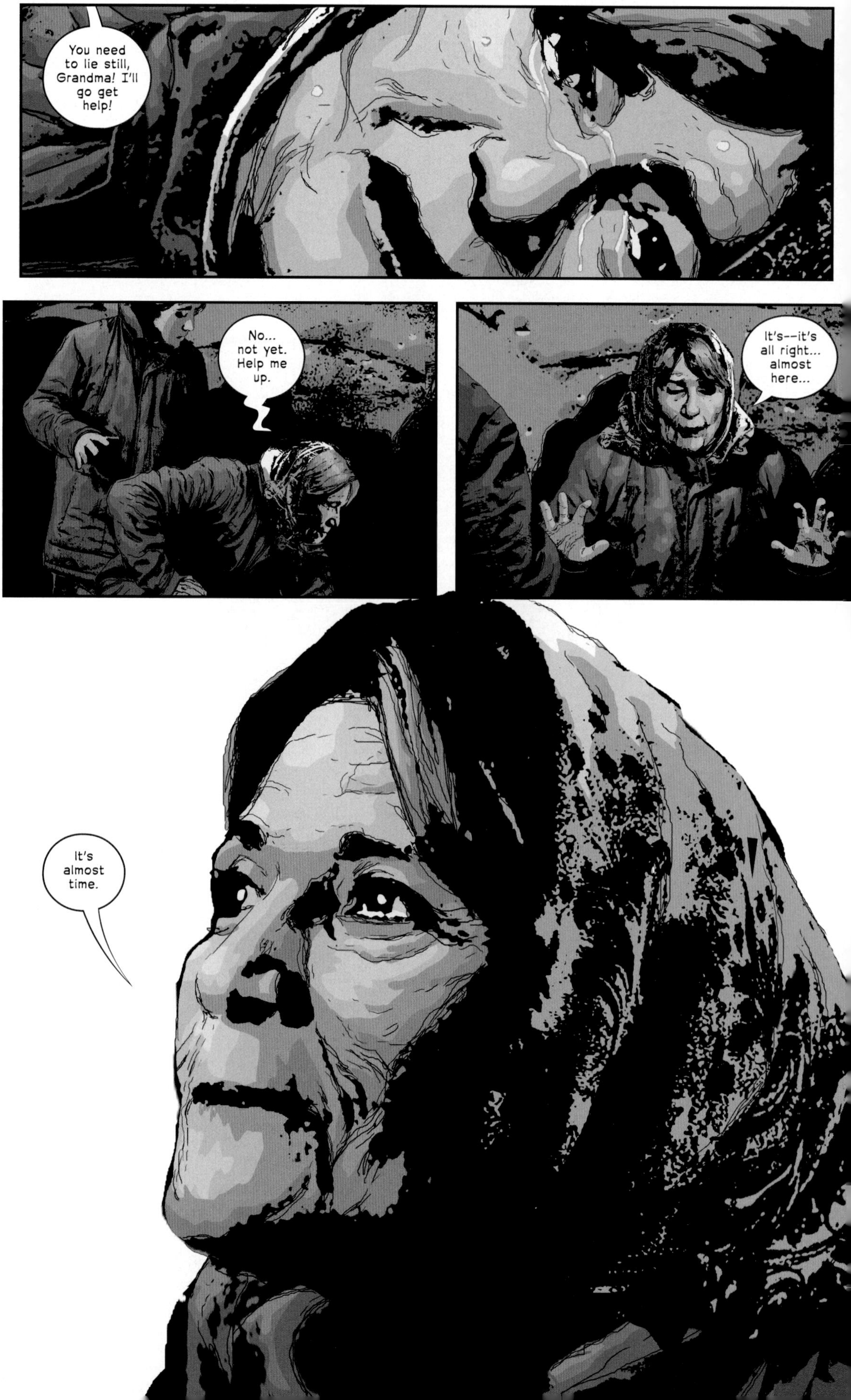
You need to lie still, Grandma! I'll go get help!
No... not yet. Help me up.
It's--it's all right... almost here...
It's almost time.

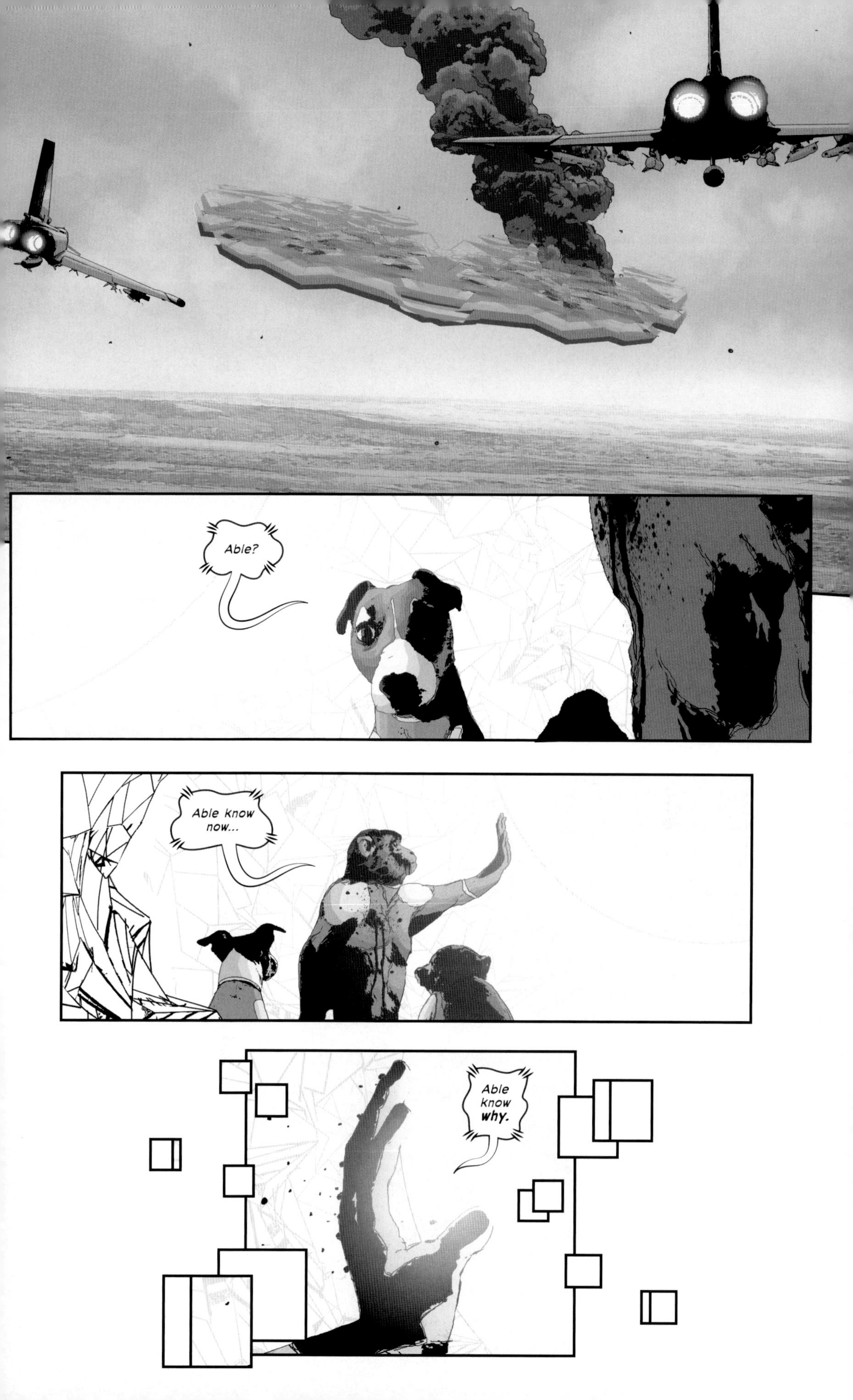
Able?
Able know now...
Able know why.

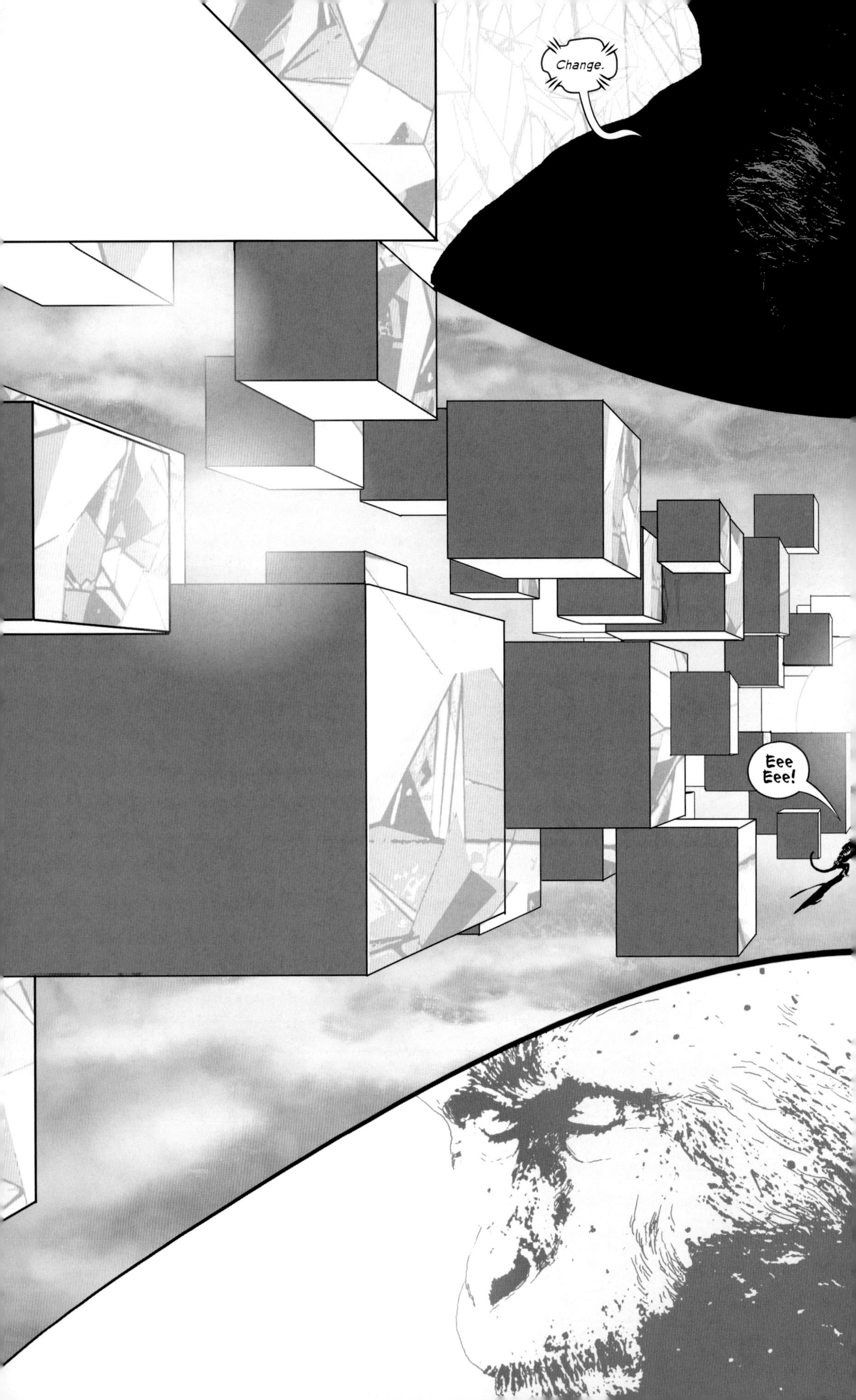
Change.
Eee Eee!

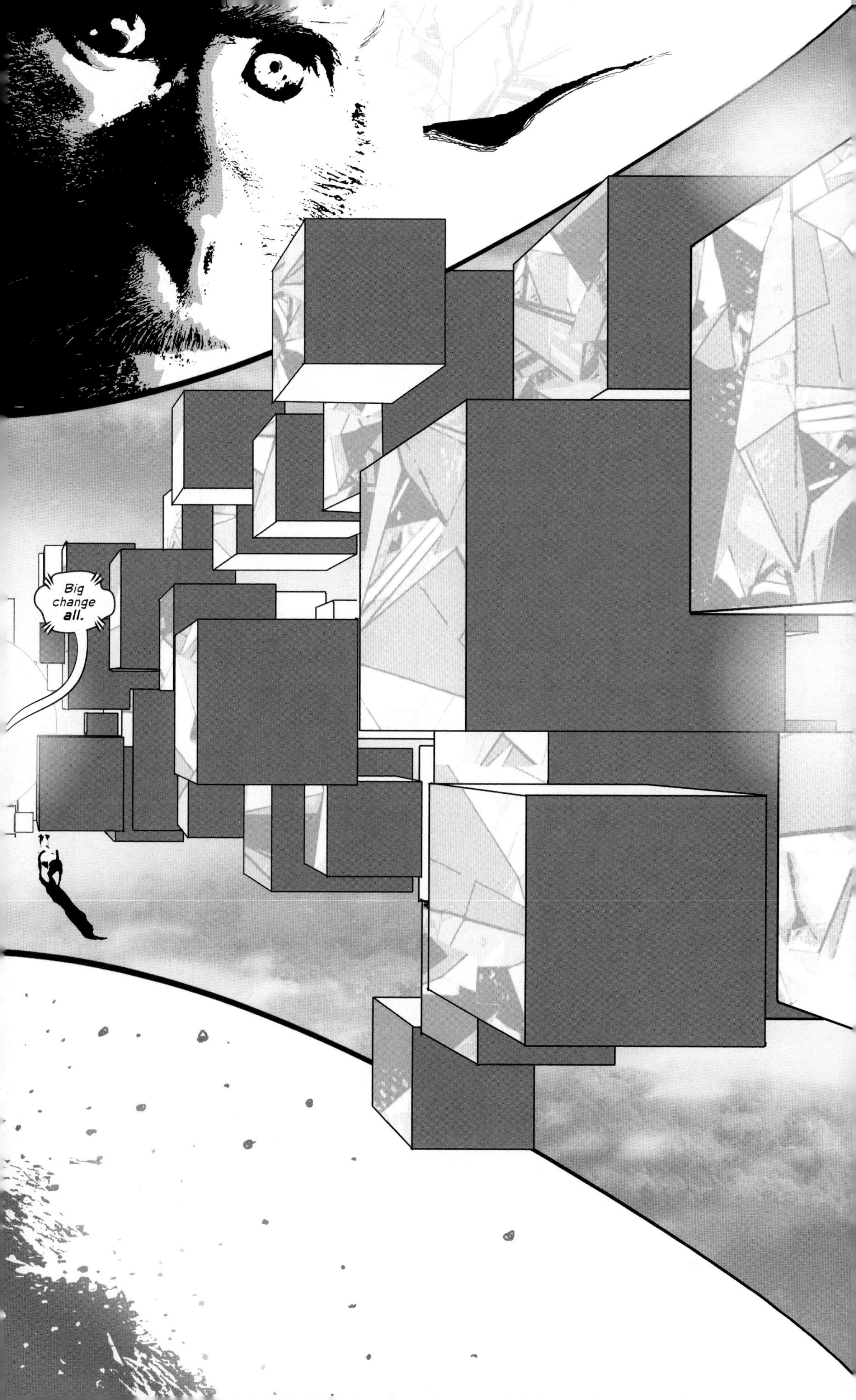
Big change all.

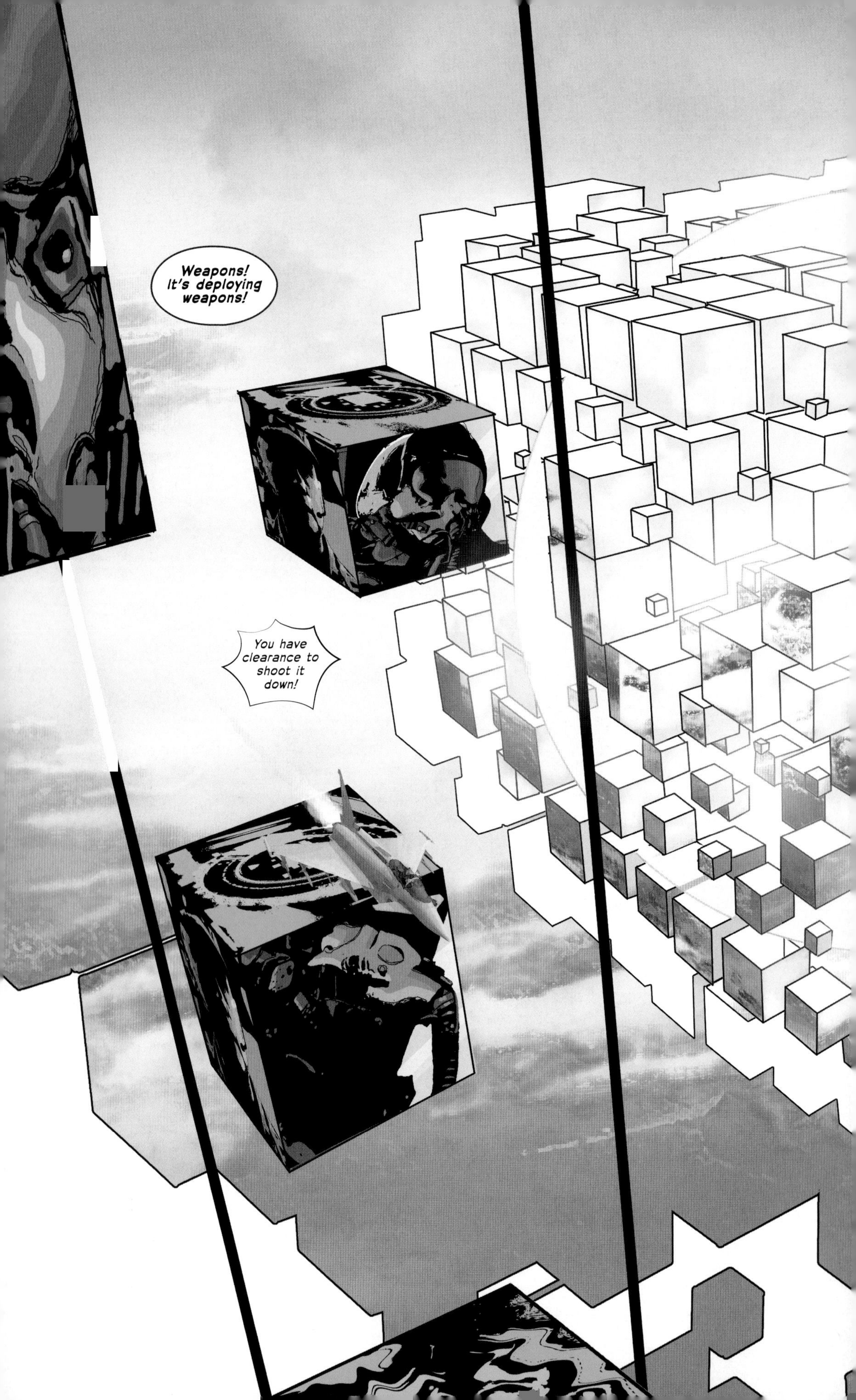
Weapons! It's deploying weapons!
You have clearance to shoot it down!

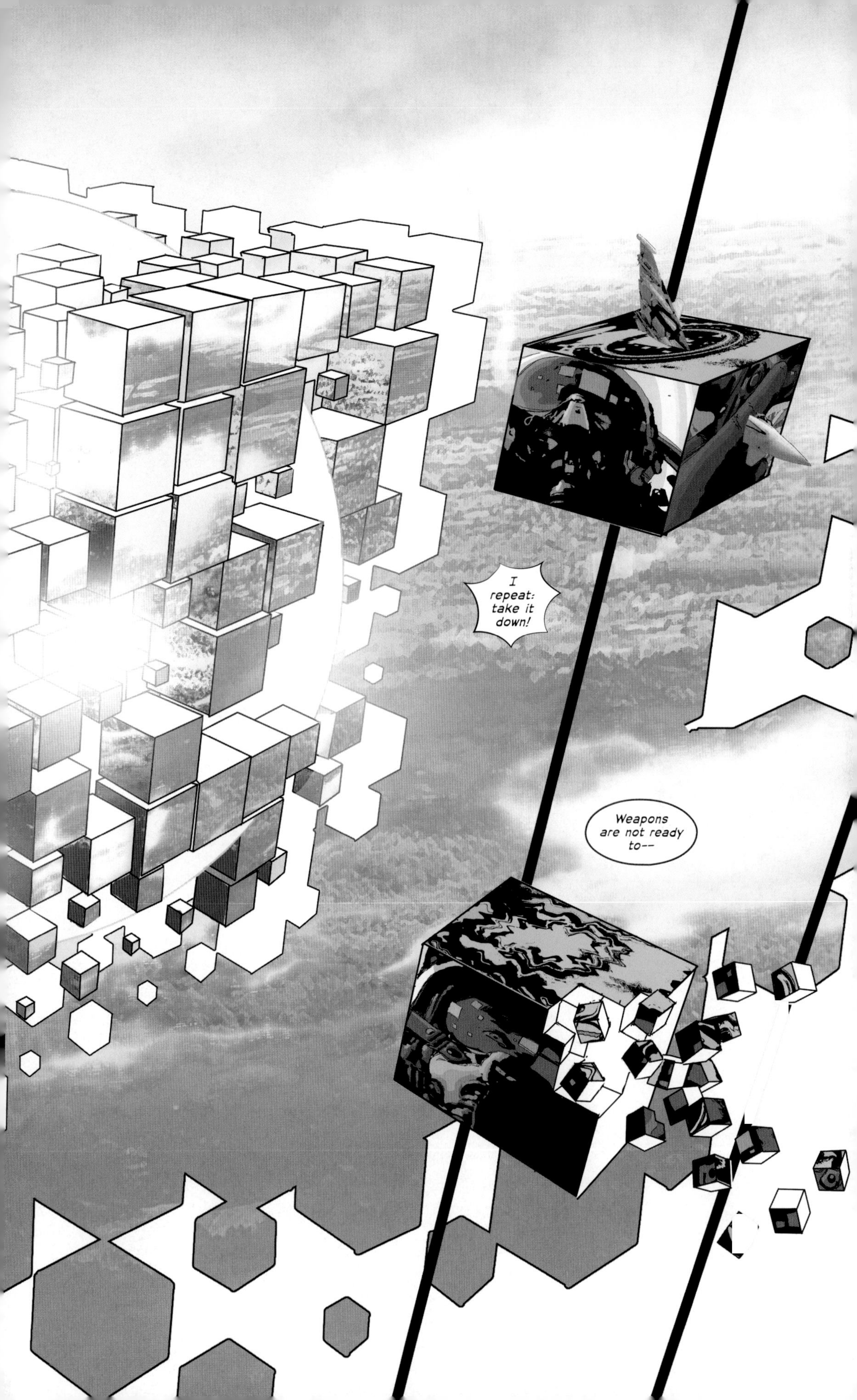
I repeat: take it down!
Weapons are not ready to--

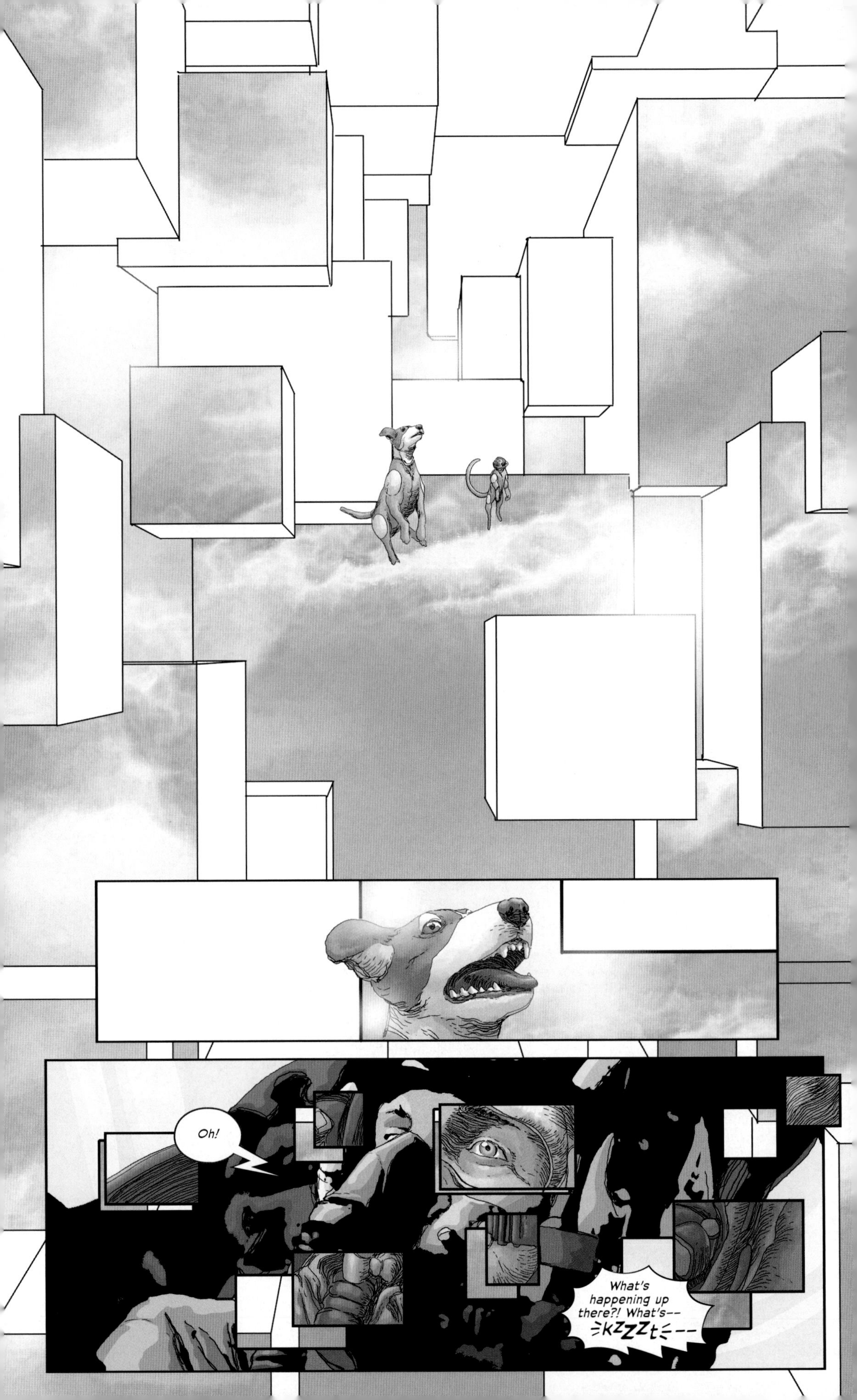
Oh!
What's happening up there?! What's--
KZZZt--

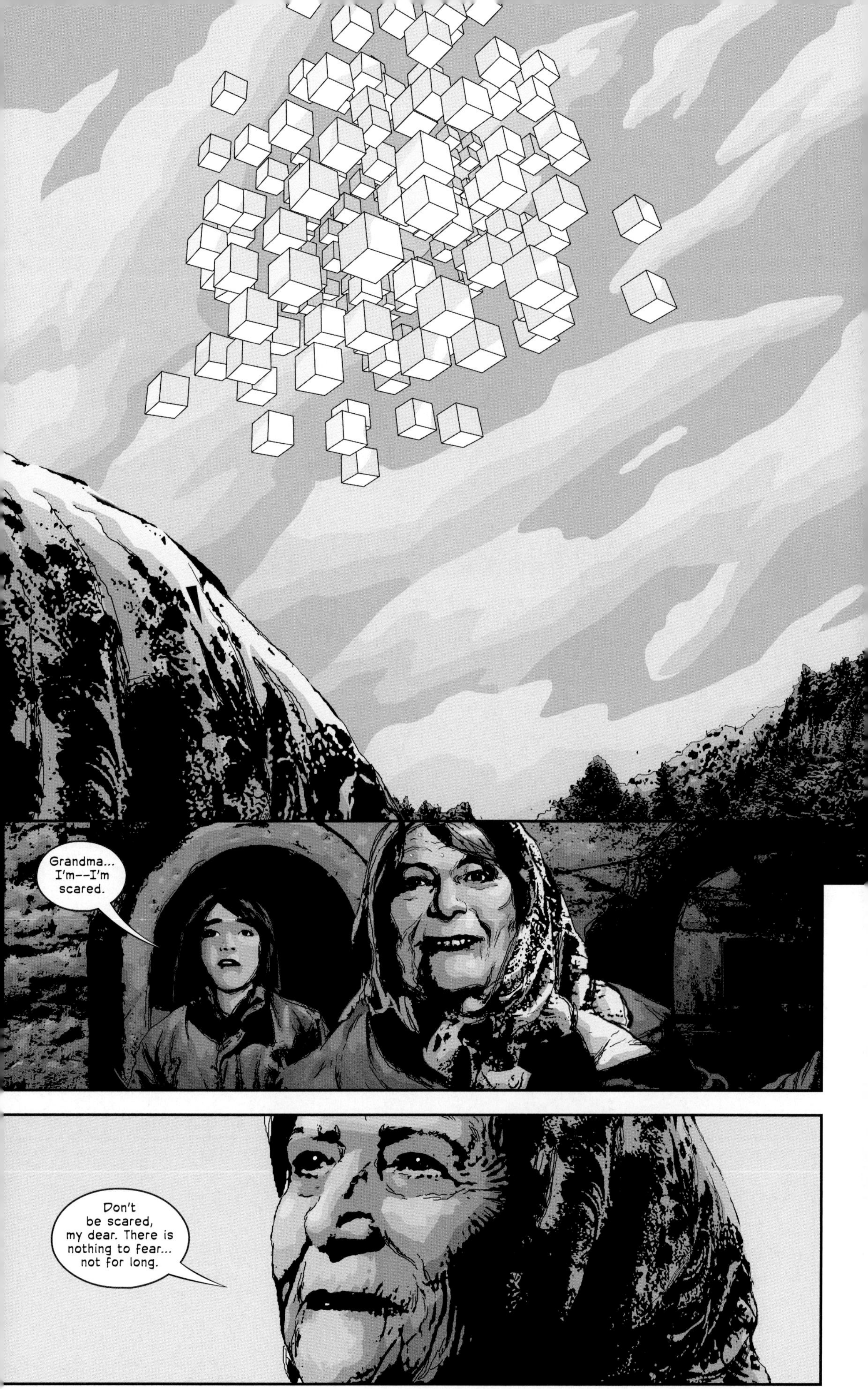
Grandma... I'm--I'm scared.
Don't be scared, my dear. There is nothing to fear... not for long.

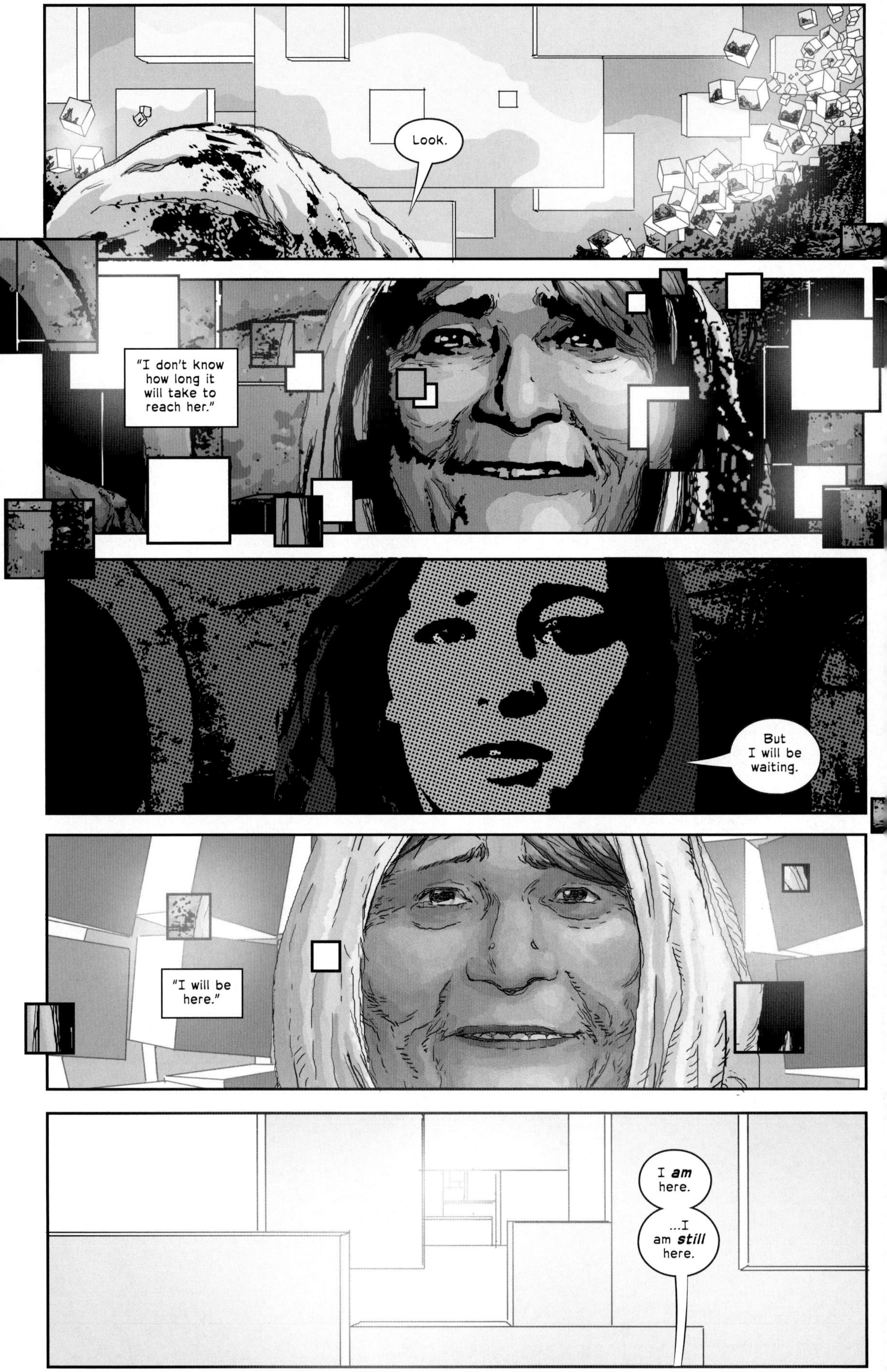
Look.
"I don't know how long it will take to reach her."
But I will be waiting.
"I will be here."
I *am* here.
...I am *still* here.

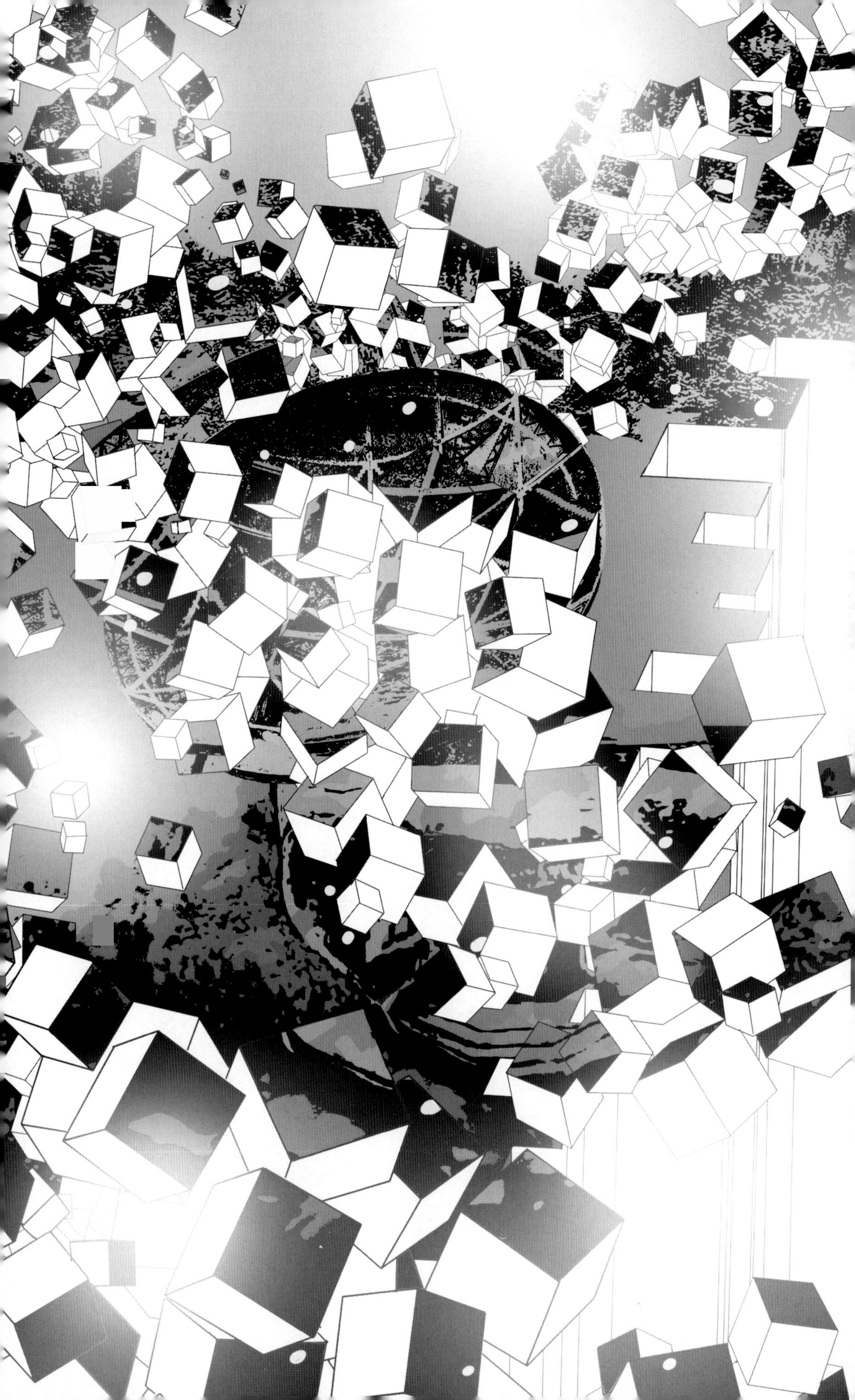

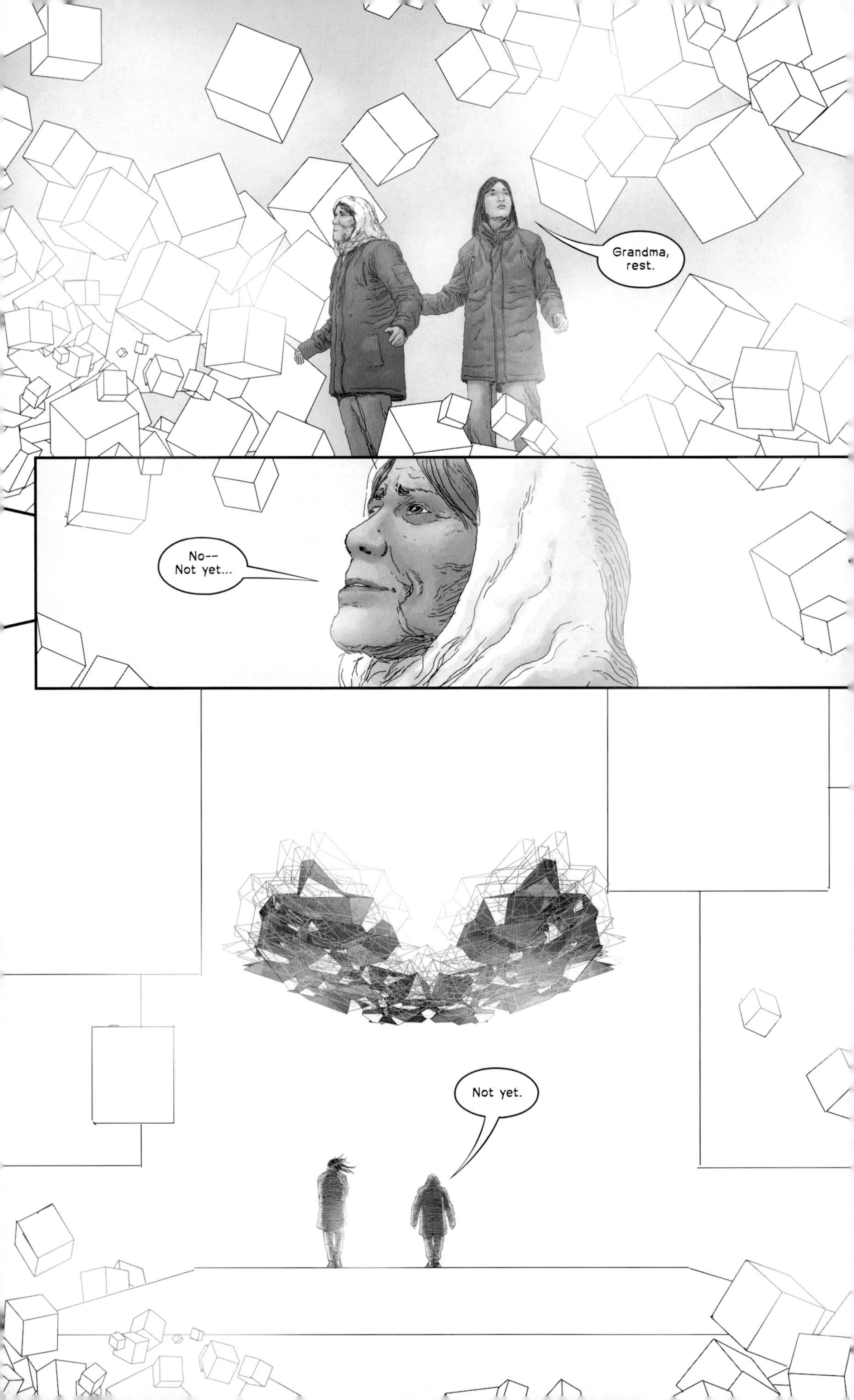
Grandma, rest.
No-- Not yet...
Not yet.

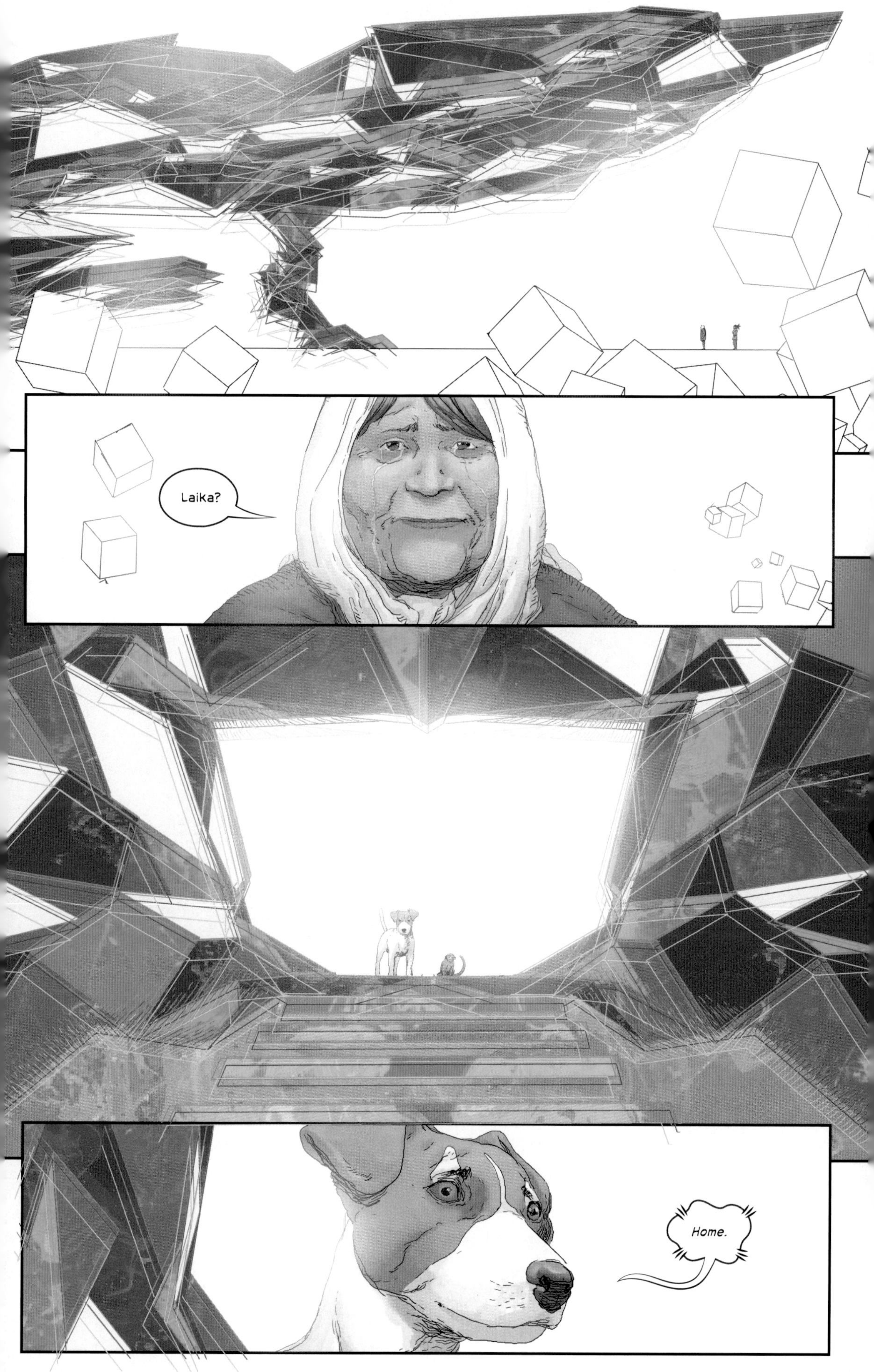
Laika?
Home.

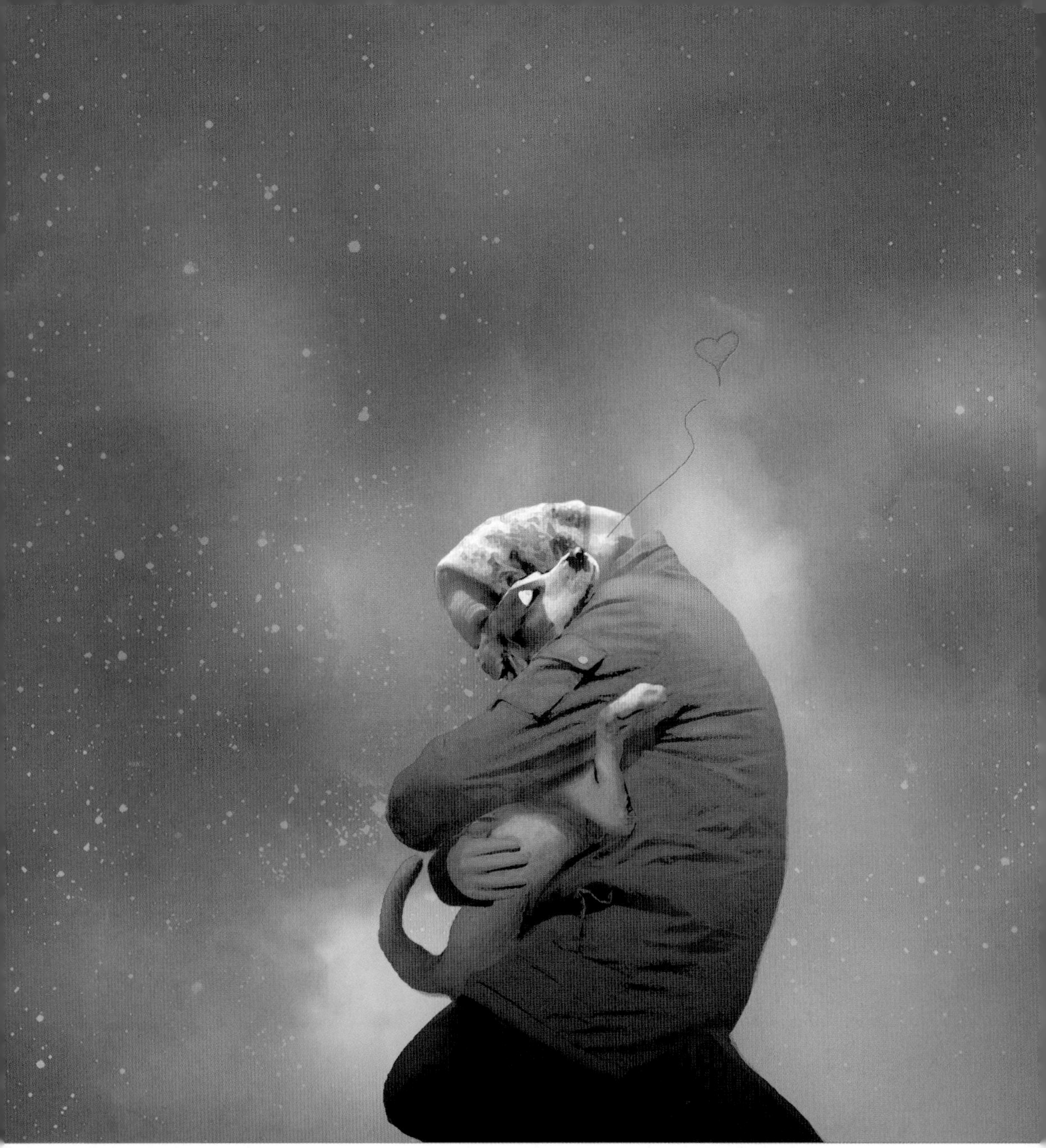

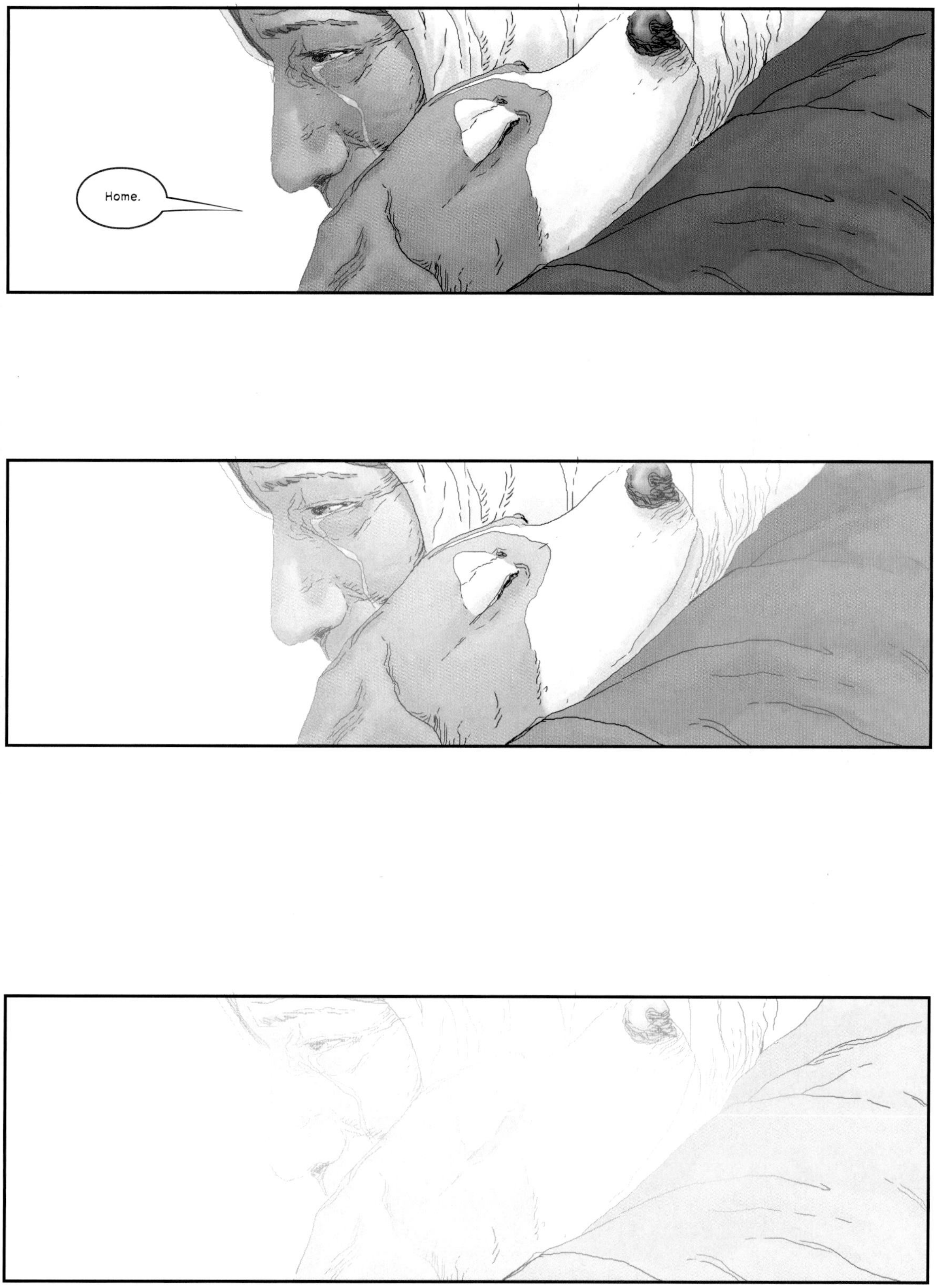
Home.

The End

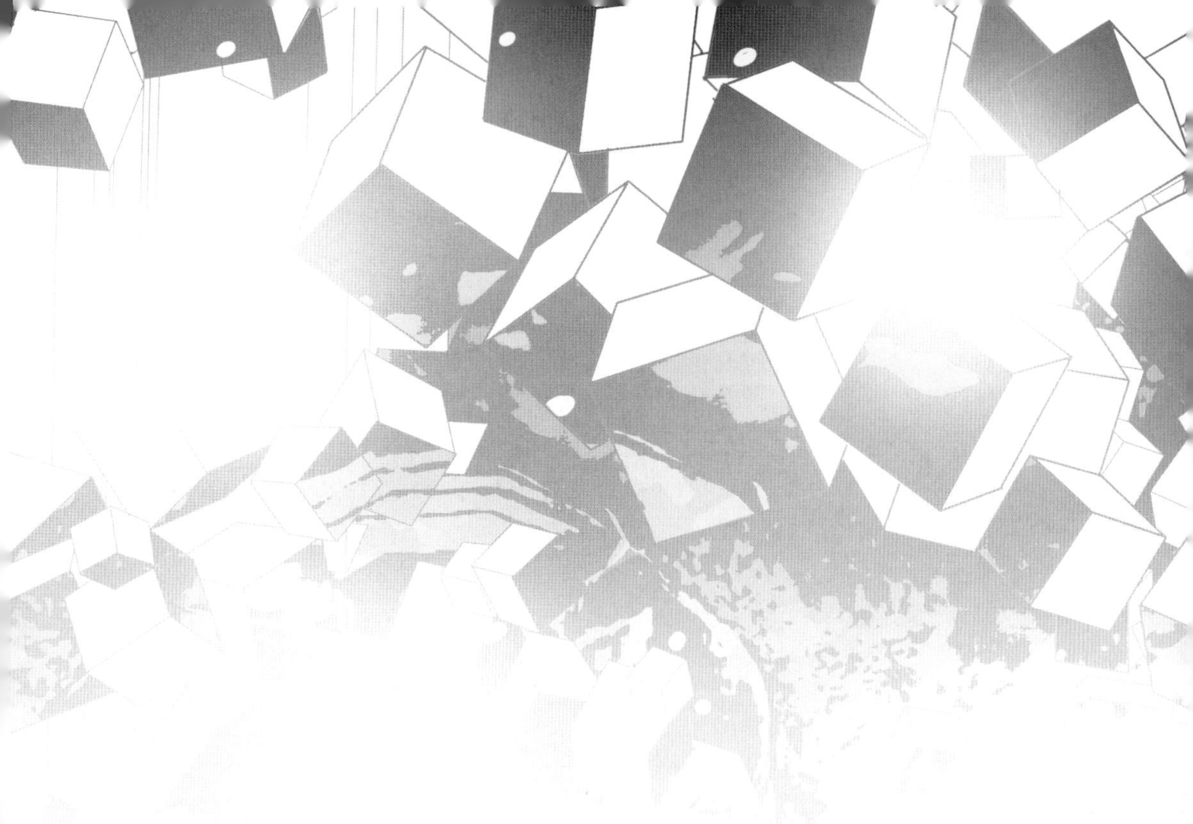

Cover Gallery

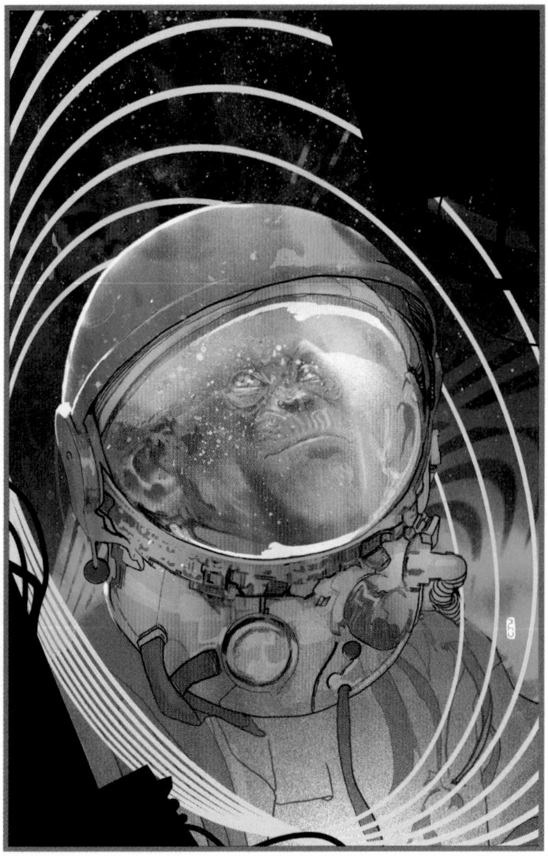

#1B | Christian Ward

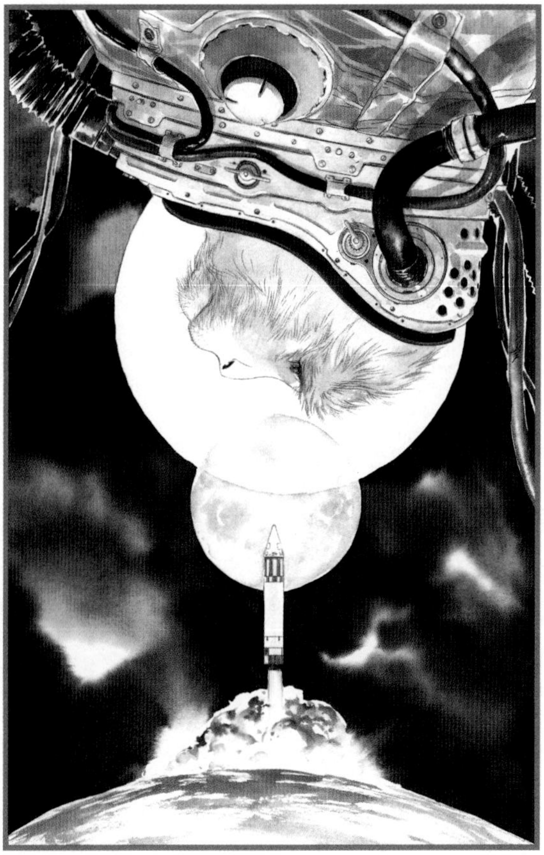

#1C | Dustin Nguyen

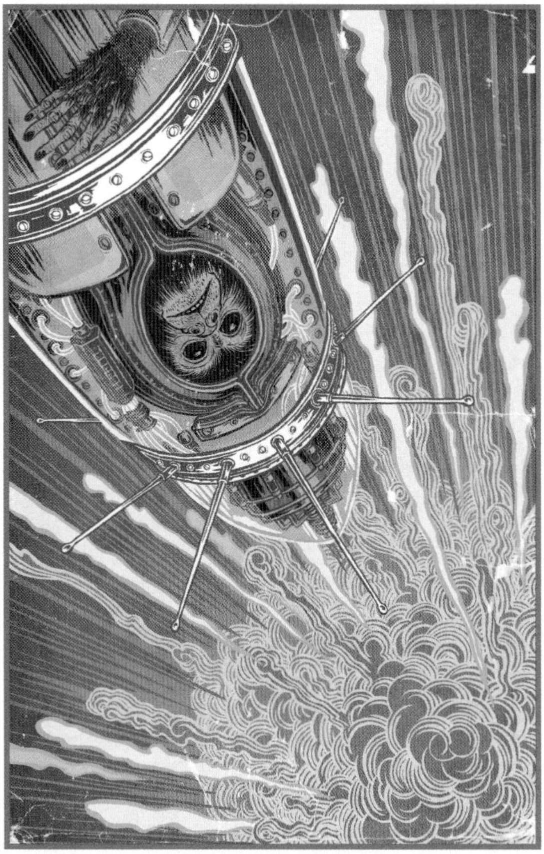

#1 D | Yuko Shimizu

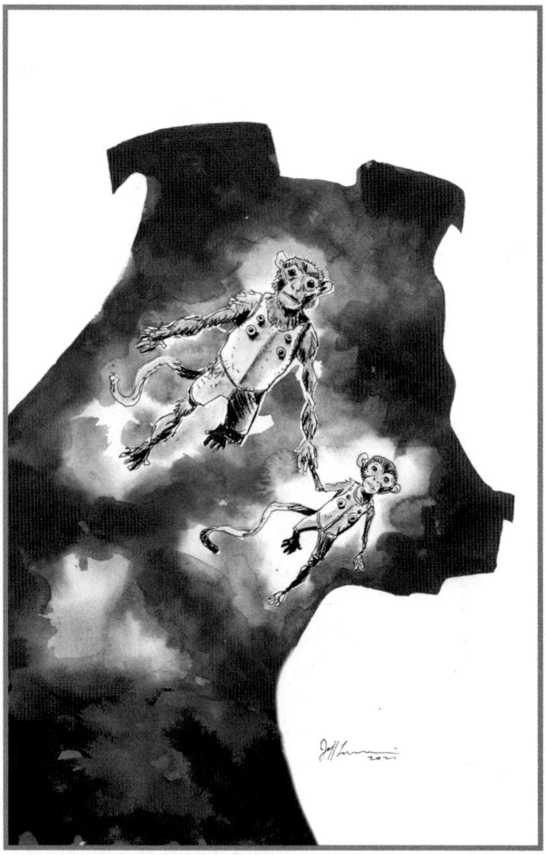

#1 1:100 | Jeff Lemire

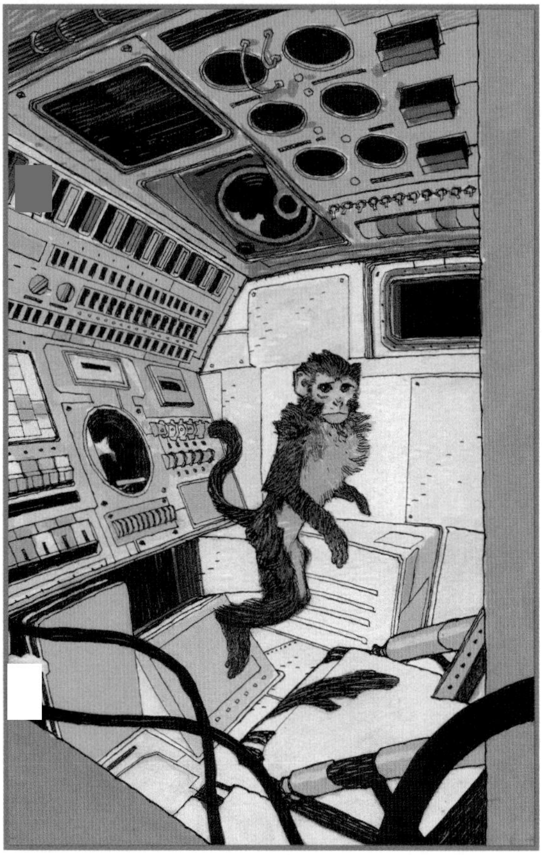

#2B | Gabriel Walta

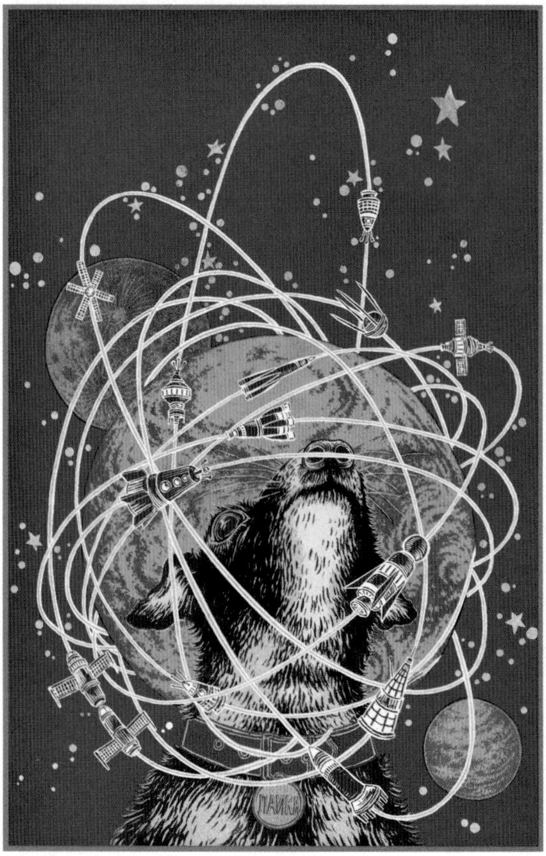

#2C | Yuko Shimizu

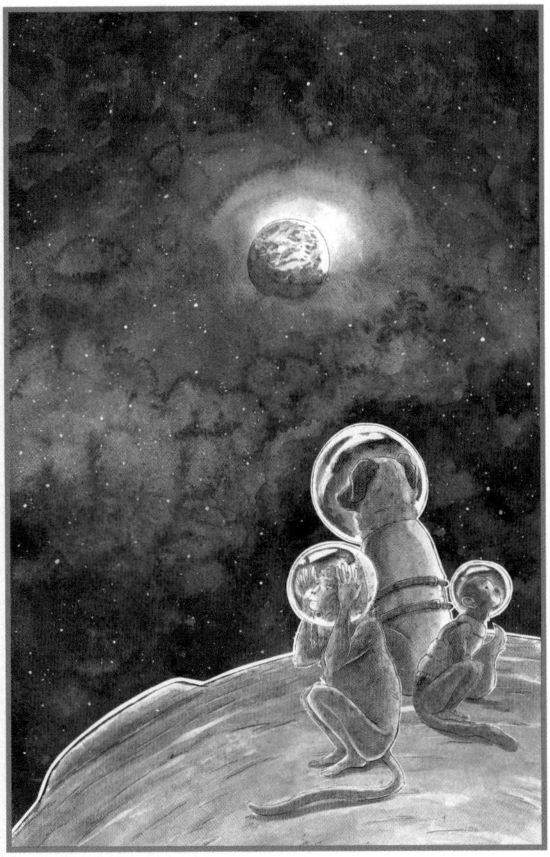

#3B | Emi Lenox

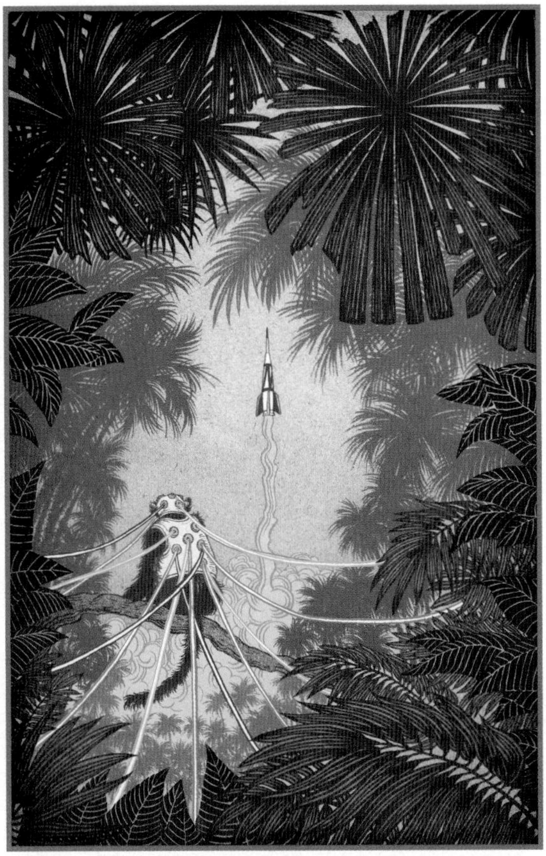

#3C | Yuko Shimizu

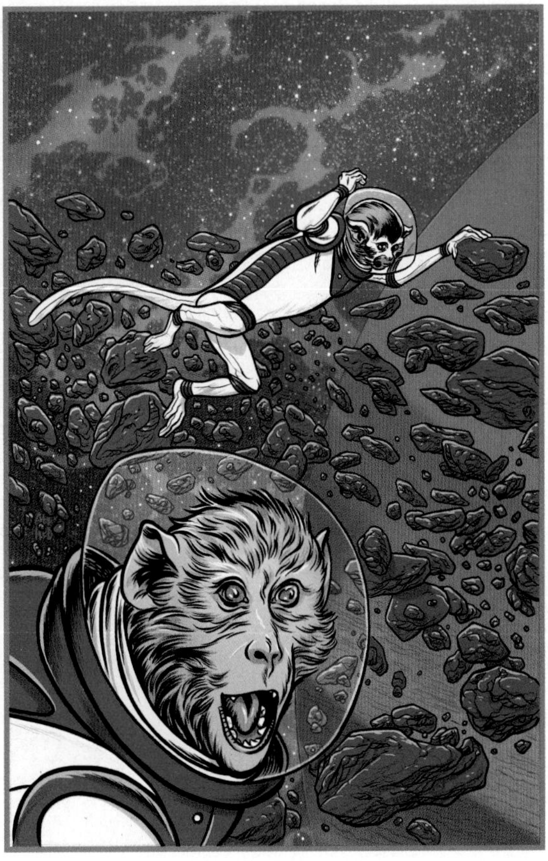

#4B | Michael Allred

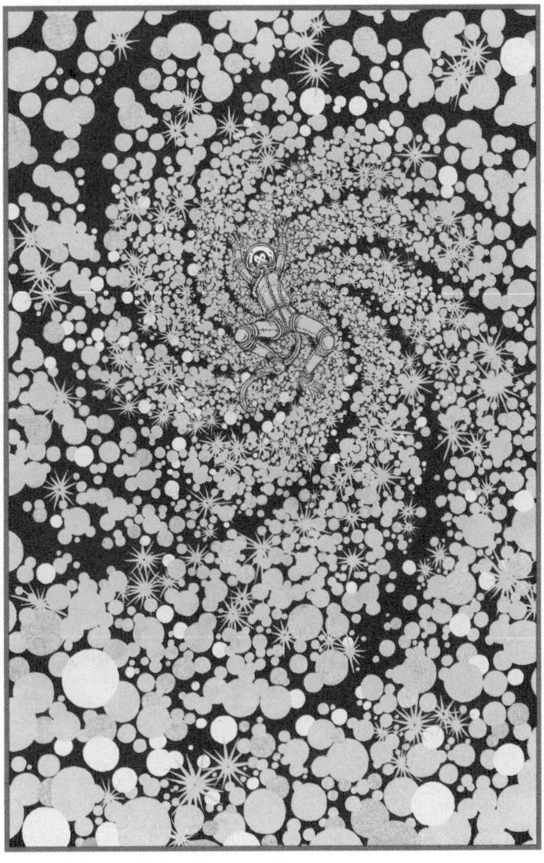

#4C | Yuko Shimizu

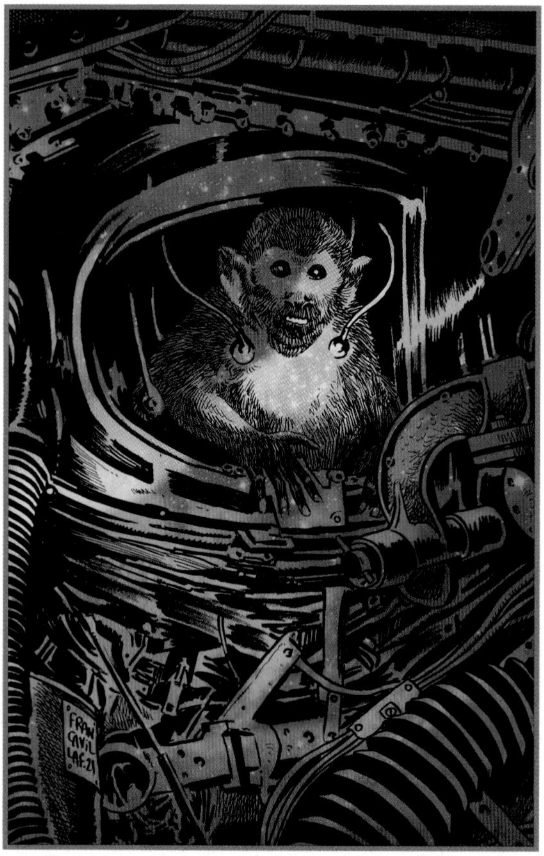

#5B | Francesco Francavilla

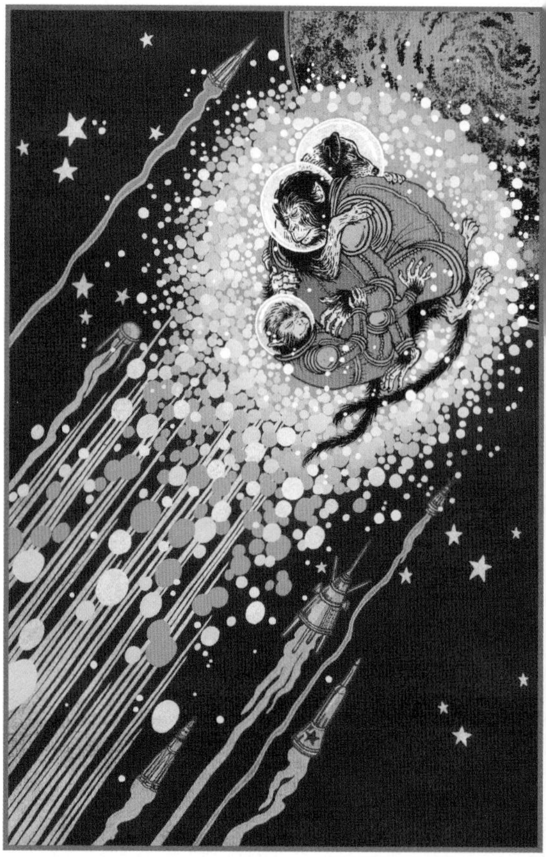

#5C | Yuko Shimizu

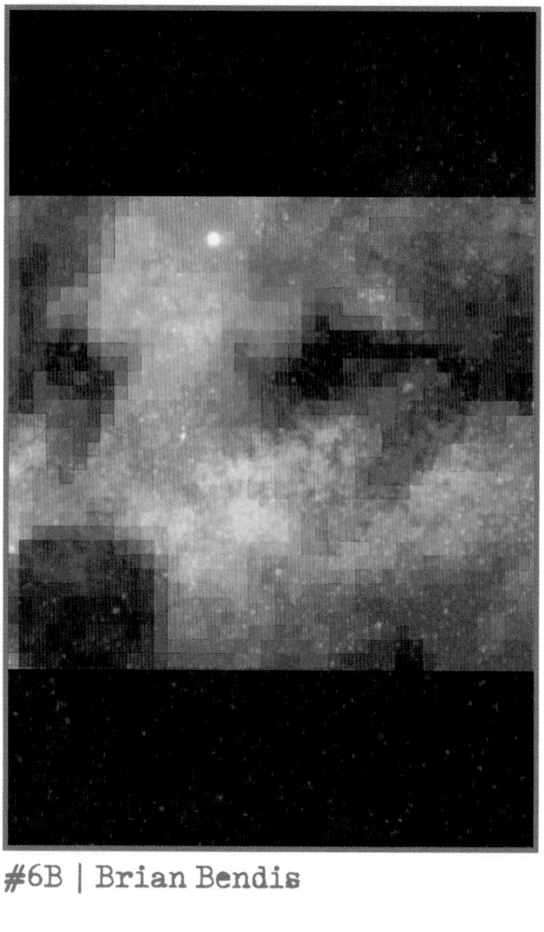

#6B | Brian Bendis

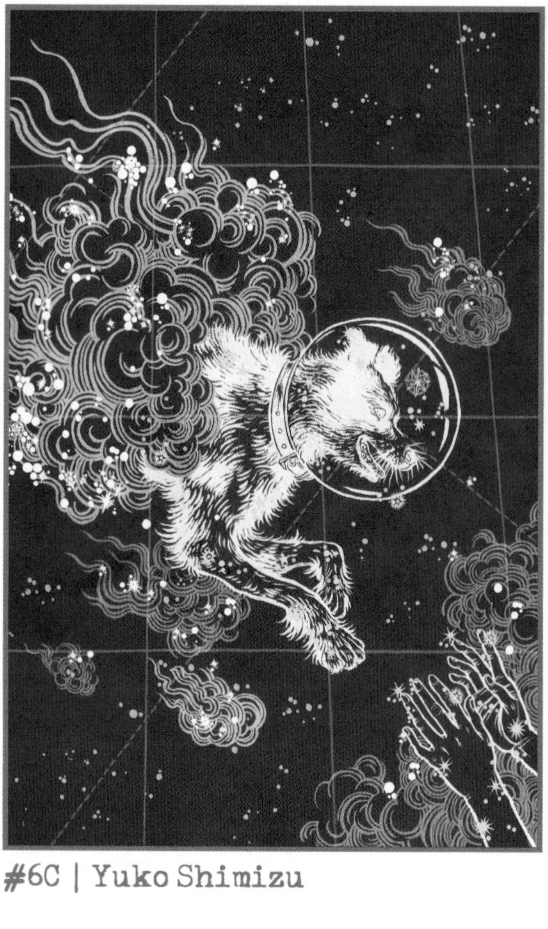

#6C | Yuko Shimizu

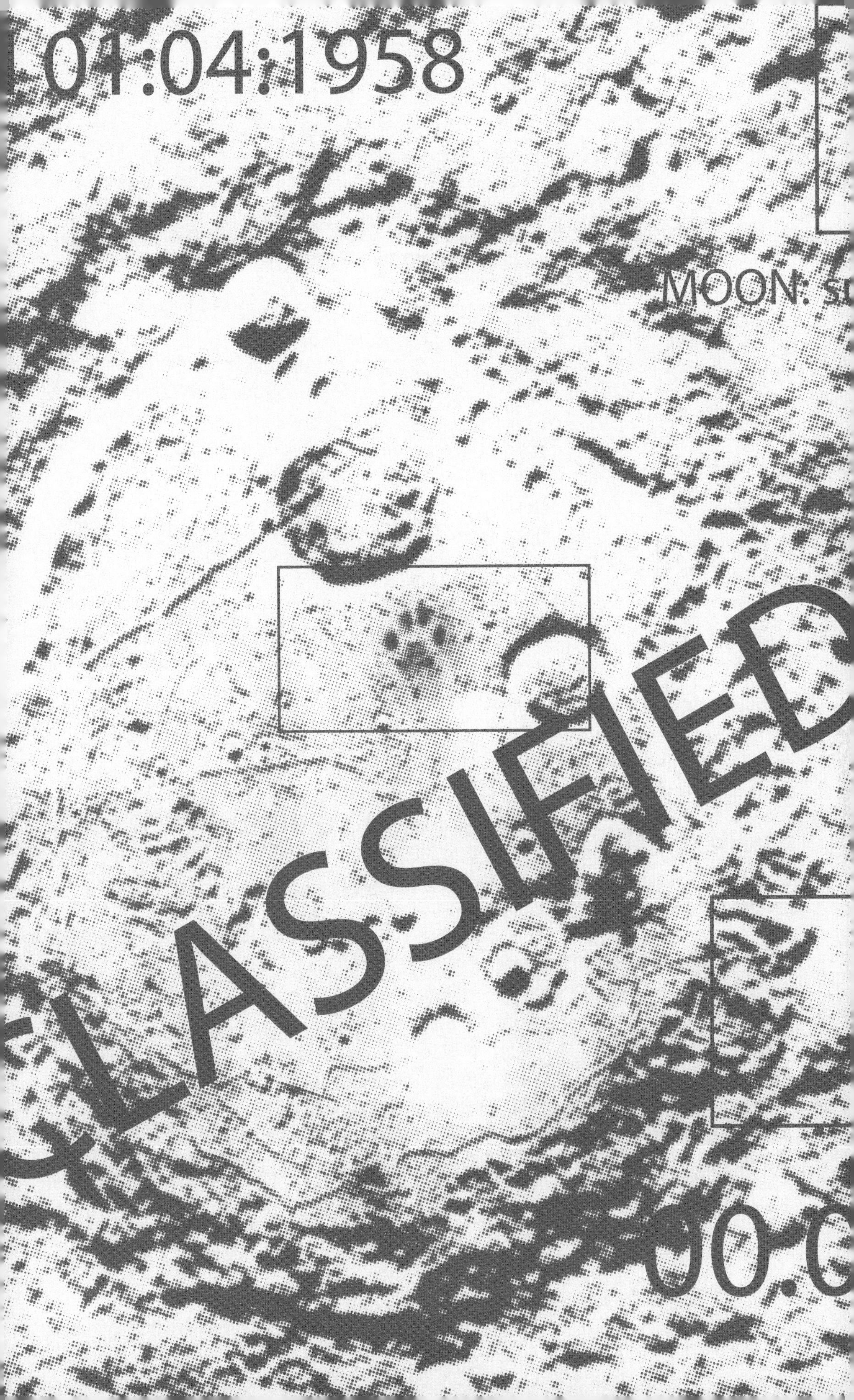
01:04:1958
MOON:
CLASSIFIED
00.

About the creators

CODENAME: [redacted]

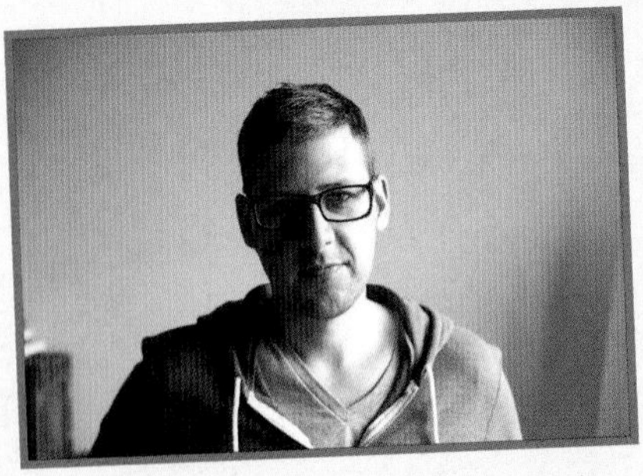

JEFF LEMIRE is the creator of the acclaimed graphic novels *Sweet Tooth* (at Netflix from Robert Downey Jr.), the *Essex County Trilogy, The Underwater Welder, Trillium* and *Roughneck,* as well as *Descender* and *Ascender* with Dustin Nguyen and *Black Hammer* with Dean Ormston. Jeff has also written *Green Arrow, Justice League* and *Animal Man* for DC Comics and *Hawkeye* for Marvel Comics. He's also part of the creative team on *Cosmic Detective,* which he recently Kickstarted with Matt Kindt and David Rubín.

In 2008 and in 2013 Jeff won the Shuster Award for Best Canadian Cartoonist. He has also received the Doug Wright Award for Best Emerging Talent and the American Library Association's prestigious Alex Award, recognizing books for adults with specific teen appeal. He has also been nominated for 8 Eisner awards, 7 Harvey Awards and 8 Shuster Awards. In 2010 *Essex County* was named as one of the five Essential Canadian Novels of the Decade. He currently lives and works in Toronto with his wife and son.

CODENAME: [redacted]

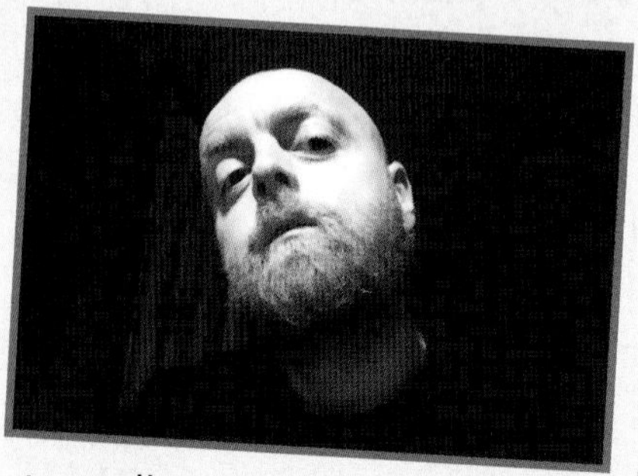

ANDREA SORRENTINO is the artist and co-creator of the critically praised and Eisner Award-winning *Gideon Falls* as well as the artist of other DC and Marvel hits like *Joker: Killer Smile, Batman: The Imposter* and *Wolverine: Old Man Logan.* He's renowned in the comic world for his tense, moody and suspenseful art and creative layouts that go beyond beat-to-beat storytelling and into evocations of deep, suggestive mental states.

Sorrentino lives and works just outside of Naples, Italy, precariously close to an active volcano.

CODENAME: [redacted]

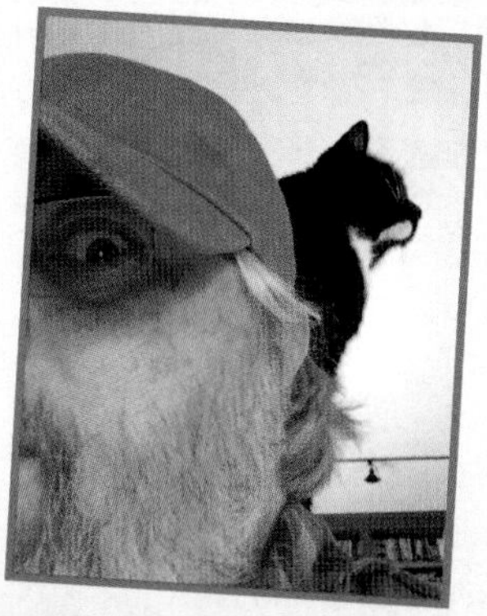

DAVID STEWART has worked as a colorist for over 20 years. He's worked on titles like *Hellboy, Shaolin Cowboy, Black Hammer* and *Ultramega*. He resides in Portland, Oregon with his wife and three black cats.

CODENAME: [redacted]

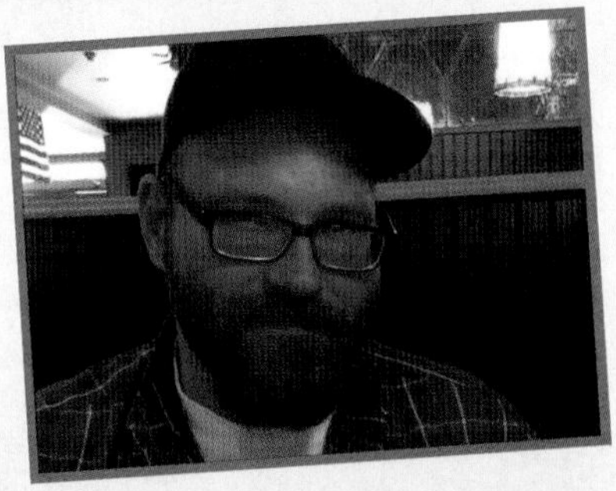

STEVE WANDS is best known as a Harvey Award-nominated and Lammy Award-winning comic book Letterer with DC Comics, Image, TKO Studios, Dark Horse and others, but he's also indie author of the *Stay Dead* series, *Night of the Drunks* and co-writer of *Trail of Blood*. When not working, he spends time with his family in New Jersey.

CODENAME: [redacted]

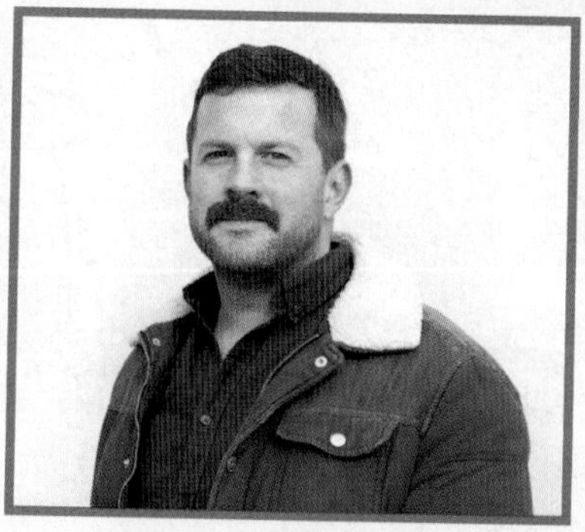

GREG LOCKARD is a comic book writer and editor. As a freelance editor, his clients have included ComiXology Originals, Image Comics, Einhorn's Epic Productions and others. As a member of the Vertigo editorial staff, he worked on a number of critically acclaimed titles including *Dial H, The Unwritten, Sweet Tooth* and many others. *Liebestrasse*, published by ComiXology Originals, is his debut graphic novel as a writer and co-creator.

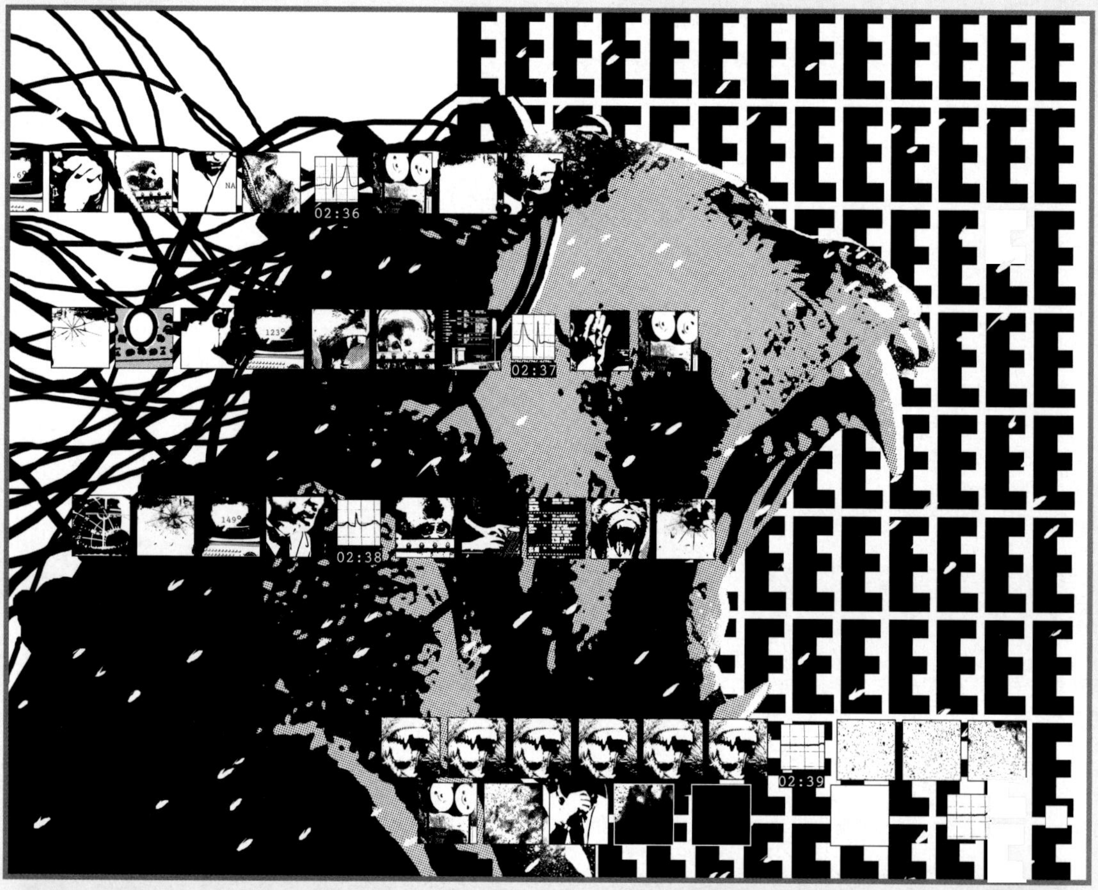
02:36
02:37
02:38
02:39

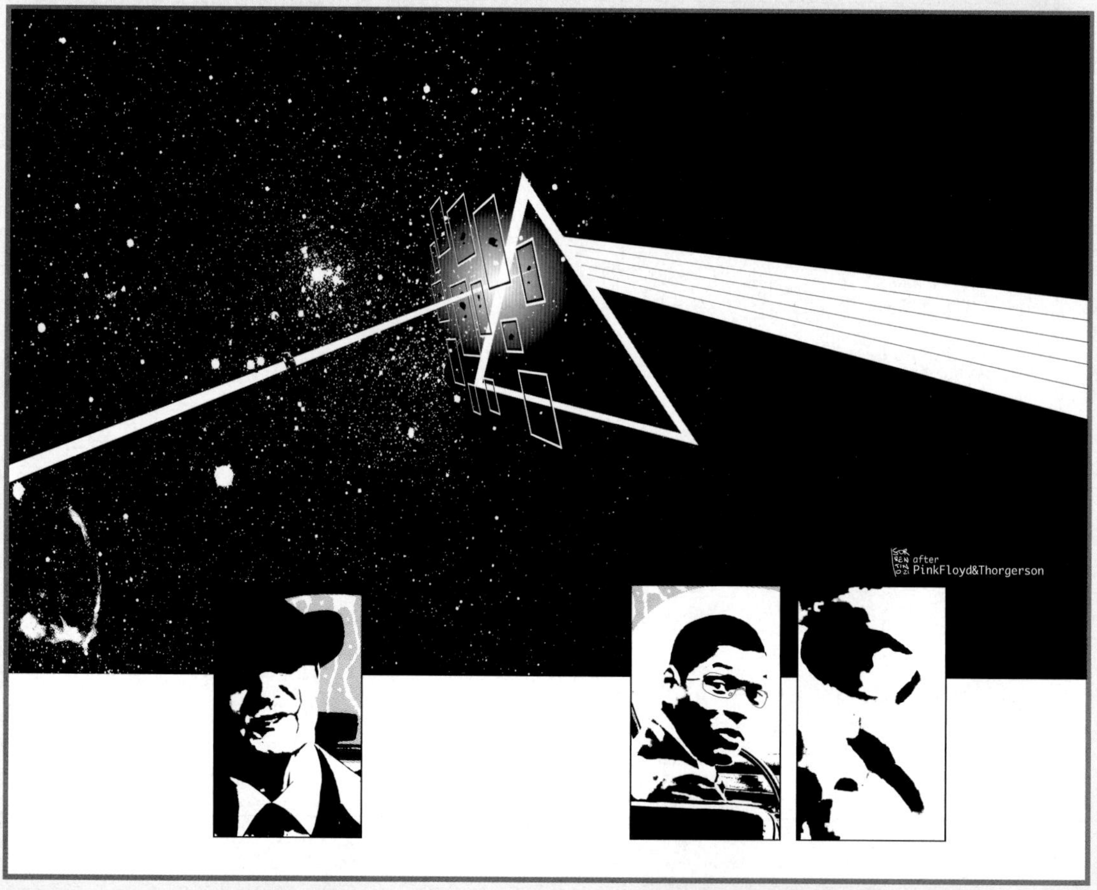
SOR
REN
TIN
after
PinkFloyd&Thorgerson

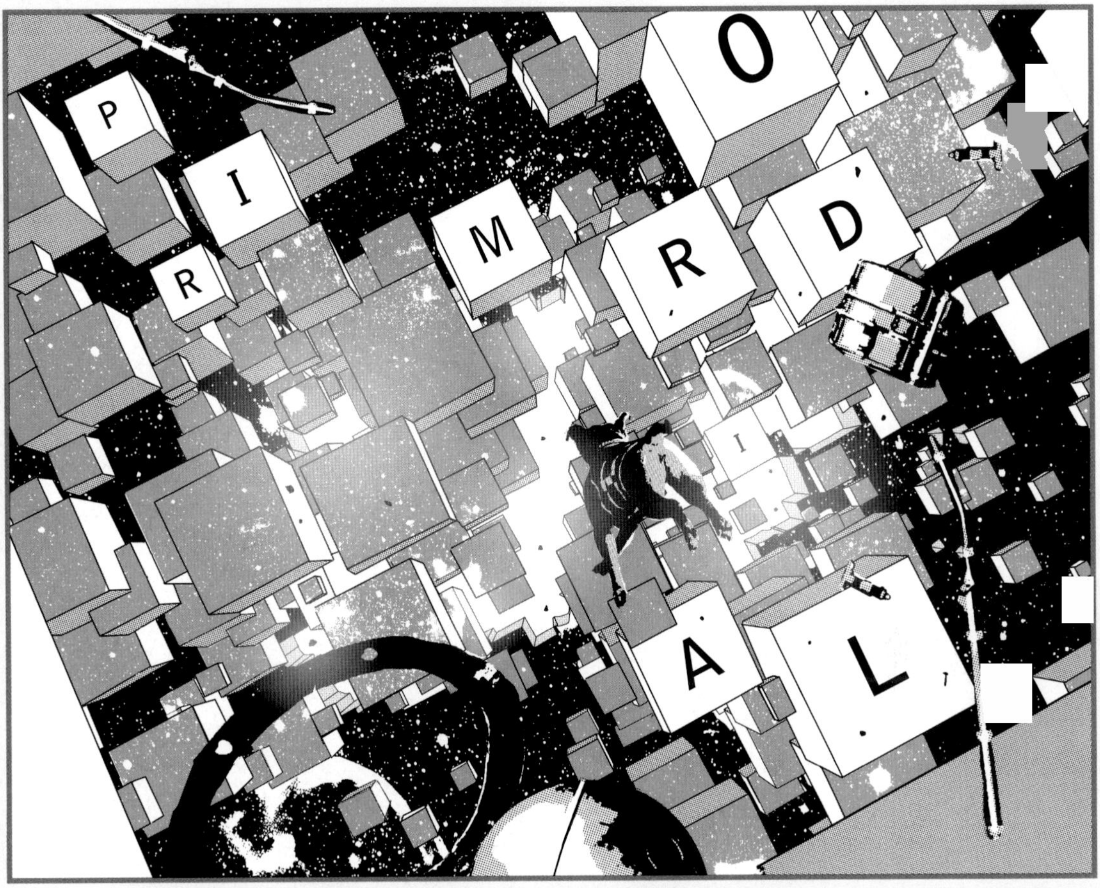
PRIMORDIAL

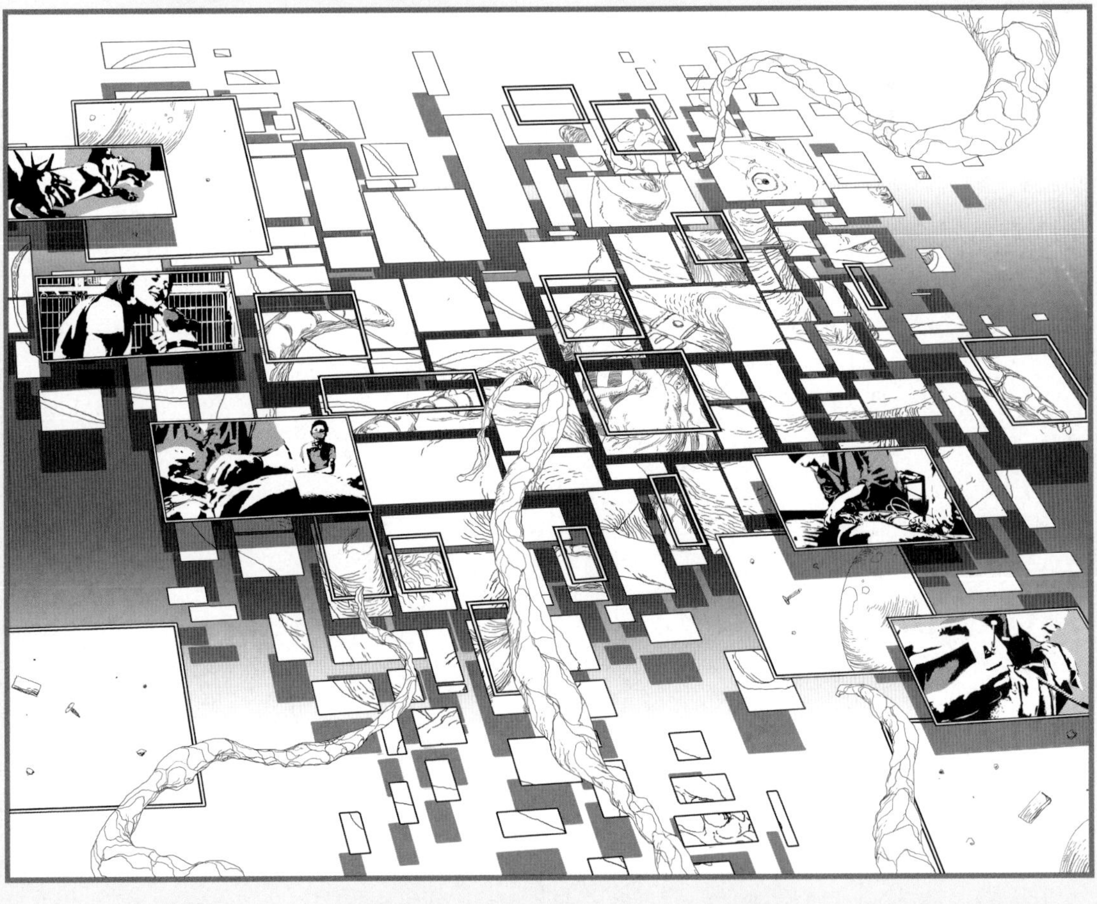

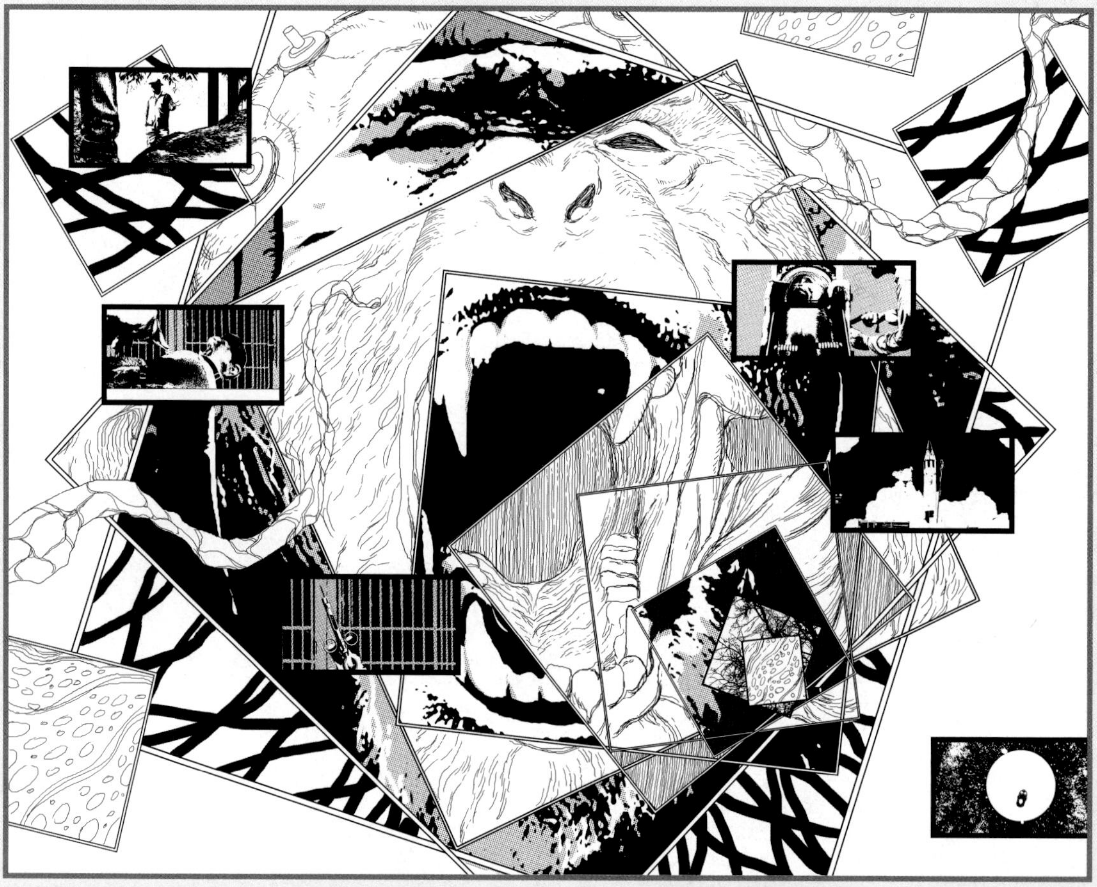

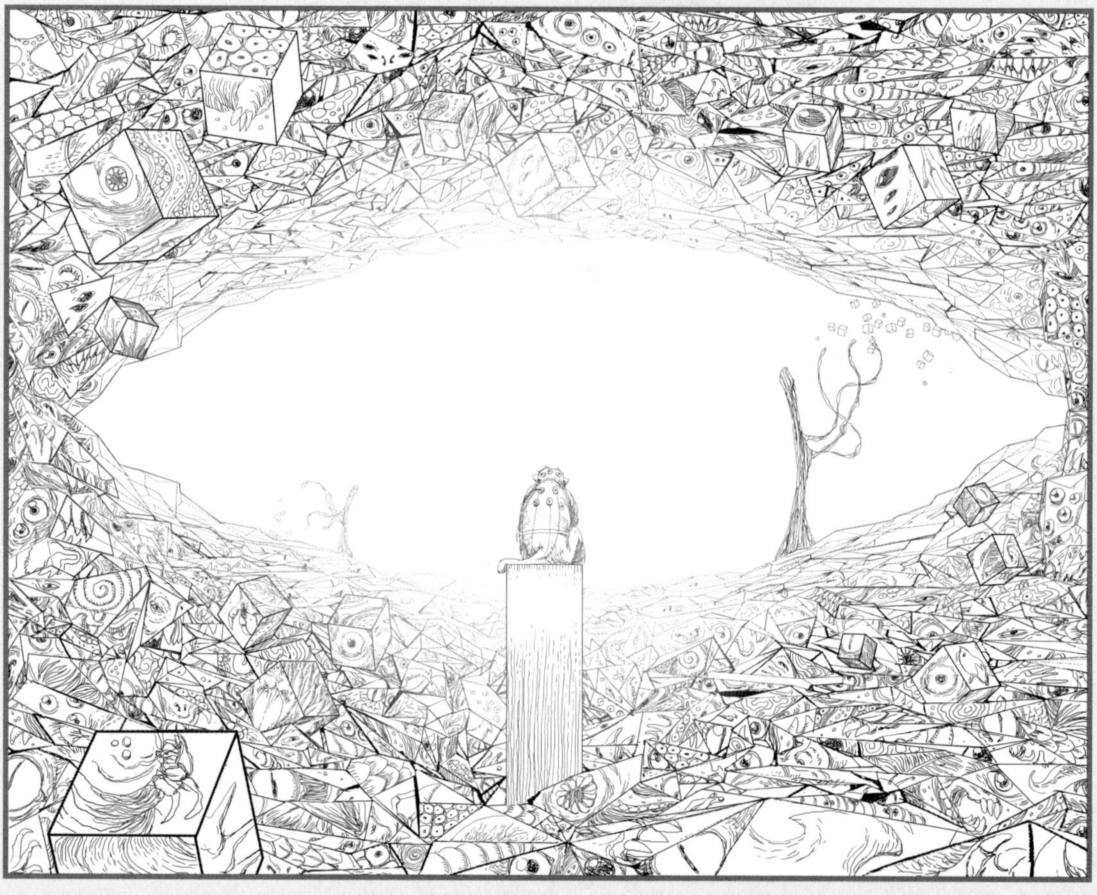

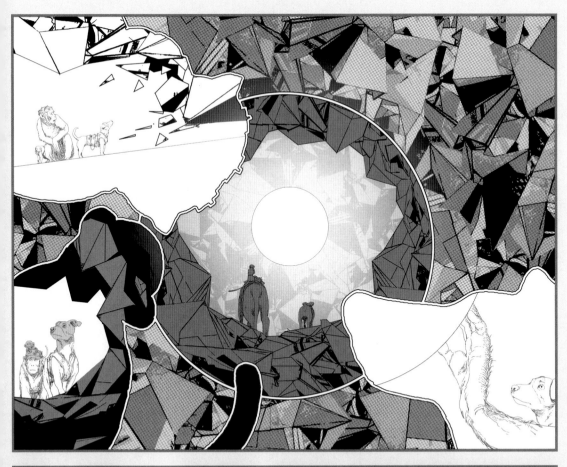

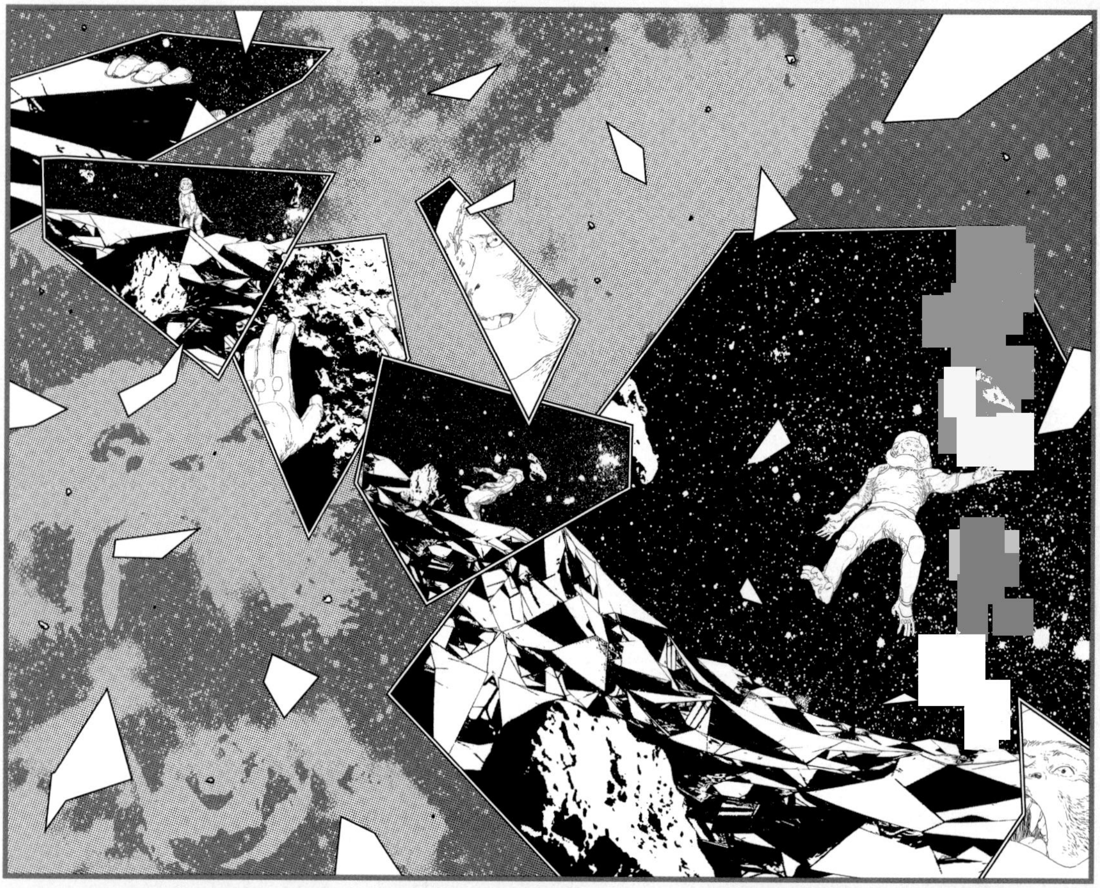

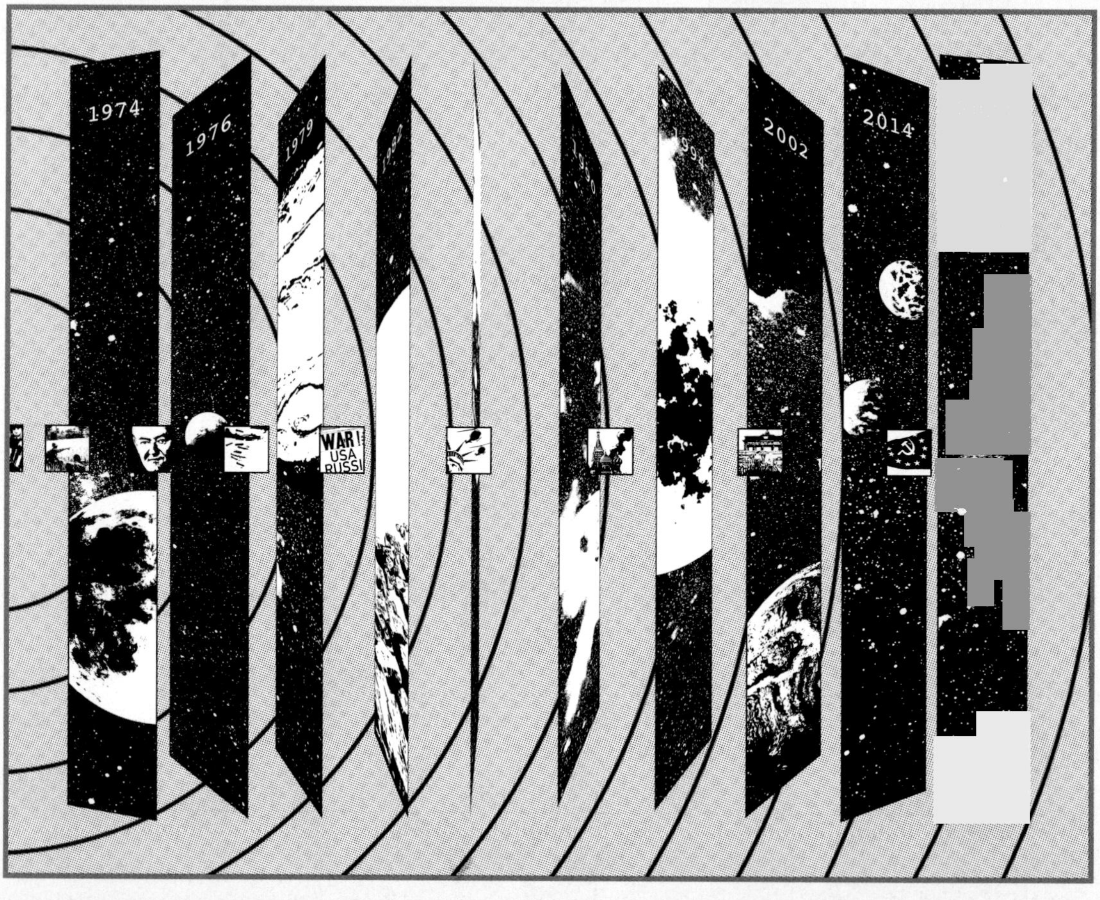

1974
1976
1979
1982
1990
1994
2002
2014
WAR!
USA
RUSSI

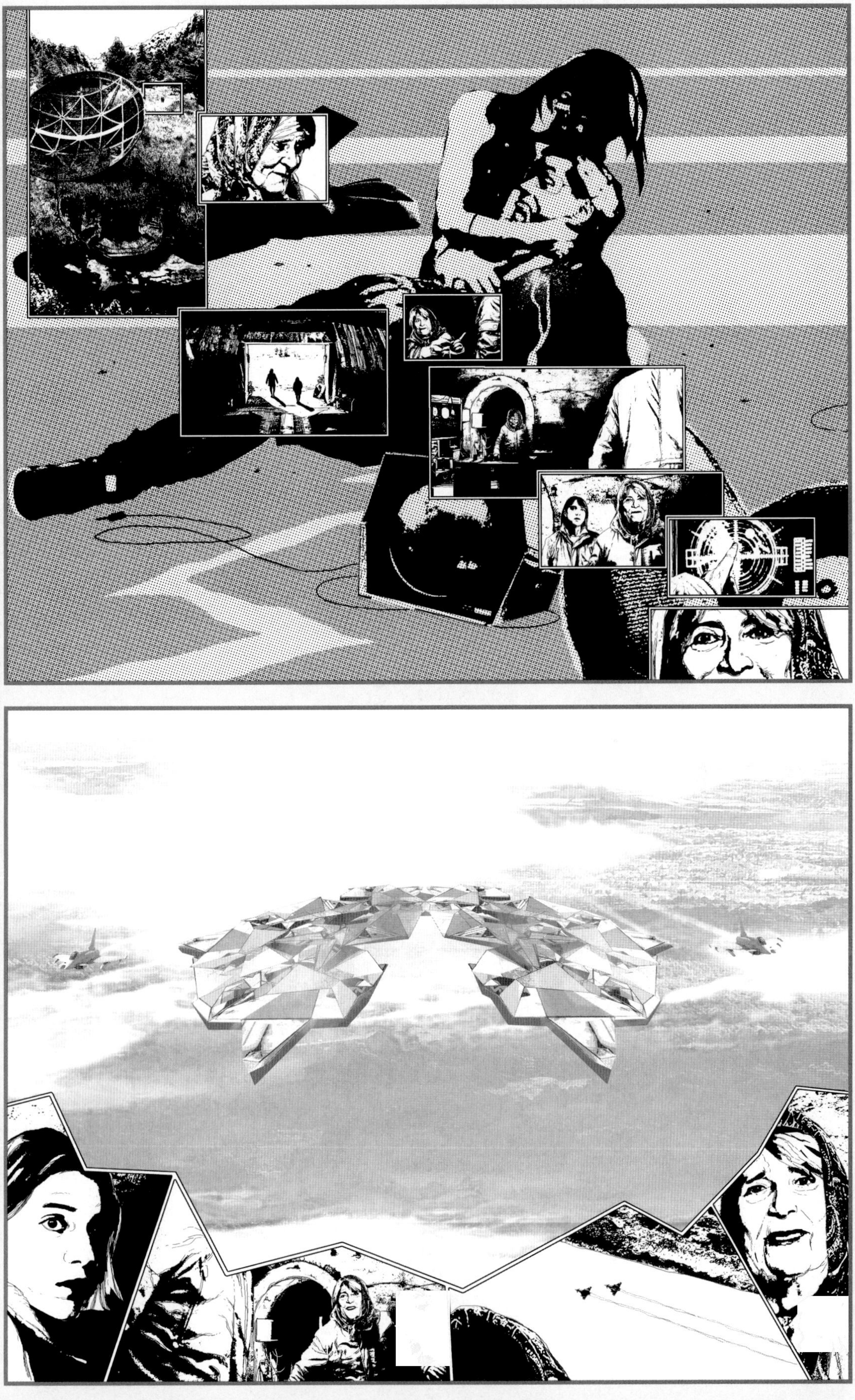

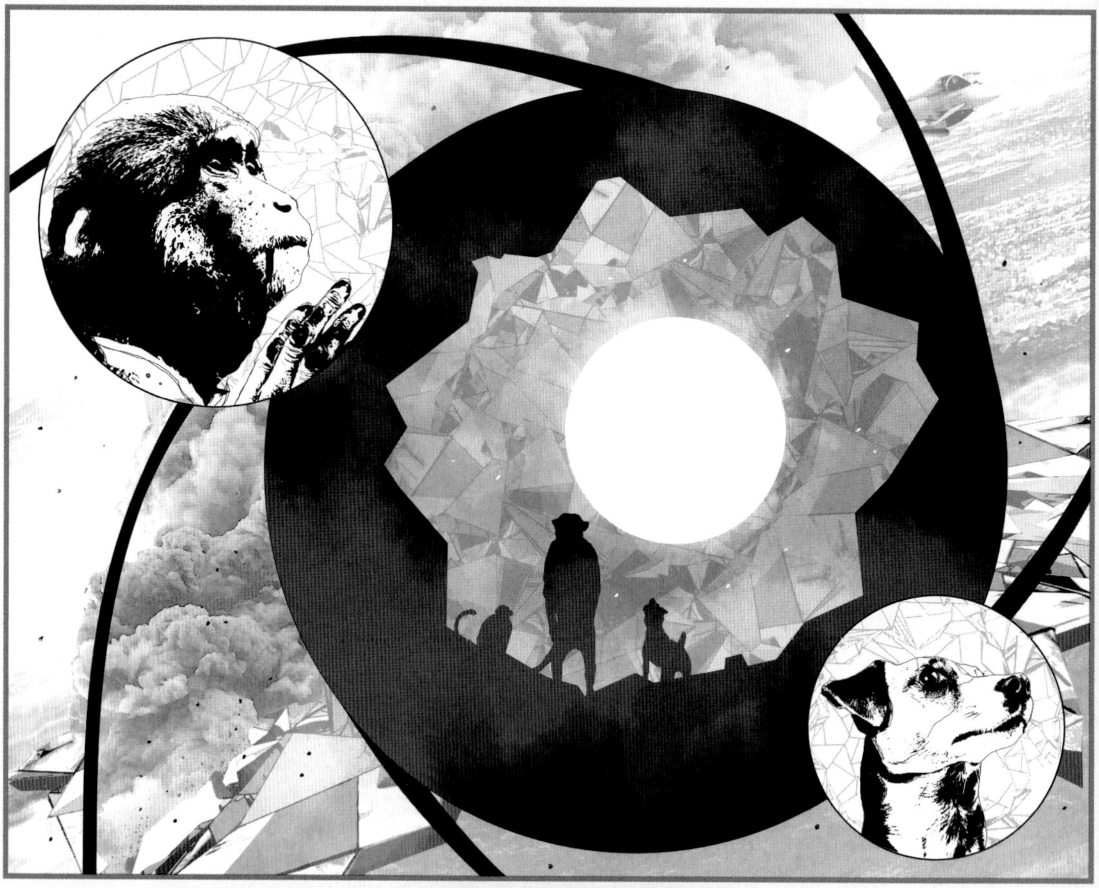
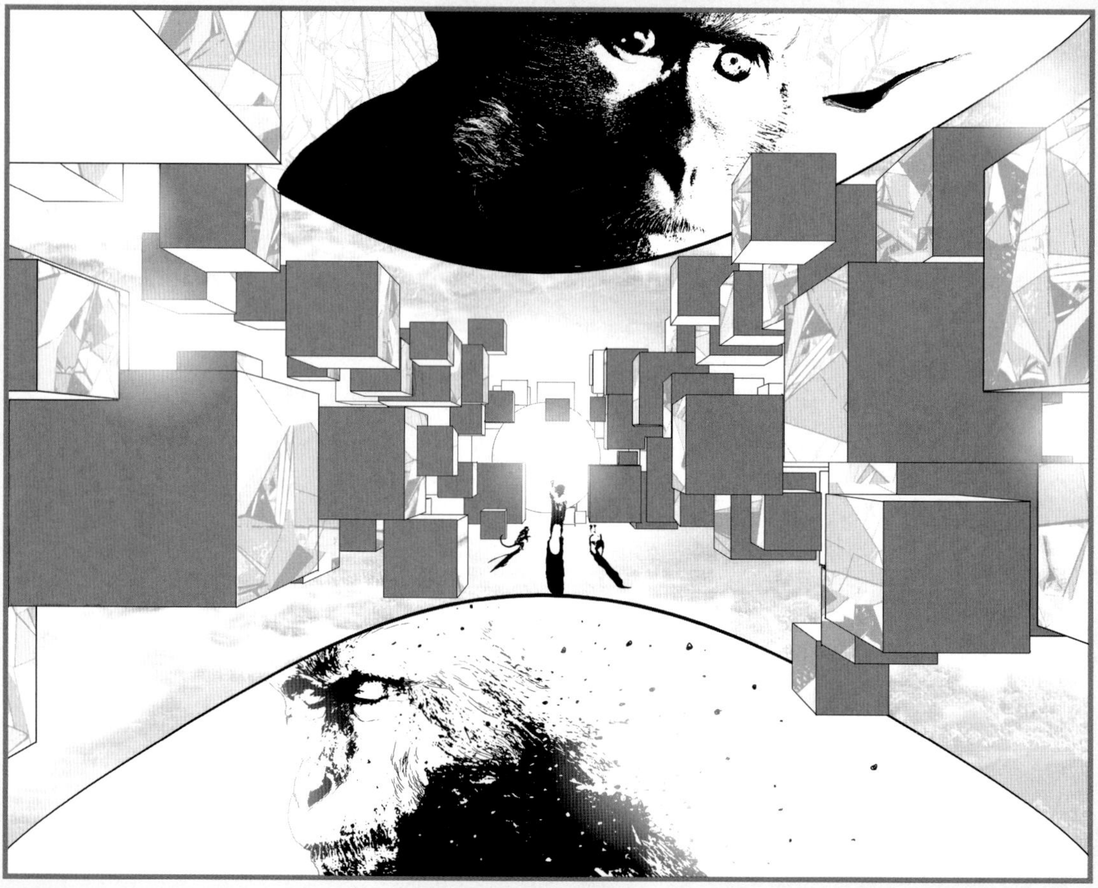

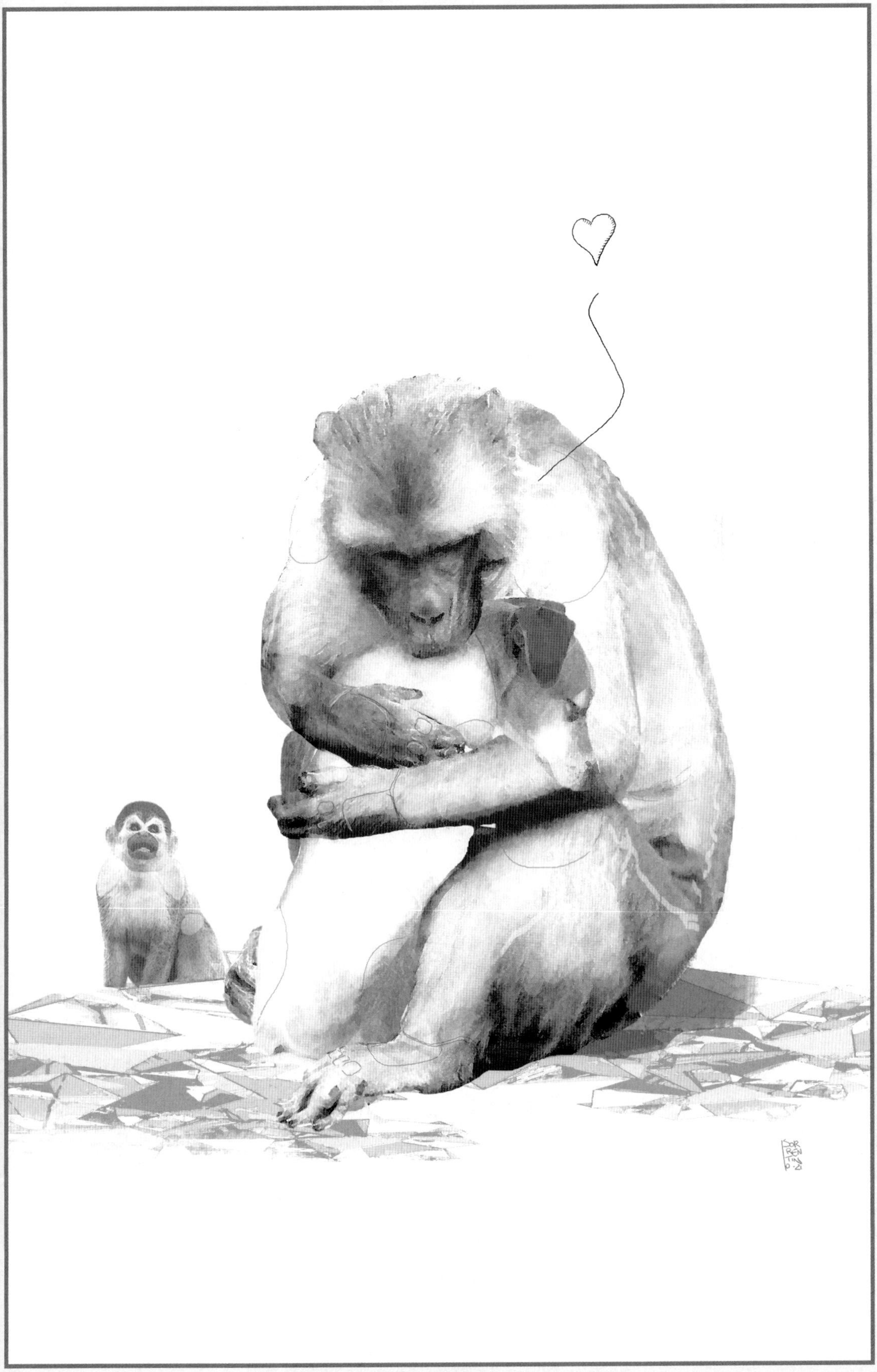

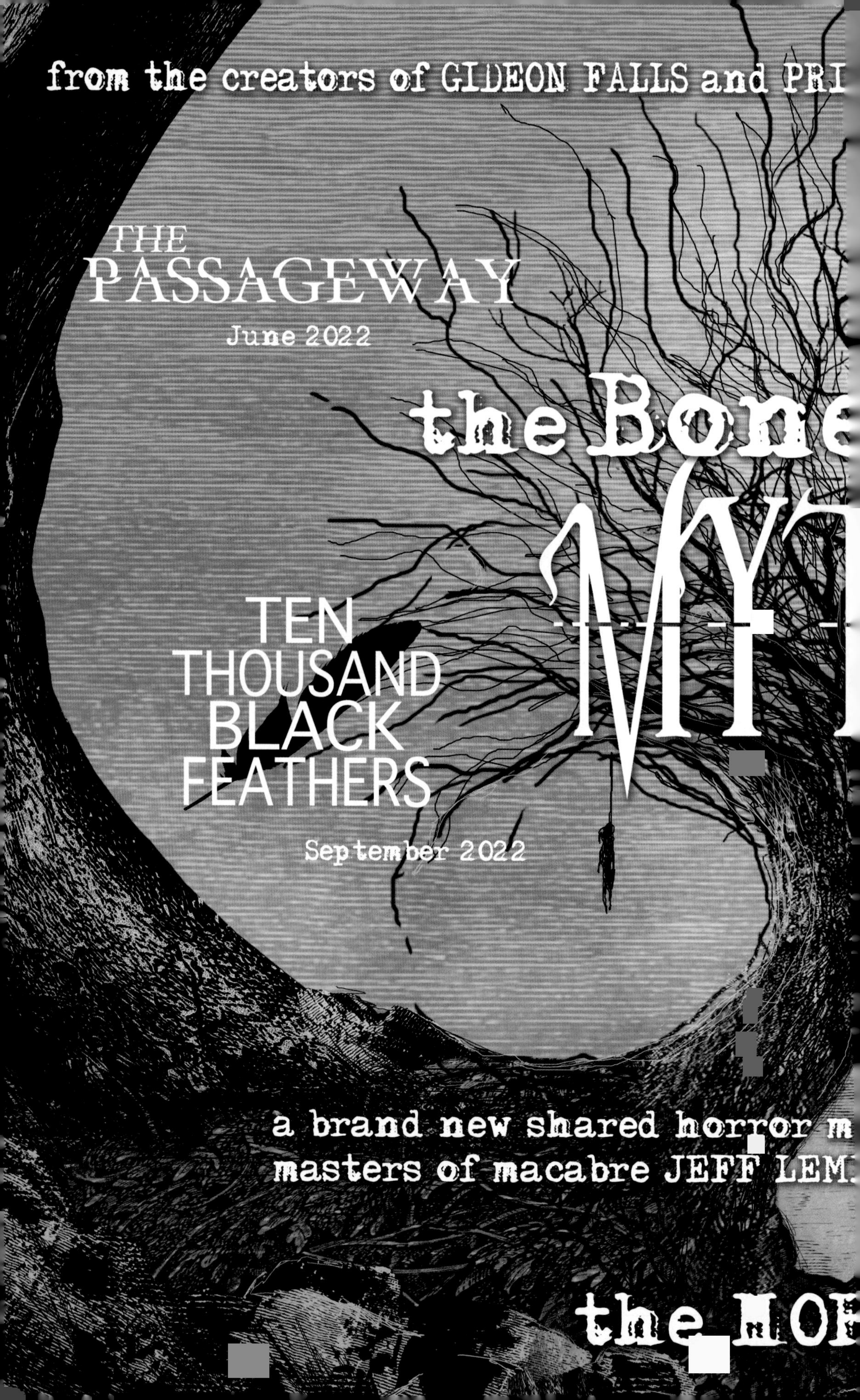

from the creators of GIDEON FALLS and PRI
THE PASSAGEWAY
June 2022
the Bone
TEN THOUSAND BLACK FEATHERS
September 2022
a brand new shared horror m
masters of macabre JEFF LEM

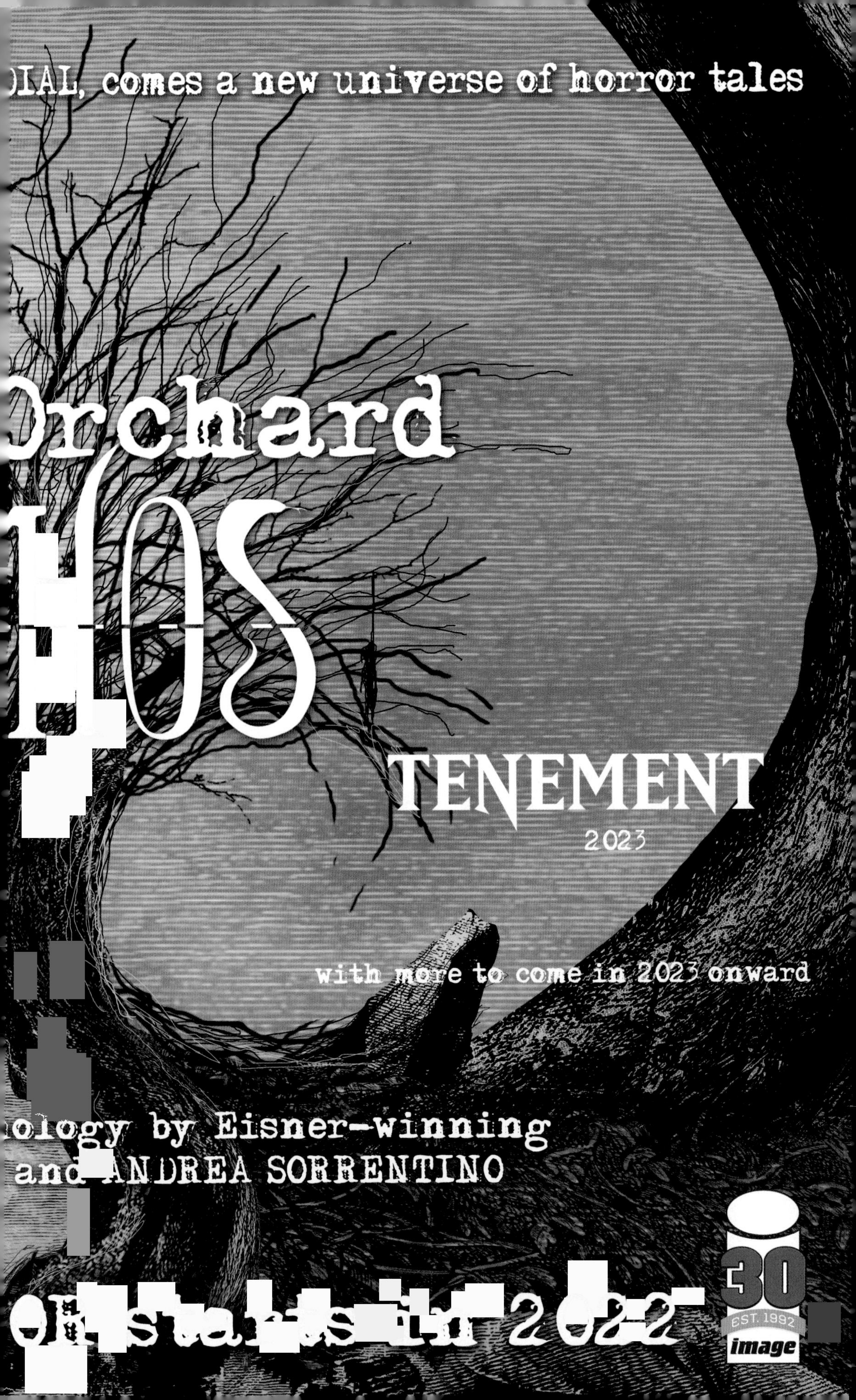
IAL, comes a new universe of horror tales
Orchard
TENEMENT
2023
with more to come in 2023 onward
ology by Eisner-winning
and ANDREA SORRENTINO
2022
30
EST. 1992
image

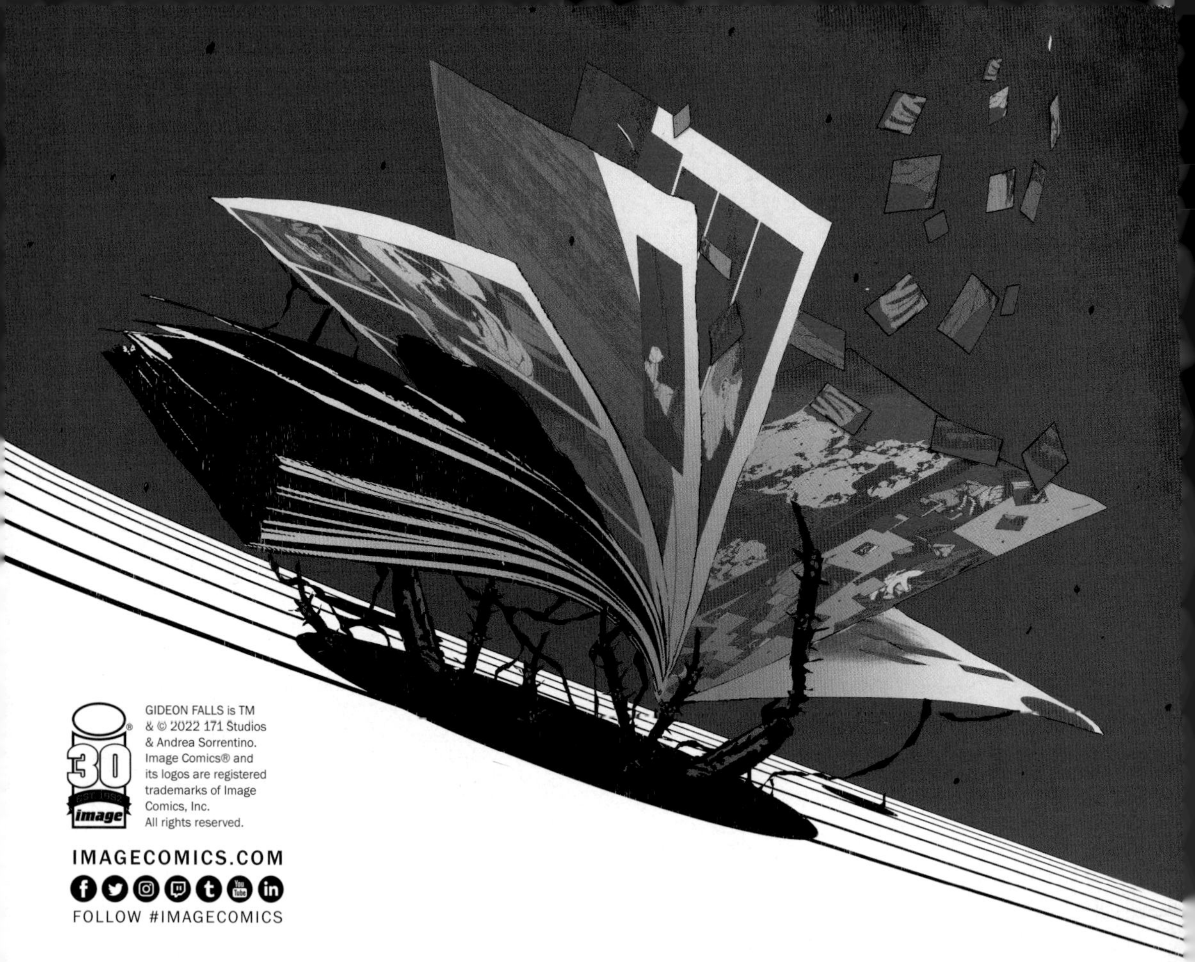

TERROR THROUGH TIME AND SPACE

GIDEON FALLS™

Experience the groundbreaking horror series in its entirety.

Volumes one through six available now in trade paperback.

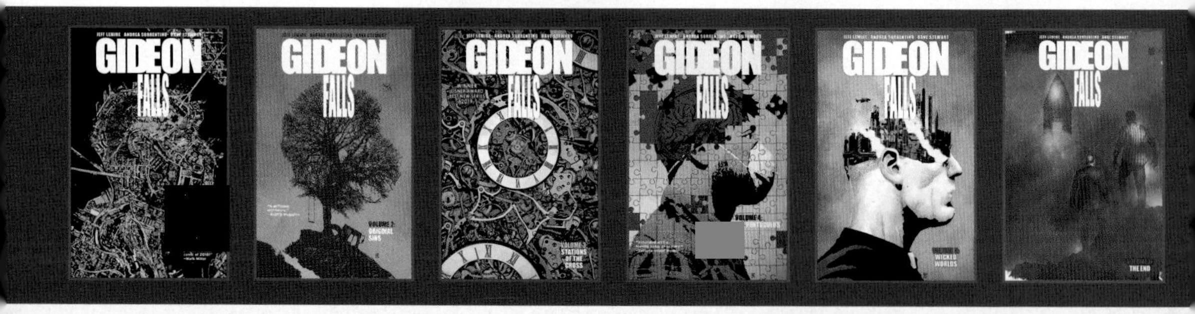

GIDEON FALLS
GIDEON FALLS
GIDEON FALLS
GIDEON FALLS
GIDEON FALLS
GIDEON FALLS